Norfolk, Marsham, Arthur T. Michell

The Parish Register of Marsham

Norfolk, from 1538 to 1836

Norfolk, Marsham, Arthur T. Michell

The Parish Register of Marsham
Norfolk, from 1538 to 1836

ISBN/EAN: 9783337378776

Printed in Europe, USA, Canada, Australia, Japan

Cover: Foto ©Andreas Hilbeck / pixelio.de

More available books at **www.hansebooks.com**

THE PARISH REGISTER

OF

MARSHAM,

NORFOLK:

FROM 1538 TO 1836.

EDITED BY

A. T. MICHELL, M.A.

ONE HUNDRED AND FIFTY COPIES PRINTED FOR SUBSCRIBERS BY

JARROLD & SONS, PRINTERS, NORWICH.

1889.

PREFACE.

The Register Books of Marsham Parish for the years comprised in this publication should have been ten in number, and appear to have been entire until about fifty years ago. But about the year 1835 the church was broken into and the Parish Chest ransacked, and the marauders, either in disappointment at finding nothing of more tangible value or in mere wanton malice, removed the whole of the Register Books, tore them from their covers, and scattered them about the churchyard and adjacent fields. With the exception of a part of the earliest Book, and one whole volume covering the interesting period, 1653—1684, the whole were recovered and very carefully sewn together, some few pages having a piece missing in the middle or a corner lost.

The first Book, 1538—1653, measures 14 inches by 6, and consists of five gatherings of vellum stitched in a limp cover of the same material. One whole gathering is missing, and the book has evidently been re-stitched and the edges pared since the loss of this part. The book is undoubtedly what the Latin title by Henry Aldred, curate, leads us to expect, a copy on vellum of the earlier paper book, and made in obedience to the injunction of 1697 : the book being of sufficient size to continue in use until nearly sixty years later. The writing of Henry Aldred is extremely clear, though his work was evidently rapid. There are indications, besides the occurrence here and there of untranslated entries, that the whole of the earlier Register was written in Latin; thus we find the copyist gradually settling down into the form " daic," though he began by writing " day," or " daye." It would seem as if his eye became so accustomed to see " *die* " in every entry, that his hand unconsciously adopted definitely the spelling which most resembled it. Each page has four vertical lines ruled in the margin, from the first of which begin the entries of Baptisms, from the second those of Marriages, and from the third those of Burials. This system redeems in some measure the inter-mixture of the three classes of entries, and is reproduced in the text by asterisks. In more than one instance these lines correct slips of the pen by which "baptized" appears for "buried," or *vice versa*, and must have formed a check in copying throughout the book. There are very few abbreviations, and those of the simplest form. They are not reproduced in print except in one instance on page 13, where Mr. Aldred was apparently himself at fault. This industrious gentleman left a few names incomplete, intending no doubt a revision, which he never made: nor did he bring his work quite down to the year in which he was writing. Possibly the entry in which his own name figures on page 31, may be held to be both a reason and an excuse for these circumstances. We have adopted the method of indicating by numbers the hands of the various writers where they can be identified. Henry Aldred is Nᵒ· 1, and deservedly holds the first place. No. 2 is Samuel Oates, Junʳ· or as he himself writes the notorious name, Otes. This gentleman took up the work where Mr. Aldred left off, having succeeded him in 1600 as curate to Samuel Otes, senior. His writing, which is of the character common to the Visitation MSS. of his time, continues to the end of the book, which brings us to the year when the registration passed for a season out of the hands of the clergy. All his pages seem to contain a fair copy of entries previously made, probably on loose sheets or "bills," or in a day book: and this remark applies to the greater part of all the earlier books. Samuel Otes died in 1658 still apparently in the possession of the benefice. But the loss of Book II. deprives us of any records of the last troubled years of his incumbency. A small portion of the contents of the last book is supplied by Register Bills. All of these that are extant are therefore printed after Book I. They are written by William Day and John Deyns, successive Rectors.

Book III. is of vellum, measuring 11 inches by 7½. It has on the cover in contemporary writing, "Marsham Register Booke Anno Dñi 1684, pretium 5s.": and added in a later hand under the above date "to 1736 inclusive": and beneath: "There must have been a gross omission in the Registration from 1729 to 1736." This last remark, which is undeniably true, must have been written soon after the year last named, since the book came into use again for Marriages from 1738 to 1754, and again deserved similar censure. The title and the entries for the first year are in the writing of John Deyns, No. 3, whose burial is recorded on page 103. In his successor, No. 4, we have Daniel Wiseman, whose work continues for twenty years without interruption. This Rector was economical in the consumption of parchment, to say the least of it, and covered every possible corner of the pages with his minute caligraphy. The friction at the extremities has consequently done more than usual damage. An idea of his power of close-packing his entries may be formed by comparing the number crowded in by him on one leaf, pages 111—118, with the use made of the same-sized leaf by a bolder hand later on, page 176, the paging of the Register being printed in the margin. Mr. Wiseman, who had formerly been Rector of Blickling,[1] held the living of Horsford together with Marsham, but resided at the latter. His practice of making the young people of Horsford come six or seven miles to Marsham to be married may have been inconvenient for subsequent searchers in that parish; and gives a hint to follow up a pluralist when his livings are not too far apart for such an expedient. He was buried at Horsford in 1707.

No. 5, a clear modern-looking hand, occurs towards the close of Wiseman's time, and now and then on the pages following. The autographs in the Archdeacon's Registry enable us to identify the writer in Thomas Fuller, curate of Marsham in 1713, and probably of some neighbouring parish during the years immediately preceding. No. 6 is Robert Dymes, Rector of Swanton Abbot and curate of Marsham, whose burial is recorded here, though it took place at Norwich. No. 7 is Robert Pate, who does not appear to have been continuously resident even for the short term of his incumbency. No. 8 is

---

[1] Some of his entries in the *Blickling Register* are very precise, e g. :—
"Daniel filius Danielis Wiseman clerici et Annæ uxoris Suæ, natus inter duodecimam et unam horam undecimi diei mensis Februarii, baptizatus fuit a patre prædicto vicesimo die mensis prædicti Anno Domini 1672."

John Spurling, curate in 1716. No. 9 is James Norris, who wrote the entries with a few exceptions throughout his incumbency. He died in 1729 and was buried in his chancel.

Down to this date the Registers have every appearance of having been punctually and carefully written up. But with the incumbency of William Harvey comes a change for the worse. As this Rector held also the living of Lyng we had, before inspecting the Register Bills, supposed that his non-residence was the cause of the defects in the parish books. But the Register Bills for the first part of his time were written by him, and contain baptisms of his children,[1] and indicate residence at Marsham from 1729 to 1736. And we recognise his hand, No. 10, in the entries of the latter part of 1729 and a part of 1730. But after that date, although he punctually delivered the bills at the general and episcopal visitations, he ceased to copy the entries into the parish book. In 1737 the name of B. Pauls, curate, appears on the Register Bill, but the contents are not to be found in the book. This gentleman, No. 11, who was probably a relative of his Rector's wife, seems to have left several pages blank with the hope that the missing years might yet be filled in, and made a start towards the end of the book with the Marriages of 1738 and 1739, after which he ceased to enter Marriages at all. For Baptisms and Burials he began a new book, and entered them in separate parts, a reform for which he deserves credit.

Book IV. thus begun is of the same size as the preceding volume, but contains a mixture of parchment and paper, a very injudicious piece of economy. The ill-matched pages have travelled down the stream of time like the brass and earthen pots, and with much the same result, the weaker material having had the rough contact of its coarse companion to contend with in addition to its natural enemies and dangers. The first leaf is lost, but can have contained nothing more important than a title. In the first few pages many items are out of their proper place, lost threads apparently being gathered up from time to

---

[1] "Wᵐ Harvey, clerk of Marsham & Elizᵗʰ Paul of Sᵗ Peters Norwich, spinster, were married 19 June 1732." (Register of Sᵗ Helen, Norwich.)

time and inserted with the current entries. This part of the
Registers therefore requires careful search. In 1743 appears the
hand of George Ray, curate, and is numbered 12. He seems to
have been punctual in registering Baptisms and Burials, and the
hope of supplying the neglected sheets of 1730 to 1736 having
been now abandoned, his hand set down the few entries on p.
171, which we may suppose him to have learnt from the relatives
of the persons named in them. But with regard to Marriages
either none were solemnised by him, or he followed the bad
example of his predecessors. The former hypothesis is quite
tenable, for we find certain parishes popular for marriages at
different times, and at this particular time many Marsham
people were married in the neighbouring parish of Brampton.

With Nathaniel Ponder, No. 13, we return to careful fulfil-
ment of all duties of registration. He became Rector in 1748,
and while he continued the use of Book IV. for Baptisms and
Burials only, he found space at the end of the third book to
enter the Marriages which took place in that and the five
following years. In 1754 Hardwicke's Act took effect, and the
book prescribed by it came into use. It contains the certificates
of publication of Banns, which form half the book, and which
have proved serviceable in corroboration of doubtful readings.
They also guide us to some marriages solemnised in other
parishes. Beyond these remarks it seems unnecessary to say
anything of this book or of the books which came into use in
1813, except that many leaves were torn or detached in the
manner described above; but no leaf was lost, and the restoration
of each portion to its proper place is rendered easy by the form
of the books. After 1754 the writers of the various parts are
easily identified, and the names are more conveniently noted in
the text. It is, therefore, needless to follow them here. From
first to last there is a rare immunity from scribblings or casual
interruptions of the text, the only examples of the former being
the autographs of the Parish clerks, generally Jeckells or Delphs;
and of the latter the Note on the Bells printed in the Appendix.
There is a Memorandum as to a right of way written on spare
leaves at the end of Book I., also given in the Appendix, and
beneath the title of the same book, written in minute and well-

formed characters of an early date, but by a hand which cannot
be identified, the following sentences :—

        .˙. legendo proficio : proficiendo lego .˙.
          .˙. mors mihi lucrum :   τα καλα δυνεσα
      .˙. premisimus non amisimus : : abiit non obiit :
    .˙. **Diabolus malum ingerere potest, cogere autem non potest**

Whether these lines had any personal allusions, or were a
mere collection of tags suitable for monumental and other
purposes, it is impossible to say. The last line certainly looks
like a hit at the Lay Register. The writer's knowledge of Greek
must have been small: he may have meant to write δυνατα, but
even that does not make a very elegant sentence.

Of the names recorded in the Registers none are widely known
to fame, but a great number will be recognised as of local
respectability. The limits of this work do not, however, admit of
much research outside the parish memorials. Of the older
inscriptions in the Church the greater number is recorded in
Blomefield, and they are only repeated here in order to show how
time and their custodians have treated them since that work was
written. When Blomefield visited the Church, if indeed the
description is his, the following were legible ; on the Rood-
screen :—*Orate pro animabus Johannis de Norton et Margaretæ
uxoris quorum animabus Deus propicietur.* Labels in windows :—
*Orate pro animabus Thome de Norton et Marie uxoris predicti
Thome.—Orate pro anima Roberti Atte Hill.—Orate pro anima
Willielmi Atte Hill.—Pray for the soule of John Belknap*, Gen.
Arms of, *Jenny, Moore*, and others, and *Bp. Wakering's* cognisance.
On a broken brass :—*Orate pro anima Johannis Bysshop qui ob.*
mccccclxxii *et pro anima Agnetis uxoris* . . . . mccccclxxxix
et pro quibus tenentur.
Of these the brass alone survives, still more broken : the frag-
ments of a few letters remain on the screen : but the whole of
the painted glass has been removed. Many of the ancient
inhabitants remember the time when almost every window
contained some " gay glass," and can tell how most of it was
removed by a so-called Antiquary, who was sometime resident in
the parish, and who was troubled by few scruples in satisfying

his thirst for collecting antiquities.[1] Dispersed by him at his various sales, it is impossible to say where most of these scrolls and coats may be now located, or whose modern villa may be borrowing an air of medieval respectability from their display. In one instance another sacrilegious hand had forestalled this depredator : and we have seen in a house at Brandiston the arms of the Plantagenet Kings in rich colours, which formerly adorned one of the clerestory windows, and the scroll mentioned above— Orate pro anima Roberti Atte Hill. These were removed by one who certainly ought to have known better, a curate of Marsham in 1836—7, who bore a somewhat similar name. Made up into one piece with the scroll beneath the regal coat, and inserted in the glazed portion of the lobby door, the effect may have been imposing. But the slammings of half a century have already made so many cracks that the whole is only held together by a back and front of plain glass, and the housemaid's broom-handle may at any time deal the finishing blow.

In Blomefield stones to the memory of the following persons are mentioned :—

> Mrs. Margaret Lyng, died, October 18, 1698, aged 74.
> * Mary, wife of Andrew Dix, 1621.
> * Thomas Grix 1720, aged 74.
> Thomas son of James Grix, 1712, aged 15.
> Susan Jeckel widow, 1704, aged 70.
> * William Jeckel, 1728, aged 68.
> John, son of James and Anne Norris, born 1721 died 1725 ; John, another son 1725 ; Thomas, another 1726.

Of these the three marked with an asterisk have either been removed or become illegible.

The following names are also to be seen :—

> John Jeckel, died 11 Nov. 1698 aged 67.
> Jacobus Tennant, Armiger, 12 July 1733, aged 61.
> Ann, wife of the above and eldest daughter of Peter Elwin late of Tuttington, 30 June 1741.
> Samuel Thorsby, Junior, 10 Oct 1733, aged 38.
> Susanna wife of Samuel Thorsby, senior 27 Jan 1747 aged 85.

---

[1] At his death no less than nine Parish Registers were found among his papers.

John Bear, 20 July 1733, aged 66.
Sarah Bear, 23 March 1757, aged 85.
James Grix, 23 May 1742, aged 85.
Jeremiah Hartley 3 Jan 1742, aged 32.
Lydia wife of Jeremiah Hartley, 6 Aug 1749, aged 63.
Samuel Dyball 22 Aug 1752, aged 63.
Mary, wife of above, 22 May 1769, aged 70.
Elizabeth, wife of Thos. Morrill, gent, of this Parish, 2 Sept 1786.
    Georgiana Elizabeth only daughter of John Morrill, surgeon,
    of Cawston, and great granddaughter of above Elizabeth, 4
    Nov. 1848, aged 5.
John Cook, 18 Nov. 1806, aged 56.
Mary Cook, sister, 13 Feb 1807, aged 41.
Ann Sophia Pike, 19 Sept. 1808, aged 38.

The large slab mentioned by Blomefield, containing the harsh inscription, "*Oblivi mi datus sum tanquam mortuus a corde*" with the word *Oblivio* repeated six times round the margin, still remains legible. *Cor* is the seat of the passions rather than the vital principle, and one wonders that the relatives of the person whose resting place is thus marked, and whose life must have been somewhat notorious, succeeded in so singular a mode of consigning to oblivion one for whom they had lost all natural affection.[1]   Readers of Foxe (Memorials pp. 465—466) have been tempted to guess at the identity, but we in Marsham have no desire to lift the veil; and the Will of the person there named not only shows that he was to be buried at Aylsham, but also tends to throw doubts upon the justice of the abuse heaped upon him by that untrustworthy writer.   By far the most ancient monument in the Church is a sepulchral stone now placed in the north-west corner of the north aisle.   This is uninscribed, but has sculptured work upon it which seems to mark a transition from the St. Cuthbert's Cross of pre-Norman times to the twelfth-century work, which has been likened to the ornamentation of ancient iron hinges.

To any one in search of details of any particular family whose name occurs in the records of this parish a hunt among the Wills preserved at Norwich would bring its reward.   The kind of information obtainable from that source is shown in the following

---

[1] Cp. "*civiliter mortuus.*"

extracts kindly supplied by Mr. Thomas Tallack. Those selected will be seen to bridge roughly the period covered by the earlier registers.

Norw. Archdeaconry Bk 1561 fol 453.

RAYNOLD BRIAN, of Marsham, worstead weaver.

> To be buried in churchyard there. To high altar 12^d To bye a greyle for the north side of the Church 10s. To a bell 6s. 8d. To church of Marsham a covering for the bearc of the poor people. To the church of Marsham a latten bason. To the church of Marsham a "howsling towlye" 3 yards in length. To poor there 40s. Legacies to CECILY, daughter; MARGARET, daughter and JOHN CRONGER, her husband, Executors. Sir John Bury, parson of Marsham, supervisor, and if he die Sir John Spewes to be so— Proved before John Bury L.L.B. 18 Aug 1561.

Norwich Archdeaconry 1605. fol 234.

ROBERT MARSHAM, husbandman—To be buried in churchyard of Marsham. To poor there 6s. 8d. To ELIZABETH, daughter, wife of CHRISTOPHER COTES, £21. To CHRISTOPHER, JOHN, ELIZABETH children of said CHRIST^R & ELIZTH £3 each. To wife of JOHN MARSHAM my brother deceased, 10s. To MARGARET WEST, my sister, 20s. To THOMAS, (son of Edmund Marsham) my grandson £5. To rest of my son Edmund's children, namely, ROBERT, MARGARET, WILLIAM, EDMUND & JOHN £3 each. To EDMUND, son, tenements in Marsham, and to be my Executor—SAM. OATES J$^{NR.}$ clerk ROB. WRIGHT, STEP. CHAPMAN, Witnesses. He surrendered his property held of the Manor of Hevingham and Marsham to JOHN WAKE to the use of his will on the said 8 July 1605—Dated 8 July 1605. Proved 1 Oct 1605.

JOHN DEYNES, clerk, late of Marsham.

> Administration granted 6 Aug 1686 to JANE DEYNES the relict, and ROBERT BANYER of Aylsham, Gent^n by the Consistory Court of Norwich.

The will of "JOHN BURY, clk., vicar of Aylsham" has also an interest for Marsham. It is dated 14 May 1558, (132 Consist) and provides :—

> To be buried in chancel of Aylsham right before the pyctor of S. Michael there by the side of the Sepulture.
> To repair of said church 20s. To Cathedral Ch. 20s. To Poor of

Aylsham £5. To twenty of the poorest householders in Marsham 3s. 4d. each. To the rest of householders there 20ᵈ· each. A solemn dirge and masse at Aylsham, and every householder and his wife to be present Except sickness letteth it, or else no partakers, inasmuch as this towne be near adjoining to Aylsham, and they have access. Legacies to ROBERT, son of ROBERT BURY, brother, the house bought of NIC BULLYN. JOHN, brother, and DOROTHY, sister, of said ROBERT ; to ELIZABETH DAVY ; to THOMAS, RICHARD, and ELIZABETH, children of said ROBERT : to brother WALTER'S children : to brother WILLIAM'S children (WILLIAM and KATHERINE excepted). To nephew WILLIAM, son of brother WILLIAM, if he be a Priest. To brother Sir THOMAS best gowne, jacket, doublet and typpet. To brother HENRY and his wife. To EWFEME METRE, JNO WOODCOKE, BRIDGET NEAVE, and JOHN her son. To Sir JOHN SPELKES. To each godchild in Aylsham, Marsham, Hevingham, and Felmingham—legacies. To Aylsham churchwardens vestment of red tissue of £10. Towards a great bell in Marsham £10, so that they will pay the rest so yᵗ it be provided within three years next after my decease. Good Mr. DR. SPENSER, supervisor. To his servants 20ᵈ· each, the coke to be one. To Mr. THOS. SYMONDS, official of Sudbury. To Mr. ATKYNS and wife, and GEO. ATKYNS godson, —legacies. Mr. THOS. SENYOLE gave a house called Wythes to me and my successors ; now I will same to next Incumbent (of Marsham) being content to acquit my Exors for Dilapidations, or else to my next kinsman. Every maid that shall be married in Marsham being dwellers to have 6s. 8d. at her marriage, for three years after decease. To Aylsham Ch. my best testor to be borne over the blessed sacrament on Corpus Christi Day, and that which remayneth at the head to make a cushin to lay in the sepulchre on Good Friday, and I will that the curtᵗyns of the same bed shall remayne in the vestry where the copes hang to drawe about Marye's bed yerely when these pageants shall go. Legacies to Sir THO. BURY, brother ; ROBERT, nephew, son to ROBERT, brother ; and WᴹBURY nephew, son to WILLIAM, brother. To Mr. Wᴹ MINGAY and each of his clerks. To free skole new erected (at Aylsham) if it go forward, 40s.

Proved 1 Dec 1558 by THOS BURY, clerk.

Extracts from the Wills of John Swan and Elizabeth his wife, benefactors of the Poor, are preserved in the deed-box of the Charities, a handy account of which has been recently printed by Mr. C. Louis Buxton of Bolwick Hall (Jarrolds, 1887). John Swan was a native of Marsham, but by a strange irony what we take to be the entry of his baptism in 1629 wants the Christian name, this having been apparently forgotten by the minister before he found time for this part of his duty. We may mention the charity accounts as an excellent source of information as to the status of various families in the Registers, lists of the recipients having been preserved from 1694.

Of the Manors we have nothing to add to Blomefield's account, except that the Advowson is now separated from the manor of Marsham, having been retained by the Anson family when they sold the Marsham part of the Paston estate.

The following list of the institutions to the Rectory, which we have extracted from the Diocesan Records will also give an outline of the descent of the manors :—

Liber :	fol :	Rectors of Marsham	Institution :
i.	48.	GEOFFRY DE NOTYNGHAM Patron. Bishop of Norwich.	4 Nov. 1312.
i.	94.	SIMON DE LAUSELLE Patron, Bp. of Norwich.	9 March 1321.
iv.	151.	ROBERT DE STRATON LL.D. Patron Bp. of Norwich.	9 Feb 1353.
vi.	316.	RICHARD SAYER. Patron Bp. of Norwich.	6 April 1405.
vii.	49.	RICHARD DE MIDDLETON, monk of Norwich Patron Bp. of Norwich.	23 Jan 1412.
ix.	90.	JOHN BENNET Patron Bp of Norwich.	13 Feb 1436.
x.	61.	JOHN BULMAN Patron Bp of Norwich.	(no date).
x.	61.	JOHN DONEWICH Patron Bp of Norwich.	18 Sept 1445.
xi.	55.	THOMAS CANDOUR LL.D. Patron Bp of Norwich.	28 Nov 1449.
xi.	84.	WILLIAM BROOKE Patron Bp of Norwich.	22 Aug. 1455.

xi.	129.	**NICHOLAS STANTON L.L.B.** Patron Bp. of Norwich.	Oct 1461.
xi.	129.	**THOMAS, L^D BP OF DROMORE** Who resigned Aylsham in exchange.	Oct 1461.
xii.	26.	**JOHN HEWYSSON** Patron Bp of Norwich.	10 May 1473.
xii.	38.	**THOMAS PALETT** Patron Bp of Norwich.	11 July 1474.
xii.	152.	**ROBERT TOMPSON** Patron Bp of Norwich.	(no date).
xii.	152.	**THOMAS SENYCLE** Patron Bp of Norwich.	6 Aug 1491.
xiv.	7.	**WILLIAM WHITE** Patron Bp of Norwich.	(no date).
xiv.	7.	**JOHN BURY LL.B.** Patron Bp of Norwich.	28 Aug 1530.
xviii.	224.	**EDMUND CHAPMAN *alias* BARKER** Patron Michael Hare, Armiger.	21 Jan 1559.
xx.	16.	**WILLIAM STONE** Patron. The Queen.	7 Sept. 1576.
xx.	16.	**SAMUELL OTES. A.B.** Patron The Queen.	6 July 1577.
xxii.	I.	**SAMUELL OTES jun^r** Patron The King.	8 May 1605.
Sparrow.		**WILLIAM DAY** Patron, John Hobart, Armiger.	25 Feb 1658.
Sparrow.		**JOHN DEYNES** Patron Sir John Hobart, Bar^t	5 Feb 1685.
Lloyd.		**DANIEL WISEMAN** Patron. Mary Hobart, widow.	4 Oct 1686.
xxix.	1.	**JOHN HAVET. A.M.** Patron. Wm Earl of Yarmouth.	18 Feb 1707.
xxix.	93.	**ROBERT PATE A.M.** Patron Wm Earl of Yarmouth.	7. Aug 1714.

| xxix. | 116. | JAMES NORRIS. A.M. | 18 May 1717. |

Patron Christopher Layer, Gent.

| xxx. | 26. | WILLIAM HARVEY, A.B. | 7 Nov. 1729. |

Patron John Bennett.

| xxx. | 131. | NATHANIEL PONDER. | 19 July 1748. |

Patron John Bennett for this turn.

| xxx. | 191. | JOHN GREENE A.M. | 12 March 1766. |

Patron. George Lord Anson.

| xxxi. | 210. | WILLIAM GOODALL, A.M. | 13 April 1787. |

Patron George Anson Esq of Shugborough.

| xxxiv. | 20. | JOHN GUNTON A.B. | 21 May 1844. |

Patrons Miss C. C. Jex Blake and others for this turn.

| xxxv. | — | WILLIAM SEDDON TRAPP; the | 3 Dec. 1886. |

present Rector.

Patron Bp of Norwich by lapse.

We can also give a tolerably long list of Assistant Curates
with the approximate dates of their labours :—Henry Aldred,
1595—1600. Samuel Otes Junr, 1600—1605. Robert Dymes,
Rector of Swanton Abbott, 1713. John Spurling, 1716. B.
Paul or Pauls, 1737. George Ray, 1742—1747. William
Gordon, 1757—1787. William Jewell, 1788—1799 (Rector of
Burgh, 1778—1829). James Bingle, 1800—1832 (died at
Hevingham, 1833, aged 65). Henry Evans, 1832—1836 (after-
wards Lombe). William Atthill, 1836—1837 (sometime Vicar
of Horsford). Henry Howes, 1838—1842 (died Rector of
Spixworth, 1888). Henry Asker, 1842—1844. Roger John
Wright, 1875—1878. Lewis Morgan, 1878—1885. W. S.
Trapp, 1885—1886 (now Rector).

The following notes on the Rectory and Parish Church are
preserved in the Tanner MS.

MARSHAM—Dedicatio Omnibus Sanctis.

    Estimatio ecclⁱᵉ præter portionem xxiii marc.

    Portio Hospitalis Normanni de Norwico in eadem xxs.

    Non visitatur Ecclia ab Archino quia est in maneriis Dni Epi.

Synodalia per annū xxii[d.]
Denarii S. Petr.   x[d.]
Duæ partes dec. de Dno Ep[o] appropr. Pr. et Can. Nor. postea ad
 firmam dimissæ Vicario pro 5 sol. annuatim prout per
 compositionem factam per Walt. Ep. 1247. tunc temp [erant]
 Rector et Vicarius in hâc Ecc[a.]

Gild of ye Trinity.	Lum. Omn[m] Sanct[m.]
,, ,, S. John.	,, B. Mariæ.
,, ,, S. Thomas.	,, S. Nicholas.

Many other lights are mentioned in Blomefield.

The Church of All Saints' consists of Chancel, Nave with N.
and S. aisles, and a square western tower, a south Porch, and a
vestry opening to the north door of the chancel. If we may
judge by the chancel and tower the plan of the present building
belongs to the latter part of the thirteenth century. In the nave
however the windows of the aisles and clerestory indicate either
a rebuilding or renovation at the close of the following century,
being of the style called perpendicular. The hammer-beam roof
of the nave belongs also to the latter period. The masonry was
not sufficiently well built to resist the thrust of this kind of roof,
and tie-beams of rough timber have at some later time been
inserted to arrest further damage. These beams naturally spoil
the appearance of the roof, and have displaced some of the
carved ornamentation. The whole church has also undergone
restoration at a recent date, and some ancient features have as
usual disappeared. The chancel especially has been much
disfigured by the levelling of the floor of the sacrarium,
and by the insertion of a new east window copied from some bad
example of the perpendicular style, the sill having been brought
some three or four feet lower than before to correspond with the
same alteration of the floor level. The Tower requires a considerable amount of repair, and it is hoped that subscribers and
readers of this Register, the printing of which has been under-
taken in hopes of helping that work, will for that reason be
lenient to its defects.

It will be gathered from what already has been said that this
church was formerly well provided both with the accompaniments
of the ancient form of worship, and with ornaments of all kinds.

The return of Church goods made in 1552 is among the number still preserved in the Record Office, and will not be without interest to many.   It runs as follows :—

Hundred of Southerpingham.

MARSHAM. This inventory indented made the first daye of September in the syxt yere of the reign of o[r] most dread souaigne Lord Edward the sixt by the grace of God Kyng of England, Fraunce and Ireland Defender of the Feyth and of the Church of England and also of Ireland on earth the supme heade. Betwixt Will[m] Faremore, John Robishart and Christofer Heydon, Knights, Robert Barney, Osbert Moundefort and John Callibut Esquiers commissioners emongs other assigned by vertu of the Kings Mat[s] commission to them directed for the survey of Churche goods in the countie of Norff. of thone ptie and Christopher Mollet, Rob. Bustang, Rob. Louth and Will[m] Batman of the seyd Towne of thother ptie Wytnessith that there remaneth in the custodie of the seyd Christofer, Robert and Will. the daye and yere aboue wrytten theis goods under wrytten.

	£	s	d
In pmis a pyx of sylver all gylt weying xix unces ev[y] once iiii[s]. iii.[d.]	iiii[li.]	ii[s.]	iiii[d.]
Itm ii chales wth patents parcell gilt weying xxiiii uncs whereof one weyeth xvi uncs thother viii uncs ev[y] unce iiis. viiiid.	iiii[li.]	viii[s.]	
Itm ii copes one of worsted another of russett sylke valued at		iiii[s.]	
Itm ii copes of velvet one redd the other blewe valued at		xi[s.]	viii[d.]
Itm ix Vestments ii of redd velvet thother of blewe, another of whit damaske one of redd bodkyn wth tunacles of the same one of blewe worsted ii othor of russet sylke thother of whit lynnen cloth valued at		xxx[s.]	
Itm ii steple bells by estimacion weying xiiii[cc] whereof thone viii[cc] thother vi[cc] valued ev[y] hundred at xv[s.] ... x[li.]		x[s.]	
Itm one clapper valued at ...		ii[s.]	viii[d.]
Itm ii hand bells weying vii[l] valued at			x[d.]
Itm certen mettell whiche were of organes valued at ...			xx[d.]
Itm iiii candlesticks of latten wth a holly water stoppe valued at		x[s.]	
Itm in Redy mony of thynges solde ...		xxx[s.]	

Whereof assigned to be occupied and used in the administracion of diuine s'vice the chales of viii uncs and the bell of vi^{cc} in the steple. In wytnes whereof the seyd comissioners and others the seyd p'sons to theis Inventories alternately have put there hand the daye and yere aboue wrytten.

per me Johannem Bury cleric.

by me Roberd Bustyng.

(*Augmentation Office Miscell. Books* 505.)

Some, however, of the property of the Church had already been disposed of, as may be seen from the following certificate belonging to an earlier year of the same reign :—

MARSHAM.   Nicholas Boleyn and William Smyth churchwardens do
(1ugworth).   present that we have sold by the consent of the Towen-
            ship there a pax of v onc. a pixt and a schipx weyenge
            together xxii onc at iiii^s vii^d ye onc.——vi^{ll} viii^s
Whereof we have bestowed upon a payer of gates for churchyard xiii^s iiii^d and reparing the lead in plummers crafte and other charges about the church xx^{s.} The residewe remayen in oure handes towards the castinge and whitinge of oure churche and to do other things according to the Kings Maiesties Injunctions.—
(Record Office. K. Edward vi. no year given).

And after the second commission there was probably little delay in the sale of what was condemned thereby. But we cannot suppose that the inhabitants, many of whose near relatives had no doubt contributed to the adornment of their place of worship, were willing to see it stripped of all but the barest necessities ; and it is not surprising to find signs in the Visitation books of the diocese that there was much quiet resistance. Thus of Marsham we find it noted in 1563, "*The Roodloft is not pluckt down.*" At what date this was accomplished we cannot say. But the Rood screen seems to have been in very good preservation as lately as 1846[1] and even now is structurally sufficiently perfect to exhibit what it has been, a good example of early fifteenth century work. On the panels of the lower part are painted the figures of four- teen Saints, seven on each side of the doorway. Although the faces have been much injured—a bench within easy reach having

---

[1] Norf. Archæol : vol. i. 240.

been thought until recently a good place to seat the school children—yet the emblems which can still be observed in several instances enable us to say with some confidence, that the figures represent the Twelve Apostles and two other saints, the latter in all probability the patron saints of John and Margaret de Norton. Beginning in the doorway and counting northward we find: 1. *S. Peter*, two Keys and Book. 2. *S. Andrew*, Cross Saltire. 3. *S. John, A. & E.*, Chalice. 4. *S. James the Greater*, Pilgrim's Staff. 5. *S. Thomas*, Lance and Book. 6. *S. James the Less*, Fullers Club. 7. *A Female Saint*, holding a crosscut saw. On the South side, 2. *S. Philip*, Basket, is the only one with a distinctive emblem. 1. 3. 4. 5. have books. 6 appears to be preaching. 7. is a *Bishop* with Mitre and Staff.

The beautiful xv century Font remains in good preservation. It is octagonal in shape, the bowl being supported by eight angels springing from an octagonal shaft. On the eight sides of the bowl in canopied panels are sculptured the seven sacraments of the Roman Church and one other subject. Baptism naturally is on the eastern side, Penance on the Western: on the northern are Eucharist, N.E., Orders, N., and Matrimony, N. W.; on the Southern, Confirmation, S.E., Extreme Unction, S., and an eighth subject, S.W., which seems to be Purgatory or perhaps the Preaching to the souls in Hades. The shaft contains in panels figures of the four Evangelists, the intervening panels having the Evangelical symbols. Blomefield can only have taken a cursory glance at this Font, as it would be impossible to mistake these symbols for Confessors, nor could the legend of St George and the Dragon be evolved from the eighth panel above. The whole stands upon an octagonal base graduated to form two steps on all sides, the second having a course of fourleaved flowers running round the face, a characteristic ornament which is also found carved on the screen. There is little else that requires description besides the peal of bells, which will be more conveniently noticed in the Appendix.

To return for one moment to the Registers it is necessary to warn those who search them that the varieties of spelling in the names of several families are very numerous, and that although the Index has been very carefully compiled, it has been found impracticable to make it a complete key to these varieties. As a rule one form of surname has been adhered to and the varieties will be found bracketed under this. But in some instances where the different forms are alphabetically far apart, it has been thought better to index them separately. Thus Ulph and Olfe are treated distinctly, and the name now stereotyped as Penton, but which appears in the registers under the forms Panten, Pantenny, Pantin, Panton, Penten, Pentein, Penteny, Pentenny, Pentin, Penton, Spantin, and Spanton, has been indexed under the three of Pantin, Penton, and Spantin: Alexander and Saunders are both indexed though they refer to the same family, as the following note in the register of the neighbouring parish of Hevingham shows:—*Memorandum: Johes Saunders vulgo vocatur, rerum nomen est Johes Alexander, patet ex Registro Haynforth ubi natus fuit A° 1634. (Hevingham Register.)*

In Christian names no distinction in indexing has been made between obvious synonyms, and Marie, Mary, Marye, Susanna, Susannah, Susanne, and like variations will be found generally under that form which occurs first.

The Editor cannot conclude this somewhat lengthy introduction without expressing his obligations to Dr Bensly and Walter Overbury, Esq., for their ready permission to make use of the records in the Registries of the Diocesan and Archdeacon respectively.

A. T. M.

November, 1889.

CONTENTS.

CORRIGENDA.

P. 1, *line* 4, *for* Baptizatorum *read* Baptizatarum.

P. 3, *line* 8, *for* thee *read* this.

P. 9, *line* 30, *for* Cabrrooke *read* Carbrooke.

P. 46, *line* 29, *for* * Thomas *read* ** Thomas.

P. 106, *line* 28, *for* Edmond *read* Edward.

P. 130, *line* 1, *The Entry should read*, James Garnutt, of S^{ct} Peter of Mancroft singleman and Mary Breese singlewoman of S^{ct} Edmond, &c.

P. 156, *line* 10, *for* Lives *read* Lines.

P. 181, *line* 25, *for* 3^d *read* S^d

P. 221, *line* 30, *for* Thomas read James.

P. 294, *line* 4, *for* Jan : *read* June.

The Marsham Parish Register

From 1538 to 1836.

REGISTERIUM OMNIUM AC SINGULORUM NOMINUM PERSON-
ARUM VIDELICET A PRIMO OCTOBRIS MENSIS DIE
ANNO MILLESIMO QUINGENTESIMO TRICESIMO[1] OCTAVO,
BAPTIZATORUM, CONJUGIO DEINDE CONIUNCTARUM, ATQUE
SEPULTARUM DENIQUE. ANNO AUTEM HENRICI OCTAVI
REGIS TRICESIMO. AD PRIMUM PLACITUM DICTI REGIS
ATQUE FORTIOREM ELIZABETHÆ REGINÆ NUNC IN . . . . . .[2]
ANNO ILLIUS REGNI CONFIRMATIONEM SUBIECTUM.
PER ME HENRICUM ALDRED CURATUM HUIUS PAROCHIÆ
FIDELITER RECOLLECTUM AC PRIMUM AUCTUM.

    CHRISTENINGS.

* *   MARRIAGES.

* * *   BURIALS.

ANNO DOMINI 1538.

John Reynolds of Alisham and Faith Persie of Marsham
wer married the 14 daie of October.

Margerie yᵉ daughter of Andrew Hobson was baptised 21
daie of October.

Margaret the daughter of John Barnye was baptised the
19 day of December.

* Cisly yᵉ daughter of John Seyve was baptised the 24 day
of December.

---

[1] This word is written in the margin.
[2] Left blank but should be again *tricesimo*.

B

* Robt. the sonne of Richard Carier was baptised y⁰ 17 day of Februarie

Anno Dni 1539.

Ciselie Kinge set under.

* * * Margaret Wyth widowe was buried xxii day Aprill.

* * Reynolde Bryan and Margaret Harvye wer married the 26 day of Aprill.

Margaret daughter of John Bustinge was baptised the x day of Maie.

Reynolde Wake y⁰ sonne of John Wake was baptised the first daye of June.

* Ciselie y⁰ daughter of Thomas Thackewey was baptised the xiii of June.

Elizabeth y⁰ wife of Thomas Thackewey was buried y⁰ xiiii of June.

Margaret the daughter of William Marshall was baptised the 4th daye of June.

Edmunde Bishoppe et Margaret Codnham of Marsham wer married the xiii of Julye.

Edmunde Carbrooke the sonne of William Carbrooke was baptised the xvii daye of August.

Moreover y⁰ Registerium Anno Dni 1539 continuatur.

Ciselie Kinge y⁰ daughter of Thomas Kinge was baptised the 14 day of March.

* * Willm Wyth and Alyce Pestell wer married in cemeterio de omnibus Sanctis y⁰ 28 day Septembris.

* John Massam y⁰ sonne of Henrye Massam was baptised y⁰ ii day of October.

* * * Bettrice Wyth was buried in cemeterio de Omnibus sanctis y⁰ viii day of November.

Thomas Smythe y⁰ sonne of Antonye Smyth was buried the xxviii of November.

* John Wake the sonne of Willm. Wake was baptised xviii day of November.

* * Simon Chapman and Helene Quitte of Marsham wer married the 24 day of November.

* * * John Bustinge was buried y⁰ xxi of December.

* Margerie Sawer ye daughter of Thomas Sawer was baptised
ye xxi daye of December.

Anno Dni 1540.

* Ciselye ye daughter of Alane Mors was baptised the vi daye
of March.

* Margerye Chapman, Simon Chapman's daughter, was baptised the xiii day of June.

This last name is set downe in thee evill order bycause that in
y^e former Register he first leaped much space inconsiderately
wh^c is after written up with this chrystenynge, which fell in the
moneth of June follow [1] . . . . . y^e place wh^c he had
leaped between y^e 13 and y_e 28 daye of . . . .

. 3. * Alan^e y^e sonne of John Barnye was baptised y^e xx of
Ma(rch).

* Agnes Hobson y^e daughter of Andrew Hobson was baptised
the xxviii daye of March.

* Robt. the sonne of Edmonde Bishoppe was baptis'd the xviii
day of Aprill.

* Audrie Tucke y^e daughter of Simon Tucke was baptised the x
of Aprill.

* Henrye the sonne of John Elvin was baptised the first of
Maye.

* Johann Marryon ye daughter of Marryon was baptised the 10
of Maye.

* * * Johann Marryon aforesaid daughter of Marryon was
buryed the 10 of Maye.

* * * Marryon Bryan was buried ye 20 daye of June.
Johan Bennit was buryed ye 14 daye of August.

* Agnes Redfen ye daughter of Willm. Redfen was baptised the
xv day of August.

* Annas Bishoppe of Marsham was baptised the 10 daye of
September.

* * * Alyce Gre [2] . . . was buried the 10 day of Oct.

* Ciselie Rogers was baptised the xiii day of October.

---

[1] Some words perished.

[2] Some letters have been erased in this name.

* * * Margaret Faror was buried yᵉ xxx day of Nov.

* * * Willm. Smithe was buried yᵉ xviii day.

* Edmunde Coates was baptised yᵉ last day of December
Moreover yᵉ Register in ano Dni 1540 is yet continued.

* * * Henrye Bryan was buried yᵉ 6 day of April.

* * Willm. Louth and Margaret Toolye wer married the xx
day of June.

* Margaret the daughter of Edmonde Bishoppe was baptised
the xxiiii of Oct.

* Margaret yᵉ daughter of John Wake was baptised the xvi of
November.

Anno Dni 1541.

* * Thomas Bryaunt and Ciselie Bennet wer married the xviii
daye of Julye.

* * Thomas Sonclaw and Dorytie Fonell wer married the xvii
daye of August.

* * Robt. Host and Margaret Coates wer married the xiii day
of November.

Nicholas the sonne of John Downinge was baptised upon
yᵉ feast day of yᵉ Nativitie of Chr.

* Edmunde yᵉ sonne of Adam Farrour was baptised yᵉ 25 of
January.

* Margaret yᵉ daughter of Alane Mors was baptised yᵉ 5 of
Februar.

* * * Richarde Riches was buried yᵉ 4 of Februar.

* * * Nicholas Downinge was buried yᵉ viii daie of March.

* Edmund yᵉ sonne of John Seyve was baptised yᵉ xx daye of
March.

Anno Dni 1542.

* Margaret yᵉ daughter of Andrew Hobson was baptised the
xxv daye of March.

P. 4. * Robt. Sawer the sonne of Thomas Sawer was baptised the
xxvi daie of March.

* Willm. the sonne of Willm. Wake was baptised the xxx daye
of Aprill.

* Thomas the sonne of Thomas Sonneinlaw was baptised the ii of Maye.

* * * Johan ye daughter of John Reynold was buried ye v daye of Maye.

Edmund ye sonne of Robt. Host was baptised ye vi day of Maye.

* * * Margaret Wake was buried the 10 day of Maye.

Thomas ye sonne of Thomas Kinge was baptised xxvi daye of Maye.

* Adam ye sonne of John Helwyns was baptised ye xxviii of Maye.

Anno Dni 1543.

* Thomas Dockin and Fabella Chapman wer married the xiiii daye of Januarie.

* * Ju Bequette was buried y^a xvii day of Januarie.

* Willm. Hackett was baptised the xx day of November.

* Margerie ye daughter of Willm. Brigges was baptised the x day of October.

Anno Dni 1544.

* Johannes Mosse was baptised the Ultimo die Januarii.

* * * Willm. Brigges was buried the xiii daye of Februarie.

* Allin Hopman was baptised ye xv day of Februarie.

* * * Edmunde Carbrooke was buried ye xxiiii day of Februarie

* * * Willm. Hewet was buried ye xxv day of Februarie.

* Margaret Bishopp was baptised ye xi daye of March.

Anno Dni 1545.

* John Hawkins was baptised the iii daye of Aprill.

* Agnes Nicholl was baptised the xxi daye of Aprill.

* * John Pye and Mautild Margerison wer married xxii daye of Aprill.

* Agnes Reynolds was baptised the xxvi daye of Maye.

* * Willm. Carbrooke and Margaret Herman wer married the vii day of June.

* * Nicholas Louth and Ursla Bayman wer married the vi daye of Julye.

Johan the daughter of Willm. Carbrooke was baptised the iii day of August.

Margareta the daughter of Thomas Bonnet was baptised the 5 day of August.

Margaret ye daughter of Henrye Marsham was baptised the xvi daye of August.

* John ye sonne of Nicholas Downinge was baptised the xi daye of September.

* Willm. the sonne of Richarde Barnye was baptised the xiii daye of September.

Edmund ye sonne of Thomas Soway was baptised the xxvii daye of September.

Margaret ye daughter of Willm Redfield was baptised the x daie of October.

* * * Johan ye daughter of Willm. Carbrooke was buried x day of October.

Anno Dni 1546.

* * * Agnes Thaxter was buried ye x of September.

* * * Johan Aunckine was buried ye xiii of Septem.

* * * Edmund Farror was buried ye xv of Septem.

* * * Helene Farror was buried xxiii of Septem.

* * * Dorothie ye daughter of one man of Cawson was buried ye xi of October.

Edmunde Pinninge and Avis Wilson wer married the 10 of October.

* Agnes Smith was baptised ye xiii of October.

* * * Clemes Farrar was buried ye 20 of October.

* * * Helene Farrar was buried xxiii of October.

* * * Ciselie Downinge was buried ye xxv day of October.

Clement Farror was baptised the xxvi of October.

* * * Clement Farror was buried ye xxx of October.

* * * Agnes Redfinne was buried the xix of November.

* * * Doritie and Sicelie Morse were buried the xx of November.

Agnes and Margerie Coate wer buried ye xxiii of
　　　November.
* 　Agnes Smith was baptised the (xxiii of November).
* * * 　Margaret Redfinne was buried the xvi daye of December.
* * * 　John Downinge and Thomasin Morse wer buried the
　　　xix of December.
* * * 　Etheldred Tucke was buried ye xxv of Decem.
* 　Thomas Downinge was baptised the xxix of December.
* * * 　Margaret Morse was buried yo xxix Decemb.
* * * 　John Morse was buried ye x day of Januarie.
* * * 　Johann Ewinch was buried ye 18 of Januarie.
* 　John Dicks was baptised the xix of Januarie.
* * * 　Agnes Redfin was buried ye xxi of Januarie.
* * * 　James Sonclaw was buried ye xxiii of Januarie.
* * * 　Thomas Downinge was buried the xxv day of Januar.
* * * 　Willm Morse was buried ye xxix of Januar.
* * * 　Peter Kinge was buried ye xxx of Januarie.
* * * 　Robt. Morse was buried ye 1 day of Februarie
P. 6. * 　Avis Wake was baptised ye xix of Februarie.
　　* 　Alice Woode was baptised ye xv of Februarie.
　　* 　Johannis Carbrooke was baptised ye xxi of March.

Anno Dni 1547.

* * * 　Agnes Mollet was buried ye xvi of March.
* * 　John Elwin and Fraunces Haulse wer married the xx of
　　　Aprill.
* 　Anna Nicolls was baptised ye xxi of Aprill.
* * 　John Pye and Matilda Margerison wer married the xxi of
　　　Aprill.
　　Alyce Coates was baptised the xv daye of Maye.
* 　Alice Hobson was baptised ye xix day of Maye.
* 　Agnes Reynolds was baptised xxvi day of Maye.
* * * 　John Carbrooke was buried ye xx of Maye.
* 　Edmund Mollett was baptised the iii of June.
* 　Elizabeth Bishoppe was baptised the xi of June.
* * 　Willm. Carbrooke and Margaret Herman wer married the
　　　vii of June.

Nicholas Louth and Ursula Bayman wer married the xvi
of Julye.

Johan Carbrooke was baptised the iii of August.

* Margaret Bennett was baptised the v of August.

Margaret Farror was baptised the vii of August.

Margaret Marsham was baptised yᵉ xvi of August.

* * * Agnes Thaxter was buried the x of September.

[* * * Johan Anckin was buried yᵉ xiii of September.

* * * Edmunde Farror was buried yᵉ xv of September.

Helene Farror was buried the xxiii of September.

These names conteined wᵗʰ this bonde which gripeth them
together, and manye other, doe belonge to the yeare 154(5)
goinge before, all yᵉ names of yᵉ wʰ said yeare wer set down
twise in yᵉ old Register, therefore these ar to be red amonge
their fellows sub titulo 154(5) whereby notwithstandinge yᵗ I
have begunne to write them here againe, you may in comparinge
yᵉ new with yᵉ old the more plainely se how truelie this new
Register is copied out and brought into better order yᵉ trueth
being kept].

* John Downinge was baptised yᵉ xi of September.

* Willm. Barnye was baptised yᵉ xiii of September.

* Edmund Sawer was baptised yᵉ xxvii of September.

* * Thoms. House and Agnes Camplyn wer married the x of
October.

* * * Johan Carbrooke was buried yᵉ 10 of October.

Continues de Anno Dni 1547 Registerium ex subicctis primis.

* Willm. Filbeck was baptised the xi of Ma(ye).

* Alyce Coates was baptised xv day of May.

* Alyce Hobson was baptised xviii day of Ma.

* * * John Cabrrooke was buried yᵉ xx of Maye.

* Edmund Mollet was baptised yᵉ iii of June.

* Elizabet Bishoppe was baptised yᵉ xi of June.

* Margerie Farror was baptised yᵉ vii of Aug.

* * Richarde Hubar and Johan Bryant wer married the xxiii of
October.

* Agnes Ascue was baptised yᵉ v of November.

* Nicholas Smith was baptised vi of December.

* * * Margareta Bryant was buried yᵉ 9 of December.

* Thomas Elwins was baptised the xix of December.
* Willm. Chapman was baptised the xxiii of December.
* Robt. Seyve was baptised the x daie of Januarie.
* Robt. Redfin was baptised ye xix of Januarie.
* John Souhelaw was baptised ye viii of March.
* Margaret Rumpe was baptised ye ix of March.
* * * Edmunde Downinge was buried the xix of March.

Anno Domini 1548.

* Willm. Morse was baptised ye xxv day of Mar.
* Andrew Bishoppe was baptised ye xxix of Mar.
* * John Lowth and Margaret Wilson were married ye x of June.
* John Carbrooke was baptised ye xv of June.
* Margaret Farror was baptised ye iii of Julye.
* * Robt. Cowper and Margaret Midleton wer married the xiii of Julye.
* * Willm. Willington and Elizabeth Crome wer married the xxiii of Septer.
* * Richard Clarke and Margaret White wer married xvii day of October.
* * Simonde Lombe and Avis Pinninge wer married ye v daye of November.
* Agnes Nicolls was baptised the xii day of November.
* Marie Elwyn was baptised ye v daie of December.
* Agnes Sawer was baptised ye xvi daie of December.
* Thomas Smyth was baptised xxix of December.
* * * Johan Marsham was buried ye v of Januarie.
* Susan Burie was baptised ye iii of Februarie.
* * * Dorithie Morse was buried ye ix of Februarie.
* Thomas Haber was baptised ye xiii of Februarie.
* * * Ketterine Towneson was buried ye viii of March.
* * * Richarde Cooke ye ix Johan Bright ye xii of March wer buried.

Anno Dni 1549.

* Simonde Lombe was baptised ye 8 day of April.
* * * John Gosse was buried ye x of Aprill.

Margaret Lowth was baptised ye xxv of Aprill.

Johanna Wake was baptised ye xxii daye of Maye.

* * *   The same Johan Wake was buried ye xxv daic of Maye.

John Willington was borne the xix daic of June.

Margaret Farror was borne the last daic of ye moneth of Julye.

Edmunde Bishoppe the sonne of Richard was borne the iiii daic of August.

Christofer and John Clarke the sonnes of Richard Clarke wer borne the xv daic of August.

Thomas the sonne of Willm. Wake was borne ye xxviii daye of August.

Edmunde ye sonne of Willm. Preston was borne the xiii of November.

William Mollet died ye iiii of November.

Ciselie Coningham died ye xviii of November.

Susan Burye died ye xxii of November.

Alyce ye wife of Edmunde Chapman was buried ye iiii daye of December.

Fraunces Elwyns was borne the iiii daic of Januarie.

* * *   Johan ye daughter of John Scyve died the vii of Januarie.

* * *   Simonde Lombe died the ix of Januarie.

Alyce Carbrooke was borne the xiiii of Februarie.

Willm. ye sonne of Thomas Waike was baptised the xviii daic of Februarie.

Agnes ye daughter of Thomas Chapman was baptised the xx daic of Februarie.

Robt. Farclay was baptised ye xx daic of Februarie.

* * *   John Walbye was buried the xvi daic of March.

* * *   Margaret Clawey was buried ye xvii daic of March.

Katherine ye daughter of John Vicne died ye xx day of March.

ANNO DNI 1550.

Thomas Bryan was buried the xxvi of March.

Edmund Wake and Nicholas Reymers wer buried ye iiii daye of Aprill.

Thomas the sonne of James Dennis was baptised xi daye of
Aprill.

John yᵉ sonne of John Wake was borne the last daie of
Maye.

Margaret yᵉ daughter of Willm. Redfin was baptised the xx
of Julye.

* Marie Rumpe was baptised yᵉ xii daie of August.

* John and Sicelie yᵉ children of Robt. Coningham wer baptised
the vi of September.

Nicholas yᵉ sonne of Thomas Askew was baptised yᵉ xx daye
of December.

Alyce Woods was baptised yᵉ xx daye of November.

Margerie Bishoppe was baptised the 10 daie of December.

* Margerie yᵉ daughter of Thomas Sawer was baptised yᵉ xviii
daye of Februarie.

Margaret yᵉ daughter of John Elwyn was baptised the xxvii
daye of Februarie.

* John yᵉ sonne of Richarde Burye was baptised yᵉ xxii daye
of March.

The Marriages be written against these in yᵉ ix leafes side
(i.e., P. 10).

Anno Dni 1551.

* Agnes yᵉ daughter of Willm. Wake was baptised the xxvi
day of March.

* Willm. Willington was baptised 6 of Aprill.

* Thomas yᵉ sonne of John Lowth was baptised yᵉ xix day of
Aprill, and

* Johan filia Thomae Farror yᵉ same daie.

* James yᵉ sonne of Richarde Haver was baptised the xxiiii of
Aprill.

* * John Dennisse and Margaret his wife were married the xiii
of August.

* Alyce yᵉ daughter of Thomas Bunnet was baptised the xx of
September.

* Alyce yᵉ daughter of Willm. Smith was baptised the xxix daie
of September.

* * Robt. Coningham and Margaret his wife wer married the xx day of October.

* * Richarde Smith and Johan his wife wer married the xxviii daic of October.

* Margerie yᵉ daughter of John Seyvc was baptised the xxviii daic of October.

* John Wake yᵉ sonne of John Wake was baptised the xxviii day of December.

* * * The aforesaide John Wake was buried the xxviii day of December.

* * * Elizabeth Halott was buried the xv of Januarie.

* * Thomas Greene and Johan Browne of Caston wer married the xxvii daic of Januarie.

* Willm. Smith yᵉ sonne of John Smith was baptised the first daye of March.

Edmunde Townesend was baptised the xv daye of March.

Anno Dni 1552.

* Alyce yᵉ daughter of Edmonde Ferror was baptised the xv daic of Aprill.

* Margerie yᵉ sonne [1] of Thomas Chapman was baptised the xxv daic of Aprill.

* John yᵉ sonne of Edmunde Rogers was baptised the xxix daic of Aprill.

* John yᵉ sonne of Robt. Veric was baptised the viii daie of Maic.

* Robt. yᵉ sonne of John Elwyns was baptised the x daie of Maic.

P. 10. * Agnes Wallbye yᵉ . . . [2] John Wallbye was baptised the xii daic of June.

* * Thomas Wood and Alice Bateman wer married the x daie of Julye.

* Johan Batteman yᵉ daughter of John Bateman was baptised the xviii daic of Julye.

---

[1] Sic in Register.
[2] Left blank in Register.

* Also againe Johan Battman yᵒ daughter of aforesaide John Bateman was baptised being another daughter of the same conception.

* Richarde yᵉ sonne of John Lowth was baptised the xxiii of Julye.

* * * Tricesimo die sepultus fuit Thomas Tyler.

* John yᵉ sonne of Thomas Thackwett was baptised the xxi daie of August.

* * Thomas Barnye and Ciselie Chapman wer married as is noted 3 names under this.

* * * Alyce Coates was buried the (vi daie of Sept.)

* * * Adam yᵉ sonne of Elwings was buried yᵉ xxiii day of September.

Thomas Barnye and Cisclie Chapman wer married the xxviii day of October.

* * * Dorithie yᵉ daughter of James Dennis was buried xxviii of November.

Avis Wiggenhall was baptised the xiii of November.

Dorytye Dennis was baptised yᵒ xvi day of November.

Margerie yᵉ daughter of Johan Typpett was baptised the xxix daye of yᵉ moneth of November.

* * Doritie yᵉ daughter of James Dennis was buried the xxviii day of November.

* Doritie yᵉ daughter of Willm. Redfin was baptised the xxiii day of December.

* * * Katharine Goodwin was buried xiii day of Januarie.

* * Robt. Battman and Olife Smith of Linge were married the xv daie of Januarie.

* * John White and Fabell Dockinge of Alisham widow wer married yᵒ xvi of Januarie.

* * Nicholas Coun'r[1] of Holt and Katherine Bishoppe widow of Marsham wer married yᵉ xi of Februarie.

* * * Alyce yᵉ wife of Robt Hervey was buryed the xvii daie of Februarie.

* Thomas Wake yᵉ sonne of Thomas Wake was baptised the xiiii daye of Februarie.

* Bryan yᵉ daughter of Edmonde Bishoppe was baptised the xxvi daie of Februarie.

---

[1] A doubtful reading.

Henric yᵉ sonne of Robt. Coningham was baptised the v daie of March.

John Hawking was buried the first daye of March.

* * * Johan Baken was buried the xviii daye of March who was yᵉ wife of Willm. Baken.

Anno Dni 1553.

* John yᵉ sonne of Robt. Haver was baptised the xvi of April.

* * * Henry yᵉ sonne of Robt. Conebye was buried yᵉ xviii day of Aprill.

P. 11.* * John Monie of Sharington and Aiothea Coates wer married yᵉ first daie of May.

Johan Hoode yᵉ daughter of John Hoode was buried the xii day of Julye.

Anno Dni 1554.

Margaret Donett was buried yᵉ xxv of October who was yᵉ wife of Thomas Bonnet.[1]

Johan Donnett their daughter was buried yᵉ same daye.

Estell yᵉ daughter of Edmunde Rogers was baptised the xxviii day of October.

* Avis yᵉ daughter of John Lowth was baptised the xxviii of October.

Willm. Bryan of Cawston and Etheldred Raymers of Marsham ([2]wer married) vi daie of November.

John yᵉ sonne of Willm. Younges was baptised the ix daie of November.

* Willm. yᵉ sonne of Thomas Woddes was baptised the ix of November.

Robt. yᵉ sonne of John Seyve was baptised yᵉ xiii of November.

* Agnes yᵉ daughter of Robert Dateman was baptised the xvii daie of November.

Margaret yᵉ daughter of Robt. Bustinge was baptised yᵉ xxvi daie of November.

---

[1] Sic in Register.

[2] The lines show this to be a marriage.

* * * Edmunde yᵉ sonne of Christopher Mollet was baptised and buried yᵉ iii daye of Januarie.

* * * John yᵉ sonne of Willm. Younges was buried yᵉ x daie of Januarie.

* * * Agnes yᵉ daughter of Robt. Bateman was buried yᵒ xiii Janu :

* * Thomas Bonnett and Margaret Gladon wer married yᵉ xv daye of Januarie.

* Margerie yᵉ daughter of Thomas Sower was baptised yᵉ xvii of Januarie.

* * * Margerie yᵉ daughter of Thomas Chapman was buried yᵉ xxvi day of Januarie.

* Margaret yᵉ daughter of Robt. Matthu was baptised yᵉ first daie of Februarie.

* Margaret Kinge gotten in base yᵒ daughter of Alyce Kinge was baptised the vi of Februarie.

* * * The saide Margaret Kinge was buried the same daie

* Avis yᵒ daughter of Thomas Farror was baptised the tertia die.

* Margaret yᵒ daughter of James Dennis was baptised the vi daie of March.

Anno Dᴺɪ 1555.

* * * Alyce yᵒ daughter of Richarde Caryer was buried yᵉ xxvi daye of Maye

* * * Alyce yᵉ daughter of Robt. Bateman was buried the xxvii of Maye.

* * * Willm. yᵒ sonne of Thomas Wake was buried the xv daie of June.

* Agnes yᵒ daughter of Thomas Downinge was baptised the vii of Julie.

* John yᵉ sonne of John Woodcocke was baptised the xiii of Julie.

* * * Marye yᵉ daughter of Stephane Hill was buried the iii daie of October.

* Willm. Joonys yᵉ sonne of Willm. Joonys was baptised the first day of Decemb.

* John yᵉ sonne of Willm. Wake was baptised yᵉ xix daie of December.

*   Avice y⁰ daughter of William Rogers was baptised the xvi of
Februarie.

* * *   Robt. y⁰ sonne of Robt. Mathew was buried the vii of
March.

Anno Dni 1556.

Edmunde the sonne of John Fynde was baptised the xxvii
of March.

*   Henrye y⁰ sonne of Edmonde Monye was baptised the xxix
of March.

* * *   Avis yᵉ daughter of Thomas Farrow was buried the x of
Maie.

Hew Lowne y⁰ sonne of John Lowne was baptised the xxviii
daie of Maie.

John yᵉ sonne of Thomas Woods was baptised the same
daie.

* *   Robt. Bishopp was buried y⁰ xxix daie of Maie.

Johan y⁰ daughter of Edmonde Bishoppe was baptised the
xxxi day of Maye.

Marie yᵉ daughter of Edmonde Bishoppe was baptised the
xxviii of Maye.

Reynold Beryan was buried the xviii of August.

* * *   Robt. y⁰ sonne of Andrew Lambarde was buried the xviii
daie of August.

*   Elizabeth Bateman y⁰ daughter of Robt. Bateman was
baptised the xxi of August.

*   *   Ciselie wife of Thomas Chapman was buried y⁰ ix daie
of September.

*   John the sonne of William Wade was buried the x daie
of September.

* *   Thomas Gills and Agnes Lowson wer married the xv daie
of September.

* * *   John y⁰ sonne of John Smith was buried y⁰ xx daie of
September.

* * *   Agnes y⁰ wife of Robt. Bishoppe was buried the xxviii
day of September.

* * *   Agnes y⁰ wife of Edmonde Chapman was buried the ii of
October.

* * * Agnes ye daughter of Thomas Chapman was buried
ye vii daye of October.

* * * Robt. Wegge was buried ye xv of October.

* * * Margaret ye daughter of Robt. Mathew was buried the
xv day of October.

* John Bonnet and Margaret Bonnet the sonne and daughter
of Thomas Bonnett wer baptised and buried the x
daie of November.

* * * John Wallbye was buried ye same daie.

* * * Willm Bryam was burid ye xii of December.

* * * Alyce Mollet was buried ye xv of December.

* * * Thomas Save was buried ye xxii of December.

* * * Margaret Marsh was buried ye xxvii of December.

* * * John Chapman was buried ye xxviii of December.

* * * Thomas Midleton was buried the v of Januarie.

* * * Edmond Farrour was buried ye ix daie of Januarie.

* * * Thomas Farrour was buried ye xxvii of Januarie.

* * Edwarde Doughtie and Audrie Bryam widow wer married
the iii daie of Februarie.

* * * John Woods was buried the x daie of Februarie.

[1]

Anno Dni 1579.

P. 24.* * John Thurston and Sara Rosier wer married the xi of
Januarie.

* * * Martin Dix was buried ye xv of Januarie.

* * * Vastian Dix was buried ye xvii daie of Januri.

* * * Ciselie Watton was buried ye viii of Februarie.

* Agnes ye daughter of Richarde Pye was baptised the iii of
Mar.

* Robt. ye sonne of John Coningham was baptised ye vi of
March.

Anno Dni 1580.

* * * Avis ye daughter of Jane Nicolls was buried ye xxv day
of Aprill.

* * Willm. Watton and Margaret Litlewodde wer married the
xxix of Aprill.

* Margerie Bunnet was baptised ye viii of Maie.

---

[1] 12 Pages are missing.

C

*   Simon y⁰ sonne of Thomas Smith was baptised y⁰ xii of Maie.

* * *   Agnes Pawlins was buried y⁰ xviii of Mayo

*   Robt. y⁰ sonne of Robt. Vout was baptised the xxii daie of Maic.

*   George y⁰ sonne of John Bery was baptised the xxii of Maie.

*   Ollie y⁰ daughter of Will. Locket was baptised the xxiii of Maie.

*   Susan Kinge was baptised y⁰ x of Julye.

*   Agnes Chambers was baptised y⁰ xvii daie of Julye.

*   Elizabeth Oliver was baptised y⁰ iiii daie of September.

Margerie Thurston was baptised y⁰ xxiii of October.

*   John Dennis was baptised y⁰ vi daie of November.

John Shorten was baptised y⁰ same daie.

*   Katherine Wake was baptised y⁰ xxvii of November.

* * *   Margaret Watson was buried y⁰ xxix of November.

* * *   Margerie Smith was buried xxviii daie of December.

* * *   George Berye was buried y⁰ xxiiii of Januarie.

* * *   Doritie Harman was buried y⁰ xxvi of Januarie.

*   ——[1]Sanders was baptised y⁰ v daie of Februarie.

Anno Dni 1581.

*   Marion Willes was baptised y⁰ xxv daie of March.

*   Bridget Watson was baptised y⁰ ii daye of Aprill.

* *   Valentine Suffolke and John Plummer wer married the v daie of Maie.

*   Edmonde y⁰ sonne of John Marsham was baptised the xiiii of Maie.

Doritie Marsham was baptised y⁰ same daie.

* * *   Isabell Rogers buried y⁰ xi of June.

* * *   Robt. Gednye was buried y⁰ xv daie of June.

*   Robt. Ryall was baptised y⁰ xvii daie of September.

Marion White was baptised the first daie of October.

*   Agnes Kinge was baptised the viii daie of October.

*   Robt. Hemminge was baptised y⁰ x daie of November.

*   Henric Harwin was baptised y꜀ xix of November.

---

[1] Left blank in Register.

* Nicholas Voute was baptised yᵉ xxvi daie of November.
* Timotheus Otes filius Samuelis Otes cler. baptizatus fuit November xxvii.
* * * Henric Harwin was buried yᵉ xxvi daie of November.

P. 25.

Anno Dni 1582.

* Alyce Spicer was baptised yᵉ first of Aprill.
* * * Elizabeth Jecks was buried yᵒ xxiii of **Aprill**.
* * * Alyce Geduye was buried xxiiii of Aprill.
* * * John Seayve was buried yᵒ v daie of Maie.
* * * Robt. Romer was buried yᵒ xii daie of Maie.
* John Tomlinson was baptised yᵒ xiii daie of Maie.
* * Frauncis Elmore Gent and Anne Ling wer married the xix of September.
* Doritie Sowthes was baptised yᵉ ii of November.
* John Chambers of yᵒ parrishe of Alisham was baptised the xxv daie of November.
* * Christopher Pye and Jhoan Pawlinge wer married the xx of Januarie.
* Thomas Harwin was baptised yᵒ xi daie of Februarie.
* Agnes Alderkare was baptised yᵒ xxiiii of Februarie.

Anno Dni 1583.

* Thomas Wake was baptised the xiiii of Aprill.
* * * Willm. Mollet was buried yᵒ xxiiii of Maie.
* Samuel Pye was baptised the xxi daie of Julye.
* John Dennis was baptised the first of (D)ecember.
* Alice Marsham was baptised yᵒ viii daie of September.
* Frauncis Kinge was baptised yᵒ vi of October.
* Marie Elmore was baptised Novembris.
* Thomas Watson was baptised yᵒ vii of November.
* Prudence Parson was baptised vi of December.
* * * Eadem Prœdicta Prudenc was buried yᵒ xii of December.
* Robt. Rannow and Margaret Rannow wer baptised yᵒ xxvi of Januarie.
* Titus Oates was baptised yᵒ same daie.
* * * Olyve Locket was buried yᵒ xii of March.

Anno Dni 1584.

*   Margaret Forrest was baptised the xx° daie of Aprill.

* * *   Marie Pye was buried y° viii daie of Maie.

* *   George Fletcher and Alice Stive wer married the xxx° daie of Maie.

* * *   John Wilton was buried y° iii of August.

* * *   Robt. Bustinge was buried y° xx° of September.

* * *   Thomas Wake was buried y° iiii of October.

Edmunde White was baptised y° xxv° daie of October.

* * *   Agnes Litlewoode was buried y° xxix of December.

* * *   Margaret Bustinge was buried ye viii daie of Januarie.

John Hemminge was baptised y° x° daie of Januarie.

*   Agnes Willes was baptised y° xvii daie of Januarie.

* * *   Elizabeth Gednye was buried y° xxi daie of Januarie.

* *   ——[1]Freeman and Margaret Tod wer married y° xvii of Januarie.

*   Elizabeth Sowthes was baptised y° xxiii of Januarie.

*   Mathias Woodstacke was baptised y° xxix of Februarie.

*   Barbarie Spicer was baptised y° xiiii daie of March.

* * *   Nicholas Winnie was buried y° xviii of March.

*   Robt. Wilton was baptised y° xxi daie of March.

P. 26.   Anno Dni 1585.

*   Samuell Marsham was baptised the xix of Aprill.

*   Edmunde Marsham was baptised the xxv daie of Aprill.

*   Peter Braser was baptised the xxv daie of Aprill.

* * *   Edmonde Stive was buried y° xvii daie of Maie.

* *   Willm. Wake and Elizabeth Bustinge wer married the xxiii daie of Maie.

*   Willm. Ryall was baptised the viii of June.

*   Richarde Bateman was baptised y° iii daie of Julye.

* *   Robt. Newman and Anne Pickrell wer married the xii of Julie.

* *   John Wake and Doritie Stive wer married the first daie of August.

---

[1] Left blank in Register.

* John Fletcher was baptised ye viii daie of August.

* Margaret Alderkar was baptised y^o xxii of August.

* * * Margerie Marshall was buried ye first of September.

* Robt. Wild and Agnes Chapman wer married the xxvii daie of September.

* Richarde Conabie was baptised ye x^o of October.

* Edward Suffolke was baptised the xxi daie of November.

* * * The same Edwarde was buried the xxviii of November.

* Richarde Bell was baptised y^o xxviii daie of November.

* * * Agnes Wilde was buried ye xx^o daie of December.

* Marie Pye was baptised the ix daie of Januarie.

* Prudene Freeman was baptised y^o ix daie of Januarie.

* Robt. Otes was baptised the xiii daie of Februarie.

* Robt. Tomlinson was baptised ye xiiii of Februarie.

* John Watson was baptised ye xx^o daie of March.

Anno Dni 1586.

["This year I do not finde that any were Registered."[1]]
Here follows Note on Bells, see Appendix.

P. 27.　　　　　　　### Anno Dni 1587.

* Robt. ye sonne of Edmonde Marsham was baptised the vii daie of Maie.

* Anne y^o daughter of Edmonde Elwarde was baptised the first daie of (June)

* Elizabeth ye daughter of John Riston was baptised ye first daie of June.

* Barbarie Aldercar was baptised ye ix daie of Julie.

* Sara ye daughter of Thomas Greene was baptised y^o xxx^o daie of Julie.

* * * Winfridd Bishoppe was buried ye xii daie of August.

* * John Grony and Margaret Gednye wer married the xxiiii daie of September.

* * Richard Pearce and Margaret Lowth wer married the v daie of November.

---

[1] In Handwriting No. 2.

* Willm. yͤ sonne of John Harwen was baptised the xᵒ daie of November.

* Elizabeth yͤ daughter of Edmonde Bel was baptised the first daie of Jannarie.

* Thomas yͤ sonne of George Marsham was baptised the xᵒ daie of Januarie.

* Marie yͤ daughter of Willm. Fletcher was baptised the xiiii daie of Jannarie.

* Elizabeth yͤ daughter of Robt. Hemmen was baptised the iiii daie of Februarie.

* * * James the sonne of John Gronye was buried the xi daie of Februarie.

* * Willm. Gednie and Margaret Franke wer married the xxᵒ daie of Februarie.

* Elizabeth yͤ daughter of John Wake was baptised yᵒ xxiiii daie of March.

Anno Dni 1588.

* Willm. Dennis was baptised yͤ i daie of Aprill.

* * * Christopher Coates was buried yᵒ xii of Aprill.

* Martha Sowthes was baptised yͤ xii of Maie.

* Thomas Fletcher was baptised yͤ xixᵒ daie of Maie.

* * Thomas Moses and Johan Keede wer married yᵒ ixᵒ daie of June.

* * * Robt. Tomlinson was buried the ixᵒ daie of June.

* Doritie Moses was baptised yͤ iiii daie of August.

* * * Willm. Swan was buried yͤ xvii daie of August.

* Doritie Otes was baptised the vii daie of September.

* Thomason Bacon was baptised yͤ xvᵒ daie of September.

* Martha Pie was baptised the xvᵒ daie of November.

* John Berye was baptised yͤ same daye.

* Margaret Watson was baptised yͤ same daie.

* * James Greene and Doritie Bustinge wer married yͤ xv of December.

Blyth Woodstacke was baptised yͤ vi daie of Jannarie.

P. 28. * * Thomas Amis and Elizabeth Coleman wer married yͤ vi daie of Jannarie.

* Margaret Marsham was baptised yͤ xxiii of Februarie.

* Alice Willis was baptised ye ix daie of March.

Martha Greene was baptised ye xvi daie of March.

Anno Dni 1589.

Ciselie ye daughter of John Marsham was baptised ye viii of Maie.

* * Christopher Coates and Elizabeth Marsham wer married ye first daie of June.

Thomas ye sonne of John Conabye was baptised the xv^o daie of June.

* * * Willm. Waltam was buried ye ii daie of Julie.

* Matthie ye daughter of Willm. Geduye was baptised the xx^o daie of Julye.

* Willm. Rogers and Doritie Willis wer married i daie of August.

* Margaret ye daughter of Richarde Webster was baptised vii of September.

Avis ye daughter of Thomas Amis was baptised the xxvi daie of October.

James ye sonne of James Greene was baptised ye viii of of December.

* Willm. ye sonne of George Fletcher was baptised ye same daie ye viii of December.

* Willm. ye sonne of John Gronie was baptised ye ii daie of Februarie.

* John ye sonne of Thomas Moises was baptised ye xv^o daie of Februarie.

* Willm ye sonne of Willm Wake was baptised the first daie of March.

Robt. ye sonne of John Harwin was baptised the xv daie of March.

Anno Dni 1590.

* James ye sonne of Robt. Fletcher was baptised ye x daie of Maie.

* Doritie Bacon was baptised ye same daie.

* Margaret Kotes was baptised the iiii daie of June.

* * * James Smith was buried ye x daie of Julie.

* John y⁰ sonne of Willm. Rogers was baptised ye xx⁰ of Julie.

* Bennit Sowthes was baptised y⁰ ii daie of August.

* Johan y⁰ daughter of John Chapman was baptised y⁰ ix daie of August.

* Elizabeth Armes was baptised y⁰ xxx⁰ daie of August.

* Agnes Amis was baptised y⁰ xx⁰ daie of September.

* Abigall Daines was baptised y⁰ iiii daie of October.

* * Robt. Pickeringe and Johan Church wer married the first daie of November.

* Thomas y⁰ sonne of John Wake was baptised the viii of November.

* Beniamin Ryall y⁰ sonne of John Ryall was baptised the xxiiii daie of December.

* Rebecca Greene was baptised y⁰ xxviii of December.

Susan Edwarde was baptised y⁰ x⁰ daie of Januarie.

Willm. Hemmen was baptised y⁰ first daie of Februarie.

* * * Margaret y⁰ wife of Stephane Chapman was buried y⁰ same daie.

P. 29.* Beeffersou y⁰ sonne of Worlde was baptised y⁰ x⁰ daie of Februarie.

* Alyce Emerson was baptised y⁰ xi daie of Februarie.

* Mathie Marsham and Grace Marsham y⁰ sonne and daughter of George Marsham wer baptised y⁰ xix of Februarie.

* * * Elizabeth Wright was buried y⁰ xxvi daie of Februarie.

* Margaret Breese was baptised y⁰ xii of March.

* * * The same Margaret was buried y⁰ xvi of March.

Anno Dni 1591.

* Thomas y⁰ sonne of Edmonde Marsham was baptised y⁰ iiii daie of Aprill.

* * * Willm. Griffing was buried y⁰ xiii of Aprill.

* Richarde y⁰ sonne of Thomas Watson was baptised the xvi of Aprill.

Richarde Pye was baptised y⁰ xviii daie of Aprill.

John y⁰ sonne of James Greene was baptised the xxiii daie of Maie.

* * * John Lowe was buried y⁰ xvii daie of June.

Dorithie ye daughter of Thomas Conibye was baptised ye xx°
daie of June.

Stephane Chapman and Agnes Saive wer married the xxi
daie of June.

Peter Wilsie and Elizabeth Pickeringe wer married the iiii
daie of Julye.

Elizabeth ye daughter of Willm. Wake was baptised the
xxv° daie of Julie.

* Ciselie ye daughter of Richarde Kinge was baptised ye xviii of
August.

Christopher Coates ye sonne of Christopher Coates was
baptised ye xxxi daie of December.

Thomas ye sonne of Willm. Sowthies was baptised ye xx of
(Januarie).

Margaret ye daughter of Peter Wilsye was baptised the xxviii
of Januarie.

Drusilla ye daughter of Willm. Rogers was baptised the xi
daie of March.

Henrie ye sonne of John Vaile was baptised the xi daie of
March.

John ye sonne of Thomas Green was baptised ye xiiii daie of
March.

Anno Dni 1592.

* * * Avis ye wife of Richard Pye was buried ye iiii daie of
September.

Richarde Reade and Ciselie Estwicke wer married ye xxiiii
daie of September

* * * Robt. Fenne was buried ye ix daie of Februarie.

* * * Moother Kinge was buried ye xvi daie of March.

P. 80.   ### Anno Dni 1593.

* Elizabeth ye daughter of James Greene was baptised ye first
daie of Aprill.

* * * John Spicer was buried ye xi daie of Mai.

Mary ye daughter of John Frostwicke was baptised ye xx° daie
of Maie.

* * John Hemminge and Dorithie Waltam wer married the xxvii daie of Maie.

* * * Moother Waltam was buried yᵉ iii daie of June.

Willm. yᵉ sonne of Richard Reade was baptised yᵉ same daie.

Agnes yᵉ daughter of John Marsham was baptised yᵉ x daie of Ju.

* Thomas yᵉ sonne of Thomas Breese was baptised the xxix daie of Julye.

* Josua yᵉ sonne of Clement Free was baptised yᵉ xix of August.

* Margaret yᵉ daughter of Robt. Wilde was baptised yᵉ xxvi daie of August.

* Willm. yᵉ sonne of Thomas Moses was baptised yᵉ iii daie of November.

* Willm. yᵉ sonne of Edmonde Marsham was baptized the if daie of December.

* Agnes yᵉ daughter of ~J. Wi¹~ Read was baptised yᵉ same daie.

Elizabeth yᵉ daughter of Peter Wileye was baptised the xx° daie of Januarie.

Antonie yᵉ sonne of Willm. Mollet was baptised yᵉ iii daie of March.

Doritye yᵉ daughter of John Hemminge was baptised the ix daie of March.

* * * Dorithie Hemminge was buried yᵉ xx° daie of March.

Anno Dni 1594.

* Robt. yᵉ sonne of ——² Fletcher was baptised yᵉ ii daie of Aprill.

* Robt. yᵉ sonne of James Greene was baptised yᵉ ii daie of Aprill.

* Margaret yᵉ daughter of Robt. Fletcher was baptised the xiii daie of Aprill.

* Margerie yᵉ daughter of Thomas Watson was baptised yᵉ seconde daie of June.

* Dorithie yᵉ daughter of John Leech was baptised the first daie of Julie.

---

[1] Christian name incomplete in Register.
[2] Left blank in Register.

* Elizabeth ye daughter of George Blofeilde was baptised the xviii daie of August.

* Sara ye daughter of John Harwin was baptised ye same daie.

* John ye sonne of Thomas Lee was baptised ye xxi of September.

* * * Margaret ye wife of Fraunces Armes was buried the xxv daie of September.

* Johan ye daughter of John Gronye was baptised ye v daie of November.

* Amye ye daughter of Thomas Conibye was baptised the first daie of December.

* George ye sonne of Willm. Bateman was baptised the xxii daie of December.

* * Thomas Browne and Marie Wrenham wer married the vi daie of Januarie.

* William ye sonne of Edmonde Spinke was baptised ye xii of Januarie.

P. 31.* Stephane ye sonne of Richard Read was baptised the xix daie of ——[1]

* Alice ye daughter of Willm. Gednye was baptised the xxiii daie of March.

Anno Dni 1595.

* Richarde ye sonne of Robt. Wilde was baptised the iiii daie of May.

* John ye sonne of Christopher Coates was baptised the xxix daie of June.

* * * Robt. Vickeringe was buried ye xii daie of Julie.

* Amye ye daughter of John Bustinge was baptised ye xx daie of Julie.

* Margaret ye daughter of Robt. Hemminge was baptised xxxi daie of August.

* * * The wife of Robert Dye was buried ye vi daie of September.

---

[1] Left blank in Register.

* John y° sonne of Thomas Moses was baptised the xxii daie of September.

* * Robt. Hardinge and Agnes Campe wer married the xii daie of October.

* * John Barningham and Johan Younges wer married the xxvi daie of October.

* * Matthew Castle and Anne Dix wer married the xvi daie of November.

* Marie y° daughter of John Linge baptised the xvi daie of November also.

* Marie y° daughter of John Barningham was baptised the xxiii daie of November.

* * John Hardinge and Ellen Waltam wer married ye xxiiii daie of November.

* Thomas y° sonne of James Greene was baptised the xxx° daie of November.

* * * Marie y° daughter of John Linge was buried the ii daie of Januarie.

* Nicholas y° sonne of Willm. Gillet was baptised the vii daie of March.

* Marie y° daughter of Clement Free was baptised the xiii daie of March.

Anno Dni 1596.

* Margaret y° daughter of Thomas Goram was baptised the xviii daie of Aprill.

Elizabeth y° daughter of Thomas Browne was baptised y° ii daie of Maie.

* Thomas y° sonne of Willm. Mollet was baptised the same seconde daie of Maie.

* John y° sonne of John Frostwicke was baptised the same ii daie of Maie.

* John y° sonne of Willm. Gednye was baptised the vi daie of June.

* Johan y° daughter of Robt. Harwin was baptised the first daie of August.

* Thomas y° sonne of John Bustinge was baptised the viii daie of August.

P. 32.* Thomas yͤ sonne of Peter Wilcye was baptised yᵉ xvᵒ daic of August.

* Margaret yͤ daughter of Robt. Hardinge was baptised the xxii daie of August.

* Amy yͤ daughter of Thomas Watson was baptised yᵉ v daie of September.

* * * John Dennis was buried yᵉ vᵒ daie of October.

* * * John Rishtone was buried yᵉ ——[1]

* * * Elizabeth Lee was buried yᵒ xxvi daie of October.

* * * John Lee was buried yᵉ iiii daie of November.

* * * The Widow Wekuoles was buried yᵒ first daie of Januarie

* * * The Widowe Sower was buried yᵒ ii of Februarie.

* * * Edmunde yᵒ sonne of Edmonde Marsham was baptised[2] the xix daie of March.

Anno Dni 1797.

* Dorithic yͤ daughter of ——[1] Mortoft was baptised xᵒ daie of Aprill.

* Alice yͤ daughter of John Barningham was baptised the xvii daie of Aprill.

* * * John Wakerson was buried the xxvi daie of April.

* * * The Wife of Willm. Elwin was buried the xxix daie of Aprill.

* John yᵒ sonne of Thomas Wells was baptised the v daie of Maie.

* * * John yᵒ sonne of Goodwife Bacon was buried the viii daie of Maie.

* * * Willm. yᵒ sonne of John Gronie was buried the first daie of August.

* * * James yᵒ sonne of John Gronie was buried the vᵒ daie of August.

* * * Willm. Walton was buried the xii daie of August.

* * * Margaret yͤ daughter of John Gronie was buried the xiiii daie of August.

---

[1] Blank in Register.
[2] The lines indicate a Burial.

* * * Alice Barningham y⁰ daughter of John Barningham buried y⁰ vii daie of October.

P. 33.* Anne y⁰ daughter of John Gronye was baptised the xvi daie of October.

* * * Alice y⁰ wife of John Bateman was buried the xxi daie of October.

* Rafe y⁰ sonne of Thomas Moses was baptised the xxiii daie of October.

* John y⁰ sonne of George Winnye was baptised the xxx daie of October.

* * * George y⁰ sonne of George Fletcher was buried the x daie of December.

* * * John y⁰ sonne of John Winnye was buried the xxiii of December.

* * * Margaret y⁰ wife of Robt. Coningham was buried y⁰ first daie of Januarie.

Anno Dni 1598.

* Zara y⁰ daughter of Robt. Briggon was baptised the ii daie of Aprill.

* * * Christopher y⁰ sonne of Robt. Horne was buried the xviii daie of June.

* * * Hester Durrant y⁰ daughter of Edwarde Durrant was buried the xxiii daie of June.

* John y⁰ sonne of Willm. Mollet was baptised the v⁰ daie of Julye.

* * * The same John Mollet was buried y⁰ vii daie of Julye.

* * * The wife of John Riston was buried y⁰ xv of August.

* Alice y⁰ daughter of Christopher Coates was baptised the xx⁰ daie of August.

* * * The Widow Dennis was buried the first day of September.

* Fraunces y⁰ daughter of Erasmus Dynne, Gent, was baptised the first of October.

* Thomas y⁰ sonne of Richarde Clarke was baptised the xv⁰ daie of October.

Anne ye daughter of John Barningham was baptised the xxii
daie of October.

* *   Stephane Gednye and Katherine Bunne wer married the
xxii daie of October.

* * *   Alice Coates was buried the xx° daie of November.

* * *   Alice y° daughter of Willm. Wilton was buried the xxii
daie of December.

Robt. y° sonne of George Fletcher was baptised the xvii daie
of Januarie.

*   Sara y° daughter of John Frostwicke was baptised the xi daie
of Februarie.

P. 34.*   Bridget y° daughter of Robt. Hardinge was baptised y° fourth
daie of March.

* * *   The same Bridget was buried y° viii daie of March.[1]

Anno Dni 1599.

George the sonne of Myles Holl was baptised the first day of
Aprill.

*   Fraunces and Ciselie the sonne and daughter of Clement
Free bapt. 18 of Aprill.

* * *   John Bateman widdower was buried 18 of Aprill.

Thomas the sonne of Thomas Same bapt. xiiith of Maye.

* *   Henry Aldred Clerke then Curate here and Margrett
Browne wer married 4 day of June.

*   Thomas Gedny the sonne of Willm. Gedny Jⁿ was baptized
xxth day of June.

* * *   The wife of Thomas Same buried 4 day of August.

Margrett the daughter of John Exham bapt. y° xii day of
August.

*   John the sonne of Thomas Wilkinson bapt. y° xixth of
August.

* *   Robert Marsham and Agnes Litlewood wer married the
xxiiiith September.

*   Elizabeth the daughter of Willm. Mollet was baptised the
viith of October.

---

[1] Handwriting No. 1 ends and No. 2 begins.

* Dorathie the daughter of Christopher Cotes was baptised the iiiith day of November.

* Richard the sonne of Thomas Moyses was bapt. the iith of Decemb.

* * * Elizabeth the wife of John Withe was buried xxviiith of Decemb.

* * * Elizabeth the daughter of Willm. Mollet was buried the xxxith of Decemb.

* * * Elizabeth Oates widdow was buried the viiith of January.

* * * Agnes Coates was buried xxxth of January.

* Winnethred the daughter of John Colbye was bapt. the xth of Febr.

* John the sonne of Robert Hardinge was bapt. the xviith of Febr.

John the sonne of John Barningham was bapt. the ixth day of March.

Robert the sonne of John Harwin bapt. xvith of March.

* * * Willm. Mollet was buried the xvith day of March.

ANNO DNI 1600.

* * * Hewe Moses was buried vth day of Aprill.

* John and Alice Bateman the sonne and daughter of Will. Bateman bapt. xviith of Maye.

* John the sonne of John Jaruis was bapt. xxiiith day of Aug:

* Marye the daughter of Robt. Marsham was bapt. xviiith day of September.

* Bridget the daughter of Danye Guddins[1] was bapt. ye the . xiiiith day of Sept.

P. 35.* Thomas the sonne of ——[2] Mortoft was baptized the xxvi day of Novem.

* Alice the daughter of Alice Pickeringe was baptised the same day.

* Edwarde the sonne of ——[2] Reade bapt. ye first of November.

* John the sonne of Edmund Marsham bapt xxvth day of Janu :

---

[1] *Goodwin* in Transcript.

[2] Left blank in Register.

John the sonne of John Downinge gent was baptized the xxii of March.

Willm. the sonne of Willm. Smith was baptized the same day.

Anno Dni 1601.

Samuell Otes cler. began this yeare beinge the first yeare of his cominge to Marsham.

* * * Alice Pickeringe widdow was buried the 2nd of Aprill.

Robert Exham the sonne of John Exham was baptized the xxith day of Maye.

* Thomas Saunders the sonne of Robert Saunders was baptized the xith of Aprill. this should have com in before.

Elizabeth Otes daughter of Will : Otes was baptized ye xixth of June.

* John the sonne of John Bustinge bapt. xixth of June.

* * * Elizabeth Otes the daughter of Willm. Otes was buried xixth of Julye.

Robert the sonne of Robt. Osborne bapt. xiiith of Sept.

John the sonne of John Ryall bapt. xxith of Sept.

Sara the daughter of Thomas Wilkinson was bapt. the xxvth of October.

* * * Robt. Osborne the sonne of Robt. Osborne was buried viiith of October.

* * * Agnes Rogers the wife of Robt. Rogers was buried xixth of October.

Brigget Bustinge the wife of John Bustinge was buried xiiiith of December.

* * * George Marsham was buried xvth of December.

Thomas the sonne of John Barningham was bapt. the xxth of December.

Margrett Moyses was buried vth of Janu :

John *Dewin* was buried xth of Janu :

Margret[1] Watton was buried xith of Janu :

* * Stephen Angell[2] and Margerie Osborne were married ye xiiii of January.

---

[1] Left blank in Register, but supplied by Transcript.
[2] *Anger* in Transcript.

* * * John Marsham was buried 5 of Febr.

* * John Buslinge and Auice[1] Browne were married the xvth day of February.

(page signed) per me Samuelem Otes cler.

P. 36. * * * John Ryall was buryed xxi day of February.

* Martha ye daughter of Robt. Tylny bapt. March i.

* * * Margret the daughter of Willyam Streek was buryed March xi.

* * * John Cunningham was buryed March xvth.

* * * Alice[2] the daughter of Christopher Cotes was buryed March xviith.

* * * Marrian Bacon wid: buryed Martii 22.

* * * Willyam Reede was buryed Martii 24.

Anno Dni 1602.

* * * Richarde Reede was buryed Aprilis 2.

* * * Margrit Browne was buryed the same day.

* * * Susan ye daughter of Thomas Akers was buryed Maii 3.

* * * John Conningham was buryed Maii 5.

* * * Hwe[3] Younge was buryed Maii 29.

* Robert ye sonne of Robt. Bensly was baptized Maii 25.

* * Willyam Wake singleman & Margrett Glouer singlewoman were marryed Junii 20.

* * Robert Bensly & Agnes Wyly were married Junii 21.

* * John Lound singleman & Katherine Bincke singlewoman married Julii 4.

* * * Robert ye sonne of Robert Benslye was buryed August xxii.

* Katherine the daughter of Thomas darnes was baptized the same day.

* * * *Widow Reade was buried August 22.*[4]

* * * Dorathie Bustinge widdowe was buryed August xxiiii.

---

[1] *Amie* in Transcript.

[2] *Dorathie* in Transcript.

[3] *Hugo* in Transcript.

[4] An additional entry in Transcript.

*   *John*[1] Morse the sonne of Stephen Morse was baptized Sept. xi[th].

Robert the sonne of John Bustinge & (? Amie or) Auice his wife was bapt. Sept. xxvi[th].

Susan the daughter of Thomas Moyses was bapt. the same day.

Elizabeth the daughter of Christopher Cotes and Elizabeth his wife bapt. October xx.

* * *   Agnes the daughter of George Dennis was buryed the xxvii[th] of October.

*   Robert the sonne of Robert Osborne was baptised Nov. 23.

Willyam the sonne of Willyam Otes & Katherine his wif was baptised Decembr 5.

   Per me Samuelem Otes Rectorem ibid. Rob Perse. John Wyth gardeani. *

P. 37. *   Laurente the sonne of George Fletcher was baptised Decembr 5.

*   Robert the sonne of Robt. Marsham bapt. Janu 9.

*   Robert the sonne of Robt. Wright baptised the same day.

* * *   Willym the sonne of Willm. Otes was buried January 14.

* * *   Robt. the sonne of Robert Osborne was buryed January 15.

*   Elizabeth the daughter of Clement Free was baptised Febr. 5.

1335235

Anno Dni 1603.

* * *   John ye sonne of Willm. Gedny was buried Mariti 31.

John the sonne of Robt. Case baptised Aprill 3.

Samuell the sonne of John Downinge & Emme his wif was bapt. Aprill xvii[th].

* *   Robert Motts singleman & Alice Winny singlewoman were married Maii ix[th].

Dorathie the daughter of Robert Hardinge J[u] was baptized Maii xv[th].

Agnes ye daughter of John Exham & Anne his wif was bapt. Maii xxii.

---

[1] Left blank in Register but supplied by Transcript.

* Katherine ye daughter of Willyam Wake bapt. Aug. xxviii^{th.}

* ——[1] the daughter of Thomas Goram was baptised Sept. 4.

* Auphillis daughter of Stephen Anger was bapt. Sept. 25.

* * Willyam Bond singleman & Bridgett Smith singlewoman married Octobr 3.

* * Henry Kinge and Agnes Reade were married Janu 16.

Nicholas the sonne of Willm Exham was bapt. January xxii^{th.}

* Joane the daughter of Robert Osborne was bapt. Janu 24.

* * * Edmund Smith was buryed Janu 27.

* * * Robt. Croskin was buryed Janu xxix^{th.}

Timothie the sonne of Willyam Otes was bapt. Martii 4.

* * * Agnes the daughter of John Exham was buryed Martii 8.

John the sonne of Anthonie Burlye was bapt. Martii 25.

Anno Dni 1604.

John the sonne of John Dix & Rebecca his wif was bapt. Aprill xxvi^{th.}

* Robt. the sonne of Robt. Hardinge ye younger was bapt. Julii 15.

* * * Robt. Hardinge ye younger was buryed Sept. 2.

Samuell the sonne of Robt. Wright & Anne his wif was bapt. Sept. 16.

(page signed) per me Samuelem Otes Rectorem ibidem...Ro. Perse —John Wyth—gard^{s.}

P. 38.* Elizabeth the daughter of Philip Keede was bapt. Octob. 7.

* Dorathie the daughter of Willm Wake was baptized Nov 4.

Laurence the sonne of Thomas Moyses was bapt. Nov. xi^{th.}

Robert the sonne of Robt. Motts & Mary his wife bapt. Dec. 2.

John the sonne of Henry Rysinge was baptised January xx^{th.}

Millicent the daughter of Robt. Sanders was bapt. Martii x.

* * John Boswell and Joane Smith were marryed Martii xxviii^{th.}

---

[1] Left blank in Register.

Anno Dni 1605.

Thomas the sonne of Thomas Wilkinson was baptized Aprilis secundo.

* * Willyam Muse & Susan Kinge single persons were married Maii xii[th].

Thomas the sonne of John Boswell was baptized Maii xx.

Thomasin the daughter of Thomas Derne was baptized June ix[th].

* Agnes the daughter of Stephen Kempe was bapt. June xvi[th].

Thomas the sonne of John Downinge was baptized June xxiii[th].

* * Thomas Horne & Elizabeth his wife were married Julii ii.

* * Thomas Croxton and Millicent Black were married Julii xxi[th].

* * Stephen Kempe and Mary Borne were married Julii xxix[th].

* * * Robert Marsham y[e] elder was buried Sept. xviii.

* Mary the daughter of Edmund Marsham was baptized Sept. xxix[th].

Margery Exham y[e] daughter of Willm. Exham was bapt. Nov. i.

Robt. Osborne the sonne of Robt. Osborne was bapt. January xii[th].

* Richard Anger the sonne of Stephen Anger was bapt. the same day.

* Rebecca the daughter of John Bustinge was bapt. Feb. xvi[th].

* Margrett the daughter of Robt. Royall was bapt. Martii ix[th].

* * * Thomasin Derne was buryed December 24

(page signed) per me Sam. Otes Rectorem ibid—Rob. Perse—John Wyth—Gard.

P. 39.

Anno Dni 1606.

* * * Ursely the wife of Robt. Wilkinson was buryed the 31 of Maye.

John the sonne of Robt. Marsham was bapt. June xxix[th].

* Willm. the sonne of Willm. Bustinge was bapt. Julii 8.

* Elizabeth the daughter of Thomas Croxton was baptized
    Julye xiii[th].

* Katherine the daughter of Willm. Otes and Katherine his
    wife was bapt. July xx.

* John the sonne of Robt. Wright was bap. Aug. 24.

* Katherine the daughter of Willm. Wake was bapt. Octob. 29.

* * Robt. Anger[1] & Martha Otes single persons were married
    Novemb. xvi[th].

* Millicent the daughter of Anthonie Burly was bap. Janu. 18.

* Elizabeth the daughter of Thomas Goram was bap. the same
    day.

Robert the sonne of John Dix & Rebecca his wife was bapt.
    February 1.

Anne the daughter of Andrewe Dix & Mary his wife bapt.
    Martii 8.

Anno Dni 1607.

* Robert the sonne of Robt. Hawud was bapt. Martii 19.

* * * Robert the sonne of widdowe Hardinge was buryed
    Aprill xxiii[th].

* Elizabeth the daughter Thomas Wilkinson was bapt.
    Aprill xxvi[th].

* Mary the daughter of Henry Rysinge was bapt. Maye 24.

* * * John the sonne of Robt. Marsham was buryed June 3.

Margrett the daughter of Tho. Derne was bapt. June 24.

* * Willyam Osborne & Anne Hardinge widdowe were married
    Aug. 2.

* * Robt. Hemminge & Margrett his wife were married
    Sept. xxi.

* Mathewe the daughter of Stephen Morse was bapt. Sept.
    xxix[th].

* * * Willm. Wake was buryed Octo 7.

* Edmunde the sonne of John Bustinge & Amie (or ? Auice)
    his wife was bapt. November i.

---

[1] *Angell* in Transcript.

*   John Cusshin & Elizabeth Wake single persons were
married Nov. 15.

*   Mary the daughter of Willm. Osborne bapt. the same day.

* * *   Thomas Allen was buryed Nov. xx.

Willm. the sonne of Stephen Kempe was bapt. Nov. 28.

Richard the sonne of Andrewe Coventry & Adry his wife bapt.
Decemb. 27.

(page signed) per me Samuelem Otes Rectorem ibid.

P. 40.   Anno Dni 1608.

Robert the sonne of Nathaniell Waker was bapt. Maii i.

* * *   Willm. the sonne of Stephen Kempe was buryed Maii
xix.

Margret the daughter of Edmund Marsham was bapt.
Maii xxii.

* * *   Robt. the sonne of Nath. Waker buryed June 21.

*   Katherine the daughter of Jo. Lound & Katherine his wife
bapt. July 3.

* * *   Willm. Fletcher was buryed July x[th.]

* * *   Briggett Watson was buryed Aug. 28.

Robert the sonne of Stephen Angell was bapt. Aug. xxx.

Willm the sonne of Robt. Osborne was baptized September
xi[th.]

Sara the daughter of Robt. Marsham was bapt. Sept. 18.

Anne the daughter of Robt. Hemminge & Marg. his wife
bapt. Sept. 25.

* *   Willm. Algate & Mary Sayue single persons were married
Octo. 16.

John the sonne of Willm. Otes was baptized Octo. 23.

* *   Samuell Otes clerk parson of Marsham & Anne Dix of
heavingham both single persons were marryed att
heavingham November the third day.

* *   Willyam Lambe & Margerye Motts single persons were
marryed Nov. vii[th.]

* * *   ——[1] Spicer widdowe buryed Nov. 16.

---

[1] Left blank in Register.

* *   Robt. Bonde and Ciselye Willisse were marryed Nov. xx[th].

Martha the daughter of Thomas Croxton was bapt. Nov. 27.

* John the sonne of Willm. Muse bapt. Dec. xi.

* John the sonne of John Cusshin & Elizabeth his wife was
bapt. Janu 1.

* Elizabeth the daughter of Henry Rysinge was bapt. Janu. 15.

* * *   Martha the daughter of Thomas Croxton was buryed
Janu. 16.

Elizabeth the daughter of Willm. Algate was baptized
Martii 14.

* Anne the daughter of Robt. Anger and Martha his wife was
bapt Aprill 2.

* Rebecca the daughter of Edmund hawud was baptised
Aprill 9.

(page signed) per me Samuelem Otes Rectorem ibid—Thomas
Moyses—John Wake—Gardians.

P. 41.   Anno Dni 1609.

* Mary the daughter of Andrewe Dix & Mary his wife was bapt.
Maii 21.

* * * Stephen Chapman was buryed July 5.

* * * Robert Hanes was buryed July xx.

* * John Exham & Margrett Marsham single persons were
marryed October i.

Dorathie the daughter of Willm. Lambe bapt. October 8.

* * * Robert Willis was buryed Nov : 15.

* Margret the daughter of John Tomlinson and Marget his wife
was bapt. Nov : 30.

* * * Robert hardinge was buryed Dec : 12.

Samuell Otes the sonne of Samuel Otes & Anne his wife was
baptized December xix.

* * * and was buried the next day.

* * * Alice the wife of Andrewe Sanders was buryed Dec. xxx.

* * * Mary Wynnye widdowe was buried Janu : xxviii[th].

* * * Stephen Marsh was buryed Janu : 30.

Anno Dni 1610.

* John the sonne of John Boswell was bapt. Martii xxv.

* * * Henry Lusher was buryed Martii 29.

* * * ——[1] the wife of Thomas Pamer was buryed the same day.

Anne the daughter of John Exham Ju: was baptized April vi[th].

* * * Willyam Phillips was buryed Aprill vii[th].

* * * Willyam Gedny Ju: was buryed April xii[th].

Andrewe Sanders widdower and Elizabeth Leatherpoole singlewoman were marryed Aprill xiii[th].

' * * * John Cusshin was buryed Aprill 18.

* Anne the daughter of Willm. Osborne was baptised Aprill 22.

* * * Anne the daughter of John Exham Ju: was buryed June i.

* * Jacob Cooke Singleman & Margrett hope widdowe were married June xi[th].

John Woodhowse singleman & Rebecca Hardinge widdowe wer married June xi.

John Whale & Dorathie Sothis single persons were married June 28.

Willyam Streek & Anne Carr single persons were marryed October xxii[th].

Samuell Otes the son of Samuell Otes clerk and Anne his wife was baptized Nov: xx.[2]

(page signed) per me Samuelem Otes Rectorem ibid—Robt. Perse —Jo: Wyth—yard.

P. 42.* * Edmunde hardinge and Elizabethe wadron single persons were married Novemb. xii[th].

* * * Willyam Lynge Gent dyed the 2[d] of dec[r]. and was buryed December 5.

Laurence the sonne of Henrye Rumpe was bap. Decemb: 9.

* * * John the sonne of John Boswell buryed Dec. xi.

---

[1] Left blank in Register.
[2] The Transcript adds "borne Nov: 18 att 7 att night."

* *Rebecca*[1] the wife of Willyam Wilton was buryed Janu :
  15.
Willyam the sonne of Andrewe Dix was baptized feb. 3.
* * * *Christopher Dye was buried Nov : 29.*[2]
* Alice the daughter of Willyam Muse bapt. the same day.
* * * Robert Rogers was buryed febru : 16.
* * * Margret Sayve was buryed feb : 24.
* Willyam the sonne of John Whale was bapt. Martii x^th.

Anno Dni 1611.

* * * John Ristoe gent was buryed Martii 25.
Richard the sonne of Richard Lusher bapt. Martii 31.
* * * Willyam the sonne of John Whale was buryed Aprill
  vi^th.
* * * Margrett Griphin widdowe buryed Aprill xx^th.
* * * James fletcher was buryed May 2.
* Jacob the sonne of Jacob Cooke and Margrett his wife was
  bapt. Maie 5.
* Elizabeth the daughter of Edmund Medow & Mary his wife
  was bapt. the same day.
Thomas the sonne of Stephen Anger & Margerie his wife
  bapt. May xix^th.
Nicholas the sonne of John Exham Ju : & Margrett his wif
  was bapt. Maye xxiiii.
* * * John Hemminge singleman was buryed June 8.
John the sonne of John Lound and Katherine his wife was
  bapt. June xvi^th.
Richard the sonne of John Dix clerk was baptised Aug : 4.
Andrewe the sonne of Thomas Wilkinson was bapt. Aug : 25.
* Edmunde Smith & Anne horne single persons were
  married Sept. xxii^th.
* * * John Browne gent was buryed Novem. 3.
* Elizabeth the daughter of Willyam Black was bapt. Nov : 17.

---

[1] Left blank in Register but supplied from Transcript.
[2] An additional entry in Transcript.

* Elizabeth the daughter of Robt. Hemminge Ju: was bapt. Dec: 8.

Clemens the daughter of Willyam Streek Ju. was bapt. the same day.

* * Robt. Dowsinge & Anne hallifax single persons married Janu: 13.

* * Christopher Welch & Anne Ristoe married Febr. 2.

(page signed) per me Samuelem Otes Rector ibid :

P. 43.　　　　　　　　Anno Dni 1612.

* John the sonne of Ralf Skeete & Margrett his wife was baptized Martii 29.

* * * Rebecca Woodhouse the wife of John Woodhouse was buryed Aprill 22.

* * * Alice Jeckyl widdowe was buryed May 4.

* * * Willyam Dix the sonne of Andrewe Dix was buryed Maye 6.

* * * Thomas Pamer widdower buryed May 9.

* * * Elizabeth Sothis singlewooman was buryed May x.

* Ellener the daughter of John Whale was baptized Aprill 19.

* * * Richard Kinge was buryed May 21.

* Amie the daughter of Willyam Algate was baptized May 25.

* * * Richard Osborne was buryed the same day.

* Rebecca the daughter of Willyam Osborne was baptized May 31.

* * * Margerie the wife of Thomas Cunnybye was baptized[1] June 1.

* * * Thomas Cunnybye was buryed June 3.

* * * Willyam Streeke was buryed the same day.

* * * John Wyth widdower was buryed June 9.

* * * Robert the sonne of Henry Rysinge was buryed June 28.

* * Thomas Maxe widdower and Jeane Fletcher widdowe were married June 29.

* Andrewe the sonne of Edmund Smithe was baptized July 13.

* * * and was buryed July xx.

---

[1] The lines show this to be a burial.

* * *   Robert Sower was buryed Aug : 5.

John the sonne of John Lound baptized Aug : 9.

* *   Willyam Wilton & Marrian Jordan were married Aug : 24.

* * *   Richard Chaplin was buryed Sept. 17.

* * *   Margrett the wife of Clement Free was buried Octo : 25.

* * *   Willyam Wilton was buried Octo xxxi.

Fraunces the daughter of Christopher Welch was bapt. Nov. 22.

*   Nicholas the sonne of John Bustinge bapt. Nov. 28.

* * *   Joane the wife of John Dowsinge buryed Dec. 8.

* *   Stephen hardinge singleman and Elizabeth Cusshin Widdowe were married Dec. 13.

*   John the sonne of Robt. Dowsinge & Anne his wife was bapt. Dec. xx[th].

* * *   John Dowsinge before named was buryed Dec. 31.

* * *   ——[1] Elson[2] was buryed Febr. 3.

Grace the daughter of Willm. Ryall bapt. Febr. 7.

Oliver the sonne of John Exham babt. febr. 9.

* *   Robert Marsham & Martha Sothis were married febr : 14.

(page signed) per me Sam : Otes Rector : ibid :

P. 44.   ANNO DNI 1613.

Anne the daughter of Henry Rumpe and Mary his wife was bapt. Martii 25.

Robt. Forrest and Dorathie Chapman single persons were married Aprill 5.

*   Willyam the sonne of Willm. Streek Ju : was baptized April 18.

* *   John Woodhouse widdower & Alice Smith singlewooman married Aprill 25.

Martha the daughter of Andrewe Dix & Mary his wife was baptized May 30.

* * *   Anne the wife of Martin Hambleton was buryed Octob : 4.

* * *   Andrewe Saunders was buryed Octo : 7.

---

[1] Left blank in register.   [2] A doubtful reading.

* * *   Edwarde Samson was buryed Octob : 29.

*   Elizabeth the daughter of Willm. Muse bapt. Octo : 30.

* *   Willm. Harwin and Anne Colls single persons were married Nov : 18.

*   Dorathie the daughter of Stephen Harding was bapt. Nov : 20.

Thomas Marsham & Elizabeth Graner single persons were married Novemb : 30.

* * *   Robert Perse was buryed Dec : 8.

* * *   Elizabeth Bannyard was buryed Dec : 11.

*   John the sonne of Robert Jayry bapt. December 12.

* * *   Richard Ristoe was buryed the same day.

*   Elizabeth the daughter of John Tomlinson & Margrett his wife bapt. Janu : 2.

*   John the sonne of John Exham sen. and Anne his wife was bapt. Janu : 6.

John the sonne of John Wak & Elizabeth his wife bapt. Janu : 9.

*   Andrewe the sonne of Willm. Harwin & Anne his wife was bapt. and was buryed Janu : 13.

* * *   John Wake was buryed Janu : 21.

Anne the daughter of John Gedge was bapt. Janu : 30.

* * *   Edmund Marsham was buryed Janu. 31.

James the sonne of Stephen Anger was baptized feb : 13.

Christopher yᵉ sonne of Robt. Dowsinge & Anne his wife was bapt. feb : 28.

*   Phillip the sonne of Robt. Reade bapt. the same day.

*   Dorathie the daughter of John Boswell & Joane his wife was bapt. Martii vii^th.

(page signed) per me Samuelem Otes Rector : ibid.

P. 45.   Anno Dni 1614.

*   Thomas the sonne of Richard Lusher was bapt. Martii 27.

*   John the sonne of Samuell Otes clerke & Anne his wife was borne Apr. 13 being Wednesday about midnight and was bapt. upon palme sonday vid.[1] Aprill xvii^th.

---

[1] i.e., *videlicet.*

Willm. the sonne of Willm. Otes & Katherine his wife was
    bapt. Aprill 26.
    James Horne singleman and Bridget Alcock singlewooman
    were married May 23.
Thomas the sonne of Willm. Streek was baptized June xix[th.]
* * Thomas Watson singleman and Dorathie Greene were
    married July 3.
Margret the daughter of Robt. Forrest was bapt. July 10.
Robert the sonne of Edmund Smith was baptized the same
    day.
* * * Margret Pye widdowe buryed Aug. 14.
James the sonne of John Bustinge and Amie his wife was
    bapt. Sept. xi[th.]
    Adam Chambers and Joane Chapman single persons were
    married Oct: ix[th.]
    James Fletcher singleman and Dorathie Connyby single-
    wooman were married the Nov: x[th.]
* Debora the daughter of ——[1] Thexton was baptized Nov:
    xx[th.]
* Nicholas the sonne of Robert Vowte was baptized feb: xii[th.]
* * * Margerie the wife of Stephen Anger was buryed
    February xxvii[th.]
* John the sonne of Willm. Streeke Ju: was bapt. Martii xii[th.]
* * * Anne Chapman widdowe was buryed the same day.
    (page signed) per me Samuelem Otes Rectorem ibid.

P. 46.   A_NNO_ D_NI_ 1615.

* * Stephen Anger widdower and Cicely Read widdowe were
    married Aprill xviii[th.]
    Thomas Akers widdower and Christian Portland wid. were
    married Aprill xx[th.]
* * Thomas Conningham & Alice Browne single persons were
    married Aprill xxiii[th.]
Robert the sonne of Thomas Watson was bapt. May vii[th.]
Thomas the sonne of Henry Rumpe was baptized May 14.

---

[1] Left Blank in Register.

John the sonne of Robert Forrest was baptized Aug : xx[th].

* * * Anne Osborne widdowe buryed Aug. 25.

* Robert the sonne of Christopher Welch was bapt. Sept : x[th].

* Faithe the daughter of John Exham the younger was baptized Octo : viii.

Elizabeth the daughter of Adam Chambers was bapt. Octo : xxii[th].

* Alice the daughter of Richard Bell & Margrett his wife was bapt. October xxx[th].

* * * Elizabeth the wife of Willm. Streek was buryed Janu : 6.

John the sonne of Robt. Dowsinge was baptized Janu : 7.

Henry Rysinge the sonne of Henry Rysinge was bapt. febr : 2.

Thomas the sonne of John Lound was baptized febr : xi[th].

Robert the sonne of James fletcher was baptized feb : 25.

John the sonne of Edward Umphry was baptized febr : xxviii[th].

(page signed) per me Samuel Otes Rectorem ibid.

P. 47.   Anno Dni 1616.

* * Thomas Watson the elder was buryed Aprill 1.

Dorathie the daughter of John Wake was baptized Apr. 17.

* * * Marriam Willisse was buryed May 30.

Brigget Boswell and Katherine Boswell the daughters of John Boswell and Joane his wife were bapt. June 2.

Katherine Algate the daughter of Willm. Algate was bapt. June ix[th].

Anne Oliver the wife of Thomas Oliver was buryed June xxii[th].

* * * Ciselie the wife of Robt. Bonde was buryed June xxx[th].

* * * Nicholas the sonne of Robt. Vowte was buryed Aug : 14.

* * * Augustine Nun was buryed Aug : 18.

Richard the sonne of Robt. Jayry and Elizabeth his wife was bapt. the same day.

Fraunces the daughter of Christopher Welch was buryed Aug : xxii[th].

* * * Alice Pickeringe was buryed Aug : 25.

Anne Otes the daughter of Samuell Otes clerk and Anne his wife was borne the 27 day of September about midnight and bapt. October vi^th.

Anphillis the daughter of John Woodhouse & Alice his wife was bapt. the same day vid : Octo : vi.

Peter Greene was buryed Octob. x^th.

Dorathie the wife of Thomas Watson Ju : was buryed Octo : xi^th.

* * * Peter Black was buryed Octo : xxi.

Richarde the sonne of Willm. Oakes bapt. Octo : 23.

* * * and buryed the xxv^th day.

* * * Thomas Tyler was buryed Nov : 5.

Anne the daughter of Christopher Cotes was bapt. Nov : 17.

* * * Alice the wife of Thomas Wilkinson was buryed Nov : 24.

Nicholas the sonne of Tho : Hardinge bapt. Dec : 1.

Thomas the sonne of Edmund Smith bapt. Dec : 15.

Robert the sonne of James Horne was bapt. Janu : 22.

Wyborowghe the daughter of James Horne bapt. the same day.

* * * Both these children beinge twins were buryed Janu : 27.

* * * Elizabeth Dewin widow was buryed febr : xvi^th.

(page signed) per me Samuelem Otes Rectorem ibid.

P. 48.   ANNO DNI 1617.

* * * Elizabeth Destinie was buryed May 1.

* * * Willyam Browne sen : buryed May 15.

James Vowte the sonne of Robert Vowte was bapt. June 22.

* * * George fletcher was buryed June 28.

* * * Mary fletcher singlewooman was buryed Julye x^th.

Mary Lusher the daughter of Richard Lusher was bapt. July xx.

Anne Wright ye daughter of Robt. Wright & Anne his wife was bapt. Aug : x^th.

Willm. Reade & Alice Gedny single persons were married Aug : 18.

* * Joseph Free & Sara Woodhouse were married Aug : xxv^th.

* George Bell the sonne of Richard Bell & Margrett his wife was bapt. Sept: 7.

* * Thomas Wilkinson widdower & Joane Maxie widdowe were married Sept: 8.

Umphry the sonne of Willm. Streek was bapt. Sept: xxi[th.]

* Willyam Oakes the sonne of Willm. Oakes was bapt. Octob: 5.

* John the sonne of John Tomlinson was bapt. Octo: 26.

* * * Alice fletcher widdowe was buryed Octo: 28.

* Robt. the sonne of Willm. Browne was bapt. Nov: xvi[th.]

* Margret y[e] daughter of Henry Rumpe bapt. Nov: 80.

* Margret the daughter of John Exham bapt. Dec: 7.

* Robt. Free the sonne of Joseph Free bapt. Decemb: 14.

* * * Cicelie Lusher widdowe buryed Dec: 24.

* * * Willm. Sothis was buryed Janu: 5.

* John Chambers the sonne of Adam Chambers bapt. Janu: xi[th.]

Willyam Pestill y[e] sonne of hen: Pestill bapt. Janu: 25.

* * * Margret the daughter of John Exham the younger was buryed febr: ix[th.]

* * * John the sonne of Adam Chambers was buryed feb: xix[th.]

* Anne the daughter of Simont Pratt & Jane his wife was bapt. Martii x.

* Anne the daughter of Robert Forrest & Dorathie his wife bapt. Martii 15.

(page signed) **per me Samuelem Otes Rectorem ibid.**

P. 49.   ANNO DNI 1618.

* Willm. the sonne of Christopher Welch bapt. Aprill xix[th.]

* Thomas the sonne of Edward Umphry bapt. the same day.

* * * Elizabeth Rysinge the wife of henry Rysinge was buryed May 5.

* * * Elizabeth Chambers was buryed May 6.

* * * Umphry Streek was buryed May 17.

* * * henry Rysinge the sonne of henry Rysinge was buryed May 23.

* Willm. the sonne of Willm. Reade & Alice his wife was bapt. May 24.

* Anne the daughter of Stephen hardinge & Elizabeth his wife bapt. June 21.

* Margrett hemminge the daughter of Robt. hemminge Ju. was bapt. Julye 25.

Willm. the sonne of John Whale was bapt. August 2.

Anne Dowsinge the daughter of Robt. Dowsinge & Anne his wife bapt. Sept: 27.

Margrett Marsham the daughter of Thomas Marsham bapt. Octo: 4.

* * Katherine Boswell the daughter of John Boswell was buryed Octo 18.

* * * Willm. the sonne of Christopher Welch was buryed the same day Octo: 18.

* * * Christian Cutts widdowe buryed Octo: 25.

* * Robert Bond widdower & Margret Watson singlewooman were married Nov: xvth.

John Pigeon the sonne of Willm. Pigeon & Bennet his wife was bap. Nov: xxixth.

Nicholas Cotes the sonne of Christopher Cotes was bap^t. Dec: 13.

* Willm. Browne the sonne of Willm. Browne was bapt. the same day.

* Anne Richford the daughter of James Richford was bapt. Janu: ixth.

* Simont Woodhouse the sonne of John Woodhouse & Alice his wife was bapt. Janu: 24.

* John Cunningham the sonne of Thomas Cunningham was bapt. february 14.

* * * Margret Loue the daughter of ——[1] Loue was buryed feb: 18.

* Christopher the sonne of John Lound was baptized febr: 22.

(page signed) per me Samuelem Otes Rectorem ibid—John Exham —John Chapman—gard.

---

[1] Left blank in Register.

P. 50.   Anno Dni 1619.

* Adam Chambers the sonne of Adam Chambers and Joane his wife was bapt. Aprill xi[th].

* Rachel Marsham the daughter of Robert Marsham was bapt. the same day.

* * * Willm. Kinge was buried Aprill xvi[th].

James Smith the sonne of Edmund Smith was bapt. Aprill 18.

Willm. the sonne of John Wake was bapt. May 2.

Richard the sonne of Willm. Strecke was bapt. May xvii[th].

* * Willm. Hemminge and Mary Hallifaxe were marryed June xx[th].

Robert Exham the sonne of Jo : Exham Ju : bapt. June 29.

* * * Anphillis Woodhowse was buryed July x[th].

* * Robert Greene and Anne Gryme single persons were married July 18.

* * Mary Guddins was buryed the same day.

* * * Richard Jayry was buryed July xx[th].

* * * Robt. hemminge sen : was buryed July xxx[th].

* * * Christopher Cotes sen : was buryed Aug : 6

* * * Mary y[e] wife of willm. hemminge was buried Aug : 13.

* Anne the daughter of Edw. Umphry was bapt. Sept : 26.

* Anne the daughter of Christopher Welch bapt. Octo : 17.

* * * John Woodhowse was buryed October 31.

* Joane Fletcher the daughter of James Fletcher and Dorathie his wife was bapt. Novemb. 14.

Margret Skeete was buryed November 15.

* * * Emme Sayue wid : was buryed Nov : 24.

* * * John Dowsinge was buryed Decem : 21.

Margret Otes the daughter of Sam : Otes clerk & Anne his wife was borne Jan : 3. about 7 att night being monday & was bapt. January ix[th].

* * * George Dennis was buryed Janu : xix[th].

Robert Boswell the sonne of John Boswell & Joane his wife was bapt. Janu : 23.

* * John Woodhowse widdower and Mary Kinge widdowe were married febr : 3.

* * Willm. hemminge widdower and Alice Woodhowse widdowe were married febr : x^{th.}

* * * Willm. Osborne was buryed febr : 17.

* Rose Vowte the daughter of Robt. Vowte was bapt. febr : 27.

* Brigget Lusher the daughter of Richard Lusher was bapt. Martii 5.

* Ellen Richford the daughter of James Richford was bapt. Martii xii^{th.}

(page signed) per me Samuelem Otes Rectorem ibid—John Exham gard.

P. 51.   ANNO DOMINI 1620.

* Elizabeth Pratt the daughter of Simont Pratt was bapt. Aprill 2.

* * * Cicely Cunningham widdowe was buryed Aprill 4.

John Stockinge the sonne of Richard Stocking was bapt. Aprill 23.

Brigget Bond the daughter of Robt. Bond bapt. June xi^{th.}

* * Willm. Marsham and Elizabeth Hix single persons were married June xi^{th.}

* * Richard Watson and Susan Perse single persons were married June 18.

Richard Swan singleman & Amie Cunnyby singlewooman were married June 29.

John Whale the sonne of John Whale was bapt. July 2.

Dorathie Greene the daughter of Robt. Greene was bapt. July 2. also

* * Jeremie Blisse and Amie Grunye single persons were married July 3.

* * * John Whitinge was buried July 15.

Anne Bell the daughter of Richard Bell and Margrett his wife was bapt. July 18.

* * * John Whale the sonne of Jo : Whale was buryed July 25.

Susan hardinge the daughter of Thomas hardinge was bapt. Aug : 6.

* * * Mary Dix the wife of Andrewe Dix wss buried Aug : 23.

* * * Mary Marsham singlewooman was buryed Aug : 24.

* Robert Forrest the sonne of Rob : Forrest and Dorathie his wife was bapt. Octo : 8.

* Richard Coates the sonne of Christopher Cotes was bapt. Octo : 15.

Elizabeth the daughter of Willyam Browne was bapt. Dec : 3.

* * * Robert horne was buryed December 28.

* Robert Reade the sonne of Willm. Reade was bapt. Decem : 31.

* * * and was buryed Janu : viiith.

Christopher the sonne of Thomas Watson & Mathewe his wife was bapt. feb : 2.

* * * Joane Barningham widdowe was buried feb 3.

* * * Thomasin Ruckwood the wife of Robt. Ruckwood gent was buryed febr : 5.

* Amie Watson the daughter of Richard Watson and Susan his wife was bapt. february xith.

* Susan hemminge the daughter of Willm. hemminge was bapt. Martii 14.

(page signed) per me Samuelem Otes Rectorem ibid.

P. 52.   Anno Domini 1621.

Willm. Pigeon the sonne of Willm. Pigeon & Benedick his wife was bapt. Aprill 2.

Elizabeth the daughter of Stephen hardinge was bapt. Aprill 8.

* * Thomas Suggatt and Sara Jeckill single persons were married Aprill ixth.

* Margret the daughter of Richard Swan & Amie his wife was bapt. May 13.

* Amie Blisse the daughter of Jerimie Blisse was bapt. June xth.

* * Nicholas Springall and Anne Barningham single persons were married July 15.

* John Whale the sonne of John Whale was baptized July 22.

* * John Greene and Elizabeth Exham single persons were married Aug : 5.

* Judith the daughter of Edward Umphry was bapt. Sept : 2.

* Faithe Greene the daughter of Robt. Greene was bapt. Octo : 7.

* * * Katherine Lound the wife of John Lound was buryed Octo : xx[th].

Edmund Smith the sonne of Edmund Smith was bapt. Nov : 4.

* Andrewe Delf the sonne of John Delf was bapt. Nov : xi[th].

* * Nicholas Exham and Anne Gedge single persons were married Nov : xxv[th].

* Anne Chambers the daughter of Adam Chambers & Joane his wif bapt. Dec : 26.

John Barningham the sonne of John Barningham was bapt. Dec xviii.

* Robt. Dowsinge the sonne of Robt. Dowsinge and Alice his wife was bapt. Janu : 2.

* Andrewe Exham the sonne of John Exham & Margret his wife was bapt Janu : 6.

(page signed) per me Samuelem Otes Rectorem ibid.—Richard Bell —Nicholas Exham—gard :

P. 53.* Katherine Browne the daughter of Willm. Browne was bapt. Janu : 13.

* * * and buryed the 15 of Jan :

* Thomasin hemminge the daughter of Robt. hemminge was bapt. Janu : xx[th].

* Anne Free the daughter of Joseph Freo was bapt. the same day.

* Margrett Bell the daughter of Richard Bell was bapt. febr : 4.

* Margerie the daughter of John Tomlinson was bapt. febr : x[th].

* * * Willm. Plowman was buryed Martii 19.

Anno Domini 1622.

* Elizabeth Jeckill the daughter of Robt. Jeckill was bapt. Aprill 7.

* Jane Welch the daughter of Christopher Welch and Anne his wife was bapt. Aprill 22.

* Elizabeth the daughter of Robt. Vowte & Susan his wife was bapt. Aprill 28.

* Willyam Lusher the sonne of Richard Lusher was bapt. May 5.

* Susan fletcher ye daughter of James fletcher was baptized the same day vid. May 5.

* Willm. Parker the sonne of Thomas Parker was bapt. May xix[th].

* * * Elizabeth the wife of John Greene was buried May xx[th].

* John Greene the sonne of John Greene & Elizabeth his wife was bapt. May 20 also

* * * and was buried June 15.

* * * Susan Lound the daughter of John Lound was buryed June 18.

Andrewe Suggatt the sonne of Thomas Suggatt & Sara his wife was bapt. June 23.

* * * ——[1] Sutton widdowe buried the same day.

* Margerie the daughter of John Wake was bapt. July xx.

* Elizabeth Cotes the daughter of Christopher Cotes was bapt. Aug: 21.

* * * Thomas hardinge was buryed Sept: 4.

* * * Andrewe Delf sonne of John Delf was buried September xi[th].

* * * Elizabeth hardinge the wife of Stephen hardinge was buried Sept: 14.

* Peter Bond the sonne of Robt. Bond was bapt. Sept: 29.

* John Marsham the sonne of Willm. Marsham & Elizabeth his wife was bapt. Octo: 14.

* Richard Otes the sonne of Samuell Otes clerk & Anne his wife was borne Nov: 2 about noone and baptized Nov: x[th].

(page signed) per me Samuelem Otes Rectorem ibid—Richard Bell—Nicholas Exham—gard.

P. 54.* Willyam the sonne of John Paretree was bapt. Nov: x[th].

---

[1] Left blank in Register.

* Elizabeth Swan the daughter of Richard Swan & Amie his wife was bapt. the same day vid: Nov: x.

* Margrett Exham the daughter of Nicholas Exham bapt. Dec: 23.

* Elizabeth hemminge the daughter of Willm. hemminge was bapt. Janu: 5.

* Rachell the daughter of henry Cotes and Thomasin his wife was bapt. Janu: 12.

* * * Margret Gedny widdowe was buryed Janu: 14.

* Willm. Forrest y° sonne of Robt. Forrest & Dorathie his wife was bapt. Martii 16.

Anno Domini 1623.

* * * Richard Cotes[1] was buried Martii 27.

* Thomas the sonne of Willyam Pigeon & Benedict his wife was bapt. Martii 30.

* * * and was buried the same day.

* Edmund Read[2] the sonne of Edmund Read[2] gent & Mary his wife was bapt. May 2.

Richard Dowsinge the sonne of Robt. Dowsinge & Alice his wife was bapt. May xi[th].

* *Henry*[3] the sonne of Jeremie Blisse was bapt. June 1.

* Briggett Chambers the daughter of Adam Chambers was bapt. August x[th].

* * Edward Nikerson & Elizabeth Allens single persons were married Octo: 7.

* * Willm. Barker & Susan Busting single persons were married Octo: 14.

* * * Henry Greene was buryed Nov: 7.

* * * Thomas fletcher was buryed Nov: 16.

* Elizabeth Greene the daughter of Robt. Greene was bapt. Dec: vii[th].

---

[1] The Transcript adds " singleman."
[2] *Reve* in Transcript.
[3] Left blank in Register but supplied from Transcript.

* Adam Watson the sonne of Richard Watson was bapt. Dec : 14.

* Thomas Springall the sonne of Nicholas Springall & Anne his wife bapt. Dec : xxii^{th.}

* * * ——[1] the wife of Thomas Emmes was buryed Dec : 24.

* * * Anthonie Burly was buryed Dec : 29.

* John Paretree the sonne of Robt. Paretree was baptized Janu : 25.

* * * Edward Marsham was buried Janu : 28.

* * * Thomas Bosse was buried Janu : 29.

* Agnes Smith the daughter of Edmund Smith & Anne his wife bapt. febr : 15.

* * * Anne horne widdowe was buried Martii xx^{th.}

  (page signed) per me Samuelem Otes Rectorem ibid—Thomas
—Moyses—Robert Vowte—gard.

P. 55.   Anno Domini 1624.

* Richard Bell the sonne of Richard Bell & Margrett his wife was bapt. Maii 4.

* Thomas Boswell the sonne of Richard Boswell & Dorathie his wife was bapt. Maii 16.

* John Bull the sonne of John Bull was bapt. Julye 4.

* Mary Watson the daughter of Thomas Watson & Mathewe his wife bapt. July 4.

* * Robert Moyses & Elizabeth Cotes single persons were married July xi^{th.}

* Margrett Lynge the daughter of John Lynge gent. and Elizabeth his wife was bapt. July xvi^{th.}

* Mary the daughter of Edward Nikerson was baptized Aug : xxiii^{th.}

* Fraunces Cotes the sonne of henry Cotes was baptized Octo : 3.

* * Thomas Gedny and Mary Bareway were married Octob : 4.

* Susan Vowte the daughter of Robt. Vowte was baptized Octob. 13.

---

[1] Left blank in Register.

Mary the daughter of Willm. Browne was baptized Octob : 17.

* * * John Exham was buryed Octo : 17. also

Elizabeth the wife of Willm. Marsham was buryed Octo 26.

Judeth the daughter of Nicholas Exham & Anne his wife was bapt. Nov : 1.

* * * Elizabeth Exham widdowe was buryed Nov : 5.

Richard Jeckill the sonne of Robt. Jeckill was bapt. Nov : 21·

* * Erasmus hallifax and Mary Marsham single persons were married Janu : 24.

* * * Brigget Lusher the daughter of Richard Lusher was buried Janu : 29.

* * Mathewe Marsham and Elizabeth Clemens were married febr : 12.

* * Thomas Childe & Margrett Greene single persons were married febr : 17.

* * * Joseph Free was buryed feb : 18.

Thomas Child ye sonne of Thomas child was bapt Martii 17..

* * * Rachel Marsham was buried Martii 23.

* * * Thomas Springall was buried Martii 24.

(page signed) per me Samuelem Otes Rectorem ibid.   Tho : Moyses —Ro : Vowte—gard.

P. 56.   ANNO DOMINI 1625.

Jane Welch the daughter of Christopher Welch & Anne his wife was bapt. Aprill 3.

Willm. Moyses the sonne of Tho : Moyses & Thomasin his wife was bapt. Aprill 19.

* * * Dorathie Croskin widdowe was buried Aprill 22.

* * * Elizabeth Pratt was buried Aprill 23.

* Susan Welch the daughter of Christopher Welch & Anne his wife was bapt. May 8.

* Robert Suggatt the sonne of Thomas Suggatt was bapt. May 15.

* * * Henrye Pestill was buryed May 16.

* * * Sara Suggatt the wife of Thomas Suggatt was buried May 18.

* Eue Watson the daughter of John Watson & Eue his wife was bapt. June 12.

Edmund Dallida and Elizabeth Bustinge single persons were married June 13.

* * * John Whale was buried June xx^th.

Robert Paretree the sonne of Robt. Paretree was baptized Octo : ix^th.

* John the sonne of Erasmus hallifax was baptized Octob : 16.

* * * and was buried the 18 of Nov:

* * * Richard Streek was buryed Janu : 5.

Margrett Greene the daughter of Robt. Greene was baptized Janu : 8.

* * * Richard Bosse was buried Janu : xii^th.

* Thomas Watson was Buried Janu : 23.

* * Cicelie Browne widdowe was buried Martii xi^th.

Anno Domini 1626.

John Brandon was buryed Aprill 5.

* * * Elizabeth Bosse widdowe was buried Aprill 22.

* Anne Strecke the daughter of willm. Strecke was baptized Aprill xxx.

Thomas Chambers the sonne of Adam Chambers was bapt. July 9.

Thomas Dowsinge the sonne of Robt. Dowsinge was baptized July 22.

* * * Anne Watson widdowe was buried July 31.

Anne Exham the daughter of Robt. Exham was bapt. August 24.

* * Thomas Greene and Elizabeth Jeckill single persons were married October xxi^th.

Thomas hallifax the sonne of Erasmus hallifax was baptized Janu vii^th.

(page signed) per me Samuelem Otes Rectorem ibid.

P. 57.* Thomas Cotes the sonne of henry Cotes was baptized Janu : 14.

* * John, the reputed sonne of John Bustinge, & Mary Cotes single persons were married Janu : 26.

* * *   Margrett Blisse was buried feb: 3.

* * *   Anne the wife of Edmund Smithe was buryed febr: 14.

*   Christopher Exham the sonne of Nicholas Exham was baptized Martii 4.

* * *   Robert Chapman singleman was buryed Martii 15.

* * *   Henry Cotes was buryed Martii 19.

* * *   Fraunces Cotes was buryed Martii 24.

Anno Domini 1627.

John Bell the sonne of Richard Bell and Margrett his wife was bapt. Martii 27.

* *   Richarde Stockinge was buryed Aprill 9.

Robt. Bustinge and Susan Moyses single persons were married Aprill 23.

* *   Thomas Boswell the sonne of Richard Boswell was buryed Aprill 24.

Edward Cubit and Elizabeth Bareway single persons were maried Maye 21.

Margrett Greene the daughter of John Greene was baptized June 17.

*   Robt. Welch the sonne of Christopher Welch & Anne his wife was baptized July 5.

*   Anphillis Paretree the daughter of Robt. Paretree was bapt. July 29.

* *   Thomas Barker and Anne Curtisse single persons both of Alisham, but married by license, were married att this parishe July 26——This ought to have been placed in the lyne beforegoinge.

* * *   Anne Welch was buryed Aug: xi[th.]

* * *   Robert Dowsinge was buryed August xii[th.]

* *   Edmund Smith widdower and Alice Whitehead widdowe were married Aug: 13.

*   John Bustinge the sonne of Robt. Bustinge was baptized Sept: 23.

* * *   John hunt singleman was buryed Sept: 25.

*   Margret Jeckill the daughter of Robt. Jeckill was bapt. Sept: 30.

* *　Willyam Isbell of horsham St. Faithes & Elizabeth
　　　Croxton were married Nov : 16.
* * *　———[1] the wife of Edward Umphry was buryed Nov : 17.
　　(page signed) per me Samuelem Otes Rectorem ibid :—Thomas
Moyses—Jam : Horne—gard.

P. 58.*　Samuell Exham the sonne of John Exham was baptised
　　　Nov : 25.
*　———[1] the daughter of Thomas hardinge baptized Dec : 9.
Margrett Greene the daughter of Thomas Greene and
　　　Elizabeth his wife bapt. Dec : 26.
*　Thomas Browne the sonne of Willm. Browne was bapt.
　　　Dec : 25.
* * *　Margret Exham was buryed the same day.
John Medcalf the sonne of Edmund Medcalf was bapt.
　　　Janu : 1.
*　Robert Otes the sonne of Samuell Otes clerk and Anne his
　　　wife was borne feb : 23 about 4 of the clock in
　　　y[e] morninge & bapt. february xxviii[th.]
Robert Bustinge the sonne of John y[e] reputed sonne of John
　　　Bustinge & Mary his wife was baptiz. Martii ix[th.]
*　Willm. Ling the sonne of John Ling gent. and Elizabeth his
　　　wife was baptized November the first.

Anno Dni 1628.

John Watson the sonne of Jo : Watson & Eue his wife was
　　　bapt. Apr : 15.
George Greene the sonne of Ro : Greene and Anne his wife
　　　bapt. Apr : 17.
*　Thomas Blisse the sonne of Jerrimie Blisse was bapt.
　　　May 20.
*　Willm. the sonne of Willm. Hemminge and Alice his wife
　　　was bapt. June 29.
*　Dorathie the daughter of Edward Cubit & Anne his wife bapt.
　　　the same day June 29.

---

[1] Left blank in register.

*　——[1] the sonne of Tho : Child was bapt. sept : 6.

John the sonne of John Rysinge and Dorathie his wife was
　　　bapt. Nov : 2.

James Bull the sonne of John Bull was bapt. Nov : 23.

*　henry the sonne of Adam Chambers & Joane his wife was
　　　bapt. Nov : 30.

John the sonne of Richard Boswell & Dorathie his wife bapt.
　　　Dec : 7.

*　Fraunces Swan the daughter of Rich : Swan & Amie his wife
　　　bapt. Dec : 21.

*　Stephen Jeckill the sonne of Robt. Jeckill was bapt. Janu : 2.

*　John the sonne of Anne Dewin a base child by Jo : Ryall
　　　ye reputed father was baptized Janu : 28.

*　Thomas Watson the sonne of Richard Watson & Susan his
　　　wife was bapt. feb : 2.

　　(page signed) per me Samuelem Otes Rectorem ibid : Tho : Moyses
—Ja : H.—gards.

P. 59.*　Marie the daughter of Erasmus hallifax was bapt. feb : 15.

*　Marie Slatter the daughter of Robt. Slatter & Margerie his
　　　wife was bapt. feb : 22.

Margrett Brandon the daughter of Tho : Brandon & Eliz^{th.}
　　　his wife bapt. Martii 15.

Thomas Bosse the sonne of Jo : Bosse & Thomasin his wife
　　　was bapt. Martii 22.

* *　Henry Toll singleman and Mary Keed singlewooman were
　　　married Apr : 30.

* *　Thomas Brandon singleman & Elizabeth Bustinge single-
　　　wooman married May 18.

* *　Clement Spanton singleman and Anne Springall wid :
　　　married June 24.

* *　John Ryall singleman & Elizabeth Tomson singlewooman
　　　were married Sept : 27.

* * *　Daniell Dowsinge was buried May 30.

* * *　Thomas Blisse was buried May 30.

* * *　Edmund Marsham singleman buried Mart : 17.

* * *　Willm. Elvin was buried Mart : 21.

* * *　Cicely ye wife of Step : Angell buried Mart : 23.

---

[1] Left blank in Register.

Anno Domini 1629.

* Grace the daughter of Robt. Forrest & Dorathie his wife bapt. Aprill 12.

* Elizabeth Bustinge the daughter of Robt. Bustinge & Susan his wife bapt. Apr: 19.

* Marie the daughter of Robt. Moyses was bapt. Apr: 26.

* Thomas Paretree the sonne of John Paretree was bapt. May 20.

* James Bell the sonne of Rich: Bell and Margrett his wife was bapt. May 28.

* Edward Warnes[1] the sonne of Robt. Warnes was bapt. June 1.

* ——[2] Swan the sonne of Richard Swan & Amie his wife bapt. Janu: 8.

* John Bustinge & George Bustinge the sonnes of John Bustinge were bapt. Decem: 20.

* Margrett the daughter of Thomas Gedny & Mary his wife was bapt. Octo: 4.

* Blyth the daughter of Edmund Medcave & Margrett his wife was bapt. Octo: 15.

(page signed) per me Samuelem Otes Rectorem ibid :—Richard Bell—James Horne—gard :

P. 60.* * Stephen Angell widdower and Alice Tomson singlewooman were married Sept: 20.

* * * Margrett Jeckill ye daughter of Robt. Jeckill was buried June 6.

* * * widdowe Fen was buried December 18.

* * * ——[2] ye wife of Willm. Welch was buried Martii 20.

Anno Dni 1630.

* Peter harwin the sonne of Thomas hardwin was bapt. July 4.

* Margrett Marsham the daughter of Robt. Marsham was bapt. Octo: 3.

---

[1] *Edward Dye* in Transcript.
[2] Left blank in Register.

* Anne Greene the daughter of Robt. Greene was bapt. Octo : 24.

* John the sonne of Robt. Exham & Anne his wife was bapt. Octo : 28.

* Brigget the daughter of Robt. Bustinge was bapt. Octo : 31.

* Samuell Chambers the sonne of Adam Chambers & Joane his wife bapt. Nov : 28.

* Robt : Slatter the sonne of Robt : Slatter & Margerie his wife bapt. Nov : 30.

* John the sonne of Thomas Ixford was bapt. Janu : 7.

* Samuell Angell the sonne of Stephen Angell was bapt. Janu : 27.

* James the sonne of John Watson bapt. Janu : 27.

* * henry Love singleman & Mathewe Mason singlewooman were married Octo : 6.

* * Willm. Wake singleman & Amie Watson singlewooman were married Nov : 19.

* * Edmund Leman singleman and Rebecca Reynolds singlewooman were married Janu : 23.

* * Thomas hardinge singleman and Mary Mason singlewooman were married Janu : 27.

* * * Alice Perse widdowe was buried July 24.

* * * John Reynolds was buried Janu : 14.

(page signed) **per me Samuelem Otes Rectorem ibid :—Adam Chambers—John Greene—gard :**

P. 61.　　　　　　　　ANNO DOMINI 1631.

* Willyam Bell yͦ sonne of Rich : Bell & Margrett his wife was bapt. May 30.

* Thomas hardinge the sonne of Tho. hardinge & Mary his wife was bapt. the same day.

Willm. Claxton the sonne of Tho. Claxton and Margret his wife were bapt. June 14.

Mary the daughter of Willm. hemminge and Alice his wife was bapt. July 17.

James Childe the sonne of Thomas Child & Margret his wife was bapt. July 31.

* Thomasin Bosse the daughter of Jo : Bosse & Thomasin his
wife was bapt. Octo : 16.

* Thomas Betts the sonne of Robert Betts of Bollick[1] hall was
bapt. Nov : 1.

* Edmund Warnes the sonne of Robt. Warnes was bapt.
Nov : 27.

* Anne hallifax the daughter of Erasmus hallifax was bapt.
Janu : 1.

* Mary Lubbock the daughter of Christopher Lubbock &
Mathewe his wife bapt. Janu : 8.

* Thomas Lemman y⁰ sonne of Edmund Lemman & Rebecca
his wife was bapt. febr : 12.

* John harwin the sonne of Tho : harwin was baptized
May 4.

* Margret Rysinge the daughter of John Rysinge & Dorathie his
wife was bapt. May 11.

* * Laurance Moyses singleman & Ursely Cotes singlewooman
were married Octo : 6.

* * Willm. Bustinge singleman & Elizabeth Dye singlewooman
were married Nov : xx.

* * Richard Jeckill singleman & Elizabeth Keed singlewooman
were married Janu : 29.

* Margrett Metton daughter of Robt. Metton bapt Martii 17.

* * * Dorathie Wake wid. was buried April 23.

* * * Samuell Cartor was buryed May 28.

* * * Elizabeth Bustinge was buried July 25.

* Rebecca hardinge daughter of John hardinge was baptized
Martii xᵗʰ.

* * * ——[2] the wife of Thomas Moyses the elder was buried
Octo : 1.

* * * Anis Griphin was buried Octo : 2.

* * * John Fletcher was buried Octo : 8.

* * * Frauncis Free singleman was buried Octo : 25.

* * * Willm. Parker the sonne of Thomas Parker was buried
Dec : 8.

* * * Edmund Warnes was buried Dec ; 14.

---

[1] Now Bolwick Hall.
[2] Left blank in Register.

* * *   Dorathie the wife of James fletcher buried Dec : 31.
* * *   Richard Watson was buried feb : 1.
* * *   Dorathie hardinge was buried feb : 4.
* * *   Robt. Marsham sen : was buried feb : 24.
* * *   Katherine Elvin widdowe was buried upon good fryday.
* * *   Mathewe Greene yᵉ daughter of Jo : Greene was buried
          Martii 17.

(page signed) per me Samuelem Otes Rectorem ibid : Adam Chambers, John Greene—gard.

P. 62.   Anno Domini 1632.

*   Thomas Moyses the sonne of Robt. Moyses was baptized
    May 13.

*   James Toll the sonne of Henry Toll & Mary his wife was
    bapt. May 27.

*   John Ryall the sonne of John Ryall & Eliza : his wife was
    bapt June 17.

*   Thomas Jeckill the sonne of Richard Jeckill & Eliz : his wife
    was bapt. July 1.

*   Elizabeth Bustinge the daughter of John Bustinge & Mary
    his wife was bapt. July 22.

*   Henry Slatter the sonne of Robt. Slatter & Margerie his wife
    was bapt. Aug. 26.

*   John Browne the sonne of Thomas Browne was bapt.
    Sept : 23.

*   Mihill Ixford the sonne of Thomas Ixford was baptized
    Octob : 7.

*   Willm. Cusshinge the sonne of John Cusshinge was bapt.
    Nov : 4.

*   Fraunces Moses the daughter of Laurance Moses was bapt.
    Novemb : 18.

*   Cicely Betts the daughter of Robert Betts was baptized
    Dec 3.

*   Anne Warnes the daughter of Robt : Warnes was bapt.
    Decemb : 16.

*   Elizabeth Bustinge the daughter of Willm : Bustinge bapt.
    Janu : 13.

*   Brigget Wright the daughter of John Wright bapt. Janu : 27.

* *   Willm Jeckill singleman & Fraunces Bird singlewooman
married May 1.

* *   Thomas Scottowe widdower & Elizab : north singlewooman
maried Nov : xi.

* * *   James Greene the elder was buried April 2.

* * *   John Bustinge the sonne of Thomas Bustinge was buried
Aprill 20.

* * *   ——[1] the wife of Robt. Dye was buried Aprill 21.

* * *   Thomas Gurny the sonne of Willm. Gurny was buried
May 27.

* * *   Emme Tylor widdowe buried June 3.

* * *   Robt : Fen was buried June 13.

* * *   ——[1] the wife of Tho : Scottowe was buried July 8.

(page signed) per me Samuelem Otes Rectorem ibid : James ¦Horne
—Richard Swann—gard.

P. 63.* * *   Henry Green was buried July 14.

* * *   Katherine the wife of Clement Free was buried feb : 15.

* * *   Millicent Sanders was buried feb : 16.

Anno Domini 1633.

*   Anne Greene the daughter of John Greene was bapt. Martii
xxxi[th].

*   Robert Swan the sonne of Richard Swan & Amie his wife
was bapt. May xii[th].

*   Elizabeth Barnes the daughter of Willm. Barnes was bapt.
May xix[th].

*   Anne Blisse y[e] daughter of Jeremie Blisse was bapt. Aug :
xi[th].

*   Thomas Browne the sonne of Thomas Browne was bapt.
Octob. xiii[th].

*   Elizabeth Hopkin the daughter of John Hopkin was bapt.
the same day Octo xiii.

*   Thomas Greene the sonne of Thomas Greene & Elizabeth his
wife was bapt. Decem : 1.

---

[1] Left blank in Register.

*   ——[1] the ——[1] of Thomas harwin was bapt. Decem: xxvi[th].

*   Henry Jeckill the sonne of Willm. Jeckill was bapt. Janu. xii[th].

*   Alice Harwood the daughter of Henry harwood was bapt. feb: xiiii[th].

*   Anne Scottowe the daughter of Thomas Scottowe was bapt. febr: xvi[th].

*   Joane Wake the daughter of Willm: Wake & Amie his wife was bapt. february xxvi[th].

*   Isabell Betts the daughter of Robert Betts was bapt. febru: xvii[th].

this should have cam in before Wakes next to Scottowes.

* *   Thomas Davye singleman & Susan Stibnam singlewooman were married Sept. xxii[th].

* *   James Fletcher widdower & Faith Bosse singlewooman were married Octob: xiiii[th].

* *   John Otes singleman, y° sonne of Willm. Otes, & Elizabeth Solamon[2] singlewooman married Nov: x[th].

* *   Willm: Keede singleman & Thomasin Woodhowse singlewooman were married Novemb: xxvii[th].

* *   Thomas Gilberd singleman & Mary Free singlewooman were married Janu: xiiii[th].

(page signed) per me Samuelem Otes Rectorem ibid James Horne— Willm. Barnes—gard:

P. 64. * * *   ——[1] the wife of Oliver Smith was buried Aprill xxii[th].

* * *   Rebecca hardinge the daughter of Thomas hardinge buried May xxi[th].

* * *   Thomas Allin widdower was buried May xxx[th].

* * *   Amie y° wife of Richard Swan was buried July 4.

* * *   Clement Free widdower was buried July xxxi[th].

* * *   ——[1] the wife of Willm. Dalliday was buried Sept. vi[th].

* * *   Mary the wife of Willm. Algate was buried Nov: 1.

* * *   Thomas Moyses the sonne of Robt. Moyses was buried Decemb: vi[th].

---

[1] Left blank in Register.
[2] Salomon in Transcript.

* * * Thomas Moyses the elder was buried Decemb. xvi[th].

* * * Anne Reynoldes widdowe was buried Martii vii[th].

* Briggett Watson the daughter of John Watson was bapt. Martii ix[th].

* John Bosse the sonne of John Bosse was baptized Martii xvi[th].

* Robert Toll the sonne of henry Toll was baptized the same day.

Thomas Bell the sonne of Richard Bell & margrett his wife bapt. xxi[th] Martii.

ANNO DOMINI 1634.

* Robert Jeckill the sonne of Robt. Jeckill and Margrett his wife was bapt. Aprill vi[th].

* * Willm. Raynoldes singleman and Alice Allens singlewooman were married Aprill xv[th].

* Alice Exham the daughter of Nicholas Exham & Anne his wife was bapt. the xx of Aprill.

* Dorathie Lubbock the daughter of Christopher Lovick bapt. the same day Aprill xx.

* Dorathie Keede the sonne[1] of Willm. Keede & Thomasine his wife was bapt. May vi[th].

* Thomas Brandon the sonne of Thomas Brandon & Elizabeth his wife was bapt. May xviii[th].

(page signed) per me Samuelem Otes Rectorem ibid : John Lynge, gent,—Thomas Harwin—gard.

P. 65.* Thomas Ryall the sonne of John Ryall and Elizabeth his wife was bapt. the same day vid : May xviii[th].

* * * Robert Marsham was buried May xxvi[th].

* Richard Lemman the sonne of Edmund Lemman & Rebecca his wife was bapt. June y[e] first.

* * * Anne Exham widdowe was buried June xviii[th].

* * * henry Jeckill was buried July vi[th].

* * * John Forrest y[e] elder was buried July viii[th].

* Mary hardinge the daughter of Thomas hardinge & Marie his wife was bapt. August y[e] iii.

---

[1] Sic in Register.

* Alice ye daughter of James Fletcher and Faithe his wife was bapt. Sept: vii[th].

Elizabeth Smithe ye daughter of Oliver Smithe & Alice his wife was bapt. Sept: xii[th].

* Christopher Bustinge the sonne of Thomas Bustinge was bapt. Sept: 14.

* Elizabeth Jeckill the daughter of Richard Jeckill & Elizabeth his wife was bapt. Septem xx[th].

* * Richard Angill singleman & Brigget Woodrowe singlewooman were married Sept: xxviii[th].

* * Frauncis Abbs singleman & Millicent Burly singlewooman were married Octob: iii.

Dorathie Smith the Daughter of Edmund Smith was baptised Octo: xxvi[th].

* Andrewe Greene the sonne of John Greene was baptized November the 2[d].

* * * John Jayry the sonne of Robert Jayry was buried November v[th].

* Robert Bustinge the sonne of Robt. Bustinge was baptized November xxx[th].

* John Tramplinge the sonne of Richard Tramplinge was baptized December v[th].

* John Wright ye sonne of John Wright and Anne his wife was baptized January xviii[th].

* Anne Childe ye daughter of Thomas Childe and Margrett his wife was baptized the same day.

* John Haselop the sonne of John Haselop was baptized January xx[th].

* John Davy the sonne of John Davy was bapt. the same day.

* Robt. Moyses the sonne of Robt. Moyses & Elizabeth his wife was bapt. february xxii[th].

* Mary Spanton the daughter of Clement Spanton & Anne his wife was bapt. Martii xxii[th].

(page signed) per me Samuelem Otes Rectorem ibid : John Lynge, gent :—Tho : Harwin—gard.

P. 66.   ANNO DOMINI 1685.

* Willyam Barnes the son of Willyam Barnes was bapt. Martii xxvi[th].

* * * Elizabeth Jeckill the daughter of Richard Jeckill was buried Aprill xxiiii[th].

* * * Dorathie Green widdowe was buried April xix[th].

* Edmund Angell the sonne of Stephen Angell & Alice his wife was baptized the same day.

* Anne Betts the daughter of Robt. Betts & Katherine his wife was bapt. Aprill xx[th].

* * * Margrett wife of Robt: Forrest was buried Maii xxiiii[th].

* * * Elizabeth Keede widdowe was buried Junii vii[th].

* * * Robert Marsham singleman was buried July xxvii[th].

* * * Robert Dye was buried August iii[th].

* * * Robt. Motts was buried Aug: iiii[th].

* Brigget Angell the daughter of Richard Angell and Brigget his wife was bapt. August iv[th].

* Richard Riches the sonne of Thomas Riches & Margret his wife was bapt. August xxi[th].

* * Robert Mauges singleman and Sara Wilkinson single-wooman married June vii[th]. this should have cam in before.

* * * ——[1] the wife of John Munsons was buried August xvii[th].

* * * Margret Tramplin was buried Sept: iiii[th].

* John Browne the sonne of Tho: Browne was bapt. Sept: vi[th].

* John Jeckill the sonne of Willm. Jeckill and Fraunces his wife was bapt. Sept. xx[th].

* Laurance Bustinge the sonne of John Bustinge the reputed sonne of John Bustinge the elder was bapt. the same day.

* Mathewe Otes the daughter of John Otes and Elizabeth his wife was bapt. Sept. xxvii[th].

* Mihell Cusshinge the sonne of John Cusshinge & Dorathie his wife was bapt. Octo: 4.

* Fraunces Bustinge the daughter of Willm. Bustinge bapt. the same day.

---

[1] Left blank in Register.

* *　John Hardinge and Margrett hooks single persons were married Octo: vii[th].

×　Margrett harwin the daughter of Tho: harwin & Elizabeth his wife bapt. Octob: xxx[th].

*　Brigget the daughter of Robt. Exham & Amic his wife bapt. Octob. xxx[th].

* * *　Marie the wife of Robt. Slatter sen: was buried November v[th].

* * *　Anne Wright singlewooman was buried on fryday vid: Novemb: xiii[th].

　　(page signed) per me Samuelem Otes Rectorem ibid:—Richard Bell—Thomas Green—gard:

P. 67.*　Susan Medcalf the daughter of Edmund Medcalf and Margrett his wife was bapt. Dec: vi[th].

*　John Warnes the sonne of Robt. Warnes & Anne his wife was bapt. Dec: viii[th].

*　Thomas Staines the sonne of John Stains & Alice his wife was bapt. Dec: xx[th].

* * *　Marie the wife of Tho: Gedny was buried Dec: 1.

* * *　James Angell the sonne of Stephen Angell was buried Janu: 2.

*　Anne Metton y[e] daughter of Robt. Metton and Margrett his wife was bapt. Janu: 3.

*　———[1] of ———[1] hopkins & ———.[1] his wife was bapt. Janu: x[th].

* * *　Brigget Bustinge y[e] daughter of Robt. Bustinge & Susan his wife was buried Janu: 17.

*　Anne Rysinge the daughter of John Rysinge and Dorathie his wife was bapt. Janu: xxviii[th].

* * *　Samuell Exham the sonne of John Exham & Margrett his wife was buried Janu: xxv[th].

* * *　Stephen Angell was buried feb: 1.

Anno Domini 1636.

*　Edmund the sonne of Robt: Maugs & Sara his wife was bapt. Aprill 18.

---

[1] Left blank in Register.

* Alice the daughter of Christopher Lubbock & Mathewe his
  wife bapt : Aprill 24.

* Frauncis Keede the sonne of Willm. Keed was bapt.
  Maii 21.

* John Lemman the sonne of Edmund Lemman & Rebecca his
  wife bapt. Junii : 26.

* Michaell Warnes the sonne of Thomas Warnes was bapt.
  odem die.

* Cicelie Betts the daughter of Robt : Betts & Katherine his wife
  was bapt. Junii 30.

* Anne Woods the daughter of Daniell Woods was bapt.
  October 2.

* Henry Bosse the sonne of John Bosse & Thomasin his wife
  was bapt. Nov : 13.

* Elizabeth Blisse the daughter of Jeremie Blisse & Anne his
  wife bapt. Nov : 20.

  (page signed) per me Sam : Otes Rectorem ibid : Richard Bell—
Tho : Greene—gard :

P. 68.* Robt : Ryall the sonne of Jo. Royall was bapt. December 4.

* James Haselop the sonne of Jo : haslop was bapt. January 1.

* Edmund Bustinge the sonne of Robt : Bustinge & Susan his
  wife bapt. Janu : 22.

* Mathewe the sonne of Tho : hardinge & Marie his wife was
  bapt. January 26.

* Laurance hallifax the sonne of Erasmus hallifax & Marie his
  wife bapt. feb : 12.
  this should have cam in before ye last.

* Thomas the sonne of Richard Angell & Brigget his wife bapt.
  Martii 12.

* Anne the daughter of Willm. Wake bapt. Martii 19.

* Mathewe Gibson the sonne of peter Gibson was bapt.
  Janu : 29.

* * Richard Jeckill widdower & prudence Goodins (?) singlewooman were married Julii 3.

* * Peter Gibson singleman & Anne Wright singlewooman
  married Junii 30.
  this ought to have bin first.

* * Thomas Gedny widdower & Margrett Loue singlewooman
  married Nov : 1.

* *   Robt. Forrest widdower and Joane Boswell widdowe maried
        feb : 21.
* * *   Margrett hemminge widd : was buried Aprill 11.
* * *   Adam Abbs was buried Apr. 12.
* * *   Elizabeth the wife of Willm. Bustinge was buried
        Aprill 24.
* * *   Michaell the sonne of John Cusshinge was buried
        Maii 5.
* * *   Susan Watson widdowe was buried Junii 27.
* * *   Marie the wife of Jo : Cusshinge was buried Aug : x[th.]
* * *   John Bustinge the elder was buried Aug : xii[th.]
* * *   Elizabeth y⁰ daughter of Oliver Smithe was buried
        Aug : 14.
* * *   John harding sen : was buried Nov : 18.
* * *   Thomas Scottow y⁰ sonne of Tho : Scottowe was buried
        Nov : 26.
* * *   Margrett Sothis widdowe was buried Martii 14.
        (page signed) per me Sam : Otes Rectorem ibid : Rich : Bell—
Tho : Greene—gard :

P. 69.   Anno Domini 1637.

*   John Greene the sonne of John Greene bapt. Maii 28.
*   Friswed Browne the daughter of Thomas Browne was bapt.
        Junii 4.
*   Thomas the sonne of John Rysinge bapt. Junii 8.
*   Thomas Manges the sonne of Robt. Mangs was bapt.
        Julii 22.
*   James the sonne of James Fletcher bapt. Julii 30.
*   Robt. the sonne of Richard Jeckill bapt. Aug : 13.
*   John the sonne of John Lound was bapt. Sept : 17.
*   Rachell the daughter of Edmund Jollye was bapt. Sept : 24.
*   Katherine the daughter of John Otes sen : was bapt. Octo : 1·
*   Willyam the sonne of willm : Jeckill bapt. Octo : 22.
*   Susan the daughter of Richard Bell was bapt. Nov : 30.
*   John y⁰ sonne of John Hardinge bapt. Janu : 7.
*   Robt. the sonne of Christopher Lubbock was bapt. febr : 4.

Margrett the daughter of Clement Spanton was bapt. febr : 11.

* Mathewe Betts the sonne of Robt. Betts was bapt. febr : 16.

* Elizabeth the daughter of Thomas Greene was baptized Martii 4.

* John the Base sonne of Margrett Forrest was bapt. Martii 7.

* Peter the sonne of Thomas Scottowe was bapt. Martii 18.

* * Edmund Jollie and Ellen Whale singlepersons were married Junii 26.

* * John Exham widdower and Elizabeth Rysinge singlewooman were married Nov : 1.

* * John Hunt widdower and mary hooke widdowe were married Janu : 14.

* * John Wake singleman and Elizabeth Mack singlewooman were married the same day vid : Janu : 14.

* * * Amie the wife of Nicholas Bennett was buried Aprill 3.

* * * Joane the wife of Thomas Wilkinson was buried Apr : 13.

* * * Richard Lusher the elder was buried Apr : 16.

(page signed) per me Samuelem Otes Rectorem ibid : John Haslop —Tho : Warnes—gard.

P. 70.* * * Mary the daughter of henry Toll was buried Aprill 20.

* * * John Chapman was buried Maii 13.

* * * henry Toll was buried Junii 9.

* * * Thomas Wake was buried Aug : 6.

* * * Thomas the sonne of John Royall was buried Sept. 24.

* * * Anne the daughter of Thomas Childe was buried Octo : 2.

* * * Jane the wife of Simont Pratt was buried Nov : 23.

* * * John Lounde ye elder was buried Nov : 26.

* * * Robt : the sonne of Richard Jeckill was buried Dec : 3.

* * * Anne the wife of John hunt was buried Dec : 15.

* * * Edmund Dallidas was buried Dec : 30.

* * * Cicelie Marsham was buried Janu : 15.

* * * Edmund ye sonne of Robt. Maugs was buried Janu : 24.

* * * Elizabeth the daughter of Robt. Jeckill was buried feb : 7.

Anno Domini 1638.

Marke Moses yᵉ sonne of Robt. Moses bapt. Apr : 29.
*   Richard yᵉ sonne of Tho : harwin bapt. Janu : 8.
*   Clemens yᵉ daughter of John Munson bapt. Junii 24.
*   Fraunces yᵉ daughter of Robt. Metton bapt. Nov : 11.
*   Peter yᵉ sonne of John Exham sen : bapt. Nov : 30.
*   James yᵉ sonne of Robt. Warnes bapt. Dec. 24.
*   Alice yᵉ daughter of Olliver Smith was bapt. Janu : 6.
*   Robt. yᵉ sonne of Richard Angell bapt. Janu : 20.
*   Susan yᵉ daughter of Laurance Moses bapt. feb : 3.
*   Margrett the daughter of John Staines was bapt. feb : 17.
*   Christopher the sonne of Robt. Betts was bapt. Martii 14.
*   Anne the daughter of will : haynes was bapt. Martii 17.
*   Richard the sonne of John Wake was bapt. Martii 24.
* *   John Cusshinge widdower & Margrett Tomlinson single-
       wooman were married Maii 2.
* *   Willm : haynes singleman & Fayth Exham singlewooman
       were married Junii 17.   verte[1]

(page signed) per me Samuelem Otes Rectorem ibid : John
Tomlinson—Edmund Bustinge—gard :

P. 71.* *   Fraunces Marsham singleman and Anthoine Burwell
       singlewooman were married Sept : 16.
* *   James Bustinge singleman & Ancoris Suggatt single-
       wooman were married Octo : 6.
* *   Olliver Exham singleman and Sara Bustinge singlewooman
       married Nov : 1.
* * *   John Bosse was buried Maii 3.
* * *   ——[2] the base sonne of Margret Forrest was buried
       Maii 6.
* * *   Elizabeth yᵉ daughter of Jo : hopkin was buried Aug : 5.
* * *   John haslope was buried Aug : 9.
* * *   henry hopkin & Ann hopkin buried Aug. 25.
* * *   Ann Brandon widdowe buried Aug : 27.
* * *   Margrett Greene was buried Aug : 30.
* * *   Thomas Wilkinson widdower buried Sept : 2.

---

[1] Probably refers to page.
[2] Left blank in Register.

* * * Nicholas Exham singleman buried Sept: 3.

* * * Robert Jayrye was buried Sept: 10.

* * * Elizabeth Bustinge yᵉ daughter of Will: Bustinge Ju: buried Sept: 12.

* * * Thomas yᵉ sonne of Tho: Greene was buried Sept: 15.

* * * John the sonne of John Wright buried Sept: 17.

* * * Anne the daughter of Thomas Greene buried Sept. 18.

* * * Thomas Greene yᵉ elder buried Sept: 26.

* * * Alice Lound widdowe was buried Octo: 2.

* * * Robt. Slatter yᵉ elder buried Octo: 19.

* * * Dorathie Keed was buried Octo: 22.

* * * Marie yᵉ daughter of John Bull was buried Octo: 25.

* * * Barbarie Grunnye widdowe was buried Nov: 3.

* * * Marye the wife of will: Keed buried Nov: 3.

* * * James the sonne of Richard Bell was buried Nov: 11.

* * * Ann yᵉ wife of John Exham buried Nov. 16.

* * * Margrett Chapman widdowe buried Nov: 25.

* * * Susan ye daughter of Richard Bell was buried Dec: 17.

(page signed) per me Samuelem Otes Rectorem ibid: John Tomlinson—Ed. Bustinge—gard.

P. 72.* * * Margrett Gedny was buried Dec: 19.

* * * ——[1] the wife of Stephen hall was buried Dec. 22.

* * * Olliver Smith was buried Janu: 2.

* * * Nicholas Bennett was buried Janu: 13.

* * * Marie the daughter of John Freeman was buried feb: 8.

* * * John yᵉ sonne of Mihell Smith buried feb: 15.

* * * John Wake yᵉ elder was buried feb: 18.

* * * Robt. yᵉ sonne of henry Toll was buried Martii 20.

* * * Katherine the daughter of John Otes sen: was buried Martii 22.

Anno Dni 1689.

* John the sonne of Peter Gibson was bapt. Martii 31.

* John the sonne of Edmund Jolly was bapt. the same day.

* Elizabeth the daughter of Edmund Bustinge bapt. Aprill 16.

---

[1] Left blank in Register.

* John yᵉ sonne of Jo : Otes yᵉ elder was bapt. the same day.

* Anne the daughter of Will : Bustinge was bapt. Aprill 21.

* ——[1] the daughter of Robt : Exham bapt. Aprill 28.

* Susan yᵉ daughter of Jo : Royall was bapt. June 16.

* Elizabeth yᵉ daughter of Tho : hardinge bapt. July 7.

* Thomas yᵉ sonne of Fraunces Marsham was bapt : July 14.

* Anne the daughter of Edm. Lemman was bapt. Aug : 11.

Edmund the sonne of Rich : Jeckill was bapt. Aug : 25.

* Edmund the sonne of James Bustinge was bapt. Sept : 15.

* Daniell yᵉ sonne of Daniell Woods was bapt. Janu : 6.

* Elizabeth the daughter of Jo : Wake was bapt. feb : 9.

* Elizabeth the daughter of Christop : Lubbock was bapt. Martii 8.

* Mathewe yᵉ sonne of Jo : Rysinge was bapt. Martii 19.

* * John Moses singleman and Grace Bennett widdowe were married June 17.

* * Mihill Smith widdower & Cicelie Rix singlewooman were married feb : 2.

* * * Joane Wake the daughter of Will : Wake was buryed Aprill 17.

* * * Willm. Davy yᵉ elder was buryed Apr : 19.

* * * John yᵉ sonne of peter Gibson was buried the same day.

* * * henry yᵉ sonne of Jo : Bosse was buried Apr : 25.

* * * ——[1] the wife of Robt. Plattin was buried Aug : 11.

* * * Elizabeth the daughter of Tho : harding buryed Aug : 23.

(page signed) per me Sam : Otes Rectorem ibid :—Edm. Bustinge, Jo : Tomlinson—gard.

P. 73. * * * Anne the daughter of Edm. Lemman was buried Aug : 23.

* * * Judethe the wife of Mihill Smith buried Octo : 12.

* * * Margrett Fletcher yᵉ elder widdowe was buried Nov : 17.

* * * Susan yᵉ daughter of Jo : Royall was buried feb : 6.

* * * John yᵉ sonne of Edmund Jolly was buried feb : 26.

* * * Elizabeth the daughter of John Bustinge was buried Mart 9.

---

[1] Left blank in Register.

* * * Thomas Evererd was buried Mart: 13.

* * * Joane yᵉ wife of Robt. Forrest was buried Martii 15.

Anno Domini 1640.

* * * John Exham yᵉ elder was buried Aprill 8.

* * * Thomas Marsham was buried Aprill 19.

* Elizabeth yᵉ daughter of John Exham & Elizabeth his wife was baptized Aprill 19.

* * * Elizabeth yᵉ daughter of John Wake buried Aprill 20.

* * * Ursely yᵉ wife of Willm. Wilde was buried Apr: 22.

* * * John the sonne of John Ryall was buried Apr: 26.

* Margret yᵉ daughter of Jeremie Blisse was bapt. the same day.

* Anne yᵉ daughter of John Otes & Dionis his wife was bapt. Maii 1.

* * * Marke yᵉ sonne of Robt. Moses was buried Maii 3.

* Elizabeth yᵉ daughter of Thomas Davy was bapt. the same day.

* Elizabeth hatinge yᵉ daughter of John hatinge was bapt. Maii 17.

* * * Robt. Plattin was buried Maii 23.

* * * Judeth Exham the daughter of Nicholas Exham was buried the same day.

* * * Thomasin Bosse widdowe was buried Maii 27.

* * * John the sonne of Edmund Lemman was buried Junii 7.

* * * Elizabeth the daughter of Jo: hatinge buried Junii 26.

* * Willm: Wilde widdower & Alice Angell widdowe were married Julii 19.

* * * Laurance yᵉ sonne of Erasmus hallifax buried Julii 24.

* Sara yᵉ daughter of Willm. Jeckill bapt. Julii 25.

* * * Rachel Cotes singlewooman was buried Aug: 3.

* * John Twe singleman & Katherine Moone singlewooman both of Oxned were married here with a lycense August 4.

* * * John yᵉ sonne of John Otes yᵉ elder buried Aug: 24.

(page signed) per me Samuelem Otes Rectorem ibid.

P. 74.   Anno Domini 1641.

* Margrett Fletcher the daughter of James Fletcher was baptized Aprill 25.

* Elizabeth Ryall daughter of John Ryall was bapt. Maii 2.

* Anne Gibson the daughter of Peter Gibson & Anne his wife was bapt. Junii 6.

* Margrett ye daughter of Will: Wilde & Alice his wife was bapt. Julii 5.

* Dorathie Betts the daughter of Robt. Betts bapt. August 1.

* Mathewe Wake ye sonne of John Wake was bapt. Aug: 7.

* Elizabeth Hanes the daughter of Will: hanes bapt. Aug: 25.

* Katherine Marsham the sonne[1] of Fraunces Marsham was bapt. Sept: 13.

* Mathewe hatinge the daughter of Richard hatinge was baptized Oct: 3.

* Thomas hall ye sonne of Tho: hall was bapt. Octo: 10.

* John Bell ye sonne of George Bell was bapt. Nov: 14.

* Robt: Delf ye sonne of Robt: Delf was bapt. Nov. 21.

* Anne ye daughter of Christopher Lubbock bapt. the same day.

* Margerie the daughter of Jo: Tomlinson Ju: bapt. Nov: 28.

* Robt. Skeete ye sonne of Jo: Skeete was bapt. Dec: 5.

* John Otes ye sonne of Jo: Otes sen. bapt. Janu: 16.

* Susan Maugs ye daughter of Robt. Maugs bapt. Janu: 23.

* Samuell Otes ye sonne of Jo: Otes Ju. bapt. feb: 2.

* Thomas ye sonne of Daniell Woods was bapt. feb. 13.

* Susan daughter of Nicholas Marsham bapt. Martii 11.

* Marie the daughter of Jo: Bustinge bapt. Martii 13.

* [2]Robt. the son of Willm. Searle & Anne his wife was bapt. Spt: 22.

* * Willyam Pestill and Jane Brett single persons were married Maii 28.

* * John Skeete & Elizabeth Burman single persons were married June 27.

---

[1] *Sic* in Register.

[2] This entry is added by a different hand.

* * Thomas hall & Grace Paretree single persons were married the same day.

* * Richard Swan widdower & Cicelie Claxton widdowe were married July 5.

* * Thomas Lusher and Anne Sulsam single persons were married Aug : vii[th.]

* * Edmund Rogers & Elizabeth Sherringham single persons were married Aug : 31.

* * Robt : Smithe & Elizabeth Algate single persons were married february 2.

* * * Mary y[e] wife of Erasmus hallifax buryed Aprill 4.

* * * Mathewe y[e] sonne of John Wake was buried Aug : 15.

* * * Fraunces y[e] daughter of Robt. Metton buried Sept : 5.

* * * ——[1] y[e] wife of Robt. Warnes was buried Decem. 14.

* * * Elizabeth the daughter of John Ryall was buried Martii 20

(page signed) per me Samuelem Otes Rectorem ibid :

P 75. **ANNO DOMINI 1642.**

* Marye y[e] daughter of John Staines was bapt. Martii 27.

* Anne y[e] daughter of Willm. Pestill bapt. the same day.

* Henry the sonne of John Rysinge was bapt. Maii 19.

* Anne y[e] daughter of Simont Barber was baptized Julii 3.

* Willm. the sonne of Edmund Bustinge bapt. Aug : 21.

* Dorathie y[e] daughter of John Wake bapt. the same day.

* Debora y[e] daughter of Tho : Tomson was bapt. Sept. 4.

* Anne y[e] daughter of Tho : harwin bapt. Nov : 22.

* Katherine y[e] daughter of Robt. Exham bapt. Octo : 30.

* Fraunces y[e] daughter of Tho : Lusher bapt. Nov : 6.

* Elizabeth the daughter of Edward Wright was bapt. Nov. xx.

* Margrett the daughter of Jo : Cusshing was bapt. Decem : 4.

* Brigget the daughter of Robt. Smithe—

* Faythe the daughter of John Skeete—all theise 3 bapt. in one day Decem : 4.

* Nicholas the sonne of Edmund Jolly was bapt. Dec : 11.

---

[1] Left blank in register.

* Thomas yᵉ sonne of Robt. harwin was bapt. Dec : 26.

* Thomas yᵉ sonne of Robt. Delfe was bapt. Janu : 8.

* Richard yᵉ sonne of George Bell was bapt : Janu : 12.

* Margrett the daughter of John Exham bapt. Janu : 20.

* Samuell yᵉ sonne of Thomas hall was bapt. feb. 22.

* Katherine yᵉ daughter of Robt. Betts bapt. Martii 5.

* John yᵉ sonne of John Connyby was bapt. Martii 12.

* *   Robart harwin and Susan Smithe single persons were married Maii 15.

* *   Willm. Whale & Margerie Palmer single persons were married June 5.

* *   John Larwood & Anne Marsham single persons were married June 19.

* *   Thomas Bloome clerk & Katherine Burges single persons were married Decem : 8.

* *   Robt. Watson & Margrett Copland single persons were married Janu : 16.

* * *   John Bell sonne of George Bell was buried Martii 27.

* * *   Thomas yᵉ sonne of Richard Angell was buried Apr : 24.

* * *   Robt. Warnes was buried Maii 30.

* * *   Susan the daughter of Nicholas Marsham was buried June 26.

* * *   Erasmus hallifax was buried Julii 12.

* * *   Anne ywife of Clemen t Spanton was buried Aug : 7.

* * *   Thomas yᵉ sonne of Willm. Bustinge buried Nov : 27.

* * *   Anne yᵉ daughter of Tho : harwin was buried Nov : 28.

* * *   Faith the daughter of Jo : Skeete was buried Dec : 17.

* * *   Robt. the sonne of Rich : Angell was buried Janu : 3.

* * *   Willm. yᵉ sonne of Robt. Warnes was buried Janu : 7.

(page signed)   per me Samuelem Otes Rectorem ibid :

P. 76.   ANNO DOMINI 1643.

* Elizabeth harding daughter of Jo. harding bapt. Apr. 1.

* Cicely daughter of Tho : harding bapt. June 14.

* Sara daughter of Will : Jeckill bapt. Aug : 5.

* John sonne of Richard Angell bapt. Sep : 22.

* Thomas sonne of Willm. Bustinge bapt. ye same day.

* Elizabeth daughter of Fra : Marsham Nov : 12.

* Mary daughter of Will : hanes bapt. Dec : 10.

* Agnes daughter of Peter Gibson bapt. Dec : 15.

* Thomas sonne of Ro : Grym bapt. Dec : 30.

* Mary daughter of Rich : hating bapt. Janu : 14.

* Adam sonne of Will : Wake bapt. Janu : 28.

* John sonne of Robt. Delfe bapt. the same day.

* Thomas sonne of Robt : Browne bapt. Feb : 2.

* Mary daughter of Jo : Tomlinson bapt. Feb : 4.

* Ciprian sonne of Robt. Fletcher bapt. Feb : 24.

* Samuell sonne of Tho : hall bapt. Maii 16.

* * Willm. Wake singleman & Eliz. Exham widdowe were married Aprill 29.

* * Thomas Bryam singleman & Anne Blisse singlewooman married Maii 2.

* * Oliuer Exham widdower & Thomasin hemming single wooman were married Sept : 29.

* * Robt : Fletcher singleman & Eliz : Jeckill were married Janu : 14.

* * * Samuell hall was buried Aprill 2.

* * * Edmund harding buried Apr. 9.

* * * Rich : sonne of George bell buried Maii 5.

* * * Edmund Lemman was buried Maii 28.

* * * Olipher Exhams wife buried June 13.

* * * Widdowe More buried July 16.

* * * Edmund Smithe was buried Aug : 25.

* * * Thomas Busting was buried Dec : 13.

* * * Wid. Marsham sen. was buried Maii 11.

* * * [1]Oliuer Exhams wife buried June 13.

* * * Nicholas Busting was buried Janu : 22.

* * * John Delf ye sonne of Ro : Delf buried feb : 14.

* * * Amie Busting wid : buried feb : 22.

* * * Ciprian Fletcher was buried Martii 22.

Anno Domini 1644.

* Simont sonne of John Otes was bapt. Aprill 4.

---

[1] A double entry.

* James Smithe sonne of Robt. Smith bapt. Apr : 7.

* Edmund sonne of Tho : Bryam bapt. the same day.

* John the sonne of Olipher Exham bapt. June 23.

* Elizabeth daughter of John Ryall bapt. Sept : 11.

Margrett daughter of Ro : Maugs Nov : 24.

* Grace daughter of Robt. Moyses bapt. Dec : 8.

* Dorathie daughter of Will. pestill bapt. Janu : 12.

* Anne daughter of Rich. Bygraue bapt. Janu : 30.

* Richard sonne of Tho : Lusher bapt. feb : 5.

Willm. sonne of Robt. harwin bapt. feb : 9.

* John ye sonne of John Staynes—

* Elizabeth ye daughter of Jo : Otes—both baptized ye same day vid : feb : 9.

* Laurance sonne of Edmund Busting bapt. feb : 12.

* Mathewe daughter of Christopher Lubbock bapt. Martii 9.

* Fraunces sonne of Will : Jeckill bapt. Martii 14.

* Elizabeth daughter of Jo : Rysinge was bapt. Martii 16.

* * Andrewe Dix widdower & ——[1] Tomson widdowe were married Aug : 26.

* * Willm. Whall & Margrett Scottowe single persons were married Octo : 27.

* * Andrewe Exham & Elizabeth Greene single persons were married Dec : 26.

* * Thomas Gedny & wid. Gasely were married Janu : 14.

* * Thomas Slight & Susan hemming were married Sept : 28.

* * * ——[1] the wife of Robt. Watson was buried Maii 13.

* * * Robt. Exham the elder was buried Maii 24.

* * * Mary Bustinge was buried June 28.

* * * Will : Whales wife buried July 21.

* * Robt. Bond was buryed July 28.

* * * Skeetes wife was buried Aug : 25.

* * * John Bulls wife was buried Dec : 24.

* * * Eliz : Ryall was buried Oct : 19.

* * * Thomas harwin sen : was buried Dec : 7.

* * * Robt. Delf ye sonne of Ro : Delf buried Dec : 20.

* * Robt. Swan sen. was buried Janu : 11.

---

[1] Left blank in Register.

* * *　Adam Wake was buried Janu : 5.
* * *　Willm. harwin was buried Janu : 14.
* * *　Edmund Medcalf his wife buried Janu : 24.
* * *　wid. Marsham wife of Tho : Marsham buried Janu : 31.
* * *　Thomas Woods was buried feb : 9.
* * *　Robt. Browne sonne of Ro : Browne buried Martii 13.
* * *　Clement Spanton was buried Martii 19.
　　　(page signed) per me Sam : Otes Rectorem ibid.

P. 78.　　　　　　　　　Anno Domini 1645.

*　Willm. the sonne of Ro : Delfe was bapt. Martii 30.
*　Richard yᵉ sonne of Rich Jeckill was bapt. Apr : 7.
*　Anne yᵉ daughter of John hardinge bapt. the same day.
*　Willm. the sonne of Jo : Busting bapt. Aprill 20.
*　Richard Langood yᵉ sonne of Gregorie Langood bapt.
　　　　Sept : 8.
*　Thomas yᵉ sonne of Will : Wake bapt. the same day.
*　Robt. the sonne of Robt. Fletcher bapt. Sept : 22.
*　Elizabeth yᵉ daughter of Tho : Tomson bapt. Octo : 5.
*　Robt. yᵉ sonne of Daniell Woods bapt. Octo : 16.
*　Katherine yᵉ daughter of Jo : Exham was bapt. Nov : 30.
*　Katherine the daughter of Will : Wake bapt. the same day.
*　Bennet the daughter of Robt : Exham was bapt. Dec : 21.
*　Elizabeth the daughter of Ro : Boswell bapt. Dec : 28.
*　Margrett yᵉ daughter of Jo : Wake bapt. Janu : 4.
*　Henry sonne of Tho : Bryant bapt. Janu : 18.
*　Elizabeth daughter of henry Blisse bapt. feb : 15.
* *　Adam Chambers & Elizabethe Swan single persons were
　　　　married Octo. 6.
* *　Robt. Everett & Alice Bryam were married Nov : 10.
* * *　Anne Free was buried Maii 4.
* * *　Willm. Delfe was buried Maii 18.
* * *　Adam Jeckill was buried June 3.
* * *　Susan Medcalf was buried June 20.
* * *　Robt. Wright sen. was buried July 31.
* * *　Bartholmewe Raynolds was buried Aug : 31.

* widdowe Burly was buried Sept : 3.

* * * Thomas Wall sonne of Will : Whall buried Nov : 24.

* * * John Otes the sonne of Samuell Otes & Anne his wife was buried Dec. 4.

Katherine Exham was buried Janu : 7.

* * * ——[1] the wife of John Whale was buried feb : 25.

Willm. Algate was buried Martii 16.

(page signed) per me Samuelem Otes Rectorem ibid :

P. 79.   ANNO DOMINI 1646.

* Anne the daughter of Willm. Jeckill bapt. Aprill 1.

* Katherine Smith ye daughter of Ro : Smith bapt. June 14.

* Elizabeth daughter of Laurance Busting bapt. Ap. 17.

Peter ye sonne of Robt. Watson bapt. June 29.

Margret daughter of Thomas hardinge bapt. June 30.

Mathewe Marsham sonne of Fraunces Marsham was bapt. July 12.

Robt. ye sonne of Willm. Pestill bapt. July 19.

* Faithe daughter of Willm. hanes bapt. Sept : 6.

Margrett ye daughter of Olifer Exham bapt. the same day.

* Edward the sonne of Edward Wright bapt. Sept : 13.

Thomas ye sonne of Edmund Jolly bapt. Sept : 27.

Margery ye daughter of Jo : Exham bapt. Nov : 1.

* Elizabeth Gibson was bapt. the same day.

* Elizabeth hating was bapt. Nov : 8.

* Willm. Whale was baptised Nov : 15.

* henry Grym ye sonne of Ro : Grim was bapt. Nov : 22.

* Robt. the sonne of Tho : hall was bapt. the same day.

* Robt. the sonne of Richard Jeckill Ju : bapt. Janu : 30.

* Elizabeth the daughter of Adam Chambers the younger was bapt. feb : 18.

* Edmund the sonne of Edmund Bustinge bapt. feb : 24.

* John ye sonne of Jo : Tomlinson Ju : bapt. Martii 14.

* Parnill Langood daughter of Gregorie Langood bapt. Martii 23

---

[1] Left blank in Register.

* * John Whale & Widdowe Free were married Maii 18.

* * Richard Langood & Margrett Burly married June 20.

* * John Ryall & Margrett hemminge were married Sept: 28.

* * Simont Pratt & Anne Scottowe wid. were married Janu: 1.

* * Samuell Danye & Susan Fletcher single persons were
married January 14.

* * Thomas Brett & Katherine Algate were married Febr: 25.

* * * widdowe Rogers was buried Martii 28.

* * * Alice Slatter wid. was buried Apr: 15.

* * * Peter Watson y⁰ sonne of Rob: Watson was buried
June 29.

* * * ——[1] the wife of John Ryall buried July 22.

* * * Thomas Scottowe was buried Aug: 9.

* * * Edmund Angell was buried Octob: 7.

* * * Dorathie Wake was buried Novemb: 18.

* * * Robt. Jeckill y⁰ sonne of Richard Jeckill Ju: was buried
feb: 14.

(page signed) per me Samuelem Otes.

P. 80. ANNO DOMINI 1647.

* Elizabethe daughter of John Cushin bapt. Martii 28.

* Robt. Ryall sonne of Jo: Ryall was bapt. June 14.

* John Fletcher sonne of Ro: Fletcher was bapt. July 10.

* Robt. Harwin sonne of Ro: harwin was bapt. July 17.

* Elizabeth Connyby was bapt. Aug: 2.
Mathewe daughter of Richard Bigrave bapt. that day.
henry sonne of Christopher Lubbock bapt: Aug: 15.
Richard Otes sonne of Richard Otes was bapt. Sept: 3.
Elizabeth daughter of Jo: harding bapt. Novemb: 2.

* Cicely Davye daughter of Sam. Davy Nov: 7.

* Elizabethe daughter of Willm. Jeckill bapt. Janu: 4.

* Fraunces Smithe sonne of Robt. Smithe was bapt. Martii 7.

* * Thomas hemminge & Clement Streck single persons were
married feb: 14.

---

[1] Left blank in Register.

* * * Edward sonne of Edward Write was buried Apr : 25.
* * * henry sonne of John Rysinge was buried June 29.
* * * John Bustinge was buried July 1.
* * * Widdowe Forrest was buried July 15.
* * * Willm. Jeckill was buried July 18.
* * * Margrett daughter of Rich : Bell was buried Aug : 19.
* * * Robt : hall sonne of Tho : hall was buried Nov : 1.
* * * Laurance sonne of Ed. Busting buried Nov : 14.
* * * Anne daughter of Nicholas Exham buried Janu : 13.

ANNO DOMINI 1648.

* Richard Angell sonne of Rich. Angell was bapt. Maii 25.
Anne daughter of John Wake was bapt. July 22.
* Robt. sonne of Isaack Wiggen was bapt. July 23.
* Willm. sonne of John Rowland was bapt. Sept. 25.
Elizabeth Otes daughter of Jo : Otes bapt. Octob : 2.
Margrett daughter of Robt. Exham was bapt. Oct : 29.
* Richard the sonne of Rich. hatinge bapt. Nov : 1.
John the sonne of Thos. hardinge was bapt. Nov : 15.
Willm. sonne of Tho : hall was bapt. Nov : 19.
* Margrett Ryall daughter of Jo : Ryall was bapt. Janu : 21.
* Margrett daughter of Edmund Bustinge bapt. Janu : 30.
* Margrett daughter of John Tomlinson bapt. Feb. 4.
* John Chambers sonne of Adam Chambers Ju : was bapt. feb. 12.
John Blisse sonne of henry Blisse bapt. Martii 18.
P. 81. * * Thomas Raymes & Elizabeth hemminge single persons were married Aprill 4.
* * * Widdowe Carter was buried Aprill 16.
* * * Robt. Royall was buried that day.
* * * Henry Bird was buried Maii 9.
* * * Edmond Medcalf was buried June 15.
* * * Susan Maugs was buried Aug : 23.
* * * John Watson ye elder was buried Aug : 30.
* * * Clement Copeman was buried Octo : 25.
* * * Margrett Gedny was buried that day.

* * * Nicholas hardinge was buried Decemb: 4.
* * * wid Fen was buried Janu: 30.
* * * John yᵉ sonne of Adam Chambers Ju: buried Martii 2.
* * * Richard Langood was buried Martii 19.

Anno Dni 1649.

* Robt. Watson sonne of Robt. Watson was bapt. Maii 6.
Richard sonne of Charles Allin was bapt. Aug: 17.
* Margret the daughter of Willm. Wake bapt. Aug: 22.
* John the sonne of Willm. Whale was bapt. Sept: 30.
* Fraunces sonne of Fraunces Marsham bapt. Nov: 30.
* Rebecca Saunders daughter of Willm. Saunders was bapt.
     Janu: 13.
* Thomas the sonne of Willm. hanes bapt. feb: 24.
* * * John Munson was buried Martii 24.
* * * The wife of Thomas Coe was buried Aprill 3.
* * * Willm. Bustinge yᵉ elder was buried Aprill 13.
     * Elizabeth daughter of Jo: harding buried Maii 4.
John Angell was buried Maii 9.
Willm. Wild was buried Sept: 14.
Richard Bell yᵉ elder was buried Octo: 1.
* * * The wife of Edward Umphry buried Janu: 31.
The wife of Robt. Jeckill was buried Martii 2.

Anno Dni 1650.

Fraunces the sonne of Fraunces Marsham bapt. Aprill 5.
Margrett Davy yᵉ daughter of Sam: Davy bapt. Aprill
     20.
Samuell Otes sonne of Richard Otes was bapt. Aprill 21.
Fraunces Chambers daughter of Adam Chambers was bapt
     the same day.
Robt. sonne of John Exham was bapt. July 27.
* Richard harwin sonne of Robt. harwin bapt. Sept. 22.
* Robt. Rixe sonne of John Rixe was bapt. the same day.

P. 82.*   Susan hardinge was bapt. Sept: 27.
      *   Thomas the sonne of Robt. Smithe was bapt. Sept: 29.
           Amie Fen was bapt. Octo: 14.
           hanna Lubbock was baptized Decem: 22.
           Anne Wiggen was baptized Janu: 6.
           Robt. Bustinge sonne of John Bustinge Ju: bapt. feb: 17.
   * *   Edward Umphry & widdowe Wilde married Maii 1.
           Henrye Ableswathe & Fayth Greene were married Aug: 2.
           John Bisshop & widdowe Pamer were married Nov: 10.
           John Medcalf & Amie Mackin were married feb 5.
   *   *   Samuell Otes sonne of John Otes was buried June 10.
           Elizabeth Whale was buried Sept. 3.
      *   Widdowe Streek was buried Octo: 13.
           Anne ye wife of Willyam Paretree was buried the same
               day vid: Oct. 3.
           Dorathie Otes daughter of John Otes Ju: buried
               Oct: 21.
           Thomas Lemman was buried Octo. 23.
 * * *   Robt. Greene was buried Nov: 5.
           John Browne was buried Nov: 15.
 * * *   Widdowe Jayry was buried Decemb: 30.

Anno Domini 1651.

           Philip the daughter of George Grene baptized Maii 4.
      *   Plesans daughter of Mark Bell was bapt. Janu: 2.
      *   Thomas ye sonne of Peter Gibson was bapt. Janu: 22.
           Olly the daughter of Edmund Busting bapt. Aprill 30.
      *   Elizabeth the daughter of John Wake was bapt. Maii 9.
           Thomas ye sonne of Tho: harding Ju: bapt. Maii 17.
           Mary the daughter of Frannces Marsham bapt. Aug: 4.
           Elizabethe ye daughter of Tho: Harding bapt. Sept: 4.
           Robt. ye sonne of Robt. Cob was bapt. Octo: 8.
           Thomas ye sonne of Tho: hemminge was bapt. Octo: 25.
      *   Anne ye daughter of Simont Ablesway bapt. the same day.
      *   Robt. the sonne of Edward Creede was bapt. Nov: 15.
      *   John ye sonne of Thomas hall was bapt. Nov: 30.

*　Phillip yͤ daughter of Roger Carter bapt. Dec : 20.
*　Robt. the sonne of John Royall was bapt. feb : 18.
*　Laurence the sonne of Laurence Bustinge bapt. Martii 14.
*　Phillip the sonne of Christopher Buck bapt. Martii 15.
* *　Willm. Paretree widdower & Susan Withe single wooman
were married October 17.

(page signed) per me Samuelem Otes C. rectorem.

P. 83.* * *　Edmund Bryant yͤ elder was buried Aprill 27.
* * *　Thomas Hardinge was buried Maii 27.
* * *　Mary the wife of Thomas Harding buried Maii 29.
* * *　Edward Umphry was buried Aug : 28.
* * *　Katherine Otes widdowe was buried Sept. 23.
* * *　Elizabeth Watson was buried Nov : 14.
* * *　Elizabethe yͤ wife of Willm. Wake buried Martii 20.

? Anno Domini 1652.[1]

*　Elizabethe the daughter of Henry Walby bapt. Aprill 10.
*　Mathewe daughter of Edmund Tuck bapt. Aprill 11.
*　Anne yͤ daughter of Ollifer Exham bat. Aprill 27.
Margrett yͤ daughter of Robt. Fletcher bapt. Apr. 28.
*　John yͤ sonne of Richard Hatinge was bapt. Maii 12.
Marye daughter of Willm. Sanders bapt. Maii 14.
Margrett daughter of Charles Allin bapt. Maii 18.
Marye daughter of Daniell Wells bapt. June 23.
Rich. sonne of willm. Pestill bapt. Aug : 11.
*　Margrett, this should be Mary,[2] daughter of Willm. Whale
bapt. Sept: 8.
Edward sonne of Willm. Paretree bapt. Sept : 11.
*　Faithe daughter of Robt. Exham bapt. Sept 15.
*　Frances daughter of Henry Chambers bapt. Octo 20.
*　Thomas sonne of Robt. Watson was bapt. Octo 24.
*　Rachel Martius daughter of Roger Martius bapt Janu : 22.
*　Richard sonne of John Bull was bapt. Janu : 24.

---

[1] The date here *follows* the entries.
[2] Added by same hand.

*   John ye sonne of John Bustinge bapt. feb : 12.
*   Elizabeth daughter of John Coe was bapt. Martii 14.
* * *   Widdowe Wake was buried Aprill 2.
* * *   Robt. Smithe was buried Octob : 28.
* * *   Willm. sonne of John Cusshing buried Octo : 30.
* * *   wid. Midleton was buried feb. 28. [1]

---

[1] End of Book I, and of handwriting No. 2. The Rev. Samuel Otes, Rector, whose pen has filled so many of these pages, was no doubt superseded in that part of his duties by the Lay Register of 1653. He seems, however, to have kept possession of his rectory and other property till his death. He was the son of the Rev. Samuel Otes, Rector of Marsham 1577 to 1605 and of North Repps 1588 to 1620. Born about 1578, he was ordained Priest by William, Bishop of Norwich, 21 Dec. 1601, having been Curate of Marsham since the beginning of that year. On the cession of his father he was presented by the king to the Rectory, and was instituted by the Archbishop of the Province 8 May 1605: and was licensed to preach throughout the diocese by John, Bp. of Norwich, 22 Nov 1608. After an incumbency of 53 years he died in 1658. His Will, dated 15 Oct. 1658, and proved, *at London*, 9 March 1658-9, provides as follows :—" To be buried in the chancel of Marsham church.—*Anne*, wife, to be sole Executrix.— to have messuage late purchased of one Andrew Dix wherein one Allen now dwelleth, and the 7 acres of land with it, for her life, and then to *Samuel*, son— *Robert*, son, to have 10 acres of land called Firmans.—*Richard*, son, to have 5 acres near above—*Samuel* the son to have library of books, bedstead and bedding, & also all the other lumber therein, also a tapestry carpet sometime my father's. *Richard*, son, to have 1½ acres of free land abutting upon Woodgate-greene & lying by Crane's lane, now occupied by Roger Carter.—To *Poor* of *parish church* of Marsham 20s. at my burial.—*Anne*, daughter, my best tapestry coverlit.—*Margaret*, daughter, a featherbed.—*Wm Searles*, clerk, *Tho. Parker*, *Richd Allen*, *Oliver Exham*, Witnesses." (Institution Books, Liber 22— Norwich Archd. Wills. fol 585. 1658.)

REGISTER BILL 1665.

CHRISTNINGS.

Mary y^e *daughter of John Harwin baptized March 26.*

Elizabeth y^e *daughter of John Jeckill & Anne his wife baptized Aprill 4.*

William y^e *sonne of William Jeckill & Susan his wife baptized May 7.*

Anna y^e *daughter of John Swan baptized June 19.*

Anne y^e *daughter of Peter Hilton was baptized June 29.*

John y^e *sonne of Daniel Hurt was baptized July 23.*

Thomas y^e *sonne of Michael Warnes & Bridget his wife was baptized August 9.*

John y^e *sonne of Thomas Havers was baptized Sept: 3.*

William y^e *sonne of John Gaze was baptized eodem die.*

John y^e *sonne of William Day clerk & Elizabeth his wife was baptized Sept: 28.*

John y^e *sonne of James Jex & Cicely his wife was baptised October 8.*

Rachel y^e *daughter of Thomas Soame & Mary his wife was baptized Oct: 15.*

Sarah y^e *daughter of Richard Jeckill jun was bapt. eodem die.*

John y^e *sonne of John Gazely was baptized Jan: 1.*

William y^e *sonne of Richard Harwin was bapt. Jan: 28.*

Anne y^e *daughter of Andrewe Greene was bapt. Feb: 4.*

Simeon y^e *sonne of Thom: Brandon & Anne his wife was baptized Feb: 25.*

Henry y^e *sonne of Thomas Woodwerke & Mary his wife was baptized eodem die.*

Isaack y^e *sonne of Thomas Harding & Mary his wife was baptized Feb: 26.*

Thomas y^e *sonne of John Harwin was baptized March 11.*

Ellen y^e *daughter of Henry Coates was baptized March 18.*

MARRIAGES Y^E SAME YEERE.

John Gazely & Anne Gibson single persons were married March 27.

Thomas Riall widdower & Margery Alborrow single woman were married July 23.

*Thomas Woodwerke & Mary Oakes single persons were married
  August 1.*

*Francis Flaxman widdower & Mary Slatter widdow were married
  September 26.*

*Henry Slatter widdower & Mary Chester single woman were married
  October 3.*

*Thomas Harding widdower & Mary Beck single woman were married
  October 10.*

*Robert Moyses single man & Sarah Busting widdow were married
  October 24.*

*Richard Anger widdower & Bridget Leeds widdow were married
  November 25.*

*Richard Smith de Blickling, Gent, & Anne Watts de Crostwicke
  single persons having a license fro ye Commissaries Court were
  married Feb : 23.*

Burialls Anno Domini 1665.

Elizabeth the daughter of Edmund Busting was buried Aprill 6.
John Moyses was buried Aprill 10.
Elizabeth ye daughter of John Jeckill was buried eodem die.
Robert Exham was buried Aprill 21.
Thomas Parker was buried June 23.
Rebecca ye daughter of Thom. Harding was buried May 23.
———[1] Witherly widdow was buried Sept : 10.
Martha ye wife of Henry Lowe was buried Sept : 30.
M^{ris} Elizabeth Ling widow was buried Nov : 21.
John the sonne of Wm Day clerk was buried Dec : 8.
Anne Gedge widow was buried December 14.
Mary Wells widow was buried January 30.
Margaret Staynes was buried February 21.
Thomas ye sonne of Michael Warnes was buried March 24.

  per me Gulielmum Day cler, Rect. ibid : Thom. Shaften—John
Exham Churchwardens.

---

[1] Left blank in Bill.

REGISTER BILL 1666.

CHRISTNINGS.

John y^e *sonne of Thom. Ryall was baptized April 6.*

Thomas y^e *sonne of Robert Moyses was baptized July 10.*

Mary y^e *daughter of Henry Slatter was baptized July 29.*

Martha y^e *daughter of John Neeve was baptized Aug: 19.*

Anne y^e *daughter of Peter Scottow was baptized Sept: 9.*

John y^e *sonne of Robert Starling & Thomasin his wife was baptized
    Sept: 23.*

Frances y^e *daughter of John Jeckill & Anne his wife was baptized
    October 17.*

Frances y^e *daughter of Francis Coates was bapt. Oct: 21.*

Robert y^e *sonne of Will*^m *Day clerk & Elizabeth his wife was baptized
    January 3.*

Matthew y^e *sonne of Matthew Gibson was baptized Jan: 6.*

Charles y^e *sonne of Will*^m *Busting was bapt. March 17.*

Anne y^e *daughter of John Tramplet was baptized March 24.*

MARRIAGES Y^E SAME YEERE 1666.

*Thomas Warner of Erpingham & Hannah Woolsey of Aylesham
    single persons having a license fro y*^e *Commissaries Court were
    married in y*^e *Parish Church of Marsham Sept: 6.*

*William Busting & Mary Shaften single persons were married
    Oct: 2.*

Simon Oates & Elizabeth Tubby single persons were married Nov: 4.

BURIALS 1666.

Anne y^e *daughter of John Swan was buried May 6.*

Mary Staynes was buried May 20.

Bridget y^e *wife of Michael Warnes was buried Aug: 7.*

Mr^s *Anne Oats widdow was buried Sept 30.*

Anne y^e *wife of Thom. Read was buried Nov: 3.*

Elizabeth Busting widdow was buried Nov: 6.

Margarett Ryall widdow was buried Nov: 14.

———[1] Witlingham widdow was buried Nov: 15.

---

[1] Left blank in Bill

Robert Jeckill junior was buried Jan: 16.
Robert Watson was buried February 17.
*Henry y*e* sonne of Thom. Woodwerk was buried Feb 20.*
    per me GULIELMUM DAY cler, Rect: ibid: JOHN EXHAM—THOMAS SHAFTEN—ROBERT SWAN—ROBERT MOYSES.

REGISTER BILL 1668.

CHRISTNINGS.

*Stephen y*e* sonne of Edmund Jeckill & Philippa his wife was baptized Aprill 12.*
*Henry y*e* sonne of Henry Loue was baptized May 7.*
*Mary y*e* daughter of James Jex was baptized May 27.*
*Alice y*e* daughter of Henry Hudson was baptized Aug: 9.*
*Mary y*e* daughter of Thom. Bensly was baptized Aug: 16.*
*John y*e* sonne of John Jeckill jun. was baptized Sept: 27.*
*William y*e* sonne of John Gazely was baptized October 5.*
*Margaret y*e* daughter of John Bland was baptized eodem die.*
*Anne y*e* daughter of Thomas Grime was baptized Nov: 8.*
*Mary y*e* daughter of Robert Busting was baptized Nov: 28.*
*John y*e* sonne of Robert Moyses was baptized Dec: 28.*
*William y*e* sonne of Henry Slatter was baptized January 3.*
*Anne y*e* daughter of Ralph Green was baptized Jan: 31.*
*Thomas y*e* sonne of Thom. Starly was baptized Feb: 28.*
*Anne y*e* daughter of Henry Cotes was baptized eodem die.*
*Daniel y*e* sonne of Will*m* Day clerk & Elizabeth his wife was baptized March 16.*
*William y*e* sonne of Richard Boswell was bapt. March 21.*

MARRIAGES 1668.

John Bland & Frances Freeman single persons were married Aprill 12.
John Read & Anne Heaslup single persons were married June 16.
Thomas Goldsmith & Mary Tomlinson single persons were married October 16.
Thomas Read jun. widdower & Sarah Brand single woman were married Nov: 28.

Edmund Spark & Elizabeth Otes single persons were married Dec: 8.

George Crome de Banningham singleman & Mary Sewell single woman of ye Parish of St Saviour in ye City of Norwich having a license from ye Commissaries Court were married in ye Parish Church of Marsham Dec 30 by me Willm Day, Rector.

BURIALLS 1668.

Robert Sterling was buried Aprill 3.
Mary ye wife of John Busting was buried Aprill 11.
Susan Harwin was buried Aprill 11.
Cicely ye wife of James Jex was buried May 25.
Margrett ye daughter of John Wake was buried June 21.
Margery ye daughter of Willm Wake was buried Aug: 31.
Fayth ye wife of James Fletcher was buried Sept: 5.
John Whalle was buried Sept: 28.
Elizabeth ye daughter of Christopher Lubbucke was buried February 6.
John ye sonne of Simon Oats was buried eodem die.
Christopher Lubbuck was buried March 18.
John Coe was buried March 23.

per me GULIELM. DAY Rectorem ibid: JAMES JEX—JAMES GEDGE Churchwardens.

REGISTER BILL 1670.

CHRISTNINGS A.D. 1670.

John ye sonne of Henry Hudson was baptized June 12.
Robert ye sonne of Edmund Jeckill was baptized Sept: 12.
Thomas ye sonne of John Neave was baptized Sept: 4.
Elizabeth ye daughter of Thom. Harding was bapt. Sept 6.
Thomas ye sonne of John Raynolds was baptized Oct: 30.
Frances ye daughter of Willm Jeckill was baptized Nov: 27.

MARRIAGES 1670.

Gregory Langood & Frances Smith were married Aprill 4.
John Tomlinson & Martha Bigrave single persons were married
Feb: 14.

BURIALLS 1670.

John y͏ᵉ sonne of widdow Sterling was buried Aprill 25.
Thomas y͏ᵉ sonne of John Harwin was buried June 5.
John y͏ᵉ sonne of Robert Busting was buried Aug: 16.
Robert y͏ᵉ sonne of John Tramplett was buried Aug: 23.
Daniel y͏ᵉ sonne Will͏ᵐ Day clerk & Elizabeth his wife was buried
October 3.
Alice Barningham widdow was buried Sept: 9.
Edmund Jell was buried October 24.
Robert y͏ᵉ sonne of Edmund Jeckill was buried Nov: 16.
Samuel Davy was buried November 30.
Robert Slatter was buried January 15.
Thomas Sharpin was buried January 30.
John Exham jun. was buried March 12.
    per me GUILIELMUM DAY Rect. ibid. THOMAS ROYALL—THOMAS
——[1] Churchwarden.

REGISTER BILL 1675.

CHRISTNINGS 1675.

John y͏ᵉ sonne of Edmund Jeckill was baptized Aprill 18.
Elizabeth y͏ᵉ daughter of Henry Lowe was baptized Aprill 19.
Anne y͏ᵉ daughter of Simon Brewster was baptized May 16.
Mary y͏ᵉ daughter of Richard Otes was baptized Sept: 16.
Elizabeth y͏ᵉ daughter of John Neeve was baptized Oct: 3.
Robert y͏ᵉ sonne of Thomas Bensly was baptized Nov: 14.
Mary y͏ᵉ daughter of John Rice was baptized Dec: 27.
Mary y͏ᵉ daughter of Will͏ᵐ Burroughs was baptized Feb: 20.
Elizabeth y͏ᵉ daughter of Thom. Delfe was baptized March 19.

---

[1] An illegible autograph.

MARRIAGES 1675.

John Rice of Marsham & Rebecca Saunders of Aylesham single persons having a license were married Aprill 6.

Matthew Goss widdower & Bridget Tibbengham wid. having a license were married July 11.

Thomas Tubby & Elizabeth Copping of Langley both single persons having a license were married Sept: 26.

John Sterling & Sarah Barnes single persons both, & of ye Parish of Banningham were married in ye Parish Church of Marsham October 26.

BURIALLS 1675.

Dorothy Heeslop was buried Aprill 11.

Elizabeth Max was buried May 7.

Mary Read widow was buried Aug: 7.

Elizabeth Jell widow was buried October 23.

Mary ye wife of Francis Flaxman was buried Nov: 9.

Fayth ye wife of Willm Haynes was buried Nov: 22.

Robert Busting jun. was buried December 3.

Mary ye wife of Stephen Jeckill was buried Dec: 23.

William Haynes was buried January 1.

Henry Slatter was buried January 10.

Lucie Gedney widdow was buried Janu: 17.

John Gazely was buried January 20.

Elizabeth ye wife of William Andrews January 29.

Sarah ye daughter of Richard Jeckill was buried Jan: 24.

Edmund Jolly was buried January 30.

Henry Love was buried March 5.

per me W^m. DAY Rect.   CHARLES ALLEN. Church W.

REGISTER BILL OF 1677.

CHRISTNINGS 1677.

Elizabeth ye daughter of Robt. Fletcher was baptized Aprill 1.

Mary ye daughter of Nathaniel Bell was baptized July 5.

Robert ye sonne of Robt. Woods was baptized August 19.

John ye sonne of John Green was baptized September 30.
Michael ye sonne of Willm. Andrews was baptized October 7.
James ye sonne of Nicholaus Jolly was baptized Oct: 28.
Elizabeth ye daughter of Richard Otes was baptized Nov: 5.
Mary ye daughter of Simon Brewster was baptized Dec: 23.
Elizabeth ye daughter of John Bland was baptized Feb: 3.
John ye sonne of John Tomlinson was baptized March 3.
Anne ye daughter of Willm. Burroughs was baptized eodem die.

MARRIAGES 1677.

Miles Cooke & Margaret Cushen single persons were married Oct: 6.
William Hayne & Frances Bens single persons were married January 1.

BURIALLS IN 1677.

Susan ye wife of Willm. Jeckill was buried Aprill 15.
Alice ye wife of John Bustin was buried May 26.
Widdow Bliss was buried September 15.
Alice Bustin widdow was buried October 15.

per me W^{m.} DAY Rect.   NATHANIEL BELL.   Church W.
                                    JAMES GEDGE.

REGISTER BILL OF 1678.

CHRISTNINGS 1678.

John ye sonne of Richard Harper was baptized March 30.
Samuell ye sonne of Richard Jeckell was baptized Aprill 21.
Thomas ye sonne of Thomas Sterman was baptized April 28.
William ye sonne of John Neeve was baptized May 5.
Thomas ye sonne of Thomas Delfe was baptized August 3.
Isaac ye sonne of Thomas Read was baptized August 10.
Thomas ye sonne of Thomas Havers was baptized Sept: 15.
Ann ye daughter of John Sharpin was baptized Dec: 25.
Robert ye sonne of Stephen Jeckell & Ellen his wife was baptized February 23.
John ye sonne of John Busting was baptized March 3.

MARRIAGES—NONE AT ALL.

BURIALLS IN 1678.

Elizabeth Parker widdow was buried March 31.
Richard Hateing was buried May 21.
John Tomlinson was buried August 3.
William Day clerke was buried August 31.
Robert Slater was buried October 17.
Robert Jeckell was buried October 14.
Catherine Greene widdow was buried October 14.
William Paretree was buried October 27.
Elizabeth ·ye daughter of Richard Oates was buried Nov : 15.
Mary Woods widdow was buried January 30.·
Willaim ye sonne of Edward Paretree was buried Feb : 2.
Christopher ye sonne of Matthew Gibson was buried Feb : 5.
John ye sonne of John Rice was buried Feb : 27.
Grace ye wife of Thomas Hall was buried March 8.
Robert Mengs was buried March 9.
Alice ye daughter of Thomas Hall was buried March 11.

JOHN DEYNS Rector.
EDWARD JECKS—JAMES GEDGE Ch : wardens.

1692.   BURIALS.[1]   *Edmund inf^{t.} son of Will. Davy Feb 12.*
Sarah wife of Samuel Brigs March 23.

---

[1] Not preserved in the parish books.

[Book 3. 1684—1754.]

[1] *THE NAMES OF THOSE PERSONS WHO WERE BAPTIZED, MARRYED, & BURIED IN THE PARISH OF MARSHAM IN Y*^E *COUNTY OF NORFOLKE & IN THE DIOCESSE OF NORWICH IN Y*^E *YEARE OF OUR LORD 1684.*

BAPTIZINGS 1684.

Elizabeth ye daughter of Jo : Havers April 21.
Tho : ye son of Tho : Thornton July 3.
Tho : ye son of Tho : Watson Aug : 10.
Elizabeth ye daughter of James Deeker Aug : 10.
John ye son of James Corke Sept : 7.
Mary ye daugh : of Tho : Scott Sept : 14
Elizabeth ye daugh : James Starling Sept : 21.
Ann ye daughter of Tho : Delfe Sept 24.
Charles & Richard sons of Rich : Press Octob : 8.
John ye son of John Green Octob : 10.
Susan ye daughter of Robert fletcher Octob : 19.
Mary ye daughter of John Sharpine Nov : 16.
Elizabeth ye daughter of John Dearth Nov : 26.
Robert ye son of John Marsham Nov : 30.
Tho : ye son of John Colye Jan : 12.
Maxye Fox ye daughter of John Feb : 15.

MARRIAGES ANNO DOMINI 1684.

James Green widower and Ann Hust singlewooman June 29th.

BURIALLS 1684.

Will : Saunders April 1.
Henry Chambers May. 19.
Ann Gilbert June 6.

[1] Handwriting No. 3 for this heading and the entries for 1684.

Amye yͤ daughter of will: Burroghs June 25.
Mary Lubbocke June 25.
John Fox July 28.
Ann Green widow Aug: 14.
Elizabeth yͤ daughter of Daniell Hart Aug: 15.
John Dearth Aug: 21.
Mary yͤ daugh: of Tho: Scott Sept: 23.
Thomas Macke Oct: 3.
Alice yͤ daugh: of Mary Death widow Oct: 11.
Elizabeth[1] yͤ daugh: of Jo:[1] Havers. Nov: 7.
Margery[1] Cotes widow Jan: 15.
Mary yͤ daugh: of Roger Neeve[1] March 10.
Elizabeth yͤ daugh of Tho: Brandon March 10.

[2] Burialls Anno Domini 1686.

John the sonne of Richard Trampling May 5th.
Robert Exham was buried July 24th.
Mary Tybbenham yͤ daughter of John Tybbenham was buried
    July 26th.
John Deyns, Clerk, Rector of Marsham, was buried August 3d.
Will: Peartree the sonne of Will: Peartree was buried Aug 4th.
Will: Jeckell was buried August 20th.
Martha Lubbock daughter of Joseph Lubbock was buried
    Sept 6th.
John Greenwood was buried Sept 8th.
Elizabeth Jeckell was buried Decemb. 8.
Elizabeth Dearth the daughter of John Dearth was buried
    Jan 28.
Sara the daughter of Henry Jeckill buried March 6th.
John Cushion was buried (bapt 10th.) March 16th.
Richard the infant sonne of Richard Otes buried March 25th.

Burialls Anno Domini 1687.

John Green was buried March 27th.
John the infant sonne of Joshua Blackbourne buried April 25th.

---

[1] Almost rubbed out but verified by Transcript.
[2] Handwriting No. 4, begins & follows continuously for 20 years.

Philip Sturman widdow buried April 28th.

Elizabeth the infant daughter of Thomas Scott April 13th.

Elizabeth the wife of John Spencer July 12th.

Thomazine the wife of Matthew Bateman May 7th.

Mary the daughter of Thomas Thornton & Elizabeth his wife
      May 17.

Martha Burton singlewooman October 20th.

Mary the daughter of Thomas Watson & Elizabeth his wife
      Novemb : 4th.

Susanne Sturman widdowe Decemb : 1.

Amy the daughter of John Hanes & Elizabeth his wife
      Decemb : 17th.

Frances the wife of John Bland January 1.

Miles the sonne of James Corke & Elizabeth his wife Feb : 3rd.

John one of the twin sons of Thomas Smith & Mary his wife
      Feb : . .[1]

Anne the wife of James Starling March 6th.

John the son of Thomas Worms & Margarett his wife March
      10th.   affidavit made hereof before Will : Heylett cler :
      Rector of Heavingham March 15th.

Simon Brereton was buried May 25 affidavit made hereof befor
      Will : Heylett Rector of heavingham May . .[1]

Marriages Anno Domini 1686.

Samuel Sayers & Mary Smith single persons of Blickling were
      married April 22d.

Christopher Jeffrys of Newton St. Faithes & Elizabeth Haryson
      of Horsford were married June 16th.

Jonathan Church of Lammas singleman & Elizabeth Bonner of
      Worstead singlewoman were married Sept 23d.

Roger Catley of St. Martins of Coslany in Norwich & Gurtrude
      Elsing of Horsford married Octo. 1st.

Marriages Anno Domini 1687.

Gregory Marsham & Judith Green both single persons of this
      Parish were married May 16th.

---

[1] Numerals worn out.

Marriages Anno Domini 1688.

Isaac Harding & Sarah Jeckell both single persons of this Parish
    were married April 1st.
Thomas Watson widdouer & Mary Harding widdow both of this
    Parish August 19th.
Henry Gill of Burrow widdower & Martha Lubbock of this Parish
    singlewoman December 12.
William Jeckell of Marsham singleman & Martha Lubbock of
    Heydon singlewoman[1] March 11th.

P. 2.   ## Baptizings Anno Domini 1685.

Elizabeth the daughter of William Matthew & Anne his wife was
    baptized Jan : 7.
Mary[1] the daughter of Edmond Exham & Frances his wife
    April 13.
Jane[1] the daughter of Richard Tills & Anne his wife May 17th.
Amy the daughter of Edward Peartree & Amy his wife Sept : 24th.
Anne the daughter of Isaack Blythe & Anne his wife October 4.
John the sonne of Robert Harwin & Grace his wife October 15.
John the sonne of Will : Andrews November 15.
John the sonne of Richard Otes & Mary his wife Novemb. 16.
Mary the daughter of Thomas Scott & Mary his wife January 5.
Anne the daughter of Roger Lolham & Dorothye his wife
    January 14th.
Phillip the daughter of John Green & Frances his wife
    March[1] . .[2]

Baptizings Anno Domini 1686.

Richard the sonne of Joshua Blackbourne & Agnes his wife
    March 28.
James the sonne of Daniell Beck April 5.
Mary the daughter of Thomas Thornton & Elizabeth his wife
    April 6.
Thomas the sonne of John Spencer & Elizabeth his wife April 6.

---

[1] Much worn but verified by the transcript.
[2] Numerals worn out.

Will: the sonne of Will: Peartree & Mary his wife April 11th.

John the sonne of John Havers & Sarah his wife May 1st.

Anne the daughter of Robert Fletcher & Elizabeth his wife July 8th.

Mary the daughter of Thomas Watson & Elizabeth his wife July 8th.

Elizabeth the daughter of James Corke & Elizabeth his wife October 4th.

Rebecca the daughter of James Dyker Novemb: 28th.

John the sonne of John Leake & Mary his wife Decemb: 4th.

Elizabeth the daughter of Thomas Scott & Mary his wife Decemb: 20th.

John the sonne of John Daglis & Mary his wife Februa. 21st.

John the sonne of Roger Neave March 20th.

Elizabeth the daughter of Richard Presse & Margarett his wife Sept. 5.

Martha the daughter of William Jeckell & Anne his wife was baptized.

Baptizings anno Domini 1687.

Thomas the sonne of Thomas Fox & Margery his wife May 15th.

Mary the daughter of Richard Harper & Anne his wife May 15.

Richard the sonne of Richard Tramplett & Elizabeth his wife July 3.

Richard the sonne of Richard Tills & Anne his wife July 17th.

Will: the sonne of Thomas Delph & Elizabeth his wife August 21st.

Susanna the daughter of Will. Peartree & Marye August 28.

Elizabeth the daughter of Edmond Peartree & Amy his wife Sept. 18th.

Anne the daughter of John Green & Frances his wife Sept: 30.

William the sonne of John Cecly & Susanne his wife Octob: 2.

Richard the sonne of Richard Barney & Elizabeth his wife Octob: 24th.

Cornelius the sonne of Stephen Streeck & Susanne his wife Octob 28th.

Ursula the daughter of John Gibson & Elizabeth his wife
　　　Novemb : 27th.
Thomas the sonne of Thomas Thornton & Elizabeth his wife
　　　Decemb 11th.
Elizabeth the daughter of Joshua Blackbourne & Agnes his wife
　　　Decemb : 11th.
Amy the daughter of John Haynes & Elizabeth his wife
　　　Decemb : 26th.
Mary the daughter of Matthew Parker & Margery his wife
　　　Decemb : 27th.
Frances the daughter of John Bland & Frances his wife
　　　Jan : 5th.
Thomas the sonne of John Havers & Sarah his wife Feb : 5th.
Robert the sonne of Will Jeckill & Anne his wife Feb 15th.
John & Thomas the twin sons of Thomas Scott & Mary his wife
　　　Feb 25th.
William the sonne of James Starling & Anne his wife Feb 27.
Elizabeth the daughter of John Marsham & Elizabeth his wife
　　　March 4th.
Frances the daughter of Will. Andrews & Elizabeth his wife
　　　March 18th.

Baptizings Anno Domini 1688.

Richard the base sonne of Amy Sanders April 18th.
Abigail the daughter of Charles Bustinge & Elizabeth his wife
　　　April 20th.
Miles the sonne of Matthew Gibsonne & Mary his wife June
　　　24th.
Titus the sonne of Richard Otes & Mary his wife August 17th.
Samuell the sonne of William Davy & Susanne his wife
　　　October 9th.
Joseph the sonne of Samuel Briggs & Mary his wife October
　　　25th.
James the sonne of James Corke & Elizabeth his wife Feb : 3rd.
John the sonne of Richard Barney & Elizabeth his wife
　　　March 8th

Baptizings Anno Domini 1689.

Susanna the daughter of Isaack Harding & Sarah his wife April 8th.

Hannah the daughter of Richard Tramplett & Elizabeth his wife June 8th.

Edward the sonne of Thomas Thornton & Elizabeth his wife June 27th.

Frances the daughter of John Green & Francis his wife August 4th.

Joseph the sonne of Joseph Lubbock & Cicely his wife August 13th.

George the sonne of Richard Presse & Margarett his wife August 25th.

Matthew the sonne of Matthew Gibsonne & Mary his wife September 1s ·

Philip mary yᵉ base daughter of Mary Watson widdowe & Philip Tukely nominated by her the father Septem : 1st.

Anne the daughter of Roger Neave & Mary his wife Sept : 3rd.

Burialls Anno Domini 1688.

Anne the wife of Richard Harper March 29th.   affidavit made hereof before Will : Heylett Rector of Hevingham April 4.

Elizabeth the wife of Thomas Watson April 18th.

Thomas Lusher an old man April 23d.
    affidavit made of both these before Will : Heylett Rector of Hevingham April 24th.

Simon the sonne of Thomas Brandone was brought from Norwich & buried by Anne his mother May 7th.
    Affidavit made hereof before Phillip Stebbing Mayor of Norwich May 11th.

Elizabeth Cotes singlewoman May 17th.
    Affidavit made hereof before Will : Heylett Rector of Hevingham May 22d.

Frances the daughter of John Bland June yᵉ 26th.
    affidavit made hereof before Mr Heylett aforesaid July 2nd.

Miles the infant sonne of Matthew Gibson & Mary his wife July
the 22nd.
affidavit made hereof before Mter Heylett July 25th.
Elizabeth Wake widdowe August 27th.
Affidavit made hereof before Mter Heylett Sept the 1st.
Titus the infant sonne Richard Otes & Mary his wife Sept 1st.
Affidavit made hereof before Mter Heylett Sept 5th.
John Daglis Sept 25.   Affidavit made hereof before Mter Heylett
Octob : 2nd.
Anne the daughter Thomas Scott & Mary his wife Octob : 5th.
Affidavit made hereof before Mter Heylett Octob : 11th.
Mary the daughter of Will : Burrowes Nov : 12th.
Frances Langwood widdow Nov : 12th.
Affidavit made hereof before Mter Heylett Nov 19th.
Mary Day singlewoman Decemb : 5th.
Affidavit made hereof before John Wrench Mayor of Norwich
Decemb : 7th.

BURIALLS ANNO DOMINI 1689.

John the infant sonne of Daniell Beck & Mary his wife Aprill
11th.
Affidavit made hereof before Mter Heylett Aprill 20th.
Margarett the wife of John Harwin March 13th.
Affidavit made hereof before Mter Heylett March 16th.
James the sonne of Samuel Briggs & Mary his wife May ye
17th.
Affidavit made hereof before Mter Heylett May 21st.
Rebecca the daughter of James Dyker & Awdry his wife May
30th.
Affidavit made hereof before Mter Heylett June ye 4th.
Hannah the infant daughter of Richard Tramplett & Elizabeth
his wife June 24th.
Affidavit made hereof before Mter Heylett June 27th.
Samuel Davy singleman June 30th.
Affidavit made hereof before Mter Heylett July the 1st.
Elizabeth the daughter of James Diker and Awdry his wife July
the 26th.
Affidavit made hereof before Mter Heylett August 1st.

Cicely the wife of Joseph Lubbock August 12th.

    Affidavit made hereof before Mter August 16th.

Thomas Delph August 27th.

    Affidavit made hereof before Mter Heylett Sept : 3rd.

Margarett the daughter of Robert Fletcher Octob : 17th.

    Affidavit made hereof before Mter Heylett October the 21st.

Anne the daughter of Thomas Scott & Mary his wife November the 8.

    Affidavit made of her buriall in woollen before Mter Heylett Rector of Hevingham Nov : 12th.

Susanne the daughter of Edward Partree Nov : 17th.

    Affidavit made hereof before Mter Heylett Nov : 20th.

John Sharpin Decemb : .   .[1]

    Affidavit made hereof before Mter Heylett Rector of Hevingham Decemb : 10th.

Anne Sharpin his daughter Decemb 26th.

    Affidavit Jan 2nd.

Frances the wife of John Green (affidavit Jan 3d.) Decemb 30th.

Margaret the wife of Robert Swan January 12th.

    Affidavit made hereof before Mter Heylett January 18th.

Baptizings Anno Domini 1689.

Mathias the sonne of Thomas Fox and Margery his wife Sept 15th.

Margaret the daughter of Robert Fletcher & Elizabeth his wife Sept : 25th.

Joseph the sonne of James Dyker & Awdry his wife Sept [1].

Sarah the daughter of William Jeckell & Martha his wife Octob [1].

Anne the daughter of Thomas Scott & Mary his wife Octob : [1].

John the sonne of John Hanes & Elizabeth his wife oct : [1].

Susanne the daughter of Edward Partree & Amy his wife No : [1].

Martha the daughter of Joshua Blackbourne and Agnes his wife was baptized Nov : 16th.

William the sonne of John Harwin & Sarah his wife Nov : 24th.

---

[1] Numerals worn out.

Anne the daughter of Richard Oates & Anne his wife was baptized Dec: 1.[1]

(page signed) Daniel Wiseman, Rector.

Marriages Anno Domini 1689.

John[2] Blyth of Mattishall widdower & Alice Paretree of this Parish singlewoman ware married October the 15th.

Michael Pully & Jane Sutton both single persons of Horsford Decemb 9th.

Christopher Stangroome of Hellsden singleman & Elizabeth Chambers of St. Paul's in the City of Norwich were married Jan: 2d.

Thomas Chapman of Aylesham singleman & Frances Cotes of this Parish singlewoman were married upon Sct. Matthias.

Joseph Lubbock widdower & Anne Chambers singlewoman both of this Parish were married April the 22nd 1690.

Joseph the sonne of Joseph Lubbock was buried 1689 March 17th.

　　Affidavit made hereof before Mter Heylett of Hevingham March 22th.

Marriages Anno 1690.

Edward Green of Felthorp widdower & Frances Hudson of Horsford singlewoman were married July the 8th 1690.

Thomas Bullen & Elizabeth Neale single persons of Horsford married October ye 19th.

More Burialls Anno Domini 1689 looke back.

Margery the wife of Matthew Parker Jan: 16th. affidavit made before Mter Heylett Jan: 20th.

Mary the wife of Thomas Scott (affidavit of this Jan 21st) Jan: 16th.

---

[1] Numerals worn out.

[2] *George* in Transcript.

Matthew the sonne of Matthew Gibson & Mary his wife Jan:
17th.

Affidavit made of his buriall in woollen before Mter Heylett
Jan: 28th.

Philip Mary the base daughter of Mary Watson widdow & Philip
Tukely by her the nominated father was buried Feb 4th.

Affidavit made hereof before Mter Heylett of Hevingham Feb
12th.

Christopher Eswick (affidavit as beforesd. Feb 13th) Feb 17th.

Matthias the sonne of Thomas Fox & Margery his wife (Affid:
March 1st) Feb 25th.

Elizabeth the wife of Edward Jeckes senior (Affidavit March
10th) March 3d.

Elizabeth the wife of Richard Barny. (Affidavit made March
15th) March 7th.

More Christnings Anno Domini 1689.

Susanne the daughter of John Jecks & Mary his wife Feb 8d.

William the sonne of William Partree & Mary his wife Feb 6th.

William the sonne of William Jeckell & Anne his wife Feb 12th.

Elizabeth the daughter of Samuell Briggs & Mary his wife Feb
23d.

Sarah & Elizabeth the twin daughter of Richard Barny &
Elizabeth his wife March 1st.

Burialls Anno Domini 1690.

William the infant sonne of William Partre & Mary his wife was
buried April the 5th.

Affidavit made before Mter Heylett April ye 15th.

William the infant sonne of William Jeckell & Anne his wife
April ye 24th.

Affidavit made hereof before Mter Heylett April 28.

Abigail the daughter of Charles Busting & Elizabeth his wife
May 14th.

Affidavit made hereof before John Toft Curate of St Helens
Norwich May 16th.

Margarett Cushion wid. May ye 18th. Affidavit before M{ter} Heylett May 20th.

Elizabeth the infant daughter of Charles Busting & Elizabeth his wife was brought from Norwich as the former was & buried May the 25th.

Affidavit made before John Toft aforesd May 29.

Robert the sonne of John Leake & Mary his wife was buried Sept : 30th.

affidavit made before M{ter} Heylett October the 8th.

Sarah the daughter of Richard Barny Octob : 9th.

Affidavit hereof before M{ter} Heylett Octob 23d.

Margery Green widdow Octob : 28th. Affidavit made as before Nov 3d.

John Busting Decemb 17th. Affidavit made as before December the 23d.

Sarah the daughter of William Jeckell & Mary his wife Dec : 28th. Affidavit made hereof before M{ter} Heylett as aforesd. Decemb : 30th.

William the infant sonne of Robert Fletcher (Affidavit Jan 31st.) Jan : 25.

Robert the infant sonne of Richard Tramplett Jan : 26th. Affidavit Feb : 2d.

Anne the wife of Joseph Lubbock Jan : 27th. Affidavit Jan : 30th.

Helen Jolly widdow Feb 20th. Affidavit before M{ter} Heylett Feb 24th.

John the sonne of John Marsham & Elizabeth his wife Feb : 24th.

Affidavit made hereof before M{ter} Heylett Rector of Hevingham March 2d.

Sarah Bland an orphan Town child (Affidavit March 13) March 11.

Will : the infant sonne of Will : Davy & Susanne his wife March 24.

Affidavit made hereof before M{ter} Heylett March the 28th.

ANNO DOMINI 1691.

Michael the sonne of William Andrews was buried April the 5th.

Affidavit made hereof before M{ter} Heylett April the 7th.

Rachel Saunders widdow April the 7th·   Affidavit as before April 13th·

Anna the daughter of Richard Otes & Mary his wife was buried May yo 1st·

Affidavit made before John Tofts Clerk May the 7th·

Elizabeth the infant daughter of Thomas Thornton & Elizabeth his wife May 10th·

Affidavit as aforesd· May the 12th·

Amy the wife of John Medcalfe June 27th·   Affidavit June 20.

MARRIAGES ANNO DOMINI 1690.

Richard Barny widdower & Susanne Scott widdowe both of this Parish were married Novemb 8th·

Thomas Gymby of Tuttington singleman & Thomazine Sutton of Horsford singlewoman were married Novemb 10th·

Thomas Scott widdower & Elizabeth Cushion singlewoman both of this Parish were married Feb 23d·

MARRIAGES ANNO DOMINI 1691.

John Hutchinsonne widdower & Mary Tompson singlewoman both of Horsham Sct· Faith were married April 17th·

Edward Jeeks & Elizabeth Sharpin both single persons of this Parish were married May yo 5th·

Stephen Jeckell & Margarett Riseborough single persons of this Parish were married June 2d·

Thomas Thaxter of Blickling & Mary Marsh of Tuttington were married June 5th·

BAPTIZINGS ANNO DOMINI 1690.

Anne the daughter of George Blyth & Alice his wife August yo 8th·

Mary the daughter of Isaack Harding & Sarah his wife Sept yo 15th·

John the sonne of John Marsham & Elizabeth his wife Novemb 5th·

Anne the daughter of John Smith & Elizabeth his wife Novemb :
17th.

William the sonne of Robert Fletcher & Elizabeth his wife
January 14th.

Robert the sonne of Richard Tramplett & Elizabeth his wife Jan :
19th.

John the sonne of James Dyker & Awdry his wife Feb 1st.

Martha the daughter of William Jeckell & Martha his wife Feb
24th.

William the sonne of William Davy & Susanne his wife March
10th.

BAPTIZINGS ANNO DOMINI 1691.

Robert the sonne of James Starling & Mary his wife April
yo 5th.

Charles & Sarah the twin sonne & daughter of Richard Presse
& Margarett his wife were baptized April the .1

Elizabeth the daughter of Will. Andrews & Elizabeth his wife
Apr : 19.

Elizabeth the daughter of Thomas Thornton & Elizabeth his wife
April 20.

Robert the sonne of Matthew Gibson & Mary his wife April 2.

Ralph the sonne of John Gibson & Elizabeth his wife May the
1st.

John the sonne of William Jeckell & Anne his wife July the 5th.

Susan the daughter of Samuel Briggs & Mary his wife was
baptized October the 19th buried Oct 26 (? as before).

John the infant sonne of John Leake & Mary his wife . . .[1]

Will : the sonne of Stephen Jeckell junior & Margarett his wife
Dec : . . .[1]

Sarah the daughter of Isaack Harding & Sarah his wife Dec :

Robert the sonne of Richard Tills & Ann his wife Feb : the 16th.

John the sonne of Edward Jecks junior & Elizabeth his wife Feb
18th.

William the sonne of George Blyth & Alice his wife March
the 9.

---

[1] Numerals worn out.

BAPTIZINGS ANNO DOMINI 1692.

James the sonne of James Starling & Mary his wife April the
  17th.

Elizabeth the daughter of James Dyker & Awdry his wife May
  the 8.

Isaac the sonne of Isaac Blyth & Anne his wife June ye 19th.

John the sonne of Thomas Thornton & Elizabeth his wife July
  the 5th.

Francis the sonne of John Marsham & Elizabeth his wife July
  13th.

BURIALLS ANNO DOMINI 1691.

Will: Wake widdower was buried July ye 4th.   Affidavit
  July 7th.

Charles the infant sonne of Richard Presse & Margaret his wife
  July 11th.
    Affidavit made hereof before Mter Heylett as of ye next
    July 17th.

Joseph the sonne of James Dyker & Awdry his wife July . . .[1]
    Affidavit of its buriall in woollen before Mter Heylett
    July .¹

Elizabeth the daughter of Richard Barny July the .¹
    Affidavit made as before August 2d.

James the infant sonne of John Leake & Mary his wife was
  buried Nov: 21st.   Affidavit as before Nov: the .¹

John Jeeks was buried December 15th.   Affidavit before . . .[1]

Thomas Havers was buried Dec: 16th.   Affid. before Mter Heylett
  same day.

John the infant son of Joshua Blackbourne Jan: 4th.   affid: the
  morrow (?)

BURIALS ANNO DOMINI 1692.

Elizabeth Watson singlewoman March 27.   Affidavit April
  the 1st.

---

¹ Worn out.

John Harwing wid : April yᵒ 21ˢᵗ·

Anne Read singlewoman April 24ᵗʰ· Affidavit of both April 28ᵗʰ·

Joan Jell was buried May the 17ᵗʰ· Affidavit before Mᵗᵉʳ Heylett .¹

Thomas the son of Thomas Bensly May the 28ᵗʰ· Affidavit June yᵒ . . .¹

John the sonne of Daniel Hart June 25ᵗʰ· Affidavit June the 28.

James Backhouse Sept : 21ˢᵗ· Affidavit yᵉ 27ᵗʰ· of the same.

Marriages Anno Domini 1691.

John Metcalfe widdower & Mary Jolly singlewoman both of this Parish were married August the 17ᵗʰ·

Matthew Parker widdower & Anne Leman singlewoman both of this Parish were married October 8ᵗʰ·

Richard Harper widdower & Anne Gazely widdowe both of this Parish were married November the 2ᵈ·

Joseph Marshall of Aylesham singleman & Anne Busting of this Parish singlewoman were married February the second.

Marriages Anno Domini 1692.

Robert Shaftin & Anne Jarvis single persons of Horsford April yᵉ 18.

Richard Whall singleman & Elizabeth Green wid of Marsham May yᵉ 4ᵗʰ·

Thomas Greenwood & Frances Jeckell single persons of Marsham May yᵒ .¹

William Woods & Mary Bensly single persons of Marsham July 30.

Thomas Chadley & Frances Breese single persons of Horsford Octob 22ᵈ·

John Hagon of St. Martins at the Palace in Norwich singleman & Susanne Jeckill of this Parish singlewoman Oct : 30.

Thomas Bayst of Sᶜᵗ· Edmonds in Norwich singleman & Lydia Barnham of Horsford Sᶜᵗ· Faithe singlewoman were married January the third.

---

¹ Dates worn out.

Adam Chambers & Amy Bland both single persons of this Parish
were married February the fifth.

Joseph Lubbock widdower & *Margaret*[1] Carter single woman both
of this Parish were married feb :

(page signed) Daniel Wiseman Rector—James Gedge—John Jeckell,
Churchwns.

P. 4.   BAPTIZINGS ANNO DOMINI 1692.

Susanna the daughter of Will: Jeckell junior & Martha his wife
July 28th.

(buried Aug 7th. affidavit made aug : 10th.)

Sarah the daughter of Edward Partre & Amy his wife
August 2d.

Mary the daughter of John Hanes & Elizabeth his wife Octo
4th.

Edmond the sonne of Stephen Jeckell & Margarett his wife
Dec. 28.

John the sonne of Richard Tramplin & Elizabeth his wife Jan :
14th & buried Jan : 18th. Affidavit made hereof January
the 24th.

Arthur the sonne of John Leeke & Mary his wife bapt
Jan 22d.

Edmond the sonne of William Davy & Susanne his wife Feb :
7th. Buried Feb 12th. Affidavit hereof Feb : 20th.

Sarah the daughter of Samuel Brigs & Mary his wife was
baptized March the 9th buried March 23d.. affidavit 22th.

William the sonne of William Bowen & Mary his wife March the
12th.

Sarah Moyses the base daughter of Elizabeth Ryall & Robert
Moyses nominated to be the father was baptized March
the 23d.

(page signed) Daniel Wiseman Rector—James Gedge—John Jeckell
Churchwardens.

---

[1] Restored from Transcript.

Burials Anno Domini 1692.

Susanne the daughter of Samuel Brigs octob: 17.   Affid. 22d.

Thomas the sonne of Mary Dagliss widdow octob: 20th.   Affid:
24th.

Elizabeth the wife of John Goodman of Sct. Andrews in Norwich
& Ursula her infant child were buried Novemb: 6th.
Affiid. made hereof before Samuell Bull, clerk november
10th.

William Jeckell Junior buried Nov: 8th.   Affid: Novemb: 12th.

Anne the wife of Richard Tills Nov: 20th.   Affid Nov: 26th.

Samuel Oates Feb 18th.   Affidavit hereof Feb 24th.

John Exham March the 8th.   Affidavit before Mter Heylett the
same day.

Burialls Anno Domini 1693.

Ann the infant daughter of Richard Otes & Mary his wife was
buried April the 1st.   Affid: the 7th.

Baptizings Anno Domini 1693.

John the sonne of John Smith & Elizabeth his wife was baptized
March the 27th.

Robert the sonne of Thomas Greenwood & Frances his wife was
baptized August 11th buried Octo 7th.   Affidavit 11th.

Thomas the sonne of Isaac Harding & Sarah his wife was
baptized November the fifth.

William the sonne of William Jeckell & Anne his wife was
baptized November the twelfth.

Thomas the sonne of John Gibson & Elizabeth his wife was
baptized December the second. buried the 12.   Aff.
20th.

Robert the sonne of Joseph Lubbock & Margarett his wife was
baptized January the first.

James the sonne of James Dyker & Awdry his wife was baptized
at the same time & place aforesd.

Ursula the daughter of Richard Otes & Mary his wife was
baptized February the 24th buried the 26th. Affid March
2d.

John the sonne of Thomas Fox & Margery his wife was baptized
March the 10th buried the 15th. Affid: yo 25th.

Baptizings Anno Domini 1694.

Anne the daughter of Edward Jecks Junior & Elizabeth his wife
was baptized March the 25th.

Isaac the sonne of George Blyth & Alice his wife was baptized
September the seconde.

Brigett[1] the daughter of John Hanes & Elizabeth his wife was
baptized September the 23.

Matthias[1] the sonne of Stephen Jeckell & Margrett his wife was
baptized October the 7th.

Robert the sonne of John Beare & Sarah his wife Nov: 15th.

Robert the sonne of Thomas Thornton & Elizabeth his wife was
baptized November the 25th.

Mary[2] the daughter of Richard Barny & Susanne his wife was
baptized December 20th.

Robert the sonne of Richard Tramplett & Elizabeth his wife
January 17th. buried . . . Affit. before Mter Heylett
January the 26th.

Gregory the sonne of John Marsham & Elizabeth his wife bapt
Jan : 27.

Abigail[2] yo d : of John Leake & Mary his wife bapt Jan 27.

Jane[2] the daughter of Thomas Greenwood & Frances his wife was
baptized February the 7th.

Richard[2] the sonne of Richarde Tills & Brigett his wife was
baptized March the 5th.

Elizabeth the daughter of Edward Jecks jun & Elizabeth his
wife was bapt. March 6th.

---

[1] Restored from the Transcript.

[2] Illegible in Register but restored from Transcript.

· Burials Anno Domini 1693.

Arthur the infant sonne of John Leake & Mary his wife April 9th.

Affidavit made hereof before Mter Heylett April yo 15th.

Elizabeth the daughter of James Dyker & Awdry his wife was buried May the 4th. Affid May the 10th.

Francis the sonne of John Marsham & Elizabeth his wife May 9th.

Affidavit hereof before Mter Heylett May yo 15th.

John Jeckell junior May the 23d. Affidavit May the 27th.

John Green October the 2d. Affidavit Octob : 10th.

Susanna the wife of Thomas Beusly Octob : 15th. Affid : Octob : 19.

Peter Whall Novemb : 26th. Affidavit Decemb : 7th.

Mary Guggle Decemb : the 7th. Affidavit Decemb : 12th.

Anne Green Decemb. the 9th. Affidavit Decemb : 15th.

Jane the daughter of Richard Tills March 21st. Affid yo . .[1]

Burials Anno Domini 1694.

William Oakes was buried April the 21st. Affid : April the 26th.

Sarah the wife of James Daniell of Sct. Michael at Plea in Norwich was buried May 22d. Affid : before William Newbury the 26th.

William the infant sonne of William Jeckell & Anne his wife was buried July 3d. Affidavit before Mter Heylett July the 16th.

Alice Staynes widdow buried July the 17th. Affid July the 20th.

William the sonne of William Bowen buried July the 19th. Affid. . . .[1]

Alice the wife of Francis Flaxman buried Decemb : the 20th. Affid. . . .[1]

Elizabeth the wife of Richard Tramplett Feb 1st. Affid Feb 7th.

Dinah Taylor widdow was buried March the 7th.

(Signed here) Daniel Wiseman Rector—James Gedge—James Dyker, Churchwardens.

---

[1] Date worn out.

Marriages Anno Domini 1693.

Thomas Bensly widdower & Rebecca Jeckill widdow both of this Parish were married January the 29th.

William Westney of Felthorpe widdower & Elizabeth Calspoulson[1] of Horsford widdowe were married March the 19th.

Marriages Anno Domini 1694.

Robert Jeckell & Susanne Wild both singlepersons of this Parish were married May 28th.

Robert Roberts of Horsham Sct. Faithe widdower & Lydia Roberts of the same singlewoman were married June the 9th.

William Colman & Brigett Browne both single persons of Horsford were married October the first.

Charles Dey of Hevingham singleman & Mary Wiseman of Marsham singlewoman were married October the seconde.

Baptizings Anno Domini 1695.

Mary the daughter of Robert Jeckell & Susanne his wife was baptized March the 26th.

Robert the sonne of Charles Busting & Elizabeth his wife was baptized May the 20th buried ye 30th.   Affid: June 3d.

Elizabeth the daughter of John Palmer & Mary his wife was baptized May the last.

Susanna the daughter of William Davy & Susanna his wife was baptized June 21st.

Anne the daughter of Matthew Gibson & Mary his wife was baptized June the last.

Robert the sonne of William Partree & Mary his wife was baptized July the 16th.

Anne the daughter of William Jeckell & Anne his wife was baptized July the 25th.

---

[1] A doubtful reading.

Anne the daughter of Thomas Raymes & Rebecca his wife was
baptized Sept : ye 22^d.

Joseph the sonne of Joseph Lubbock & Margaret his wife was
baptized October the 11th.

James the sonne of Robert Gedge & Anne his wife was baptized
October the 15th.

Thomas the sonne of John Gibson & Elizabeth his wife December
y^e . .[1]

Anne the daughter of Samuel Chapman & Elizabeth his wife was
baptized December the eighth.

Michael the sonne of James Dyker & Awdry his wife was baptized December the tenth.

Charles the sonne of Richard Presse & Margarett his wife was
baptized December the 12.

P. 5.   MARRIAGES ANNO DOMINI 1695.

Richard Tramplett widdower & Susanne Busting singlewoman
were married April the 22^d.

Richard Brand & Anne Dayns both single persons of Horsford
were married October ye 1st.

George Everett of Stratton Strawlesse widdower & Mary Whalle
of this Parish singlewoman were married October the
24th.

Thomas Adcock widdower & *Rachel*[2] Neave widdow both of
Horsford were married Decemb : 11th.

John Allen & Elizabeth Holmes single persons of Horsford were
married December the 26th.

Thomas Marsham singleman & Katharine Strike wid. both of
Marsham were married January ye first.

                    BURIALS ANNO DOMINI 1695.

Amy the wife of Robert Woods June ye 28th.
      Affidavit before M^ter Heylett July the 2^d.

---

[1] Worn out.
[2] Illegible, but found in Transcript.

Anne the daughter of Matthew Gibsonne & Mary his wife was
buried August 30th. Affidavit as before Sept: 6th.
Francis Chambers widdow buried Decemb: 11th.
Affidavit hereof before Mter Heylett Decemb: 16th.
Robert Swann widdower was buried January 11th.
Matthew Parker was buried January 16th.
Affid made for both there before Mter Heylet January 17th.
The Certificate given in to the commissioners by the Collectors of his
majesties duties upon Christnings Marriages & Burials was
upon March 30th 1696—Daniel Wiseman Rector—James Gedge,
Charles Busting Churchwardens.—James Gedge, Adam Chambers,
Collectors.

(Marriages 1695.)

Robert Woods, singleman & Prudence Downing widdow were
married January the 27th 1695.
Edmond Jeckell singleman & Sarah Havers widdow both of this
Parish were married March the third.

Baptizings Anno Domini 1695.

Ursula the daughter of Isaack Harding & Sarah his wife was
baptized December the 26th.

Baptizings Anno Domini 1696.

William the sonne of Robert Woods junior & Prudence his wife
was baptized March the 30th buried April the 10th.
Affid: before Mter Heylet April 13th.
Susanne the daughter of Richard Barny & Susanne his wife was
baptized April the 19th.
Mary the daughter of Edward Jecks junior & Elizabeth his wife
was baptized May the 15th.
Hannah the daughter of Robert Jeckell & Susanne his wife was
baptized May the 16th buried ye 17th. Affid: 22d.

Sarah the daughter of Edmond Jeckill & Sarah his wife was
    baptized June the 27th.
Mary the daughter of James Starling & Mary his wife was bap-
    tized August the 9th.
Charles the sonne of George Blyth & Alice his wife was baptized
    August the 16th.
Mary the daughter of Thomas Fox & Margery his wife was
    baptized August the 30th.
Jacob the sonne of Isaac Blyth & Anne his wife was baptized
    Sept: the 24th.
Henry the sonne of Matthew Gibson & Mary his wife was
    baptized October the fourth.
Bridgett the daughter of Richard Tills & Brigett his wife baptized
    Decemb: the 15th.
Richard the sonne of Thomas Thornton & Elizabeth his wife was
    baptized January the 5th.
Mary the daughter of Edward Peartree & Amy his wife was bap-
    tized January the 22[d].
Robert the sonne of Richard Tramplett & Susanne his wife was
    baptized January the 28th.

BURIALS ANNO DOMINI 1696.

Brigett Busting widdow was buried March y[e] 30.   Affid: April
    the 2[d].
Anne the wife of Richard Harper was buried March the 30th.
    immediately after the former.   Affidavit of this last before
    M[ter] Heylett April y[e] 1st.
Mary the daughter of Edward Partre & Amy his wife was buried
    April the 1st.   Affid: April 3[d].
Briget Bond was buried May the 24th.   Affid: the 27th.
Charles the sonne of Richard Presse & Margarett his wife was
    buried October the 8th.   Affid: y[e] 14.
Henry the sonne of Matthew Gibson was buried November the
    5th.   Affid: before M[ter] Heylett Nov: 12th.
Mary the daughter of Edward Jecks junior & Elizabeth his wife
    was buried December the 14th.   Affid: 15th.

Thomas the sonne of John Gibson & Elizabeth his wife was
    buried January y⁰ 20th.   Affid: Feb: 5.
Anne Gazely singlewoman buried Jan 24th.   Affid Feb: 8.
John Gibson was buried January the 30th.   Affid: Feb: 13.
Peter the sonne of George Everett & Mary his wife baptized Jan
    31th was buried Feb: 7: Affid.
Susanne the infant daughter of Richard Barny & Susanne his
    wife was buried Feb: 23.   Affidavit made hereof before
    Mter Heylett Feb: 28.
Margarett Yaxley wid was buried March the 9th.
Elizabeth the wife of John Tybnham buried March the 10th.
    Affid of the 1st March the 11th of y⁰ last y⁰ 15th.

Marriages Anno Domini 1696.

Michael Furnace of Heynford singleman & Anne Boroughs of
    this Parish singlewoman were married June the 15th.
John Hutchinson widdower & Mary Myles singlewoman both of
    Horsham Sct. Faithe met me at Heavingham as I was
    going to Norwich to the Funerall of Reverend Mter.
    Penning, & were married in Heavingham Church by me
    Daniell Wiseman loath to come back again to Marsham.
    October y⁰ 1st.
John Gall of Pulham Sct. Mary & Sarah Bransby of Twitshall
    single persons were married October the sixth.
Stephen Scott & Anne Smith both single persons of Horsford
    were married December 26th.
    Daniel Wiseman Rector.   William Jeckill, Charles Busting, Church-
wardens.

Baptizings more Anno Domini 1696.

Robert the sonne of Stephen Jeckell junior & Margarett his wife
    was baptized Feb: 4th.
Francis the sonne of John Palmer & Mary his wife was baptized
    February the 24th.

Elizabeth the daughter of Charles Busting & Elizabeth his wife
was baptized Apr: the 9th. & the duty paid to the King
for it & all duties unto this day.

William the sonne of Samuel Chapman & Elizabeth his wife was
baptized April the 18th.

Amy the daughter of James Dyker & Awdry his wife was baptized April the 20th.

Elizabeth the daughter of Robert Jeckell & Susanne his wife was
baptized April 30th.

P. 6.   Thomas the sonne of Thomas Greenwood & Frances his wife was
baptized July the 20th.

Thomas the sonne of John Leak & Mary his wife was baptized
October the 17th.

Margarett the daughter of Will: Busting & Mary his wife was
baptized Nov 22d.

Philippa the daughter of Edmond Jeckell & Sarah his wife was
baptized November the 28th.

Elizabeth the daughter of Richard Barny & Susanne his wife was
baptized December 26th.

Alice the daughter of Richard Tramplett & Susanne his wife was
baptized January 13th.

Isaack the sonne of Isaack Harding & Sarah his wife was
baptized February the 11th.

William the sonne of William Jeckell & Anne his wife was
baptized March the 21st.

Martha the daughter of William Davy & Susanne his wife was
baptized July the 28th.

Anne the daughter of John Marsham & Elizabeth his wife was
baptized August the 7th.

Thomas the sonne of Joseph Lubbock & Margarett his wife was
baptized August the 14th. buried the 23d.   Affid: 25th.

Samuel the sonne of Samuel Chapman & Elizabeth his wife was
 baptized December the 4th.

Miles the sonne of Roger Neave & Mary his wife was baptized
 January the 6th.

Robert the sonne of Robert Woods junior & Elizabeth his wife
 was baptized January the 22d.

Adam the sonne of Robert Gedge & Anne his wife was baptized
 March the 12th.

BURIALS ANNO DOMINI 1697.

Robert Lubbock was buried April the 12th.   Affid: ye 21th.

Prudence the wife of Robert Woods was buried April the 22d.
 Affid: the 27th.

Elizabeth the infant daughter of Charles Busting & Elizabeth
 his wife was buried July the 1st.   Affid: ye 3d.

Margarett the wife of William Westmere was buried Octob: the
 7th.   Affid: the 9th.

Elizabeth the wife of Richard Harper was buried November the
 20th.   Affid: before Mter Heylett Nov: 24th.

Anne Gibson widdow was buried January ye 14th.   Affidavit
 before Mter Heylett the 20th of the same.

Amy the daughter of James Dyker & Awdry his wife was buried
 February the 25th.   Affid: the 28th.

BURIALS ANNO DOMINI 1698.

Mary Watson was buried April the first.   Affid the 5th.

Alice the daughter of Richard Tramplett & Susann his wife was
 buried June the 24th.   Affid: the 30th.

Richard the sonne of Thomas Thornton & Elizabeth his wife was
 buried August the 5th.   Affid: the 8th. before Mter Heylett.

Richard Harwin was buried August the 26th.   Affid 29th

Margaret Lyng of Hanworth was buried October the 18th.   Affid:
 before Mter Gray Rector of little Barningham the same
 day.

John Jeckell was buried Novemb: the 14th. Affid before Mter Heylett 17th.

BURIALS ANNO DOMINI 1699.

Mary the wife of James Robins of Mundesley was buried Sept the 7th. Affid: before Mter Montfort Rector of Mundesley the same day.

Anne the infant daughter of Isaac Vertegants & Sarah his wife was buried November the 16th. Affidavit hereof before Mter Heylett 20th.

Thomas the sonne of John Marsham & Elizabeth his wife was buried February the second. Buried in linnen, certified Feb the 14th witnesse taken Feb: 18th.

Amy the infant daughter of John Green & Amy his wife was buried February the 24th. Affid: Feb 28th.

Thomas Brandon was brought from Norwich & was buried here March the 13th. Affid: March the 16th before Doctor Robert Pepper Chancellor of Norwich.

(page signed) Daniel Wiseman, Rector,—John Grand, Edward Peartre—Churchwardens.

MARRIAGES ANNO DOMINI 1697.

Richard Harper widdower & Elizabeth Gibson widdow both of this Parish were married June the 17th.

Robert Woods widdower & Elizabeth Harding singlewoman both of this Parish were married December the 7th.

MARRIAGES ANNO DOMINI 1698.

John Oliver & Martha Davy both single persons of this Parish were married May the 16th.

Richard Harper widdower & Mary Daglis widdow both of this Parish were married May the 16th.

James Garnutt of S^ct· Peter of Mancroft singleman & Mary
   Breese singlewoman of S^ct· Peter of Mancroft singleman
   & Mary Breese singlewoman of S^ct· Edmond in the city of
   Norwich were married September the sixth.
John Blyth & Elizabeth Kent both single persons of Horsford
   were married Sept : the 25th·
John Greene & Amy Sharpin both single persons of this Parish
   were married Sept : the 29th·
Richard Bell of Hevingham widdower & Katherine Bygrave of
   this Parish singlewoman were married December the 5th·
John Gibson & Philippa Green both single persons of this Parish
   were married January the 5th·

Baptizings Anno Domini 1699.

Amy the daughter of James Dyker & Awdry his wife was baptized April the 2^d·
Deborah the daughter of John Palmer & Mary his wife was
   baptized May the 8th·
Sarah the daughter of Richard Tramplett & Susanne his wife
   was baptized August the 27th·
Anne the daughter of Isaack Vertegants & Sarah his wife was
   baptized September the 12th·
Charles the sonne of Thomas Fox & Margery his wife was
   baptized September the 17th·
Stephen the sonne of Stephen Jeckell junior & Margarett his wife
   was baptized September 24th·
Amy the daughter of John Green & Amy his wife was baptized
   October the 22^d·
John the sonne of John Harison & Anne his wife & Susanne the
   daughter of Robert Jeckell & Susanne his wife were
   baptized October the 29th·
Amy the daughter of Samuel Chapman & Elizabeth his wife was
   baptized January the seventh.
Anne the daughter of John Gibson & Philippa his wife was
   baptized January the 28th·
James the sonne of John Oliver & Martha his wife was baptized
   February the 4th·

Hannah the daughter of Richard Barny & Susanne his wife was baptized at the same time last aforesd.

Anne the daughter of Robert Gedge & Anne his wife was baptized March the 19th.

BAPTIZINGS ANNO DOMINI 1700.

Anne the daughter of Thomas Gryme & Mary his wife was baptized April the 1st.

Susanne the daughter of Edmond Jeckell & Sarah his wife was baptized April the 14th.

Caleb the sonne of John Shaften & Elizabeth his wife was baptized April the 22.

Henry the sonne of Joseph Lubbock & Margarett his wife was baptized May the third day.

Mary the daughter of Edward Jecks junior & Elizabeth his wife was baptized May the 6th.

Anne the daughter of Thomas Thornton & Elizabeth his wife was baptized May the 12th.

Frances the sonne of William Jeckell & Anne his wife was baptized July the 5th.

Mary the daughter of Thomas Greenwood & Francis his wife was baptized July the 12th.

Ralph the sonne of John Jeckell & Sarah his wife Aug: 11th.

Richard the sonne of Richard Otes & Mary his wife Aug: 14th.

Lydia the daughter of John Leake & Mary his wife bapt Aug: ye 24th.

P. 7.   MARRIAGES ANNO DOMINI 1699.

Thomas Riseborroe of Aylsham singleman & Sarah Watkins of Sct. John of Mattermarkett in Norwich singlewoman were married October ye last.

MARRIAGES ANNO DOMINI 1700.

Thomas Everett & Sarah Moyses both single persons of this Parish were married April the 1st.

Richard Jeckell & Amy Park both single persons of this Parish
were married April the 17th.

William Westmer widdower & Anne Brounster singlewoman
both of this Parish were married June 10th.

Robert Tramplett & Ursula Grimme both single persons of this
Parish were married June the 18th.

William Stamp of Hevingham widdower & Mary Sutton of Horsford widdow were married June the 24th.

Stephen Scott & Mary Holl widdower & singlewoman both of
Horsford were married Sept the 12th.

Roger Fickling & Mary Hase both singlepersons of Horsford were
married September the 18th.

Burials anno Domini 1700.

John Scott was buried April the 10th.   Affid: April the 22.

Elizabeth the daughter of John Hayns & Elizabeth his wife was
buried April ye 20th.   Affid: before M^ter Heylett April the
29th.

Mary Brounster widdow was buried May the 9th.
Affidavit before M^ter Heylett May the 13th.

Ralph Gibson an orphan Town child was buried June 7th.
Affidavit hereof made before M^ter Heylett June the 10th.

Faith Scott widdow the relict of John Scott above s^d. was buried
July the 23d.   Affid: July the 30th.

Amy the wife of William Burroughs was buried August the 27th.
Affidavit the 30th day.

Caleb the sonne of John Shaften & Elizabeth his wife was buried
Sept: the 18th.   Affid: 24th.

John Metcalfe was buried October the 28th.
Affidavit made hereof before M^ter Heylett Nov: 1st.

Sarah the daughter of Richard Tramplett buried Jan: 23.
Affidavit made hereof before M^ter Heylett Jan: 31st.

John Pay was buried January the 30th.   Affid: Feb 5.

Margaret Harwin was buried March the 20th.
Affidavit made hereof before M^ter Heylett upon March the
24th.

Baptizings more Anno Domini 1700.

the (y) in the bottom of the last page more plain.

[1]Lydia the daughter of John Leake & Mary his wife bapt: Sept the 1st.

Mary Oliver the base daughter of Rose Scottow singlewoman & John Oliver a married man was baptized September the 17th.

Sarah the daughter of Thomas Everett & Sarah his wife was baptized January ye 6th.

Anne the daughter of John Green & Amy his wife was baptized February the 6th.

Thomas the sonne of Robert Woods junior & Elizabeth his wife was baptized March the 9th.

Sarah the daughter of Isaack Vertegants & Sarah his wife was baptized March the 24th.

Burials Anno Domini 1701.

William Westmer was buried April the 5th.
Affidavit before Mter Heylet April the 8th.

Brigett the wife of Matthew Gosse was buried May the 12th. Affid: before Mter Heylett May the 17th.

Ursula the wife of Henry Medler was buried Sept. 8th.
Affidavit before Mter Heylett September the 16th.

Elizabeth the wife of Samuel Chapman was buried September the 20th.

Samuel the sonne buried October the 8th.
Affidavit for this last October the 18th.

John Peartree was buried December ye 4th. Affid: 7.

Grace the wife of Robert Harwin buried December 22d. Affid ye 29th.

More Marriages Anno Domini 1700.

John Colby of Helsden & Anne Mortimer of Horsford singlewoman were married Sept: ye 30th.

---

[1] Repeated.

Francis Fillback of Felthorp widdower & Susanne Sutton of Horsford widdow were married Octob: 14th.

William Boroughs widdower & Margery Bond singlewoman both of this Parish were married November 10th.

Robert Colman widdower & Anne Parker both of this Parish were married March the seconde.

Edmond Kent & Alice Elsing both single persons of Horsford were married March the second.

John Peartree of this Parish singleman & Anne Harding of Hanworth singlewoman were married March the 11th.

The Kings duty paid to this day.

Marriages Anno Domini 1702.

Philip Jeckell & Mary Harding both single persons of this Parish were married ye 9th being Whitsun monday.

Francis Flaxman widdower & Mary Medcalfe widow both of this Parish were married September the 3d.

Edmond Rust of Reifham singleman & Mary Hall of Aylesham singlewoman were married Sept: 23.

Robert Jeckell & Mary Ducker both singlepersons of this Parish were married September the 29th.

Robert Watson & Hannah Gill both single persons of this Parish were married January the 5th.

Baptizings Anno Domini 1701.

Frances the sonne of William Purdey miller & Susanne his Wife was baptized August the 8th.

Richard the sonne of Robert Jeckell & Susanne his wife was baptized September the 7th.

Grace the daughter of Samuel Chapman & Elizabeth his wife was baptized September the 21st. was buried Sept: 26th. Affid: for this and the mother Octo: 3d.

Robert the sonne of Robert Harding & Elizabeth his wife was baptized October the 5th.

Rebeckah the daughter of Richard Jeckell & Amy his wife was baptized November the 27th.

Richard the sonne of Stephen Jeckell junior & Margaret his wife was baptized January the 4th.

James the sonne of Robert Tramplett & Ursula his wife was baptized January the 18th.

Alice the daughter of Thomas Thornton & Elizabeth his wife was baptized January the 30th.

John the sonne of Thomas Fox & Mary his wife was baptized February the 6th.

William the sonne of James Wicks & Elizabeth his wife was baptized February the 9th.

Andrew the sonne of John Gibson & Philippa his wife was baptized February the 20th.   R. C.

P. 8.   Burialls Anno Domini 1702.

Richard the sonne of Robert Jeckell & Susanne his wife was buried March the 25.   Affidavit April the 9th.

Anne Allen widdow the relict of Charles Allen was buried May the 20th.   Affid: before Mter Heylett the 26th.

Philippa the wife of John Gibson was buried May the 23d. Affidavit made hereof before Mter Heylett May ye 29th.

Francis the daughter of William Andrews was buried July the 20th.   Affid: before Mter Heylett ye 21st.

Richard Presse was buried October the 7th.   Affid: before Mter Heylett October the 12th.

William the infant sonne of James Wicks & Elizabeth his wife was buried October the 26th.   Affid: Novemb: 2d.

Edmond the sonne of Edmond Jeckell & Sarah his wife was buried February the 3d.   Affid: ye 7th.

Robert Busting of Sct. Michael at Plea in the City of Norwich was brought from thence in a Hearse and was buried here February the ninth being Shrove tuesday.   Affid: before Mter Atkinson the Maior of Norwich February the 11th.

Alice the infant daughter of Thomas Thornton & Elizabeth his wife was buried February the 10th.   Affid: of 22d.

Mary Oliver the base daughter of Rose Scottow was buried at the very same time.   Affid ye 22d.

Stephen Jeckell senior the old Clerk was buried February the 18th. Affid: before Mter Heylett February yo 21st.

Baptizings Anno Domini 1702.

Susanne the daughter of Richard Barny & Susanna his wife was baptized May the 26th.

Robert the sonne of Thomas Everett & Sarah his wife was baptized June the 13th. buried June the 25th. Affid: 28th.

Edmond the sonne of Edmond Jeckell & Sarah his wife was baptized August the 30th.

John the sonne of George Saunders & Anne his wife was baptized September the 16th.

Jemima the daughter of John palmer and Mary his wife was baptized September the 26.

John the sonne of Isaack Vertegants & Sarah his wife was baptized October the 5th.

Stephen the sonne of Robert Jeckell & Mary his wife was baptized October the 5th.

Nathanael the sonne of William Jeckell & Anne his wife was baptized October the 15th.

Mary the daughter of Robert Watson & Hannah his wife was baptized November the first.

John the sonne of John Green & Amy his wife was baptized November the 22d.

Frances the sonne of Robert Woods junior & Elizabeth his wife was baptized Dec : yo 22d.

Dorothy the daughter of Thomas Grime and Mary his wife was baptized January yo 23d. buried ye 27th. Affid: before Mter Heylet Jan : 30th.

Marriages Anno Domini 1702.

Richard Harding widower & Sarah Woodhouse singlewoman both of Aylsham were married April yo 1st.
Queens duties paid here.

John Gibson widdower & Martha Jeckell widdow both of this
Parish were married July the 19th.

Joseph Watson & Susanne Harding both single persons of this
Parish were married December ye 17th.

Baptizings Anno Domini 1703.

John the sonne of Robert Tramplett & Ursula his wife was
baptized March the 28th.

Samuel the sonne of John Leake & Mary his wife was baptized
April the eleventh.

Samuel the sonne of Philip Jeckell & Mary his wife was baptized
May ye 28th.

Samuel son of Thomas Everett & Sarah his wife was bapt.
July 9.[1]

Thomas the sonne of Joseph Watson & Susanne his wife was
baptized July ye 29th.

Anne the daughter of James Starling & Mary his wife was baptized August the 4th.

Sarah the daughter of Robert Jeckell & Susanne his wife was
baptized August the 29th.

Sarah the daughter of John Gibson & Martha his wife was baptized October the 17th.

Elizabeth the daughter of Joseph Lubbock & Margaret his wife
was baptized October the 24th.

Joseph the sonne of Joseph Thaxter & Philippa his wife was
baptized December the 27th.

Edmond the sonne of Edmond Jeckell & Sarah his wife was
baptized January ye 3d.

Sarah the daughter of Robert Jeckell, the sonne of Stephen
Jeckell the late clerk, & Mary his wife was baptized
January the 18th.

Rachel the daughter of John Rivett & Sarah his wife was baptized
Jann : 23.

Edward the sonne of Edward Dennys & Mary his wife was
baptized January the 25th.

---

[1] This is an additional entry in the Transcript.

Burials Anno Domini 1703.

Elizabeth the wife of James Wicks was buried May ye 11th.
 Affidavit before Mter Heylett Rector of Hevingham May
 ye 12.
Elizabeth the wife of Simon Otes of Hauteboys was buried July
 ye first. Affidavit before Mter Guthrie Clerk Curate of
 Lamas & Hauteboys July ye 7th.
Hannah Lubbock singlewoman was buried March ye 12th. Affi-
 davit before Mter Heylett March ye 19th.

Marriages Anno Domini 1703.

Charles Blyth & Philippa Yeames both single persons of this
 Parish were married November ye 10th. [1]

P. 9.   ### Burials Anno Domini 1704.

Sarah the daughter of Edward Peartree was buried April
 ye 24th. Affidavit ye 25th.
Dorothy Mouse widdow was buried May ye 3d. Affidavit hereof
 made before Mter Heylett May ye 8th.
Anne Fletcher the daughter of Robert Fletcher was buried May
 ye 23d. Affidavit before Mter Heylett Rector of Heving-
 ham May ye 26th.
Thomas the sonne of Thomas Thornton was buried June ye
 2d. Affidavit before Mter Heylett June 7th.
Amy the daughter of Samuel Chapman was buried December
 ye 13th. Affidavit before Mter Heylett Rector of Heving-
 ham December ye 18th.
Susanne Jeckell widdow was buried January ye 1st.
 Affid : before Mter Heylett January ye 3d.
Rebeckah Cotes widdow was buried January ye 6th.
 Affidavit before Mter Heylett January ye 6th.

---

[1] Here follow " *More Christnings* A.D. 1706." moved to follow that year.

Robert Jeckell was buried January yo 7th. Affid: January ye 11th.

Mary the wife of James Starling was buried January ye 8th. Affidavit before Mter Heylett Jan: ye 10th.

Elizabeth the daughter of James Starling was buried January ye 16th. Affid: of both these Jan: ye 23d.

Anne the infant daughter of James Starling & Mary his wife was buried January ye 22d.

Richard the young sonne of Richard Otes was buried February the 8th. Affid: before Mter Heylett ye 24th.

Anne the wife of Edward Pay was buried March ye 15th. Affidavit before Mter Heylett March ye 20th.

Baptizings Anno Domini 1704.

Margarett the daughter of Stephen Jeckell & Margaret his wife was baptized April ye last.

John the sonne of Robert Watson & Hannah his wife was baptized May ye 3d.

Edward the sonne of John Green & Amy his wife was baptized July the 12th.

Thomas the sonne of Thomas Grime & Mary his wife was baptized August ye 7th.

Anne the daughter of Charles Blyth & Philippa his wife was baptized August the 23d.

Mary the daughter of George Saunders & Anne his wife was baptized August the 24th.

Isaac the sonne of Thomas Fox & Margerie his wife was baptized November ye 5th.

Thomas the sonne of John Delph & Susanne his wife was baptized November the 10th.

Christian the base daughter of Anne Peartree widdow was baptized January ye 18th.

Edward the sonne of John Watson & Anne his wife was baptized March ye 7th.[1]

---

[1] Here follow "more Bapt: A.D. 1706" & "more Christnings do."

MARRIAGES ANNO DOMINI 1705.

John Watson & Anne Peartree both single persons of this Parish were married May ye 9th.

John Davison of Gimmingham & Elizabeth Allen of this Parish both single persons were married May ye 24th.

Frances Stowton of St Augustines in Norwich & Hester West of Aylesham both single persons were married August the 29th.

Thomas Watts widdower & Frances Bunnett widdow, both of Horsford were married September ye 28th.

Robert Caps widdower & Mary Peters singlewoman, both of Horsford were married December ye 27th.

Thomas Neale & Mary Smith both single persons of Horsford were married February the 2^d.

Richard Blyth junior & Elizabeth George both single persons of Horsford were married February ye 20th being Shrove tuesday.

BAPTIZINGS ANNO DOMINI 1705.

Anne ye daughter of John Davison & Elizabeth his wife was baptized March ye 30th.

Isaack the sonne of Isaack Vertegants & Sarah his wife was baptized August the 7th.

Susanna the daughter of Robert Jeckell & Mary his wife was baptized August ye 26th.

Arthur the sonne of John Leake & Mary his wife was baptized September the sixth.

Nathaniel the sonne of Frances Greenwood widdow relict of Thomas Greenwood lately deceased was baptized September the ninth.

Amy the daughter of John Green & Amy his wife was baptized September the 27th.

George the sonne of Thomas Everett & Sarah his wife was baptized October ye 7th.

Elizabeth the daughter of Robert Fletcher junior & Mary his wife was baptized October the 22^d.

Robert the sonn of Robert Tramplett & Ursula his wife was
baptized February yᵒ 19th.

Philippa the daughter of Charles Blyth & Philippa his wife was
baptized February yᵒ 24th.

John the sonne of John Gibson & Martha his wife was baptized
March yᶜ 14th.

Baptizings Anno Domini 1706.

Mary the daughter of Joseph Watson & Susanne his wife was
baptized March 29th.

Philemon the sonne of John Palmer & Mary his wife was baptized
April yᵒ 2ᵈ.

Elizabeth the daughter of John Davyson & Elizabeth his wife
was baptized April yᵒ 21st.

Elizabeth the base daughter of Rose Scottow was baptized April
yᵒ 24.

Robert the sonne of Edmond Jeckell & Sarah his wife was
baptized May yᵉ 14th.

Susanne the daughter of Stephen Jeckell Parish Clerk & Susanne
his wife was baptized May the 30th.

Joseph the sonne of William Jeckell & Anne his wife was baptized
August the third & born the same day.

More Baptizings Anno Domini 1706.[1]

Anne the daughter of Thomas Fox & Margery his wife was
baptized August the 11th.

Simon the sonne of George Saunders & Anne his wife was
baptized October the fifth.

More Christnings Anno Domini 1706.[1]

John the sonne of Robert Woods junior & Elizabeth his wife was
baptized December yᵉ 6th.

---

[1] These are written in spaces vacant after former years, but here put in their
own year.

Edward the sonne of Edward Jecks junior & Elizabeth his wife was baptized December y⁰ 13th.

Christian y⁰ daughter of John Watson & Mary his wife was baptized December y⁰ 27th,

MORE CHRISTNINGS ANNO DOMINI 1706.[1]

Philippa the daughter of Philip Jeckill & Mary his wife was baptized January y⁰ 13th.

Susanna the daughter of Thomas Fox & Susan his wife was baptized March the 14th.

P. 10.   MARRIAGES ANNO DOMINI 1705.

Michael Newton & Margery Brett both single persons of Horsford were married April y⁰ 9th.
    The Queens duty was paid here.

Edward Pay widdower & Frances Riseborough single woman both of this Parish were married May y⁰ 22d.

Stephen Jeckill, clerk, singleman of this Parish, & Susan Ives of Burrow singlewoman were married September the second.

Thomas Spooner of Hamblington widdower & Elizabeth Fish of Horsford widdow were married February the 5th. *Queens duty paid here.*

MARRIAGES ANNO DOMINI 1706.

Thomas Fox & Susanne Peartree, both single persons of this Parish were married May y⁰ 4th.

Stephen Carter & Ursula Brett both single persons of Horsford, were married May y⁰ 14th.—Banes—Queens duty paid here.

Henry Dunmock singleman & Margarett Murch singlewoman, both of Horsford, were married August the 19th.—Banes —Queens duty paid here.

William Fulson of Cetton singleman & Sarah Otes of this Parish singlewoman were married Sept: 11th. Bannes.

---

[1] See note on preceding page.

Joseph Hutton & Susanne Fletcher both single persons of this Parish were married Sept: y⁰ 19th.—Bannes.

Robert Locket of Irmingland singleman & Elizabeth Daglis of Marsham singlewoman were married Octob : 1st. Bannes.

Christopher Gibson & Susanne Rice single persons of this Parish were married October the 27th. Banns.

BURIALS ANNO DOMINI 1705.

Matthew Gibson was buried May the 4th. Affidavit before Mter Heylett May yᵉ 9th.

Thomas Greenwood was buried June yᵉ 15th. Affidavit before Mter Heylett June yᵉ 20th.

Helene Jeckill widdow was buried July yᵉ 21st. Affidavit before Mter Heylett July yᵉ 26th.

Thomas the sonne of Robert Woods Junior & Elizabeth his wife was buried August yᵉ 27th. Affidavit before Mter Heylett Sept: yᵉ 1st.

Mary the wife of Thomas Woodwork was buried December yᵉ 14th. Affidavit yᵒ 20th.

Anne Peartree singlewoman, the daughter of Edward Peartree, was buried January yᵉ 11th. Affidavit made hereof before Mter Heylett Jan : 14th.

Elizabeth Pay widdow was buried January yᵉ 29th. Affidavit before Frances Gardiner January yᵒ 28th.

BURIALS ANNO DOMINI 1706.

Frances Flaxman was buried April 22d. Affidavit made hereof before Mter Heylett April yᵒ 26th.

Henry Cotes was buried July the second. Affidavit before Mter Heylett July yᵉ 6th.

Elizabeth the infant daughter of Robert Fletcher junior & Mary his wife was buried November yᵉ 17th. Affidavit before Mter Heylett Nov : yᵉ 25th.

Burials Anno Domini 1707.

Henry the base sonne of Faith Scottow was buried March yᵉ
25th.   Affidavit before Mter Heylett April yᵉ 1st.

Parnell Langwood singlewoman was buried April yᵉ 22d.
Affidavit made hereof before Mter Heylett April yᵉ 28th.

John Marsham was buried May yᵉ 18th.   Affidavit yᵉ 19th.

Frances Shreeve widdow was buried July yᵉ 24th.

Francis the sonne of John Delph & Susanne his wife was buried
July yᵉ 27th.   Affidavit of yᵉ former of these July yᵉ 28th.
Affidavit made of the latter before Mter Heylett August yᵉ
4th.

Mary Busting widdow was brought from Norwich & buried here
August yᵉ 17th.   Affidavit before Mter Heylett August yᵉ
22d.

Amy the wife of Richard Jeckill was buried Sept: yᵉ 1st.
Affidavit made hereof before Mter Heylett September yᵉ
2d.

Baptizings Anno Domini 170(7.)[1]

John the sonne of Thomas Everett & Sarah his wife was baptized
April yᵉ ——[1]

Frances the sonne of John Delph & Susanne his wife was baptized April yᵉ 20th.

William the sonne of Richard Barney & Susanne his wife was
baptized November the 16th.

John the sonne of John Ward & Rebekah his wife was baptized
December yᵉ 14th.

Anne the daughter of Robert Fletcher junior & Mary his wife
was baptized Decemb: yᵉ 15th. [2]

Stephen the sonne of Stephen Jeckell & Susanna his wife was
baptized March yᵉ 14th 170⅞ [3]

Davy the sonne of Samuel Lubbock & Elizabeth his wife was
baptized April yᵉ 18, 1708.

---

[1] Torn off.
[2] The last Bapt. entered by No. 4.
[3] Handwriting No. 5 which occurs again occasionally.

Mary ye daughter of Joseph Lubbock & Margaret his wife was baptized May 13th 1708.

Marriages Anno Domini 1707.

John Otes & Mary Colman both single persons of this Parish were married May ye 27th.—Banes—

Samuel Lubbock & Elizabeth Castor single persons of this Parish were married July ye 1st.—Bannes—

John Riches of Borrough singleman & Anne Green of Marsham singlewoman were married September the 18th.

John Bowles of Swannington singleman & Judith Kent of Horsford singlewoman were married December the 26th. License[1]

More Burials Anno Domini 1707.

John Leake junior was buried September ye 6th.
    Affidavit Sept : 10th. [1]

[2]John Tibbinham widdower was buried ye 5th of January affidavitt made Jan ye 11th.

Daniel Wiseman Clerk Rector of Marsham was buried at Horsford Jan : ye 16th affidavit hereof before M^{ter} Heylett January ye 23.

Joseph Utting was buried March the 16 affidavit made before M^{ter} Heylett ye 25th.

P.11. Richard Harper was buried March ye 21st 1707.
    affidavit made before Mr. Heylett 22^{d.}

Burials in ye year 1708.

Susanna Chadley was buried May ye 24th.
    Affidavit made before Mr. Heylett ye 28.

Marget Exham widow buried ye 20th June.

Keren Happuch Palmer an Infant was buried ye 17th September.

---

[1] last entries of Marriages & Burials by No 4.

[2] Handwriting No 6. begins.

Stephen Jeckell an Infant was buried y⁰ 13th October.
Jacob Blye was buried y⁰ 2d Novemb:
Edward Jecks was buried 12th January.
The Widow Peartree buried 10th February.
The Widow Philippa Jeckell buried y⁰ 15th of March.

Baptizings Anno 1708.

Keren Happuch y⁰ daughter of John Palmer & Mary his wife
bapt. 25 August.
John y⁰ son of John Oats & Mary his wife baptized.
Joshua y⁰ son of Robert Tramplett & Ursula his wife baptized
9th January.
Susanna y⁰ daughter of John Delf & Susanna his wife baptized
y⁰ 10th January.
William y⁰ son of Robert Dymes & Sarah his wife baptiz'd 27th
February.
Jacob y⁰ son of Charles Blye and Philippa his wife baptz'd April
17th 1709.

1709.

Robert y⁰ son of Robert Fletcher & Mary his wife baptized April
y⁰ 24th.
John y⁰ son of John Harrowing & Ann his wife baptiz'd May y⁰
1st.
Daniel the son of Thomas Everitt & Sarah his wife baptiz'd May
y⁰ 16th.
Isaac y⁰ son of John Green & Amy his wife baptized June 26th.
Amy y⁰ daughter of Thomas Fox & Susan his wife baptized
July 3d.
Mary y⁰ daughter of John Ward & Rebekah his wife baptized
July 17th.

Marriages Anno Domini 1708.

John Green & Ann Everett of the Parish of Marsham single
persons were married y⁰ 26 July.

John Harrowing singleman & Ann Peartree widow married ye 10th August.

William Delf & Mary Dagglis single persons married ye 7th Febr:

John Edwards singleman & Susan Hutton widdow of ye parish of Marsham married ye 8th of March.

Marriages Anno 1709.

Thomas Bensley widdower married to Martha Pitching[1] widow Decembe ye 26th.

John Rudd & Martha Jeckell both single married Dec: 26th.

Burials Anno 1709.

Mary Flaxman widow buried May ye 1st.

Ann ye wife of John Green buried August ye 29.

The Widow Blythe buried August y^o 30th.

Mary ye daughter of Robert Dymes & Sarah his wife was buried August ye 30th.

The Widow Hill was buried September ye 8th.

Isaac y^o son of John Green was buried ye Septem: 18th.

Rebecca ye Wife of Thomas Bensley buried Octobr 9th.

Frances ye Wife of John Tramplet buried Octob: 12th.

Elizabeth Harper buried Novemb: 6th.

Margaret Greenwood buried Novemb: 16th.

P.12. Elizabeth Moses[2] was buried Janu: ye 20th.

Mary ye daughter of Joseph Lobock buried Feb: ye 12th.

1710.

The widow Massham buried May ye 12th.

Elizabeth wife of Robert Woods buried May y^o 13th.

Robert Jeckel buried June 17th.

Henry Everet buried June 17th.

Robert ye Son of Will: Jeckell buried June ye 30th.

Gregory Massham buried the 14th July.

---

[1] Possibly Pikeling.

[2] A very doubtful reading.

Joseph Lovock buried 23ᵈ July.
William the Son of Robert Dymes buried yᵉ 31 July.
Robert Watson buried 2ᵈ August.
William Andrews buried 10ᵗʰ October.
Elizabeth yᵉ wife of Edward Jex : & Susan his daughter buried
      26ᵗʰ October.
Mary yᵉ wife of Thomas Wattson buried yᵉ 30ᵗʰ October.
Catherine yᵉ wife of Tho : Gazeley buried Novemb : 19ᵗʰ·
Isaac Blythe buried Nov : 30ᵗʰ·
William Blythe buried Dec : 2ᵈ·
Eliz : Greene widow buried Dec : 24ᵗʰ·
Eliz : wife of Tho : Read buried Jan : 9ᵗʰ·
Clement son of Clem : Tills buried Jan 25ᵗʰ·
Mary wife of John Snelling buried March 11ᵗʰ·

Marriages 1710.

John Green widower & Elizabeth Buck were married Octob.
      3ᵈ·
Edward Peartree & Marget Fox were married Novemb : 30ᵗʰ·
Robert Woods & Elizabeth Hart married Decemb : 26ᵗʰ·

1709.

Ann the daughter of John Green & Ann his wife baptized
      August 29ᵗʰ·
Susan yᵉ base child of Sarah Press baptized yᵉ 2ᵈ September.
George yᵉ Son of George Alexander & Ann his Wife baptized
      Octob : 16ᵗʰ·
Amy yᵉ Daughter of John Edwards & Mary his Wife baptized
      Octob : 16ᵗʰ·
Martha yᵉ Base child of Abigail Wix bapt. Decemb : yᵉ 4ᵗʰ·
Ann yᵉ Daughter of Stephen Jeckell & Susanna his Wife bapt.
      Dec : 16ᵗʰ·
Elizabeth yᵉ Daughter of Joseph Watson & Susan his Wife bapt.
      January 17ᵗʰ·
Jerimy yᵉ Son of Thomas Hartley & Lydda his Wife bapt
      March 16ᵗʰ·

1710.

Jeffery yᵉ Son of John & Mary Palmer baptized yᵉ 4ᵗʰ April.

John the Son of William Burrows & Ann his Wife bapt. 29ᵗʰ May.

Elizabeth yᵉ daughter of Robert Fletcher & Mary his wife bapt. Oct: yᵉ 22ᵈ.

Susan Daughter of Edward & Elizabeth Jex bapt: 23ᵈ October.

Mary yᵉ Daughter of John Read & Martha his Wife baptized yᵉ 8ᵗʰ November.

Mary yᵉ Daughter of Robert Jeckell & Mary his Wife baptiz'd 21ᵗʰ January.

Ann yᵉ Daughter of John & Martha Daines baptiz'd 11ᵗʰ February.

Robert yᵉ Son of John & Mary Oats baptiz'd 13ᵗʰ February.

Ann yᵉ Daughter of John Watson & Ann his Wife baptiz'd 4ᵗʰ March.

P.13.   Baptizings Anno Domini 1711.

Francis yᵉ Son of Sarah Hanes a base Child baptiz'd 2ᵈ April.

Sarah yᵉ Daughter of John & Rebecca Ward baptiz'd 29ᵗʰ April.

Elizabeth yᵉ daughter of Christopher & Susan Gipson baptiz'd 6ᵗʰ May.

Sarah yᵉ daughter of John & Amy Green baptiz'd yᵉ 30ᵗʰ June.

John yᵉ Son of John Green & Elizabeth his wife baptiz'd 12ᵗʰ July.

William Son of William & Mary Delf baptiz'd yᵉ 29ᵗʰ July.

Francis son of John Delf & Susan his wife baptiz'd 26ᵗʰ August.

Mary daughter of Philip & Mary Jeckell baptiz'd 16ᵗʰ September.

Edward son of Edward & Marget Peartree baptiz'd 22ᵈ December.

Mary daughter of Thomas & Susan Fox baptiz'd yᵉ 18ᵗʰ March.

John the sonne of John gren & Elizabeth his wife baptiz January 3.

Marriages Anno 1711.

John Tramplet & Mary Woods were married 1ˢᵗ April.

Nicholas Hart & Elizabeth Groome were married 27ᵗʰ November.

Marriages Anno 1712.

Robert Smythson & Judith Wall married 30th September.
John Rix widower & Mary Peck widow married 16th February.

Burials Anno Domini 1711.

Edward son of Edw. Jex buried 25th March.
Elizabeth Wall widow buried 2d April.
Ann daughter of John Green buried 2d May.
John Busting buried 2d May.
Ann Harper buried 23d July.
Ann daughter of John Watson buried 30th July.
Elizabeth daughter of Christopher Gipson buried 2d September.
John Turner buried ye 5th October.
John Green an Infant buried October 14th.
Judith Marsham wid: buried 22 October.
Amy wife of Edward Peartree buried 17th November.
Edward son of Edw: Peartree buried 25th December.
Richard Barney buried 13th February.
John Palmer buried ye 18th February.
John Harrowing buried 15th March.
Susan wife of Thomas Fox buried 22d March.
Mary daughter of Thomas Fox buried 24th March.

Burials Anno Domini 1712.

Elizabeth Fletcher buried 4th April.
John Hanes buried 13th April.
Elizabeth Shaffton buried 27th May.
Christopher Gipson buried 31st May.
Margery wife of Thomas Fox buried 4th June.
Sarah Harding buried 7th June.
Widow Busting buried 12th June.
Sarah wife of Edm: Jeckel buried 27th June.
Stephen Hudson buried 27th June.
Elizabeth wife of Tho: Scott 29th June.
John Rudd buried 12th July.
Margaret Oats widow buried 26th July.

Mary Harding buried 23 Sept:
John Tramplett buried 11th Octo :
Mary wife of Will: Peartree 17th Octob :
Richard Tramplett buried 13th Octob :
Ann Blyhe widow buried ye 23d Octob :
Robert Tramplet buried ye 15th Novemb :
Thomas Trower buried 30th Decemb :
Philippa Jeckel buried ye 4th January.
Mary Jeckel buried ye 6th January.
Thomas Grix buried ye 14th January.
Mary Wild buried ye 8th February.

P.14. BURIALS ANNO 1713.

George Everett buried 5th April.
Daniel Everett buried 12th April.
Thomas Read buried 23d April.
John Snelling buried 13th May[1]
Elizabeth Gazely buried 19th June.
Robert Woods buried 20th June.
David Lubboik buried 13th July.
Ann Colman, ye wife of Robert Colman was buried July ye 23d.
George Alexander was buried July ye 25.
Robert Dymes, Rectr of Swanton Abbot & Curate of this Parish
  was buried at St Simons (Norwch) ye 27th of July 1713.
John ye son of Robert & Mary Fletcher was buried Novemb.
  19th.
Ann ye wife of John Grand was buried March ye 1st.

<h3 style="text-align:center">MARRIAGES 1713.</h3>

Willm. Marsham & Mary Locket were married Nov: 24th.

<h3 style="text-align:center">BAPTIZINGS ANNO 1712.</h3>

Timothy son of Charles & Philippa Blythe baptiz'd 20th April.

---

[1] Last Burial entry in Hand No. 6.

Mary daughter of William & Mary Spink baptiz'd 25th April.

Mary daughter of Michael and Elizabeth Wild baptiz'd 13th May.

John Son of John & Martha Daines baptiz'd 16 June.

Elizabeth daughter of Thomas Gazley & Elizabeth his wife baptiz'd 5 September.

Elizabeth daughter of John Green & Elizabeth his wife baptiz'd 3d November.

Sarah daughter of Robert & Ursley Tramplet, baptiz'd ye 31th January.

Martha daughter of John & Martha Rudd, baptiz'd 8th February.

Thomas son of George & Ann Alexander, baptiz'd 22d February.

Mary daughter of Michael & Elizabeth Wild, baptiz'd 6th March.

Mary daughter of John & Mary Oats baptiz'd 21th March.

BAPTIZINGS ANNO 1713.

[1]Ann daughter of Thomas Frances & Ann his wife bapt: 2d May.

Robert the Son of Stephen Jeckell & Susanna his wife was baptized 28th June.

John ye Son of Robert Fletcher & Mary his wife was baptized Oct: ye 18.

Ann ye Daughter of Robt. Smithson & Judith his wife was baptized Decr. 2d.

John, ye son of John Ives & Martha his wife, was born Decr. 25th and baptized on ye 28th of ye same.

P.15. Samuel, ye Son of Samuel and Elizabeth Lubbock, baptized Jan: 10.

Ann, ye Daughter of Edward & Margaret Peartree, was baptized Jan: 31.

Robert, ye Son of T . .[2] Gazely & Frances his wife, ...[2] baptized Feb: 8.

Isaac ye Son of J . . . .[2] d & Rebecca his wife . . . .[2] March ye 7th.

---

[1] Last baptism in handwriting No. 6.

[2] Several letters illegible; the last surname probably *Ward.*

1 . . . (1714.)

(BAPTIZINGS) . . . . . .

. . . . yᵒ sons of John . . . . lizabeth his wife were
. . . . . . April 28ᵗʰ·

Richard, yᵒ Son of John Delph & Susan his wife, was baptized
June 6.

Robert yᵉ Son of Richard Jeckell & Elizabeth his wife was
baptized June 8.

[1] Robᵗ· Pate Rectʳ·

Richard yᵒ Son of Richard Bullard and Sarah his Wife was
Baptized Sept : yᵉ 21ˢᵗ·

Robt Colman yᵉ sone of William Colman and Eliz : his Wife was
Baptized Nov : 28.

Eliz : daughter of John and Martha Ives bapt : Dec : 28.

[2] John son of Michael Wild & Elizabeth his wif was baptized
January yᵉ 15.

MARRIAGES 1714.

Thomas Scott & Anne Jolly were married Sept : 14.
Thomas Scott & Mary Tramplet were married Sept : 21.
Joshua Blog and Eliz : Jecks were married Novemb : 5.

BURIALS 1714.

John & William Haynes (two children) were buried May 2ᵈ·
Jnᵒ Havet Rector of this Town, was buried at Sᵗ· Andrews·
(Norwich) the 3ᵈ of May.
Mary, yᵉ Daughter of George Alexander & Ann his wife, was
buried May 15.
Mary Scott was buried on yᵒ 11ᵗʰ of July.
P.16. Matthew Bateman[3] was buried Decemb : yᶜ 22ᵈ·
Sarah Hains was buryed Decemb : yᵉ 22ᵈ·

---

[1] Handwriting No. 7, this and following 8 entries.
[2] Interpolated by another hand.
[3] No. 7. again till 1716 Sept. 30.

Anno 1715 Burials.

Eliz : ye wife of Robt. Fletcher buryed Febr : 14.
Robt. Colman buryed March 4.
Lydia Leak Apr : 10.
Thomas Thornton Buryed Apr 13.
Matthew Goss buryed Apr : 27.
Susan Berny buryed May 25.
Eliz : Palmer Aug : 3^{d.}

Baptizings 1715.

George ye sone of George Alexander & Anne his Wife Apr : 25.
Benjamin ye sone of Stephen Jeckel & Anne his Wife May 3^{d.}
Sarah ye Daughter of John Davison & Eliz : his Wife July
     3^{d.}
Edward ye sone of Edward Peartree & Margeret his wife
     Baptized Aug : 28.
John ye sone of John Hains & Eliz : his Wife Sept : 4th.
John ye sone of William Marsham & Mary his Wife Baptized
     Sept : 11th.

Burials 1715.

Eliz : Ives was buried Jan : 2.
Mary [1] . . . . ton was buried Ja . . . . .

A . . . . . . 15 Burials.

Joh . . . . Buryed Fe . . . .
Will . . . . ryed Ap . . . .
Robt. Co . . . . Ap.
Michael Neeve . . . . . .
Martha Peartree Aug : . .
Sarah Gedge was buryed Dec. . .
Mary Jeckell feb : 7.

---

[1] A piece of this page is lost.

Baptizings 1715.

Amy yᵉ Daughter of John Burrows and Eliz his Wife Octob:
2ᵈ·

Hannah yᵉ Daughter of Samuel Lubbock and Eliz : his Wife
Baptized Octob : 23ᵈ·

Eliz : yᵉ Daughter of Tho : Scott and Anne his Wife Aug 7ᵗʰ·

Sarah yᵉ Daughter of Robert Gedge and Mary his Wife Nov :
6ᵗʰ·

Francis yᵉ Daughter of Edmund Jeckel & Susan his Wife Nov :
20.

Robᵗ· yᵉ sone of John Ives & Martha his Wife Nov : 27.

Eliz : yᵉ daughter of Tho : Gazely & Frances his Wife Nov : 27.

—— yᵉ sone of John Edwards & Susan his Wife Dec 12.

P.17. Edward yᵉ sone of Joshua Blogue & Eliz : his Wife Jan : 15.

Mary yᵉ Daughter of Philip Jeckel and Mary his Wife Jan : 30.

John yᵉ sone of John Green Febru : 15.

Burials 1716.

Alice Harroway buryed March 29.

Marg : Press buryed March 27.

[1]Eliz : Lines Oct : 7ᵗʰ·

James Scott &

Mary Starling —— Dec 21.

Eliz : Delph Jan : 10.

Hammond Eastgate Jan : 6.

Richᵈ· Bullard Jan : 1ˢᵗ·

Ann Barney Jan : 15ᵗʰ·

Eliz : Gazle Jan : 28th.

Edward Pay March 2ᵈ·

Mary Burrows Mar. 16.

Joh : Spurling Clerk begun to Preach att Marsham as Curate
Sept : 30ᵗʰ 1716.

---

[1] Handwriting No. 8. for 10 entries.

MARRIAGES ANNO 1715.

Isaac Blyth singleman & Elizabeth Cork singlewoman married
Sept 6.
Dan : Tayler Widdower & Jane Goss Widow married Sept : 30.

MARRIAGES 1716.

[1]Edward Watts Widdower & Susan Hammond singlewoman,
married Apr : 2.

BAPTIZINGS 1716.

John ye Bastard sone of Eliz : Barker May 13.
Peter ye Bastard sone of Eliz : Love July 1.
[2]Eliz : daughtr of Eliz : & Samuel Lives Oct : 5th.
P.18. Eliz daughtr of Charles & Phillis Blyth —— ——
Eliz daughtr of Robt & Ann Flower Oc— ——
Isaac Son of Joh : & Amey Green bapt : Oct : 20.
Francis ye Son of Mial & Eliz Wile bapt : Oct 29.
Ann daughter of Isaac & Eliz : Blyth bapt. Novbr 10.
James son of Tho : & Ann Scot bap : Dec : 9.
Will : Son of Will : & Alice Colman bap Dec : 21.

BAPD. IN 1717.

Richd. Son of Eliz : & Richd. Jeckall May 9.
Sam : Son of Eliz : & Joh : Maurice May 13.
[3]Sam Son of Joh : Maris and An his wif.
[4]Joh : Son of Ann & Joh Wattson May 19.
Thomas Son of Susan : & Tho : Fox August 25.
William son of Martha & Robert Dyball Oct : 12.
Mary ye daughter of Eliz : & Sam : Lubbock Sep : 22.
Sarah ye daughter of Susan & Joshua Watson Dec : 11.

---

[1] No. 7. again.
[2] No. 8. again for 11 entries.
[3] A repetition interpolated.
[4] No. 9. begins.

Mary yᵉ daughter of Margaret & Edward Peartree Decem : 22.
William son of Susan : & Edmund Jeckell Jan : 24.
Ann daughter of Ann & Robert Flower Feb : 23.
Sarah daughter of Susan & John Delf March 2.
Samuel son of Rebecca & John Ward March 9.

Bapt : in 1718.

Thomas son of Frances & Tho : Gazely Aprill 6.
John yᵉ son of John Burroughs & Elizabeth his wife June 10.
Amy The daughter of Richᵈ & Eliza : Jeckell June 10.
Isaac yᵉ son of Isaac & Eliza : Blyth June 15.
Joseph yᵉ son of Sammuel & Elizabeth Lubbock sep : 30.
John yᵉ son of John Morris & Ann his wife dec : 19.
Mary yᵉ daughter of John Ives & Martha his wife dec : 22.
Sarah yᵉ daughter of John Daynes & Martha his wife Jan : 1.
Samuel yᵉ son of Mial & Elizabeth [1]Wild Jan : 1.
Sarah yᵉ daughter of Robert Dyball & Martha his wife March
    22.
James yᵉ son of John Ward & Rebecca his wife March 16.

P.19.   ## Marriages in 1717.[2]

William (Jeckell) Peartree[3] & Frances Pay Apr : 21.
Elijah Starly & Mary Gibson widow Aug : 12.
William bryar & Mary Hanes Aug : 23.

Marriages in 1718.

Philip Jeckell & Margaret Chapman June 17.
Joseph Watson widower & Elizabeth Love single March 30.
Edward Leake widowʳ & Sarah Press single March 30.

---

[1] Changed to Wily by a *y* written upon the *d* in darker ink.
[2] This page to Burial of M. Scot June 1ˢᵗ evidently written by a parish clerk.
[3] Peartree seems the correction of the other and is confirmed by the Transcript.

Burials in 1717.

Mary Jeckell Apr : 21.
Robt Wood of Aylsham May 15.
Peter Love Base Child May 15.
Sam : base son of Sarah Press May 4.
Richard Jeckell June 2.
An . . Blyth Jul : 4.
Ann Daverson Jul : 25.
Mary Leake Decem : 2.
Sammuell Lubbock Decem : 8.
Alice Hudson febr : 23.

Burials in 1718.

Edmund Spark May 1st.
Mary Scot an Infant June 1st.
[1]Tho : Sanders August 18.
Sammuel Lubbock sep 27.
Susanna Watson sep : 30.
Ann Peartree octo : 23.
Ester Havers Decem : 18.
P.20. Mary Jeckell Decem : 31.
Elizabeth Purdy Jan : 16.
John Ward March 18.
Isaac Ward March 20.
Mary Taylor March 17.

Baptizings from April 8 1719.

Elizabeth ye daughter of Philip & Margaret Jeckell Apr. 12.
Charles ye son of John Davyson & Elizabeth his wife May 31.
Robert ye son of William & Alice Coleman Aug : 30.
Elizabeth ye daughter of John Haines & Elizabeth his wife Aug
    30.
Mary ye daughter of Robert & Mary Gedge Sep : 27.

---

[1] No. 9 again.

Philip yᵉ son of William & Ann Andrews Sep 27.
Elizabeth yᵉ daughter of Tho: & Susanna Fox Octo 4.
Charles yᵉ son of Charles & Philippa Blyth Jan : 13.
Elizabeth yᵉ daughter of Stephen & Mary Tudenham Feb : 2.
Richard yᵉ son of Richard & Elizabeth Jeckell Feb 16.
Thomas yᵉ son of John & Martha Deines Feb 22.
Thomas yᵉ son of John & Ann Watson March 2.
Judeth yᵉ daughter of Robert & Judeth Smithson March 2.
Thomas yᵉ son of Gregory & Laseby Marsham March 16.

Burials 1719.

James Cork senʳ April 17.
James Cork Junʳ April 27.
Elizabeth Haines June 12.
William Burroughs August 4.
Margaret Cook Sep : 2.
Susanna Burston Sep 18.
Thomas Gazely Sep 21.
John Green Octo : 4.
Samuel Chapman Oct : 5.
Mary Leak Oct : 9.
Alice Thrower Oct : 22.
Martha Gibson Jan : 11.
Charles Blyth Jan : 24.

P.21. ## Marriages 1719.

Richard Bowen of Aylesham widower & Elizabeth Chapman of
Marsham widow were married the 15ᵗʰ day of febr : 17$\frac{19}{20}$

Baptizings from April 17. 1720.

Anne yᵉ daughter of Thomas & Anne Scot August 7.
Mary yᵉ daughter of Thomas & Susannah fox decemb : 1.
Samuel yᵉ son of Robert flower & Ann his wife decemb 29.

MARRIAGES 1720.

Samuel foster & Elizabeth Knapp both single persons Octo:
    9th.
John Leak widower & Mary Woodwork widow October 16.

BURIALS 1720.

Thomas Grix dec 25.
Martha Jeckell Jan: 12.
Isaac Vertegaus Jan: 20.
Robert Fletcher feb: 28.
Alice Allen March 6.
James Wix March 16.
Mary Dye March 19.
William Miles an Infant March 30, 1721.

BAPTIZINGS FROM MAY 7TH, 1721.

James ye son of John & Elizabeth Cork May 7.
John ye son Edw. Leak & Sarah his wife July 9.
Christopher ye son of John Stageman & Sarah his wife Novem:
    13.
Robert ye son of Edward Peartree & Margarett his wife Nov: 21.
Robert ye son of Robert Gedge & Mary his wife decem: 8.
John ye son of Robert Smithson & Judeth his wife decem: 26.
Philip ye son of Philip Jeckell & Margarett his wife decem: 30.
Anne ye daughter of Edmund Smith & Mary his wife feb: 6.
James ye son of Isaac Blyth & Elizabeth his wife March 5.
Mary ye daughter of Thomas Scot & Ann his wife March 6.
Mary ye daughter of John Hanes & Eliza; his wife March—
P.22. Robert ye son of Robert Dyball & Martha his wife March 23.

MARRIAGES.

Tho: Leak & Susanna Davy both single persons Dec: 25.
Daniel Taylor & Ann Jeckell both single persons March 27 1722.

BURIALS FROM MAY 1ST 1721.

John Cork May 7.
James Cork an Infant May 14.
Thomas Saunders an Infant May 18.
Edward Thornton of Hevingham May 21.
Matthew Jeckell July 16.
Isaac Green July 31.
Ann Green Aug : 7.
Elizabeth Thornton Oct : 25.
Thomas Daines an Infant Novem : 11.
Nicholas Jecks Novem : 18.
Anne Smith an Infant feb : 13.
Samuel Jeckell feb : 26.
James Blyth an Infant March 7.
Samuel Leak March 8.
Mary fox an Infant March 31.
    as to the burials turn to yᵉ other end of yᵉ Book.[1]

BAPTIZINGS FOR YᴱᴬR 1723.

Mary yᵉ daughter of Richard & Eliz : Jeckell May 13.
John yᵉ son of Gregory & Glazeby Marsham July 15.
Mary yᵉ daughter of Daniel & Anne Taylor August 3.
Elizabeth yᵉ daughter of Wᵐ & Mary Marsham Sep 6.
Elizabeth yᵉ daughter of John & Elizabeth Burrough Sep : 30.
John yᵉ son of Tho : & Susanna Leak Novem : 8.
Robert yᵉ son of Jonathan & Ann Pert Jan : 16.
John yᵉ son of Francis & Mary Jeckell Jan : 30.
Robert yᵉ son of Samuel & Eliza : Lubbock feb : 21.
Elizabeth yᵉ daughter of Will : & Mary Bryar feb 25.
John yᵉ son of John & Eliz : Green March 13.
Elizabeth yᵉ base child of Elizabeth Barker April 14, 1723.

P.23.   BURIALLS FOR Yᴱ YEAR 1722.

Nathanael Jeckell.   Buried April 19.   Affid recᵈ April 19.
Mary Smith.   Buried April 22.   Aff. recᵈ April 22.

---

[1] They are however on the opposite page.

Tho : Scott.   Buried April 23.   aff. rec^d April 23.
Anne Smithson.   Buried April 23.   aff rec^d April 23.
Sarah Delf.   Buried May 6.   aff. rec^d May 6.
Francis Wily.   Buried May 10.   aff rec^d May 15.
Francis Delf.   Buried June 2.   aff. re^d June 2.
Mary Ward.   Buried June 11.   aff re^d June 12.
Elizabeth Haynes.   Buried July 4.   aff. rec^d July 8.
John ye son of James & Anne Norris Born decem : 31. 1721
     dyed July 10.   Buried July 12. 1722.   affidav : rec^d July
     17.
Isaac Harding.   buried August 13.   affid : rec^d August 19.
Alice Bourne.   buried Sep : 5.   affida : receiv^d Sep : 6.
Ann Marsh of Aylesham.   feb 21.   affid : receiv^d feb 26.

1723.

Robert Lubbock buried feb 27.   affid : receiv^d March 3.
William Jeckell buried April 24.   affid : rece : April 25.
Robert Gedge buried May 3.   affidav : recei : May 7.
Joanna Havin buried May 24.   affi : recei : May 29.
Elizabeth Sparke widow : bur : June 14 affi : recei : June 14.
Robert Fletcher buried August 15 affi : recei : Aug : 20.
Elizabeth Andrews an Infant Aug : 17.   affi : rece : August 21.
Sarah Harding Widow—sep : 3.   affi : rec : sep : 5.
Matthias Jeckell an Infant Dec : 17 aff : rec : Dec : 20.
Philip Jeckell . . dec : 20 affi : rec : Dec : 27.
Edwd Leak buried Jan : 5 affida : Jan : 5.

1724.

Mary Rice buried May 1st.   aff : May 3.
Martha Dyball buried May 3.   aff : May 4.
Matthew Jeckell an Infant buried May 14.   Affid : rec. May 17.
Abigal Leak an Infant buried June 1st.   Affid : rec : June 16.
Simon Oats of Hauteboys[1] mag : buried June 19.   affid : rec
     June 24.
Thomas Thornton an Infant July 5.   affi : re : July 9.

---

[1] Great Hautbois.

Susanna Lockart August 25.   aff : rec : Aug 26.
John Lockart an Infant Sep : 11 : affid : rec : 14.

P.24.   BURIALLS 1724.

John Delf was buried sep : 17.   Affida received sep : 19.
John Stageman was buried Nov : 1.   affida : rec[d] Nov : 3.
John Deynes was buried Decem : 20.   affid : Decem : 24.

1725.

John y[e] base child of Margaret Jeckell March 28 1725.   Affid :
    March 30.
Francis Wily[1] was buried April 2[d.]   affi : rec[d] April 7.
david Leak was buried April 4.   Affid : rece : April 6.
Edward Blogue was buried April 11.   aff : recei : apr. 18.
John Berney was buried April 21.   affid : receiv : April 26.
Elizabeth Jeckell an Infant June 11.   affid : recei : June 15.
Mary Smithson an Infant June 12.   affi : recei : Jun : 18.
Ann Smithson an Infant June 12.   affi : recei : June 18.
Mary Everett widow July 7.   affid : rec. July 8.
John Leak buried Sep : 17.   affid : rec : Septem : 19.
Rob[t] Woods buried Oct : 7.   affid : rec : Octo : 12.
John Smithson an Infant Octo : 26.   Aff : rec : Novem : 1.
Ann Green buried Novem : 14.   affid : Novem : 20.
Mary fox an Infant decem : 19.   affid : rec : Decem : 22.
Elizabeth Peartree buried decem : 29.   affidavit Jan : 4.
William Thornton an Infant Jan : 5.   affida : Jan 8.
Mary Parmer buried March 1[st.]   affida : recei March 6.
John y[e] son of James & Ann Norris Born febr 2, 1724 died
    March 4th & buried March 6. 1725.   affid : rec : March
    13.

1726.

Isaac harding an Infant buri : April 6. 1726.   affi : rece : April
    10.

---

[1] First written *Wild.*

Francis Parmer buried April 6 1726.   affi: rec : April 10.
Elizabeth Whall buried April 19. 1726.   affida: rec: April 20.
Amy Peartree buried 22 of August.   affid : rec : august 26.
Thomas Chapman buried 6 of oct :ber aff: rec : Oct: 10th.
Daniel Taylor buried 7 of Oct: affid : rec : Oct: 11th.
Elizabeth Royal buried 26 of Novem: aff: rec : decem : 3.
Thomas ye son of James & Ann Norris Born April 18. 1726 &
    dyed December 15 & buried Decemb : 18. 1726.   affid:
    rec : decem : 23.
Ann Scot was buried feb : 12.   affida: received feb : 16.
Ann Peart was buried feb 15.   affid : received feb : 20.
Sarah Turner was buried March 8.   affid : received March 12.

1727.

Edward Peartree buried april 12.   aff: rec April 12.
Benjamin Tills an Infant buried April 20.   affid: received April
    24.
[1]—— ye daughter of John & Frances Carman April 22.[2]

P.25.   BAPTIZINGS SINCE Yᴱ BISHOPS VISITATION 1723.

[1]—— son of William & Alice Colman Sep: 26.
[1]—— ye son of Timothy & Anne Blyth Novem : 20.
[1]—— hias ye son of Robert & Susan Jeckell decem : 7.
[1]—— abeth ye base child of Anne Haines now married (to[1])
    henry Harrod of Acle alias Oakely dec : 29.
[1]—— ye son of Samuel & Elizabeth Lubbock dec : 31.
[1]—— my ye daughter of Thomas & Rebecca Harding Jan : 11.
[1]—— usanna ye daughter of Thomas & Eliza: Greenwood
    Jan : 15.
Sarah ye daughter of Mial & Elizabeth Wily feb : 6.
William ye son of Francis & Mary Jeckell March 3.
John ye son of John & Sarah Stageman March 9th.
Abigaïl ye daughter of Edward & Sarah Leak March 22.
Jemima ye daughter of Robert & Martha dyball March 23.

---

[1] Torn out.
[2] Here follow 3 entries completely erased by scraping.

1724 BAPTISMS.

Sarah yᵉ daughter of Stephen & Honour Jeckell April 3 1724.

Elizabeth & Matthew yᵉ daughter & son of Edmund & Susanna Jeckell were baptized May 7ᵗʰ 1724.

Thomas yᵉ son of Robert & Elizabeth Thornton was baptiz'd July 2. 1724.

John yᵉ son & Thomas & Susanna Lockart bapt : August 24.

Thomas yᵉ son of Daniel & Ann Taylor baptiz : sep 1ˢᵗ·

Mary yᵉ daughter of Robert & Ann flower. bap : Oct : 21.

Jonathan yᵉ son of Jonathan & Ann Pert bap : Oct : 25.

Robert yᵉ son of Edw'd & Ann Wright bap : Novem : 8.

Gregory yᵉ son of Gregory & Glasby Marsham bap : dec : 16.

John yᵉ son of James & Ann Norris was born feb : 2 & bap : feb : 7.

Matthias yᵉ son of Rob : & Sarah Jeckell bap : feb : 13.

Margaret yᵉ daughter of John & Eliza : Green bap : March 3.

Mary yᵉ daughter of Richard & Elizabeth Pert bap : March 8.

John yᵉ base child of Margaret Jeckell widow bap : March 15.

David yᵉ son of Thomas & Susanna Leak bap : March 19.

1725.

John yᵉ son of John & Margarett Berney April 6.

Anne yᵉ daughter of John & Eliz : Hanes May 16.

P.26. Elizabeth yᵉ daughter of Richard & Eliz Jeckell May 23.

Mary & Anne yᵉ daughters of Robert & Judeth Smithson June 3.

William yᵉ son of Edward & Margaret Peartree June 9.

Anne yᵉ daughter of Robert & Eliza Ha——— ——— ———[1]

Isaac yᵉ son of Tho : & Rebecca Harding ——— ———[1]

sammuell yᵉ son of Robert & Sarah dyball ——— ———[1]

Mary yᵉ daughter of Joseph & Anne Lubbock ——— ———[1]

William yᵉ son of William & Mary Bryar ——— ———[1]

William yᵉ son of Robert & Eliza : Thornton ———[1]

James yᵉ son of Robert & Tryphena Bear ———[1]

Mary yᵉ daughter of Isaac & Sarah fox feb : ———[1]

Robert yᵉ son of Edwᵈ & Ann Wright bap : feb : ———[1]

---

[1] Torn off.

Thomas yᵉ son of Thomas & Eliza: Greenwood March 9.
Sarah yᵉ daughter of William & Alice Colman March 9.
Anne yᵉ daughter of Francis & Mary Jeckell March 12.

1726.

Anne yᵉ daughter of Jonathan & Anne Peart April 1st.
Thomas yᵉ son of James & Anne Norris was born April 18 &
        baptiz: April 21. 1726.
Michael yᵉ son of Michael Wily & Elizabeth his wife April 25.
William yᵉ son of Robert & Judith Smithson July 10.
Francis yᵉ son of Francis & Ursula Parmer July 17.
John Ash yᵉ son of Ralf & Elizabeth Jeckell Aug: 9.
Mary yᵉ daughter of Robert & Ann Laxen Sep: 8.
Elizabeth yᵉ daughter of Willᵐ & Ann Andrews bap: Oct: 4.
Mary yᵉ daughter of Thomas & Susanna fox bap: Oct: 16.
Sarah yᵉ daughter of Isaac & Sarah Fox bap: Oct: 25.
Thomas yᵉ son of John & Sarah Saunders bap: Nov: 7.
Mary yᵉ daughter of Robert & Elizab: Thornton Jan: 9.

1727.

Lydda yᵉ daughter of Thomas & Susanna Leak bap: April 2.
Ann yᵉ daughter of Stephen & Honour Jeckell bap: May 22.
Susanna yᵉ daughter of Robert & Elizabeth Harding July 11.
Sarah yᵉ daughter of Robert & Eliza: Trampling August 22.
William yᵉ son of James & Ann Norris was born Septembʳ 14 &
        baptiz'd yᵉ eighth day of October 1727.

P.27.   1727 BURIALS.

Robert Harowing buried June 14.   affida: receivᵈ June 19.
Thomas Cubit (a stranger) burᵈ sep: 6.   affida: receivᵈ Sep: 12.
Ann Tramplett an Infant buriᵈ sep: 10.   affid: receiv: sep: 13.
William Ives an Infant buried sep: 18.   affidavi: recei: sep: 30.
Nicholas Jolly buried sep: 19.   affida: received sep: 22.
Mary Woods widow buried octob: 30. Affida: received 31
        october.

Cornelius Streak buried Novem: 9[th.] affidavit received 11
    Novem:
Jemmima dybal an infant buried Novem: 23. affid: recei 26
    Novem:
Thomas Lockart buried decem: 8. affida: receiv: decem: 12.
Sarah Jeckel buried decem: 17. affidavit received decem: 23.
Martha Pert buried decem: 19. affid: received decem: 22.
Sarah Jeckel an Infant buried decem: 23. aff: rec: decem: 23.
William Bryar buried decem: 24. affi: recei: decem: 28.
William Smithson buried Jan: 14. affida: receiv[d] Jan: 20.
Mary Laxon an Infant buried feb: 11. affida: recci: feb 14.
Mary daniel an Infant buried feb: 20[th.] Affi: rec: feb: 25.
Sarah Hendry buried feb: 23. Affida: rece: feb 25.
Ann Hanes an Infant buried March 1. affid: recei: March 3.
Richard Oats buried March 3. affid: recei: March 9.
Mary lake buried March 11. affidavit receive: March 17.
George Everard buried March 21. affida: receiv[d] March 24.
Susanna Streak widow bur: march 24. affid: received 29.

<h3 style="text-align:center">1728.</h3>

Elizabeth Jeckel buried March 31. affid: received 5th of April.
Elizabeth Cork widow buried April 3. affida: received 9th of
    April.
Ralph Jeckell buried April 4. affidav: received 5 of April.
Elizabeth forster buried April 7. affidav: receiv[d] 9th of April.
Elizabeth Marsham widow buried April 18. affid rec[d] 19 April.
John Gedge buried April 20[th.] affidavit receiv: 22 April.
John Colman buried April 20. Affid receiv[d] 23 April.
Mary Oliver buried April 25. affid: receis 26 April.
Elizabeth Andrews buried June 1[st.] affid: receiv[d] June 3.
Anne y[e] wife of James Norris Clerk buried July 7.
James Starling buried August 9[th.] affida: receiv[d] August 10.
Susanna Davy buried August 12. affidavit received August 15.
Ann Blyth buried August 29. affidavit received August 31.
Michael Wild buried Sept: 18. affid: received Sep: 22.
Richard Key an Infant bur: sep: 24. affid: received Sep 30[th.]
Joseph Watson buried Octo: 17. affida: received Oct: 20[th.]
John Watson buried 24th of Octo: affidavit received 28 Oct:

Mary harper widow 24th Oct:　affidavit rec : Oct : 26.

Thomas Saunders bur : 24 of Oct:　affid : rec : Oct : 28.

Sarah Vertegans widow bur : Nov : 12.　affid : rec : Novem : 16.

Hester Ives an infant buried Nov : 21.　affid : recei : Novem : 24.

P.28.　——[1] dyball an Infant buried decem : 13.　affidavi : rec. decem : ——

Thomas Fox buried decem : 19.　affida : received decem : 20.

James Oliver an infant buried decem : 22.　affid. recci[d] decem : 28.

Tho : Thornton an infant buried decem 29.　affid : recci : Jan : 2.

Mary Jeckell buried Jan : 19.　affida : received Jan : 21.

Tho : Delph Jan : 19.　affid : received Jan : 21.

Sarah Key & John Key Infants buried Jan : 26.　Affid : Jan 28.

John Hendry an Infant buried March 9.　affid : March 10.

Richard Pert buried March 21.　affid : recciv[d] March 27 1729.

1729.

Sarah Watson buried March 29 1729.　affid : March 31.

James Wild an infant buried April 2.　affid : rece : April 3.

Francis Hanes buried April 9th.　affidavit received April 16.

——[1]Key an Infant bur : April 16.　affid : rec : April 19.

Robert Ives buried May 4th.　affidav : rec : May 9.

Edward Jecks buried May 9.　affidavit receive : May 14.

Henry Thirkettle buried May 25.　affid : recci : May 30.

William Flower an Infant buried May 26.　affida : May 29.

P.29.　　　　MARRIAGES FROM MARCH 25 1723.

Richard Pert widower & Elizabeth Cork was married April 16.

Thomas Lockart singleman & Susanna Poplinton single Oct : 7.

James Oliver & abigail Leak both single persons Oct 8.

Henry Harrod widower of Acle alias Oakely & Anne Haynes of Marsham single woman was married decem : 29.

William Pearce of ye Parish of St. Andrews Norwich gen : & Judith Norris of St. John's of Madermarket Norwich married June 16. 1723.

---

[1] Left blank in Register.

Cuthbert Croskill of ye Parish of Buxton, worstead weaver & singleman & Margarett Copland of Buxton singlewoman was married March 15. 1723—4.

1724.

John Berney & Margaret Nurse both single persons & both of this Parish was married April 27. 1724.

John Scot of Lammas cum Haughteboys parva widower & Mary Littlebury of ye same singlewoman was married ye 14th of July.

John Ash & Mary Green both of Marsham were married July 21.

Ralph Smithson of Aylesham widower & Anne Ives of Marsham singlewoman were married August 5th.

Robert dyball widower & Sarah Leak widow both of this Parish were married decem : 16.

Francis Palmer & Ursula Harding both singlepersons & both of this Parish were married ye 4th of January 1724.

1725.

William Gregory of Heydon widower & Susanna Gibson of Marsham Widow were married ye 25th day of October 1725.

John saunders singleman & Sarah Stageman widow were married feb : 14.

Christopher Harrold of S^t faiths Newton singleman & Ann Sutton of Hainford wid^w were married.

1726.

John Bowden & Mary Peartree both of Marsham in ye County of Norfolk & both single persons were married at Haynford ye 9th of July 1726.

William Cubit & Elizabeth Amyas both of Aylesham in ye County of Norfolk & both single persons were married 20th of sep : 1726.

George Martins of Worstead singleman & Ann Hemsly of Horstead singlewoman were married 28 of Sep : 1726.

Richard Riseborough of Aylesham singleman & Hannah Woolsey of Aylesham Widow were married 24 of October 1726.

P.30.   1728 Marriages.

James Thargar of Edgefield singleman & Ellen Bear of Edgefield singlewoman was married y⁰ 11ᵗʰ day of September 1728.

Pointer Copping of y⁰ City of Norwich singleman & Ann Kemp of y⁰ City of Norwich singlewoman were married y⁰ 16 day of September 1728.

Sammuel Forster of Marsham Widower & Elizabeth Hart of Marsham Widow were married y⁰ 7ᵗʰ day of October 1728.[1]

²Marriages 1729.

Decʳ 29ᵗʰ Wᵐ Doughty Widdower & Eleanor Lockit singlewoman. Both of Marsham.

P. 31.   1729 Burials.

Sarah the Daughter of Isaac Fox & Sarah his wife was buried October 8.

James Norris A: M: and Rectʳ of Marsham was buried Octʳ 9ᵗʰ.

Mary Marsham was buried October 13.

Susan Watts was buried Octʳ 16.

Eliz: y⁰ wife of Wᵐ Doughty was buried Octʳ 23.

Eliz: y⁰ wife of Wᵐ Andrews was buried Nov: 20.

John Oliver was buried November 23.

John Edwards was buried Novʳ 30.

Susan Harding an Infant was buried Novʳ 30.

Sarah harding an Infant was buried Decʳ 2ᵈ

Sarah Saunders an Infant was buryed Jan: 18ᵗʰ

---

[1] Handwriting No. 9 (Marriages) here ends.

[2] Hand No. 10.

Sarah Gedge an Infant was buryed Jan : 28th.
John Gibson of Aylesham Buryed March 12th.
Anne the Wife of George Saunders. Mar : 22.
Robt. Dyball was buryed March the 22nd.

1730.

Frances Greenwood was buryed March 27th.
Martha Ives April 1st.
Susanna Delf was buryed April the 3rd.
Martha Ives an Infant buryed April 3d.

P.32.   1727 BAPTIZINGS CONTINUED.[1]

Anne ye daughter of Richard & Eliza: Peart October 17.
John ye son of John & Bridgett Pearson Nov : 5th.
Mary ye daughter of Robert & Margaret daniel Novem : 21.
Martha ye daughter of Jonathan & Anne Peart decem : 7.
Sarah ye daughter of Robert & Sarah Jeckell decem : 8.
James ye son of James Oliver & Abigail his wife decem : 19.
William ye son of Robert & Tryphena Bear feb : 7.
John ye son of Stephen & Sarah Hendry feb : 15.

1728.

William ye son of Gregory & flasby Marsham March 28.
Mary ye daughter of Robert & Sarah Dybal August 4.
James ye son of Michael & Elizabeth Wild August 12.
Thomas ye son of Robert & Eliz Thornton december 25.
Mary ye daughter of Frances & Mary Jeckell Jan : 1st.
Sarah ye daughter of James & Eliza : Key Jan : 20.
John ye son of James & Eliza : Key Jan : 20.
William ye son of John & Eliza : Watson March ——[2]

---

[1] No. 9 again to 1729. May 25. The leaves which separate these baptisms
from the rest of 1727 have evidently been misplaced in the rebinding.
[2] Left blank in Register.

1729.

Hester yᵉ daughter of Robert & Ann Laxon April 6.

Thomas yᵉ son of William & Sarah Doughty April 19.

Thomas yᵉ son of William & Mary Mack May 5.

William yᵉ son of Robert & Ann Flower May 25.

Robert the son of John & Agnes Jeckel Oct 19.

Sarah Daughter of John Saunders & Sarah his wife was privately
  Baptized October 8. 1729.

Martha Daughter of John Ives and Martha his wife was privately
  baptiz'd November 2ᵈ 1729.

Sarah yᵉ Daughter of Robert Harding and Eliz: his wife was
  baptiz'd Nov: 23 1729.

Margaret the Daughter of Stephen Jeckel & Honour his wife was
  baptiz'd Feb 10ᵗʰ 1729.

William the Son of John Pearson, & Bridget his wife was baptiz'd
  Mar: 22ᵗʰ·

P.33. John the son of John Bowden, & Mary his wife was baptiz'd
  March 22ᵗʰ·

Isaac the Son of Thoˢ Fox, & Susan his wife was baptiz'd March
  22ᵗʰ·

1730.[1]

Robert the Son of Robert Flower and Ann his wife baptized
  August 16 1730.

Susanna Dʳ of Thomas & Susanna Leake was Baptized on the
  21ˢᵗ day of November 1731.

David the Son of Samuel Lubbock & Ann his Wife was baptized
  upon the 28ᵗʰ of March 1735.

Isaac Son of John Vertegans & Amy his Wife was Baptized the
  25ᵗʰ day of August 1732.

John Son of John Vertegans & Amy his Wife was Baptized the
  12ᵗʰ day of July 1736.

James Son of James Grix and Sarah his wife was Born August
  8ᵗʰ 1733 and Baptized the 19ᵗʰ of the same month.

---

[1] Handwriting No 12 for six entries.

P.34.   MARRIAGES IN THE YEAR 1738.[1]

Edward Watts Widower & Mary Durrant Widow were married
by Banns the 6th of March.

Richard Jeckel Widower & Judith Smithson single woman were
married by Banns, the fourth of March.

1739.

John Watson Singleman & Elisabeth Reeve Singlewoman
were married by Banns the ninth of June.

Joseph Lubbock Singleman & Sarah Car singlewoman were
married by Banns the first of October.

Richard Delf & Mary Peartree both single Persons & both of this
Parish were married by Banns the 12th of October.

Benjamin Jeckel & Elizabeth Jeckell both single Persons & both
of this Parish were married the 5th of October.

P.35.   MARRIAGES 1748.[2]

John Davy and Mary Fox both Single Persons of this Parish
were married by Banns October 9th.

William Marsham and Elizabeth Bloom both single persons were
married by Banns October 21st.

Benjamin Olfe and Susanna Owsin both single Persons of this
Parish were married by Banns Novbr 27th.

Richard Bunn and Elizabeth Brier, both Single Persons of this
Parish were married by Banns Febry 6th.

SAML DYBALL, JOHN GREEN, CHURCH WARDENS, NATHL PONDER
RECTR.

MARRIAGES 1749.

James Greenwood and Mary Lake, Both single Persons were
married by Banns Octbr 10th.

---

[1] Handwriting No 11. for 5 entries, see Preface.
[2] These entries follow the last without break.   Handwriting No. 13.
begins and continues to the end of the book.

Joseph Bromley and Elizabeth Taylor Both single Persons from Felthorp the Banns being three times published in that Parish Church were married October 22.

William Watson singleman and Margaret Jeckel singlewoman Both of this Parish 'the Banns being thrice published were married Dec^{br} 26th.

John Love Singleman of Cossey and Elizabeth Howard of Swannington Widow by licence were married Dec^{br} 29th.

P.36. Francis Taylor of the Parish of Stratton Strawley singleman and Margaret Bowles of the Parish of Heydon singlewoman by Licence were married Feb^{ry} 2^d.

John Wade Singleman and Mary Miller singlewoman Both of Felthorp the Banns being three times published there were married Feb^{ry} 13th.

John Townshend of Felthorp Widower and Mary Howlett of Sparham Singlewooman were married by Licence March 18th.

SAM^L DYBALL, JOHN GREEN CHURCHWARDENS.

NATH^L PONDER REC^{TR}.

MARRIAGES 1750.

Samuel Wily Widower and Elizabeth Harding Widow Both of this Parish were married by Banns April 16th.

John Green Singleman and Bridget Lewcock singlewoman Both of this Parish the Banns being thrice published were married October 8th.

William Crane Widower and Hannah Gladdin singlewoman Both of Hevingham the Banns being three times published in that Parish Church were married October 24th.

Robert Peartree singleman and Elizabeth Alexander singlewoman Both of this Parish the Banns being three times published were married October 25th.

P.37. Joseph Hasting singleman and Elizabeth Woods singlewoman Both of this Parish the Banns being three times published were married October 29th.

Richard Ward of the Parish of Sall in the County of Norfolk singleman and Sarah Lawrence of the Parish of Brisley in the said County singlewoman by Licence were married November: 22ᵈ·

Thomas Doughty singleman & Margarett Spurrell singlewoman Both of this Parish the Banns being thrice published were married December 26ᵗʰ·

Charles Wedlock singleman & Susanna Burrage widow Both of this Parish the Banns being thrice published were married December 26ᵗʰ·

Robert Smithson Singleman & Mary Smith singlewoman Both of this Parish the Banns being thrice published were married December 27ᵗʰ·

Joseph Gibbs of the Parish of Hevingham in the County of Norfolk singleman and Elizabeth Walker of the same Parish widow by Licence were married February yᵉ 23ᵈ·

<table>
<tr><td>SAMᴸ DYBALL</td><td rowspan="2">} CHURCH
WARDENS</td><td rowspan="2">NATHᴵᴸ PONDER RECTᴿ·</td></tr>
<tr><td>JOHN GREEN</td></tr>
</table>

P.38. MARRIAGES 1751.

Isaac Everett of the Parish of Haseborough in the County of Norfolk singleman and Anne Springall of the same Parish singlewoman by Licence were married May 12ᵗʰ·

John Gallant of Heveringland Widower and Hannah More of Hevingham Singlewoman were married by Licence May 30ᵗʰ·

Thomas Smith Singleman and Mary Jary Singlewoman Both of this Parish were married the Banns being thrice published May 30ᵗʰ·

Henry Engledow Singleman of the Parish of Ling and Susanna Park of the Parish of Whitwell singlewoman by Licence were married Septᵇʳ 15ᵗʰ·

Andrew Hastings Widower, & Mary David Widow Both of this Parish, the Banns being thrice published were married October 7ᵗʰ·

Joseph Wattson, Singleman & Anne Nickols Singlewoman both
of this Parish the Banns being thrice published were
married November 18th.

Thomas Lacey of Witton, Singleman and Elizabeth Willson, of
Buxton, singlewoman, by Licence were married December
18th.

P.39. George Barton of Attlebrigg Widower and Mary Thorn of Weston
Widow by Licence were married the twenty-fourth day of
December 1751.

John Dack, Singleman & Mary Wighton singlewoman Both of
Hevingham the Banns being thrice published there were
married December 26th.

JOHN GREEN CHURCHWARDEN.

NATH^EL PONDER REC^TR.

MARRIAGES 1752.

John Daniel of Scotto widower & Amy Bly of Hevingham
singlewoman the Banns being thrice published in each of
these Parishes were married February 8th.

Thomas Plaford singleman & Mary Tuddenham singlewoman
Both of Hevingham the Banns being thrice published
there were married March 31st.

John Fox of Horsford St. Faiths Singleman and Lettice Hase
of Morton singlewoman by Licence were married April 9th.

Robert Pitcher Singleman and Anne Gladen Singlewoman Both
of Hevingham the Banns being thrice published there
were married May 10th.

John Palmer Singleman & Elizabeth Walker singlewoman Both
of Hevingham the Banns being thrice published there
were married May 17th.

P.40. Robert Wattson singleman and Susanna Blyth singlewoman
Both of this Parish the Banns being thrice published were
married October 10th.

JOHN VERTEGANS CHURCHWARDEN

NATH^EL PONDER REC^TR.

MARRIAGES 1753.

William Pye Singleman and Mary Haines singlewoman Both of this Parish the Banns being thrice published were married January 29th.

John Lubbock Singleman and Mary Warnes Singlewoman Both of this Parish the Banns being thrice published were married March 5th.

Michael Wiley Singleman and Mary Peartree Singlewoman Both of this Parish the Banns being thrice published were married March 12th.

Stephen Mann of this Parish of Crostwick Singleman and Mary Sherwood of this Parish Singlewoman the Banns being thrice published in the said Parish Churches were married May ye 22d.

Edward Drosier of Banningham Singleman and Barbara Elden of the same Parish widow by Licence were married September 26th.

Whitehead Feak of Cawston in the County of Norfolk singleman and Mary Woodrow of the same Parish Singlewoman by Licence were married November 25th.

JOHN VERTEGANS CHURCHWARDEN.

NATHEL PONDER RECTR.

P.41.
MARRIAGES 1754.

Isaac Fox Singleman and Christian Burriage Singlewoman Both of this Parish the Banns being thrice published were married January 10th.

NATHEL PONDER RECTR IBID:

REGISTER BILL EASTER 1730 TO EASTER 1731.

Baptisms—Michael, son of Michael & Eliz. Wilde Nov: 5.
James son of Thomas & Eliz: Greenwood Dec 27.
Robert son of Robert & Judith Smithson February 14.
Elizabeth daughter of John & Sarah Alexander Feb: 8.
Susan daughter of Robert & Eliz: Hardin March 1.
Sarah daughter of Isaac & Mary Bly Aprill 4. (1731.)
Marriages—Christopher Burrage & Susan Delph. Nov: 30.
Thomas ——[1] & Phillis Jeckell Dec: 27.
Robert Peartree & Mary Bryan January 12.
Burialls—Susan Barny October 4.
Abigail Olifer October 22.
Ann Bly January 8.
Thomas Marsham Aprill 22 (1731.)

REGISTER BILL EASTER 1731 TO EASTER 1732.

Baptisms—William son of Stephen & Honour Jeckel June 6.
Daniel son of Samuel & Mary Everet June 6.
Henry son of Thomas & Phillis Andrews Sept: 5.
Sarah daughter of Robert & Anne Laxen Aug: 8.
Joseph son of Thomas & Anne Watson Sept: 24.
Susan daughter of Arthur & Susan Leak Nov: 14.
Susan daughter of Thomas & Susan Leak Nov: 21.
Isaac son of Isaac & Sarah Fox Dec: 12.
Thomas son of Christopher & Susanne Burridge Jan: 2.
Burials—Stephen Jeckil April 28.
Thomas Marsham April 29.
Isaac Fox June 6.
Mary Fox June 6.
Robert Gedge June 21.
Gregory Marsham June 26.
Anne Vertegans July 30.
Elizabeth Watson November 15.
Susanna Harding December 27.

---

[1] Torn off but probably *Andrews.*

Marriages—James Grix singleman & Sarah Tramplett single woman were married June 8.

James Oliver widower & Jane Greenwood single woman Nov : 1.

John Delph & Susanna Jeckel single persons Nov : 1.

W. HARVEY MINISTER.
JAMES GRIX—ROBERT BEAR. CH : W.

REGISTER BILL EASTER 1732 TO EASTER 1733.

Baptisms—Isaac son of Isaac[1] & Amy Verteyans Jan: 10.

Phillis daughter of Nathaniel & Margaret Greenwood Feb 4.

Elizabeth daughter of Thomas & Ann Watson Feb : 16.

Robert son of Richard & Elizabeth Jeckel April 8 (1733.)

Burials—John Ives May 4.

Diana wife of John Ogden May 14.

Henry Jeckel May 22.

Sarah Thornton June 25.

Frances Peartree June 30.

Honoria Jeckel July 30.

Thomas Andrews July 6.

Phillis Andrews August 21.

William Peartree August 20.

Robert Gazely September 5.

Margaret Jeckel widow October 8.

Sarah Dyball October 28.

John Oats November 27.

Isaac Fox December 1.

Susanna Fox December 16.

John Edwards January 6.

Mary Jeckel January 21.

William Barker February 8.

Ann Purt February 18.

Amy Fox February 22.

Elizabeth Lubbock March 2.

Henry Greenwood March 10.

Stephen Jeckel March 21.

---

[1] Probably a slip of the pen for *John.*

Henry Bone March 27 (1733.)
Mary Oates March 27.
Marriages—William Farmar & Sarah his wife May 17.
Robert Applefer & Elizabeth his wife Sept: 22.
Timothy Blythe & Mary his wife May 20.
Francis Jeckil & Margaret his wife Oct: 7.
Jeremiah Hartly & Elisabeth his wife Dec: 24.

REGISTER BILL EASTER 1733 TO EASTER 1734.

Baptisms.   Robert son of John & Mary Vout May 6.
Susanna daughter of Jacob & Sarah Blyth May 13.
Amy daughter of Will[m] & Anne Jeckel May 16.
Mary daughter of Robt. & Mary Peartree May 16.
William son of Will[m] & Elisabeth Harvey June 6.
Thomas son of Tho[s] & Elisabeth Everard June 8.
John son of John & Agnes Jeckall June 24.
James son of James & Sarah Grix July 1.
James son of Robert & Ursula Jeckall October 12.
Christian daughter of Christopher & Susan Burridge Dec: 30.
Susan daughter of Arthur & Susan Lake March 31. (1734.)
Elisabeth daughter of Tho[s] & Elisabeth Greenwood Apr 14
*   (1734.)*
Burials.   George Saunders April 13.
Robert Daniel April 20.
Maxey Furnace April 23.
Francis Jeckall April 27.
Amy Jeckall June 10.
James Tennant July 21.
John Bear August 5.
Timothy Blyth September 28.
Samuel Thorisby October 12.
Joseph Blyth December 16.
Elisabeth Davison March 30 (1734.)
Anne Dudgeon March 31 (1734.)
Marriages—Thomas Fox widower & Margaret Daniel widow June 5.
Samuel Lubbock widower & Anne Flower wid: Oct: 7.

Richard Linkhorn of Thwaite & Elisabeth Howard of Calthorp Feb: 20.
Edward Fuller of Frettenham & Elis^{th} Mayes of Hainford.

W^M. HARVEY—JAMES GRIX.

"A COPY OF THE REGISTER BELONGING TO THE PARISH OF MARSHAM FROM EASTER 1734 *TO THIS PRESENT TIME."*

(Bp's Visitation 1735.)

BAPTISMS.

Elizabeth the daughter of W^m & Eliz^{th} Harvey bapt. Sept 29.
Robt son of Robt & Mary Oats Bapt. Jan. 26.
William son of W^m & Jane Greenwood March 16.
Jane daughter of W^m & Jane Greenwood March 16.
David son of Saml & Ann Lubbock Bapt. Mar. 23.
Sarah daughter of Robt & Tryphena Bear May 11. 1735.
Elizabeth daughter of Rich^d & Eliz^{th} Jeckell May 18.
Mary daughter of Hammond & Ann Smith May 25.

BURIALS.

Mary Grix buried Decr 8th.
Edward Watson buried March 15th.
Mary Thornton buried April 13.
Amy Stageman buried Apr. 20th.
Mary Neave buried June 23^{d.}

MARRIAGE.

William Barber of Hevingham in Norfolk singleman & Mary Spink of Marsham in the 3^d County singlewoman were married Novr 21st 1734.

W^M HARVEY R^B OF MARSHAM.

REGISTER BILL 1737.

Marriage. Hillary Bennet & Ellen Green October 10.
Baptisms. Robert son of John & Pettiss Tramplin Jan: 6.

Mary daughter of Tho⁸ & Ann Greenwood Jan: 6.
Samuel son of Samuel & Ann Lubbock Jan: 30.
Elizabeth daughter of John & Ann Pearson Feb: 13.
Sarah daughter of Robert & Sarah Watson Feb: 22.
Sarah Burrage July 10.
John son of John Verdegans & Ama July 10.
Abigail daughter of Arthur & Susan Lake July 27.
Burials—Sarah Watts January 3.
Hester Thornton January 30.
Thomas Balls March 16.

B. PAULS, CURATE.

REGISTER BILL 1742—3.[1]

Baptisms—Isaac son of Robert & Elizabeth Harding Ap. 28.
Nicholas son of Nicholas & Ann Man May 17.
John son of Hilary & Elizabeth Bennet Jan: 2.
Stephen son of Richard & Judah Jeykel Jan: 9.
Valentine son of Tho⁸ & Elizabeth Fox February 20.
Marriage—Isaac Bly & Mary Hindry by Banns Oct: 31. 1742.
Burials—Elizabeth Wiley September 28.
Mary Lines October 9.
John Lake November 9.
Roger Neare December 24.
Charles Bly December 24.
Jeremy Hartley January 5.

(G. RAY, CURATE.)

REGISTER BILL 1744—5.[1]

Burials—Susanna Foster February 24. 1744.
Kezia Barker March 24. 1744.　　　(G. RAY, CURATE.)

REGISTER BILL 1745—6.[1]

Burials—Sarah Fox October 3. 1745.　　　(G. RAY, CURATE.)

---

[1] The extracts from the Register Bills of these years are of those names only which are not preserved in the Parish Books.

[Book 4.]

P. 2.[1]   Baptisms 1738.

Mary the d. of John Ives & Jemima his wife April 1.
Mary the d. of John Pearson & Bridget his wife April 1.
Mary the d. of Robert Laxon & Ann his wife April 14.
Martha the d. of John Dains & Elizabeth his wife May 7.
Elisabeth the d. of Robert Thornton & Mary his wife Aug 15.
Ann the d. of Tho : Sturman & Ann his Wife November 3.
Mary the d. of Samuel Dyball & Mary his wife November 19.
Thomas the s. of Tho : Grix & Elisabeth his wife November 19.
Susanna the d. of Robert Peartree & Mary his wife Nov[r] 24.
Phebe the d. of Samuel Ward & Elisabeth his Wife January 21.
Anne d. of James Tramplett & Hannah his Wife March 6 1738.
Hannah d. of James Tramplett & Hannah his Wife Feb[ry] 2.
         1736.
P. 3. 1739.   Mary the d. of John Ward & Mary his Wife April 20.
Sarah the d. of Thomas Scott & Mary his Wife April 28.
William the s. of William Jeckel & Jane his Wife May 13.
Mary the d. of Samuel Everet & Elizabeth his Wife June 1.
Robert the s. of Robert Oats & Sarah his wife Sept[r] 13.
Webster the s. of John Everet & Mary his Wife July 4.
Hannah the d. of Robert Watson & Hannah his Wife Nov. 4.
Sarah the d. of Andrew Gibson & Sarah his Wife Feb[ry] 4.
Sarah the d. of Jacob Blyth & Sarah his Wife Feb[ry] 4.
Elizabeth the d. of John Watson & Elizabeth his Wife March 16.
John the s. of John Dains & Elizabeth his Wife March 16.
1740. Mary the d. of James Tramplet & Hannah his Wife
         June 2.
Ann the d. of Joseph Jeckel & Mary his Wife July 8.
P. 4. John the s. of Joseph Lubbock & Sarah his Wife Aug : 17.
John the s. of Richard Delf & Mary his Wife Nov[r] : 16.
Sarah the d. of Thomas Grix & Elizabeth his Wife March 29.

---

[1] P. 1 is lost.
Note.—In transcribing this book s. and d. are used for son and daughter,
and the words "was baptized" are omitted.

Nicolas s. of Nicolas Mann & Ann his Wife 29 March 1741.
Mary d. of Samuel Wild & Mary his Wife 12 May 1740.
John s. of Richard Delph & Mary his Wife 16 Aug: 1740.
John s. of Richard & Mary Jeckel 28 June 1741.
Mary d. of Robert & Elizabeth Colman 20 Jan^ry 1740.
Mary d. of Richard & Mary Oats 15 May 1743.

P. 6.[1] 1742.   Edward s. of Richard Delph & Mary his Wife Novr 17.
Jacob s. of John Vertegans & Amy his Wife Aug 14.

P. 7.   1743.   GEORGE RAY CURATE.   BAPTISMS.

Phyllis d. of Isaac Bly & Elizabeth his Wife May 22.
Elizabeth d. of Christopher West & Sarah his Wife May 23.
Hannah d. of Samuel Lubbock & Ann his Wife June 18.
Christian d. of John Watson & Elizabeth his Wife July 10.
Robert s. of John Ward & ——[2] his Wife October 16.
Robert s. of Richard Jeykel & Mary his Wife October 16.
Ann d. of Jacob Bly & Sarah his Wife Octr 16.
John s. of Nicholas Man & Ann his Wife Octr 33.
Joseph s. of Joseph Lubbock & Sarah his Wife Novr 20.
Elizabeth d. of Samuel Ward & Elizabeth his Wife Novr 27.
Phœbe d. of John Pearson & Bridget his Wife Novr 27.
Joseph s. of Thomas Grix & Elizabeth his Wife Novr 27.
P. 8. Thomas s. of John Hunt & Mary his Wife Decr 25.
Ursula d. of Robert Harding & Elizab. his Wife Jan^ry 1.
William s. of William Morris & Martha his Wife Jan^ry 8.
Sarah & Mary daughters of Samuel Wiley & Elizabeth his Wife
        Jan^ry 29.
Christopher s. of Christopher West & Sarah his Wife Feb^ry 5.
Elizabeth d. of Stephen Jeykel & Ann his Wife March 4.
Noah s. of Robert Laxon & Ann his Wife March 11.
Tryphena d. of John Everet & Mary his Wife March 11.
1744.   Elizabeth d. of Thomas Gazely & Elizabeth his Wife
        Apr. 1.
P. 9. Joseph a Man of riper years the s. of Joseph Blyth & Elizabeth
        his Wife August 12.

---

[1] P. 6 is blank.
[2] Left blank in Register.

Samuel s. of William Lubbock & Elizabeth his Wife Oct : 28.

Richard s. of Richard Delph & Mary his Wife Nov : 5.

Sarah d. of William Jeykel & Jane his Wife Dec : 9.

John s. of George Saunders & Mary his Wife Dec : 16.

Elizabeth d. of Arthur Lake & Susanna his Wife Dec : 23.

Jonathan s. of John Vertegans & Amy his Wife Dec : 25.

Elizabeth d. of Edward Watson & Ann his Wife Dec : 30.

Luke s. of Robert Edwards & Mary his Wife Jan^{ry} 27.

Charles s. of Christopher West & Sarah his Wife March 17.

Ann d. of Andrew Gibson & Sarah his Wife April 14.

P.10. 1745.   Robert s. of Robert Amplefer & Rachel his Wife July 21.

William Hyron s. of Robert Fleether & Ann his Wife June 5.

    1744.

    1742.   John s. of Robert Spurrell & Susan his wife Aug 28.

    1743.   Elizabeth d. of Robt Spurrell & Susan his Wife Jan^{ry} 9.

    1744.   James s. of John Wild & Elizabeth his Wife Aug : 19.

    1744.   Elizabeth d. of Thomas Stuart & Mary his Wife March

       5.

P.11. 1745.   Ann d. of John Watson & Elizabeth his Wife April 21.

James s. of John Verdegans & Amy his Wife Sept. 20.

George s. of George Saunders & Mary his Wife Dec : 8.

Mary d. of John Wild & Elizabeth his Wife Dec : 15.

Mary d. of Samuel Lubbock & Ann his Wife Jan^{ry} 1.

Jacob s. of Jacob Bly & Sarah his Wife Jan^{ry} 12.

Ann d. of John Oliver & Margaret his Wife Feb^{ry} 18.

Rebecca d. of Richard & Mary Jeckel Sept 26 1745.

Robert s. of Robert & Mary Edwards Novr 7. 1745.

P.12. 1746.   Sarah d. of John Watson & Elizabeth his Wife Nov 10.

Luke s. of Luke Thompson & Sarah his Wife Aug : 21.

Moses s. of Richard Delph & Mary his Wife Jan^{ry} 18.

    1747.   Elizabeth d. of Arthur Lake & Susanna his Wife March

      29.

    1746.   Sarah d. of Christopher West & Sarah his Wife July 23.

    1746.   Michall s. of John & Elizabeth Wild Jan^{ry} 23.

    1746.   Elizabeth d. of John & Elizabeth Pentency March 12.

P.13.   1747. G. RAY. curate.

    1747.   Robert s. of John Earle & Elizabeth his Wife May 14.

Caleb s. of John Everet & Mary his Wife Aug : 23.
Matthew s. of Richard Joykel & Judith his Wife Aug : 27.
Elizabeth d. of Robert Edwards & Mary his Wife Nov[r] 1.
James s. of Robert Harding & Elizabeth his Wife Nov 8.
Elizabeth d. of Stephen Ward & Elizabeth his Wife Nov: 9.
Elizabeth d. of Joseph Lubbock & Sarah his Wife Dec : 6.
Charles s. of William Lubbock & Elizabeth his Wife Jan[ry] 31.
Thomas s. of Edward & Ann Wattson Aug : 18. 1747.

P.14. 1748.   Mary d. of Luke & Sarah Tompson *born*[1] April 10.
1748.   Elizabeth d. of John & Elizabeth Wild June 20.
Solomon s. of Will : & Mary Barber October 4.
Christian d. of John Wattson & Elizabeth his Wife Oct: 9.
Anne d. of Edward & Anne Wattson Oct[r] 9.
John s. of John & Elizabeth Earl Dec[r] 9.
William s. of Will[m] & Sarah Betts Dec 11.
Charles s. of George Alexander[2] & Mary his Wife Dec[r] 29.
James s. of John & Elizabeth Daines[1] Jan[ry] 1.
Matthew s. of John & Eliz[th] Pantin Jan[ry] 1.
Elizabeth d. of W[m] & Eliz[th] Dunnit Jan[ry] 6.
Mary d. of Will[m] & Eliz[th] Dunnit Jan[ry] 6.
Caleb a man of riper years s. of Joseph Blyth & Elizabeth his
    Wife January 15.
Mary d. of John Delph & Pettis his Wife Jan[ry] 15.
John s. of John & Mary Doughty Oct : 14.
John s. of Robert & Sarah Oats Feb[ry] 14.
Sarah d. of Charles & Elizabeth Davidson Feb[ry] 19.

<table>
<tr><td>SAM[L] DYBALL</td><td rowspan="2">} CHURCHWARDENS.</td><td>NATH[EL] PONDER</td></tr>
<tr><td>JOHN GREEN</td><td>RECTOR.</td></tr>
</table>

P.15. 1749.   Samuel s. of Stephen & Eliz[th] Ward March 25.
Susanna d. of Samuel & Elizabeth Everet Apr 24.
Isaac s. of Isaac & Mary Bly May 7.
Barbara d. Thomas & Elizabeth Gazely May 30.
John s. of John & Jemima Barker May 16.
Robert s. of Robert & Anne Olfe June 8.

---

[1] Not entered as Baptized, and therefore not in the Transcript at Norwich.
[2] *Saunders* erased.

Lydia d. of James & Sarah Ward June 22.
Joseph s. of Joseph & Elizabeth Blyth July 7.
Anne d. of Willm & Mary Woods July 26.
Sarah d. of Benjamin & Susanna Olfe July 30.
Honour d. of Thomas & Sarah Greenwood Aug: 11.
Edward s. of Christopher & Anne Stageman Sep: 1.
Mary d. of Christopher & Sarah West Sep: 18.
John s. of Robert & Elizabeth Wattson Sep: 24.
Elizabeth illegitimate d. of Ruth Ash Octr 2.
Richard s. of Richard & Grace Stirman Octr 4.
John s. of John & Mary Davy Decr 1.
Mary d. of Robert Edwards & Mary his Wife Decr 10.
Mary d. of John Everit & Mary his wife Decr 20.
Mary d. of Richard Delph & Mary his Wife Decr 25.
Sarah d. of Willm Betts & Sarah his Wife Jan^ry 21.
John s. of John Wily & Eliz^th his Wife Jan^ry 22.
John s. of Luke Thompson & Sarah his Wife Jan^ry 26.
Elizabeth d. of Richard Jeckel & Mary his Wife Feb^ry 11.
Thomas s. of James Greenwood & Mary his Wife Feb: 13.
P.16. Mary d. of Robert & Deborah Pert of Hevingham March 2.
James s. of John & Margaret Oliver March 10.

| SAM^L DYBALL | | NATH^EL PONDER |
| JOHN GREEN | } CHURCHWARDENS. | RECTOR. |

1750. Isaac s. of Isaac & Elizabeth Bly April 20.
Henry s. of James & Margaret Key May 18.
Elizabeth d. of Stephen & Elizabeth Ward May 29.
John s. of John & Elizabeth Watson July 8.
James s. of William & Elizabeth Dunnitt July 9.
Richard s. of Richard & Judith Jeckil July 11.
Reuben s. of Robert & Sarah Oates August 1.
Mary d. of John & Mary Green Aug: 1.
Joseph s. of Robert & Anne Olfe Aug: 1.
Joseph s. of Caleb & Esther Blyth Aug: 2.
Robert s. of Nicholas & Anne Mann Aug: 9.
John s. of John & Elizabeth Pantin Aug: 27.
Elizabeth d. of John Green & Mary his wife Sep: 8.
William s. of Willm Sparin & Eliz^th his wife Oct. 7.

John s. of Benjamin Olfe & Susanna his wife Oct : 9.

Sarah d. of Arthur & Susanna Lake Oct : 12.

Esther d. of Tho[s] & Margaret Rice (born March 27 1749) Oct 29.

Stephen s. of John Doughty & Mary his Wife Nov[r] 1.

John s. of William & Sarah Marsham Nov[r] 18.

Solomon Illeg[te] s. of Sarah Manning Dec[r] 6.

William[1] & Honour, Twins, s. & d. of Will[m] & Eliz[th] Lubbock Dec[r] 10.

Sarah[1] d. of James & Sarah Ward Dec[r] 11.

Thomas[1] s. of John & Elizabeth Earl Dec[r] 13.

Mary[1] d. of Richard & Elizabeth Bunn Jan[ry] 9.

Anne[1] d. of Robert & Mary Smithson Jan[ry] 11.

P.17. James s. of Richard & Grace Stirman Jan[ry] 28.

John s. of Robert & Mary Edwards Feb[ry] 17.

Anne d. of Christopher & Sarah West Feb[ry] 27.

Kezia d. of John & Jemima Barker Feb[ry] 28.

Matthias s. of Christopher & Anne Stageman March 1.

SAM[L] DYBALL } CHURCHWARDENS.   NATH[EL] PONDER
JOHN GREEN } RECTOR.

1751.   Sarah d. of George & Mary Alexander[2] March 28.

John s. of William & Margaret Wattson April 7.

Joseph s. of Joseph & Sarah Lubbock April 1.

Elizabeth d. of John & Bridget Green April 9.

Samuel & Frances, Twins s. & d. of Sam[l] & Anne Lubbock April 18.

Sarah d. of William & Elizabeth Doyle from Hevingham April 23.

Thomas s. of William & Sarah Betts May 5.

John s. of Guy & Elizabeth Smith May 6.

William s. of Robert & Anne Fletcher June 27.

Abigail d. of Luke & Sarah Thompson July 7.

Amy d. of John & Mary Green Aug : 14.

James s. of John & Elizabeth Daines Sep : 3.

---

[1] Torn off but supplied from Transcript.

[2] *Saunders* erased.

James s. of Joseph & Elizabeth Hastings Aug : *9*[1]
Elizabeth d. of John & Mary Hunt Sep : *16*[1]
Joshua s. of Samuel & Elizabeth Ward Sep : *16*[1]
Edward s. of Robert & Elizabeth Peartree Sep *28*[1]
Anne d. of Robert & Anne Bear Oct[r] *16*[1]
P.18. John s. of Charles & Susanna Wedlock Nov[r] 4.
Hannah d. of Isaac & Mary Bly Nov[r] 18.
James s. of Hilary & Elizabeth Bennett Nov[r] 22.
Jonathan s. of Robert & Anne Olfe Dec[r] 14.
Thomas s. of John & Mary Davy Dec[r] 17.

JOHN GREEN—CHURCHWARDEN.   NATH^{el} PONDER
RECTOR.

[2]1752. Susanna d. of James & Mary Greenwood Jan[ry] 22.
John s. of Richard & Mary Delph Feb[ry] 2.
Caleb s. of Caleb & Esther Blyth Feb[ry] 6.
Sarah d. of Stephen & Elizabeth Ward March 6.
James, illegitimate s. of Susanna Woods Feb[ry] 22.
Elizabeth d. of Thomas & Margaret Doughty March 16.
Elizabeth d. of Benjamin & Susanna Olfe March 7.
Samuel s. of John & Martha Lillistone April 14.
Thomas s. of Joseph & Elizabeth Blyth April 15.
Thomas s. of John & Elizabeth Spantin May 9.
Sarah d. of Joseph & Anne Wattson July 20.
Samuel s. of John & Elizabeth Wily July 25.
Sarah, illegitimate d. of Mary Wattson of Hevingham July 28.
William s. of Christopher & Sarah West Aug : 5.
Anne d. of William & Elizabeth Sparin Aug : 14.
John s. of Thomas & Mary Rump Oct[r] 2.
Mary-Anne d. of Robert and Mary Smithson Oct[r] 27.
John s. of James & Margaret Key Nov[r] 7.
Esther-Allen d. of John & Anne Daniel from Hevingham Oct[r]
    16.
Rose-Anne d. of Henry & Mary Crane from Hevingham Dec[r] 27.

JOHN VERTEGANS Churchwarden.   NATH^{el} PONDER
Rector.

---

[1] Torn off but restored from Transcript.
[2] Here the present reckoning of the year begins.

P.19. 1753.   William s. of John & Elizabeth Earl Feb^{ry} 7.
John s. of Robert & Anne Pitcher from Hevingham Feb^{ry} 7.
Alice d. of Edward & Anne Snelling from Hevingham Feb^{ry} 12.
Anne d. of William & Elizabeth Dunnitt Feb^{ry} 18.
John s. of John & Bridget Green Feb^{ry} 20.
John s. of Charles & Elizabeth Davyson Feb^{ry} 23.
Edward s. of Robert & Susanna Wattson March 10.
William-Brier s. of Richard & Elizabeth Bunn March 18.
Anne d. of Robert & Anne Olfe March 18.
Mary d. of John & Mary Doughty April 2.
John s. of William & Sarah Betts April 4.
Thomasin d. of James & Sarah Ward May 4.
James s. of Benjamin & Susanna Olfe May 13.
Edmund s. of Richard & Judith Jeckell May 17.
Jonathan s. of John & Elizabeth Daines May 21.
Elizabeth d. of William & Elizabeth Lubbock June 8.
Joseph & Mary Twins, s. & d. of John & Jemima Barker June
        22.
Richard s. of Richard & Mary Jeckell August 5.
Amy d. of Christopher & Anne Stageman Aug : 26.
Barbara d. of Stephen & Elizabeth Ward Sep : 8.
John s. of Luke & Sarah Thompson Sep : 12.
Mary-Anne d. of Joseph & Anne Wattson Sep : 19.
Elizabeth Printer a woman of riper years Octr 2.
Frances d. of John & Elizabeth Spantin Octr 17.
Anne d. of Christopher & Sarah West Octr 22.
Joshua s. of Caleb & Esther Bly Novr 11.
Anne d. of Samuel & Elizabeth Ward Novr 25.
P.20. Robert s. of Robert & Sarah Oates Novr 26.
Peter s. of Joseph & Elizabeth Blyth Decr 16.
Sarah d. of William & Margaret Wattson Decr 20.

JOHN VERTEGANS   NATH^{el} PONDER
        Churchwarden.   Rector.

1754.   Samuel & Robert, Twins, ss. of Michael & Mary Wily
        Jan^{ry} 13.
Richard[1] s. of Robert & Mary Edwards Jan^{ry} 31.

---

[1] Torn off but restored from Transcript.

John s.[1] of John & Elizabeth Wattson Feb^ry 10.
Charles s.[1] of Charles & Susanna Wedlock Feb^ry 10.
Thomas s.[1] of Robert & Elizabeth Wattson Feb^ry 21.
Joseph s.[1] of Isaac & Mary Blyth Feb^ry 28.
Aaron s.[1] of Richard & Mary Delph March 17.
Phebe d.[1] of John & Mary Lubbock April 4.
William s. of William & Elizabeth Sparin May 9.
James s. of James & Mary Greenwood May 11.
Rose d. of John & Mary Davy May 26.
Aaron s. of Thomas & Sarah Greenwood June 13.
Joseph s. of Joseph & Elizabeth Hastings July 9.
Sarah d. of Thomas & Margaret Doughty July 19.
Hannah d. of Robert & Anne Fletcher July 21.
Thomas s. of Thomas & Margaret Rice from Aylsham July 28.
Zipporah d. of Stephen & Elizabeth Ward Aug: 30.
Robert s. of Robert & Anne Olfe Sept: 1.
Jacob s. of John & Elizabeth Wily Sept: 14.
(?) Hammond s. of Robert & Mary Smithson Novr 18.
(?) William, illeg^te s. of Susanna Woods Decr 28.

NATH^el PONDER
Rector.

P.21. 1755.   Elizabeth d. of John & Elizabeth Earl Jan^ry 21.
John s. of Richard & Grace Stirman Jan^ry 25.
Ezra s. of James & Margaret Key Feb^ry 10.
Elizabeth d. of Charles & Elizabeth Davidson Feb^ry 24.
Sarah d. of Robert & Elizabeth Peartree March 2.
Mary d. of Michael Wily & Mary his Wife March 3.
Sarah d. of Isaac & Christian Fox March 8.
John s. of Joseph & Sarah Lubbock May 8.
Roger s. of Roger & Mary Hammond May 14.
Mary d. of William & Sarah Betts May—
[2]Mary d. of Benjamin & Susanna Ulph May—
Elizabeth d. of John & Martha Lillistone   —   —
Mary d. of Richard & Eliz^th Jeckell in Allen's Street   —   —
Edward s. of Christopher & Anne Stageman   —   —

---

[1] Torn off but restored from Transcript.
[2] A Bill carried to the General 30 May 1755.

Sarah d. of Robert & Susanna Wattson Aug :—
Anne d. of Theophilus & Sarah Pye Aug : 25.
Thomas s. of William & Elizabeth Payne Oct 6.
John s. of John & Elizabeth Pantenny Oct 20.
John s. of Robert & Mary Edwards Oct 27.
John s. of Stephen & Elizabeth Ward Nov 7.
Thomas s. of Richard & Elizabeth Bunn Dec 5.
Anne d. of James Grix & Anne his Wife Dec 21.

NATH^{EL} PONDER
Rector.

1756.   Edward s. of John & Elizabeth Edwards from Felthorp
        Jan 1.
John s. of William & Elizabeth Spearing Jan 15.
Elizabeth, illeg d. of Frances Greenwood & Edward Palmer of
        St Stephens Norwich, supposed Father, Jan — —
Matthew s. of Joseph & Elizabeth Blyth Febr —
Thomas s. of Joseph & Anne Wattson Febr —
P.22. William s. of John & Mary Gladden March 4.
Rachel d. of Robert & Anne Thompson March 8.
Anne d. of Isaac & Mary Blyth April 14.
Lucy d. of James & Sarah Ward May 5[1]
Jemima, illeg d. of Susanna Woods May 21.
Elizabeth, d. of Robert & Anne Dix June 25.
Henry, a man of riper years & s. of Thomas Andrews & [2] — his
        Wife July 18.
John s. of William & Elizabeth Dunnit Aug : 1.
Sarah d. of Robert & Mary Smithson Aug : 23.
Esther d. of Thomas & Sarah Greenwood Aug : 30.
Mary d. of James & Mary Greenwood Oct 24.
John s. of Joseph & Elizabeth Hastings Nov 7.
Christopher, s. of Christopher & Ann Stageman Nov 14.
Abigal d. of Joseph Lake & Susan his wife Nov 21.
William s. of William Wattson & Margaret his wife Nov 26.
Mary d. of Richd Jeckell & Elizth his wife Dec 5.
Samuel s. of Robert & Susanna Wattson Dec 19.

---

[1] A Bill carried to the General 7 May 1756.
[2] Left blank in Register.

John s. of Robert & Anne Olfe Decʳ 26.

1757.   Mary d. of Thoˢ Doughty & Margaret his wife Janʳʸ 16.

Sarah d. of Richᵈ Delph & Mary his wife Febʳʸ 6.

Elizabeth d. of Robert Fletcher & Ann his wife Febʳʸ 7.

Susan d. of Michael Wily & Mary his wife March 13.

James s. of Willᵐ & Elizabeth Payne March 20.

Sarah d. of Joseph & Ann Wattson March 24.

Valentine, illegᵗᵒ s. of Mary Hunt March 26.

Ann d. of Willᵐ & Agnes Pearson March 27.

Stephen s. of John & Mary Davy April 3.

Robert s. of Stephen & Elizabeth Ward May 1.

Ann, illegᵗᵒ d. of Elizabeth Watson May 1.[1]

P.23. Bartholomew s. of John & Elizabeth Earle May 15.

Susanna d. of Roger & Mary Hammond May 29.

William s. of William & Elizabeth Masham June 26.

Sarah, illegᵗᵒ d. of Mary Harding July 10.

Thomas s. of James & Ann Grix Aug 14.

Susanna d. of Benjamin & Susanna Olfe Octʳ 2.

Ann d. of Timothy & Ann Dracket Octʳ 14.

Elizabeth d. of Robert & Mary Edwards Octʳ 30.

Mary d. of Robert & Elizabeth Peartree Novʳ 6.

John s. of Wᵐ & Elizabeth Dunnitt Novʳ 27.

Samuel s. of James & Margaret Key Decʳ 25.

Thomas s. of John & Sarah Wattson Decʳ 25.

Philis d. of Richard & Judith Jeckell Decʳ 25.

1758.   Theophilus s. of Theophilus & Sarah Pye Janʳʸ 1.

Robert s. of Robert & Ann Thompson Febʳʸ 5.

Hannah d. of Samuel & Ann Benett April 30.

Wᵐ s. of Roger & Mary Hammond May 17.

Jacob s. of Charles & Margaret Blyth July 2.

Ann d. of Wᵐ & Agnes Pearson July 2.

Elizabeth d. of Wᵐ & Elizabeth Masham Aug : 13.

Frances d. of John & Elizabeth Spantin Aug : 20.

Robert s. of John & Mary Bloy Octʳ 3.

1759.   Mary d. of Isaac & Mary Blyth Janʳʸ 21.

Amy d. of Isaac & Ann Vertegans Febʳʸ 4.

---

[1] A Bill &c. 13 May 1757.

Elizabeth d. of James & Ann Grix Feb^ry 4.
William s. of William & Elizabeth Pain Feb^ry 16.
George-Clarke s. of George & Susanna Bayfield Feb : 18.
James s. of James & Mary Greenwood Feb : 25.
John-Miller s. of John & Mary Gladden March 7.
John s. of Joseph & Elizabeth Blyth March 18.
Samuel s. of John & Bridget Greene March 18.
Charles s. of Robert & Susanna Watson March 18.
John s. of Robert & Mary Smithson April 22.
John s. of Roger & Mary Hammond April 27.
Honour d. of William & Margaret Watson May 6.[1]
P.24. John s. of John & Mary Barker May 13.
Elizabeth d. of Richard & Elizabeth Bunn May 27.
Elizabeth d. of Joseph & Elizabeth Hastings May 29.
Elizabeth d. of John & Sarah Watson Aug : 20.
John s. of Joseph & Susanna Lake Aug : 26.
Mary d. of John & Mary Andrews Oct : 8.
Stephen s. of John & Mary Sutton Nov : 18.
John s. of John Bowles & Ann his wife Nov : 25.
Elizabeth d. of Joseph & Ann Watson Decr 3.
Elizabeth d. of Henry & Mary Weeks Decr 30.
1760.   Elizabeth d. of Thomas & Margaret Doughty Jan : 6.
Leah d. of Robert & Ann Thompson Jan : 27.
Townshend s. of John & Susanna Southgate Feb 5.
James, illeg^te s. of Hannah Watson Feb : 10.
Phœbe d. of Robert & Mary Edwards March 14.
Phœbe d. of James & Sarah Ward March 9.
Elizabeth d. of Benjamin & Susanna Olfe March 30.
Sarah d. of Christopher & Ann Stageman March 30.
Mary d. of John & Elizabeth Earle April 13.
Robert s. of Robt. & Ann Pitcher from Hevingham June 1.
Ann d. of Roger & Mary Hammond June 1.
Ann, illeg^te d. of Ann Harding June 1.
Samuel s. of W^m & Mary Jeckell June 8.
Charles s. of Charles & Margaret Blyth June 8.
Lydia d. of John & Susanna Smith June 8.

---

[1] A Bill carried &c. May 11.

Mary d. of W^m & Elizabeth Parker Aug 17.[1]

William s. of W^m & Elizabeth Dunnitt Aug: 24.

Hammond s. of Robert & Mary Smithson Sep: 7.

Elizabeth d. of John & Mary Barker Sep: 14.

Sarah d. of James & Ann Grix Sep: 14.

P.25. Richard s. of W^m & Elizabeth Pain Sep 21.

Elizabeth d. of Caleb & Esther Blyth Oct: 26.

Caleb s. of Joseph & Elizabeth Blyth Nov: 16.

1761.　John s. of John & Mary Andrews Jan: 16.

William, s. of Richard & Elizabeth Bunn Feb: 22.

Edward, s. of Noah & Sarah Stone Feb: 26.

Phebe d. of W^m & Agnes Pearson March 8.

Ann d. of W^m & Margaret Watson March 29.

Thomas s. of Isaac & Mary Blyth April 5.

Amy d. of John & Elizabeth Spantin April 19.

Edward s. of Robt & Elizabeth Peartree April 29.

Sarah d. of Robt & Susanna Watson May 3.

Ann, illeg^te d. of Elizabeth Lubbock May 31.

Elizabeth d. of John & Mary Bloy June 9.

Henry s. of John & Sarah Watson July 26.

Sarah d. of Joseph & Eliz^th Hastings Aug: 9.

Martha d. of James & Eliz^th Rudd Aug: 9.

John s. of Thomas & Sarah Mack Aug: 16.

Ann d. of Roger & Mary Hammond Aug 30.

Charles s. of John & Susanna Southgate Aug: 30.

Thomas s. of John & Mary Barker Sep: 2.

Isaac s. of Isaac & Ann Vertegans Sep: 6.

Elizabeth d. of James & Mary Greenwood Oct: 18.

Thomas s. of John & Mary Moll Oct: 25.

Mary d. of James & Rebecca Crotch Nov: 1.

John s. of John & Mary Sutton Nov: 1.

Mary d. of John & Ann Lake Nov: 29.

1762.　Samuel s. of John & Elizabeth Everet Jan: 24.

Elizabeth d. of W^m & Elizabeth Pain Feb: 12.

John s. of Joseph & Ann Newman Feb: 28.

Sarah d. of Isaac & Ann Fox March 14.

---

[1] A Bill carried &c. Aug: 1760.

William s. of William & Mary Jeckell March 21.
Sarah d. of John & Mary Davy April 4.
P.26. Sarah d. of John & Ann Sherwood April 4.
Jonathan s. of Benjamin & Susanna Olfe April 4.
Robert s. of Robert & Mary Smithson April 4.
Thomas s. of Joseph & Ann Wattson April 11.
Amy d. of Robert & Mary Edwards May 2.
David s. of Solomon & Elizabeth Shreeve May 8.
Elizabeth d. of Christopher & Ann Stageman June 6.
William s. of Richard & Elizabeth Jeckell June 20.
Ann d. of Charles & Margaret Blyth June 20.
Elice d. of John & Phillis Colman July 11.
Ann d. of John & Susanna Smith July 25.
Samuel s. of John & Bridget Greene Sep: 20.
Judith d. of John & Bridget Greene Sep: 20.
John s. of Caleb & Esther Blyth Oct: 7.
Mary d. of W^m & Mary Peartree Oct: 24.
Phœbe d. of W^m & Phœbe Grand Oct: 31.
Noah s. of Noah & Sarah Stone Nov: 28.
Charlotte d. of Theophilus & Sarah Pye Dec: 5.
Christian Earle, d. of John & Elizabeth Dec: 10.
Ann Earl, d. of John & Elizabeth Dec: 10.
James s. of Robert & Ann Tompson Dec: 12.
1763.   Sarah d. of Joseph & Elizabeth Blyth Jan: 9.
Bartholina-Shreeve, d. of Thos & Sarah Mack Jan: 23.
Richard s. of Richard & Elizth Bunn Jan: 31.
Peter s. of George & Ann Jonas Feb: 6.
Thomas s. of James & Ann Grix March 3.
John s. of Michael & Mary Wiley March 6.
Samuel s. of Samuel & Elizth Wiley April 17.[1]
Mary Ann, d. of W^m & Lidia Riches July 3.
Hannah, d. of Robert & Susanna Watson July 3.
Richard, s. of W^m & Elizabeth Pain Aug 7.
P.27. William, s. of John & Elizth Stockings Oct 30.
Sarah, d. of James & Elizth Rudd Nov: 6.
Mary, d. of Solomon & Elizth Shreeve Nov: 13.

---

[1] A Bill carried to the Visitation.

John, s. of John & Mary Sutton Dec : 22.
John, s. of John & Mary Bloy Dec : 25.
William, s. of W^m & Ann Woods Dec : 25.
Mary, d. of W^m & Elizth Marsham Dec : 31.
1764.   Grace, d. of John & Elizth Lubbock Jan : 15.
Thomas, s. of Thomas & Hannah Doughty Jan : 22.
Rachel, d. of W^m & Mary Jeckell Jan : 26.
Elizabeth d. of Joseph & Lydia Watts Feb : 12
Ruben s. of W^m & Mary Peartree March 9.
Elizabeth d. of John & Sarah Wattson March 11.
Robert, s. of Roger & Mary Hammond March 11.
William, s. of Joseph & Elizth Blyth March 25.
Charles, s. of John & Elizth Earle March 16.
William, s. of Webbster & Elizth Everet March 28.
Arthur, s. of John & Ann Lake April 15.
Sarah, d. of W^m & Sarah Bear May 6.
Robert, s. of John & Susanna Smith May 6.
Robert, illeg^{te} s. of Elizabeth Gazeley May 6.
Susanna, d. of Robt & Mary Edwards May 6.[1]
Stephen s. of John & Elizabeth Everet June 24.
John s. of John & Mary Mole July 29.
Benjamin s. of Benjamin & Susanna Ulffe July 16.
James (?) s. of John & Mary Gladden Aug : 5.
Robert s. of W^m & Elizabeth Pain Sep : 23.
Mary d. of W^m & Phœbe Grand Oct : 3.
Leah & Rachel, twin dd. of James & Mary Greenwood Nov : 4.
Sarah, d. of Samuel & Elizth Wiley Nov : 11.
Robert, illeg^{te} s. of Ann Jeckell Dec : 16.
John, s. of Richard & Sarah Key Dec : 7.
1765.   Peggy d. of John & Elizth Spantin Jan 13.
James[2] s. of Joseph & Ann Newman Jan : 31.
P.28. Sarah d. of Jonathan & Elizth Crome Feb. 10.
Matthew s. of W^m & Mary Jeckell March 3.
Lelly, illeg^{te} d. of Frances Greenwood March 24.
Elizabeth d. of Richard & Elizth Dunn April 2.
William s. of Joseph & Ann Watson April 7.

---

[1] A Bill carried to the General.
[2] Illegible in Register but restored from Transcript.

Agnes d. of W^m & Agnes Pearson April 14.
Moses s. of Edward & Eliz^th Delph May 5.
Benjamin, s. of Richard & Eliz^th Jeckell May 6. [1]
Elizabeth d. of Thomas & Hannah Doughty May 26.
James s. of Christopher & Ann Stageman June 16.
Michael s. of Michael & Mary Wiley July 7.
John s. of Robert & Susanna Wattson July 21.
James s. of W^m & Lidia Riches July 15.
Hannah d. of Thomas & Sarah Mack Aug 11.
Charlotte d. of W^m & Eliz^th Masham Aug 25.
Lydia d. of Joseph & Lidia Watts Sep : 1.
Thomas, s. of Robert & Mary Smithson Sep : 15.
Thomas, s. of Tobias & Eliz^th Field Oct : 20.
Fanny, d. of W^m & Eliz^th Pain Dec : 1.
Bill, s. of John & Eliz^th Stockins Dec : 20.
Robert, s. of Robert & Eliz^th Ivory Dec : 31. 1765.
1766.   Dinah, d. of Robert & Eliz^th Rose Jan 5. [2]
James, s. of James & Mary Crotch Jan : 19.
Elizabeth d. of James & Eliz^th Rudd Feb : 9.
John s. of John & Eliz^th Lubbock March 1.
Mary d. of John & Eliz^th Everett March 21.
Mary d. of John & Mary Bloy March 30.
Mary d. of W^m & Mary Jeckell April 20. [1]
Elizabeth d. of John & Mary Sutton May 11.
Mary d. of John & Mary Lubbock June 8.
Thomas s. of Noah & Sarah Stone June 22.
Rose d. of W^m & Lydia Riches July 27.
Mary d. of John & Mary Mole Aug 24.
P.29. James s. of James & Ann Grix Sept : 21.
William s. of Robert & Mary Edwards Sep : 21.
Biddy d. of William & Augnes Pearson Sep 28.
Jonathan s. of Jonathan & Eliz^th Crome Oct : 26.
Joshua s. of Joseph & Eliz^th Blyth Nov : 27.
Arthur s. of Richard & Abigal Sendall Dec : 7.
William s. of W^m & Mary Jeckell Dec 25.
1767.   Sarah d. of James & Sarah Browne Jan : 4.

---

[1] A Bill carried to the General.
[2] This entry follows the next in the Register.

John s. of William & Eliz^th Pain Jan : 11.
Stephen s. of George & Ann Jonas Jan : 11.
Elizabeth d. of Edward & Eliz^th Delph Jan : 11.
John s. of John & Sarah Wattson Feb : 15.
Levi s. of W^m & Mary Peartree Feb : 15.
Samuel s. of John & Mary Gladden March 15.
Lydia d. of Joseph & Lydia Watts March 22.
Sarah d. of John & Eliz^th Palmer of Hevingham March 22.
Ann d. of John & Elizabeth Earle March 29.
Jacob & Esau, twin ss. of W^m & Ann Woods Apr 19.[1]
Rachel d. of James & Mary Greenwood May 10.
Richard s. of Richard & Sarah Key May 24.
Thomas s. of W^m & Margaret Watson June 7.
Elizabeth d. of William & Phœbe Grand June 9.
Elizabeth d. of John & Elizabeth Waterson July 8.
John s. of John & Susannah Lake July 12.
William s. of W^m & Eliz^th Dunnitt July 19.
Joseph s. of Joseph & Ann Newman Aug : 9.
Robert s. of Robert & Sarah Watson Aug : 30.
Mary.d. of Roger & Mary Hammond Sep : 20.
Peggy d. of Samuel & Elizabeth Lubbock Oct : 25.
P.30. *John s. of* [2] John & Elizabeth Lubbock Dec : 2.
1768.   *Mary d.* [2] of John & Susan Smith Jan : 3.
Elizabeth d. [2] of Theophilus & Sarah Pye Jan : 13.
Thomas s. [2] of Michael & Mary Wiley Jan : 17.
John s. of [2] John & Ann Crow Feb : 19.
Judith d. [2] of Richard & Eliz^th Browne Feb 28.
Thomasin d. [2] of Edward & Mary Benet March 27.
Ann d. [2] of Robert & Elizabeth Rose April 17.[1]
Sarah d. [2] of James & Sarah Crotch May 22.
Ann d. [2] of William & Mary Barnard June 19.
Ann d. [2] of Robert & Mary Smithson July 3.
Robert [2] s. of William and Mary Jeckell July 17.
James [2] s. of John & Elizabeth Barthram July 31.
Sarah [2] d. of Hannah Watson Aug : 7.
Mary [2] d. of James & Frances Vertegans Aug : 7.

---

[1] A Bill carried to the Generals.
[2] Torn off but supplied by Transcript.

John[1] s. of William & Eliz[th] Pain Aug: 14.
John,[1] s. of John & Ann Vertegans Sep : 1.
Dinah, d. of James & Mary Greenwood Oct : 2.
Hannah, d. of John & Sarah Watson Oct : 16.
Elizabeth, d. of James & Eliz[th] Rudd Oct : 30.
William, s. of Solomon & Eliz[th] Shrieve Nov : 13.
Frank, s. of John & Mary Sutton Nov : 13.
Mary, d. of Luke & Eliz[th] Edwards Nov : 20.
Thomas, s. of Edward & Eliz[th] Delph Dec : 4.
Rachel, d. of Joseph & Ann Watson Dec : 11.
1769.　Tristram, s. of John & Mary Bloy Jan : 8.
Tryphœna, d. of William & Sarah Bear Jan : 15.
Mary, d. of John & Elizabeth Lubbock Jan : 29.
Francis, s. of Joseph & Lydia Watts Feb : 5.
Sarah, d. of Jonathan & Eliz[th] Crome March 5.
James, s. of John & Eliz[th] Stockings March 26.
Ann, d. of W[m] & Phœbe Grand April 2.
John, s. of James & Ann Grix April 16.
Mark, s. of Thomas & Hannah Doughty April 30.
Amy, d. of Isaac & Mary Vertegans May 14.[2]
P.31. Stephen, s. of Noah & Sarah Stone — —[3]
Elizabeth, d. of Joseph & Eliz[th] Blyth — —[3]
George, s. of William & Eliz[th] Cory — —[3]
Spicer, s. of John & Ann Crow — —[3]
Phœbe, d. of John & Eliz[th] Everett — —[3]
Thomas, s. of John & Susanna Lake — —[3]
John-Miller, s. of James & Frances Vertegans — —[3]
Frances, d. of Samuel & Eliz[th] Lubbock — —[3]
Ann d. of George & Ann Jonas — —[3]
1770.　Charles, s. of Robert & Susanna Wattson — —[3]
Mary, d. of Joseph & Ann Newman — —[3]
Christian, d. of W[m] & Mary Jeckell — —[3]
Elizabeth d. of W[m] & Margaret Wattson — —[3]
Robert, s. of Luke & Eliz[th] Edwards March —[3]
Ann d. of W[m] & Mary Jeckell — —[3]

---

[1] Torn off but supplied by Transcript.
[2] A Bill carried to the Generals.
[3] Torn off.

Rachel, d. of Robert & Mary Amplefer March —[1]
Sarah & Susan, Twin dd. of Ann Fox March —[1]
Aaron, s. of Richard & Sarah Key April 8.
Mary, d. of John & Eliz[th] Barthram April 8.[2]
Elizabeth, d. of Robert & Ann Durrant July 8.
Elizabeth, d. of Ann Harding July 15.
Mary-Danford, d. of John & Lucy Shreeve July 22.
John, s. of John & Ann Vertegans Aug: 26.
John, s. of Joseph & Lydia Watts Sept: 30.
Susanna, d. of Mary & Edward Bennett Sept: 30.
Ann, d. of John & Eliz[th] Lubbock Oct: 21.
Elizabeth, d. of W[m] & Sarah Bear Nov: 25.
1771.   John, s. of James & Mary Crotch Jan: 6.
Timothy, s. of Abraham & Mary Blyth Jan: 6.
Ann, d. of Robert & Elizabeth Rose Jan: 13.
Robert, s. of William & Elizabeth Pain Jan: 27.
Mary, d. of Edward & Eliz[th] Delph Feb: 3.
John, s. of James & Elizabeth Rudd Feb 17.
? Mary Ann, d. of Joseph & Ann Newman Feb: 24.
P.32. John, s. of John & Susanna Daines March 17.
Stephen, s. of Robert & Mary Smithson March 24.
Elizabeth, d. of W[m] & Lydia Riches March 24.[3]
Mary, d. of William & Martha Farrow June 2.
Frances, d. of W[m] & Phœbe Grand June 2.
Mary, d. of Jonathan & Eliz[th] Crome June 2.
Sarah, d. of W[m] & Susanna Jeckell June 2.
Martha, d. of John & Mary Bloy July 7.
Matthew, s. of Thomas & Hannah Dugdale Aug: 25.
Jacob, s. of James & Frances Vertegans Sep: 29.
Elizabeth, d. of Robert & Susan Watson Oct: 27.
Hannah, d. of John & Sarah Watson Oct: 27.
Ann, d. of John & Susanna Lake Oct: 27.
Aron, s. of Thomas & Hannah Doughty Nov: 24.
Elizabeth, d. of John & Eliz[th] Stockings Dec: 1.
Benjamin, s. of W[m] & Eliz[th] Cory Dec: 8.
1772.   Elizabeth, d. of Eliz[th] & Samuel Lubbock Jan: 5.

---

[1] Torn off.
[2] A Bill delivered at the Visitation.
[3] A Bill delivered at the Generals.

Mary, d. of John & Mary Sutton Jan : 12.

John, s. of Luke & Eliz[th] Edwards Jan : 26.

Spicer, s. of John & Ann Crow Feb 16.

William, s. of John Crow—Twins—Feb 16.

Peter & Paul, twin ss. of Sarah Thurston Feb 16.

? James, s. of W[m] & Mary Jeckell Feb 23.

Edmund, s. of Richard & Mary Jeckell March 25.

James, s. of Thomas & Sarah Daines March 29.[1]

Ann, d. of Henry & Susannah Man June 14.

Benjamin, s. of James & Ann Grix June 21.

Robert, s. of Robert & Sarah Jeckell July 12.

John, s. of Robert & Sarah Jeckell July 12.

Denys, s. of W[m] & Mary Jeckell July 19.

Jonathan, s. of Joshua & Mary Everett July 19.

Robert, s. of John & Ann Woods Sep : 20.

P.33. Ann, d. of W[m] & Mary Barnard Nov : 15.

Hannah, d. of Isaac & Ann Blyth Nov : 22.

1773.   Matthias, s. of Matthew & Phœbe Jeckell Jan : 10.

Sarah, d. of James & Frances Vertegans Jan : 31.

Mary, d. of John & Eliz[th] Waterson Feb : 7.

Richard, s. of Luke & Eliz[th] Edwards Feb 14.

Susanna, d. of Robert & Ann Durrant Feb 21.

Rose, d. of Thomas & Susanna Abbs March 7.

George, s. of George & Ann Jonas March 21.

John, s. of Robert & Eliz[th] Rose April 8.

John, s. of William & Sarah Gold April 25.

Margaret, d. of James & Mary Crotch April 25.

Lydia, d. of Thomas & Ann Greenwood May 2.

Tabitha, d. of John & Lucy Shreeve May 16.[1]

Mary, d. of Barbara Gazeley May 30.

Ann, d. of William & Sarah Bear May 30.

Jemima, d. of John & Susanna Barker June 1.

William, illeg[te] s. of Ann Fox June 20.

Nathaniel, s. of Richard & Sarah Key July 4.

James, s. of Deborah Palmer July 4.

Jonathan, s. of W[m] & Eliz[th] Pain Aug : 1.

Sarah, d. of John & Ann Woods Aug : 29.

---

[1] A Bill delivered at the Generals.

Robert, s. of James & Eliz^th Rudd Sep : 5.

Lucy, d. of Henry & Jane Crane from Hevingham Oct : 3.

Rose, d. of Henry & Eliz^th Medler from Hevingham Oct : 17.

Sarah, d. of Joseph & Ann Newman Oct : 17.

Stephen, s. of Robt & Mary Smythson Oct : 18.

William, s. of W^m & Eliz^th Bell from Hevingham Oct 31.

Theophilus, s. of Luke & Sarah Thompson from Hevingham
　　　　Oct : 31.

Thomas, s. of John & Mary Watts from Hevingham Nov : 7.

Robert, s. of John & Mary Sutton Nov : 28.

John, s. of William & Phœbe Grand Dec : 26.

1774.　James, s. of W^m & Eliz^th Cory Jan : 9.

Susanna, d. of W^ml & Susannah Jeckell Jan : 16.

Ruth, d. of Thomas & Hannah Dugdale Jan : 23.

Jonathan, s. of Thomas & Sarah Daines Jan : 23.

Dorothy, d. of Joshua & Mary Everet Jan : 23.

P.34.　Arthur, s. of John & Susanna Lake Jan : 30.

John, s. of Samuel & Eliz^th Lubbock Feb 27.

Henry, s. of John & Mary Bloy Feb 27.

Elizabeth d. of John & Susanna Daines Feb : 27.

Ann d. of John & Sarah Barber Feb : 27.

Elizabeth d. of Abraham & Mary Blyth March 6.

John s. of John & Judith Wattson March 13.

Amy d. of Robert & Susanna Wattson March 27.

James s. of Robert & Hannah Durrant April 3.

Mary d. of Charles & Mary Saunders May 1.

Richard s. of Luke & Eliz^th Edwards May 8.[1]

John s. of John & Susanna Smith June 19.

Mary d. of John & Sarah Watson June 19.

John s. of Edward & Eliz^th Delph July 3.

John s. of John & Ann Crow at Aylsham July 21.

William s. of Charles & Hannah Hardy Aug : 22.

Timothy s. of Isaac & Ann Blyth Sep : 25.

Elizabeth d. of Thos & Hannah Doughty Oct : 9.

Judith d. of Edmund & Eliz^th Jeckell Oct : 17.

Hannah d. of Edmund & Mary Wittington Oct : 23.

Phœbe d. of Matthew & Phœbe Jeckell Nov : 6.

---

[1] A Bill delivered at the Generals.

Judith, d. of W^m & Mary Jeckell Dec : 4.
Robert, s. of John & Eliz^th Lubbock Dec : 25.
Samuel s. of Samuel & Martha Smith Dec : 25.
1775.   Lydia d. of W^m & Mary Barnard Jan : 15.
William s. of W^m & Sarah Bear Jan : 29.
Arabella d. of Isaac & Mary Vertegans Feb 7.
John s. of Isaac & Mary Vertegans—Twins Feb : 7.
Thomas, illeg^te s. of Susanna Thomson Feb 19.
John s. of John & Eliz^th Barthram March 26.
William s. of W^m & Ann Skinner April 9.
Caleb, s. of Joseph & Eliz^th Blyth May 7.[1]
Mary d. of John & Ann Crow Aug : 6.
James s. of Robert & Mary Smithson Oct : 15.
Martha d. of John & Susanna Dains Oct : 15.
Mary d. of W^m & Elizabeth Pain Nov : 19.
James, s. of James & Eliz^th Rudd Nov : 19.
[2]John, s. of William & Ann Jane Jewell Nov : 20.
John s. of Thos & Susanna Abbs from Hevingham Nov 26.
Mary d. of Thos & Sarah Blyth Dec : 3.
Ann d. of James & Mary Dunnitt Dec 10.
P.35. Edward s. of Edward & Mary Killegrew Dec : 25.
1776.   Theophilus s. of W^m & Ann Hastings Jan : 4.
Henry s. of Thomas & Sarah Daines Jan : 21.
Mary d. of John & Judith Wattson Feb 18.
Elias s. of W^m & Eliz^th Cory March 10.
Ann d. of W^m & Eliz^th Batchelor Feb : 28[1]
Susanna d. of Ann Fox May 19.
Elizabeth d. of Edmund & Eliz^th Jeckell May 26.
Mary d. of Charles & Mary Saunders June 9.
Peggy d. of Samuel & Eliz^th Lubbock June 9.
Hannah d. of John & Susanna Smith June 23.
James s. of John & Ann Woods May 30.
Samuel s. of Samuel & Martha Smith June 19.
Philemon, illeg^te s. of Deborah Palmer Aug : 18.
Ann d. of John & Mary Sutton Sep : 8.
Susanna d. of Robert & Hannah Durrant Sep : 15,

---

[1] A Bill delivered at the Generals.
[2] Interpolated in darker ink by same hand.

Samuel s. of Joshua & Thomasin Ward Oct : 6.
Mary d. of John & Priscilla Saunders Nov : 3.
Mary d. of Matthew & Phœbe Jeckell Nov : 17.
1777.   Sarah, illeg^te d. of Mary Greenwood Jan : 12.
David, s. of John & Mary Shreeve Jan : 22.
Elizabeth d. of Luke & Sarah Thompson Jan : 26.
William s. of W^m & Mary Jeckell Jan : 26.
Charles s. of Thomas & Hannah Dugdale Feb : 9.
Mary d. of Isaac & Ann Jeckell Feb : 9.
James s. of Thos & Ann Greenwood Feb : 23.
William s. of W^m & Ann Hastings March 30.
Mary d. of Joseph & Lydia Watts March 30.
Ann d. of Abraham & Mary Blyth March 30.
Isaac s. of Robert & Susanna Watson April 6.
Isabella d. of Edward & Mary Killegrew Apr : 20.
Ellen d. of Charles & Hannah Hardy May 4.
William s. of W^m & Phœbe Grand May 11.
Richard s. of John & Susanna Lake May 18.
Mary d. of W^m & Eliz^th Batchelor June 1.[1]
John s. of Samuel & Martha Smith June 8.
Elizabeth d. of John & Mary Sterman June 15.
P.36. Jane d. of W^m & Susanna Jeckell June 15.
John s. of John & Ann Woods June 1.
Robert s. of Thomas & Hannah Gazeley July 6.
Elizabeth d. of Thos & Sarah Blyth July 13.
Richard s. of Edmund & Eliz^th Jeckell July 27.
Joshua s. of Edward & Eliz^th Delph Sep : 14.
John s. of John & Ellen Pentein Aug : 24.
William s. of W^m & Lydia Riches Aug : 31.
Esther d. of Joseph & Eliz^th Blyth Aug : 31.
Frances d. of James & Frances Cook Sep : 7.
Samuel s. of John & Judith Watson Nov : 30.
William s. of W^m & Ann Jane Jewell Nov : 29.
1778.   Ann d. of John & Ann Watson Jan : 25.[2]
Phyllis, illeg^te d. of Sarah Thurston March 1.[2]
Robert, illeg^te s. of Hannah Fletcher March 15.

---

[1] A Bill delivered at the Visitation.
[2] Figures blotted out but supplied from Transcript.

William, s. of John & Susanna[1] Daines March 29.
Thomas s. of Tho⁸ & Sarah Daines March 29.
Sarah d. of Luke & Sarah Thompson April 19.
Joseph s. of James & Ann Grix April 26.
William s. of Luke & Elizabeth Edwards May 3.
Ann d. of James & Eliz^th Rudd May 17.[2]
Richard s. of Matthew & Phœbe Jeckell May 31.
John s. of John & Ann Woods June 14.
Sarah d. of John & Priscilla Saunders June 14.
Mary d. of Samuel & Eliz^th Lubbock Aug: 9.
John s. of James & Mary Dunnitt Aug: 23.
Charles s. of Charles & Mary Saunders June 14.
Thomas s. of W^m & Ann Hastings Sep: 13.
Martha d. of Charles & Mary Riches Nov: 15.
Mary d. of Robert & Hannah Durrant Nov: 15.
Mary d. of John & Phyllis Amis Dec: 13.
Phyllis d. of Abraham & Mary Blyth Dec: 20.
Phyllis d. of Edmund & Eliz^th Jeckell Dec: 20.
David s. of W^m & Eliz^th Pain Dec: 20.
P.38. 1779.   Mary d. of Samuel & Mary Soames Jan: 3.
Samuel s. of John & Judith Watson Jan: 3.
Elizabeth d. of John & Ellen Pentcin Jan: 31.
William s. of Edward & Deborah Killegrew Jan: 31.
Robert s. of Peter & Hannah Ives Jan: 14.
John s. of Joshua & Thomasin Ward Jan: 14.
Susanna d. of W^m & Mary Jeckell Feb 28.[2]
Elizabeth d. of Henry & Margaret Key April 18.
William s. of John & Ann Crow May 23.
Ann d. of Tho⁸ & Ann Greenwood May 30.
Amy d. of Tho⁸ & Hannah Gazely June 6.
Elizabeth d. of John & Sarah Laws June 13.
Charlotte d. of W^m & Ann Jane Jewell July 2.
William s. of Luke & Sarah Thompson July 18.
Jacob s. of Robt & Susannah Watson Aug: 1.
Robert s. of Robt & Sarah Jeckell Aug: 1.

---

[1] Written over *Elizabeth.* Transcript gives *Elizabeth.*
[2] A Bill delivered at the Generals.
* P. 37 is blank.

Mary d. of Christopher & Susanna Grix July 27.
Mary d. of John & Mary Sterman Oct: 10.
William s. of W^m & Martha Thaine Oct: 11.
Zechariah s. of Theophilus & Hester Pye Oct: 11.
James s. of John & Susanna Lake Oct: 17.
Ann d. of Isaac & Ann Blyth Oct: 24.
Ann d. of Joseph & Elizabeth Blyth Oct: 31.
Martha d. of Samuel & Martha Smith Nov: 7.
John s. of W^m & Mary Collison Nov: 14.
Elizabeth d. of W^m & Elizth Batchelor Nov: 25.
1780.   Elizabeth d. of Joseph & Hannah Blyth Feb: 13.
William s. of Edward & Ann Watson Feb: 20.
Elizabeth d. of Richard & Barbara Bulwer March 29.[1]
Eliza d. of Joseph & Ann Hastings April 16.
Samuel s. of W^m & Elizabeth Cory April 16.
William s. of John & Ann Wattson April 30.
Robert s. of James & Elizabeth Rudd May 7.
William s. of Willm & Susanna Jeckell May 21.
Susanna d. of W^m & Elizth Pain May 28.
Jane d. of Thomas & Sarah Daines June 25.
P.39. Lydia d. of Joseph & Lydia Watts July 23.
Mary d. of Benjamin & Sarah Middleton July 25.
Thomas s. of James & Frances Greenwood Aug: 6.
Ann d. of Matthew & Phœbe Jeckell Aug: 13.
Samuel s. of John & Ellen Pentein Aug: 20.
James s. of John & Susanna Stageman Sep: 15.
Mary d. of Henry & Margaret Key Sep: 11.
Sarah-Pye, d. of W^m & Ann Hastings Oct: 1.
Aaron s. of Edward & Elizth Delph Oct: 1.
Elizabeth, illeg^{te} d. of Rose Chamberlain Oct: 8.
George, s. of Charles & Mary Saunders Oct: 15.
Ann d. of Robert & Susanna Rhodes Oct: 22.
Sarah d. of Luke & Sarah Thompson Nov: 12.
Frances d. of Edward & Deborah Killigrew Nov: 19.
Edmund s. of Edmund & Elizth Jeckell Nov: 19.
Anna-Maria, natural d. of Mary Skinner Nov: 19.
Henry s. of James & Frances Cook Dec: 3.

---

[1] A Bill delivered at the Generals.

Elizabeth-Ann, d. of John & Judith Wattson Dec : 8.

Ann, d. of John & Ann Woods Dec : 8.

1781.   Frances, illeg^{to} d. of Sarah Palmer Jan : 7.

Samuel s. of Samuel & Eliz^{th} Lubbock Jan : 14.

John s. of John & Phyllis Amys Feb : 11.

George s. of John & Priscilla Saunders Feb : 18.

John s. of John & Sarah Laws Feb : 18.

Moses s. of Thomas & Ann Greenwood Feb : 25.

William s. of John & Lucy Shreeve March 11.

Sarah d. of Samuel & Mary Soame April 8.[1]

Mary d. of Abraham & Mary Blyth June 17.

Richard s. of W^m & Mary Jeckell June 17.

Sarah d. of W^m & Eliz^{th} Batchelor July 29.

Elizabeth d. of John & Susanna Dains July 29.

William s. of John & Eliz^{th} Barthram Aug : 12.

Jacob s. of Isaac & Mary Coman Aug : 19.

Sarah d. of James & Mary Dunnitt Aug : 26.

John, s. of Robert & Hannah Durrant Sep : 16.

Joshua s. of Joseph & Elizabeth Blyth Sep : 16.

P.40. [2]*John s.* of Christopher & Susanna Grix Sept : 23.

Mary d. of W^m & Elizabeth Pain Nov : 8.

Shadrach s. of Peter & Hannah Ives Nov : 13.[2]

Hannah d. of Luke & Sarah Thompson Dec 23.

Thomas s. of Joseph & Hannah Blyth Dec : 30.

? Paul[3] s. of Benjamin & Sarah Middleton Dec 30.

1782.   Charlotte d. of Theophilus & Hester Pye Jan : 6.

Charles s. of John & Susanna Lake Jan : 27.

Benjamin s. of John & Mary Gaze Feb : 18.

Thomas s. of Thomas & Hannah Gazely March 3.

Isaac s. of Isaac & Ann Blyth March 10.

Thomas s. of John & Sarah Davy March 31.[1]

Sarah d. of Joseph & Ann Hastings April 15.

Samuel s. of Robert & Susanna Rhodes May 18.

John s. of Ann Smith June 2.

Amy d. of John & Susanna Stageman June 2.

Samuel s. of Samuel & Martha Smith July 14.

---

[1] A Bill delivered at the Generals.

[2] Torn off but restored from Transcript.

[3] Or *Saul.*

Melinda d. of Edward & Deborah Killigrew July 14.
Amy d. of John & Ellen Penten July ——[2]
John s. of Samuel & Mary Soame Aug :——[2]
Samuel s. of Edmund & Eliz[th] Jeckell Aug :——[2]
Mary d. of Samuel & Eliz[th] Lubbock Aug : 25.
Elizabeth d. of James & Frances Greenwood Aug : 25.
John s. of William & Ann Hastings Oct : 2.
James s. of John & Sarah Laws Nov : 3.
Sarah d. of John & Ann Wattson Dec : 2.
1783.   Elizabeth d. of Matthew & Phœbe Jeckell Jan : 5.
Stephen s. of John & Judith Wattson Jan : 12.
Rebecca d. of W[m] & Eliz[th] Batchelor Jan : 26.
Susanna d. of John & Ann Woods Feb : 16.
Margaret d. of Henry & Margaret Key Feb : 23.[1]
William s. of Benjamin & Sarah Middleton May 30.
Frances-Ann, d. of Joseph & Ann Page July 6.
Mary d. of James & Mary Dunnett July 27.
Ann d. of Joshua & Thomasin Ward July 27.
Mary d. of Elizabeth Greene Aug : 10.
Richard s. of W[m] & Elizabeth Pain Aug 17.
Mary d. of John & Mary Gaze Aug : 17.
Hannah d. of John & Phyllis Amys Aug : — [2]
? Sarah d. of John & —— —— —— — —[2]
P.41. Michael s. of John & Sarah Davy Oct : 12.
Lydia d. of George & Sarah Drory Oct : 26.
Joseph s. of John & Mary Bransby Nov : 9.
? Elizabeth d. of John & Ellen Pentein Dec : —[2]
William s. of Samuel & Martha Smith Dec : 14.
John s. of John & Susanna Smithson (c)[3] Dec : 14.
Ann d. of John & Susanna Stageman Dec : 21.
Mary d. of Rob[t] & Susanna Rhodes Dec : 21.
? Hannah d. of Abraham & Mary Blyth Dec : 21.
1784.   John s. of Joseph & Hannah Blyth Feb : 15.
John s. of John & Mary Hunt March 12.
? Sarah d. of Elizabeth Grix March 21.

---

[1] Bill delivered at the Generals.
[2] Torn off.
[3] Collectioner.

Robert s. of Ann Durrant March 28.

Sarah d. of Edward & Elizabeth Delph March 28.

Sarah d. of Sarah Rudd April 4.

Benjamin s. of John & Susanna Lake April 4.

Mary d. of Thomas & Ann Greenwood April 4.

? Esther d. of Christopher & Susanna Grix April 11.

Lydia d. of Henry & Ann Edridge April 11.

Samuel s. of Henry & Margaret Key May 2.

Susanna d. of Samuel & Mary Soame May 23.[1]

Samuel s. of Wm & Susanna Jeckell June 6.

? Henry s. of Wm & Elizabeth Cory Aug: 22.

——[2] d. of John & Judith Wattson Aug: 29.

Isaac s. of Isaac & Ann Blyth Sept: 19.

? Mary d. of James & Frances Cook Nov: 28.[3]

Agatha d. of Luke & Sarah Thompson Dec: 25.

1785.   John s. of Thomas & Sarah Dains (c.) March 6.[1]

Margaret d. of Wm & Ann Hasting May 29.

? Sarah d. of John & Susanna Smithson May 29.

William-Gay s. of Alexander & Sarah Robertson June 19.

Martha d. of John & Mary Gaze July 10.

——[2] & Thomas, twin ss. of Thos & Elizth Morrill July 13.

— ne d. of Wm & Mary Ann Meads July 17.

? Hester d. of John & Ellen Pentein July 17.

Elizabeth d. of Samuel & Martha Smith July 17.

P.44.   Robert s. of John & Sarah Minns July 31.

John s. of Joseph & Ann Blyth Aug. 21.

Henry s. of James & Abigail Stearman Sep: 18.

Judith d. of Matthew & Phœbe Jeckell Oct: 23.

Elizabeth d. of Joseph & Elizth Blyth Dec: 18.

1786.   Hannah d. of Joseph & Hannah Blyth Jan: 8.

Frances d. of John & Ann Wattson Feb: 12.

William s. of Wm & Elizth Batchelor Feb: 19.

William s. of Christopher & Susanna Grix Feb: 19.[5]

---

[1] A Bill delivered at the Visitation.   [2] Torn off.

[3] Paid six shillings for the Duty on Births from Oct: 1 1783 to Oct 1 1784. Robt. Francis for John Gay Junr Collector.

[4] So marked but the entries continuous.

[5] A Bill delivered at the Generals.

Maria d. of John & Mary Bransby May 7.

Ann d. of Leah Wild (c.) June 25.

Elizabeth d. of W^m & Sarah Colman July 2.

Sarah d. of John & Mary Hunt July 16.

Caleb s. of Rose Davy July 30.

Elizabeth d. of Samuel & Mary Soame Aug : 6.

Elizabeth d. of John & Esther Kiddle Aug : 6.

Mary & Elizabeth, twin dd. of John & Ann Woods Aug : 27.

John s. of Edward & Margaret Wattson Sep : 3.

Ann d. of W^m & Elizabeth Pain Sep : 10.

Elizabeth d. of John & Phyllis Amys Sep : 17.

Robert s. of Samuel & Martha Smith Sep : 17.

Mary d. of Henry & Ann Edridge Sep : 17.

Frances d. of Jonathan & Frances Ulph Oct : 1.

Aaron s. of Thos & Ann Greenwood Oct : 8.

Joseph s. of Thomas & Martha Grix Oct : 29.

William s. of John & Susanna Lake Nov : 5.

William s. of Mary Jeckell Nov : 12.

Thomas s. of James & Abigall Lake Dec 25.

1787. Carolina d. of Alexander & Sarah Robertson Jan : 25.

Margaret d. of James & Frances Greenwood Feb : 4.

John s. of Robert & Susanna Rhodes Feb : 4.

James s. of Henry & Margaret Key Feb : 4.

Joseph s. of Ann King March 6.

James s. of James & Frances Cook April 8.

Mary d. of John & Sarah Davy April 18.

Sarah d. of John & Susanna Stageman April 29.

[1] P.46. Susannah, d. of Wm Batchelor & Elizabeth his Wife (late Eliz. Skinner spinster) born Aug 14. bap : 19.

Isaac s. of John Penten & Helen his Wife, late Helen Knott, spinster,—born Aug : 23 bap : Sep 2.

Sarah d. of Robert Smithson & Mary his Wife born Sep : 8. bap : 9.

John s. of John Kiddle & Esther his Wife, late Esther Barber spinster, born Sep 7. bap : 9.

---

[1] Page 45 is blank.

Mary Ann, d. of James Gladden & Elizabeth his Wife, late Eliz. Peters spinster, born Sep: 18. bap 23.[1]

Richard, s. of John Watson & his Wife, late Hannah Heath spinster, born Dec: 2 bap same day (P.)[2]

1788.   Honour d. of John Watson & Ann his Wife, late Ann Green spinster, born 31 Dec 1787 bap Jan 13 (P.)

Ann d. of Wᵐ Hastings & Ann his Wife, late Ann Pye spinster, born Jan: 6 bap: 13.[3]

P.47. Thomas s. of Wᵐ Payne & Elizabeth his Wife late Eliz. Dicks spinster, born Feb: 9 bap 10 (P.)

John s. of Thomas Grix & Martha his Wife, late Martha Plumb spinster, born Feb: 3 bap. 10.

Agnes d. of John Everett & Ann his Wife, late Ann Jeary spinster born Feb: 8 bap.10.

Mary d. of James & Frances Greenwood born Feb 8. bap. 10.

Martha d. of John Gaze & Mary his Wife, late Mary Playford spinster, born Feb: 24 bap. Mar. 2.

Elizabeth d. of Caleb Blyth & Alice his Wife, late Alice Colman spinster, born Feb 28 bap. Mar. 2.

Mariah d. of John Sutton & Mary Ann his Wife late Mary Ann Riches spinster, born March 21 bap 30.

Samuel s. of Richard Bunn & Mary his Wife, late Mary Jeckell spinster, born April 8, bap. 13.

Sarah d. of Lydia Crome, born April 7 bap 13.

Diana d. of Samuel Soame & Mary his Wife, late Mary Greenwood spinster born Apr. 18 bap. 20.

P.50. John s. of Samuel Smith & Martha his wife, late Martha Rogers spinster born Apr: 24 bap. 27.

Maria d. of John Bransby & Mary his Wife, late Mary Plane spinster born May 12 bap. 25 (P.)

Judith d. of John Amiss & Phillis his Wife, late Phillis Jeckel spinster, born June 7, bap. 8. (P.)

John s. of Sarah Grix born June 13. bap 15 (P.)

Mary d. of Mary Everett of Hevingham born July 2 bap. 4.

---

[1] Duty paid to 1 Oct. N.B.

[2] P.—pauper.

[3] This page & 28 following signed Wᴹ JEWELL, Curate.

[4] So numbered but there is no break in the continuity.

Robert Tilyard, s. of John Woods & Ann his Wife, late Ann Bear
    spinster, born Aug: 21 bap. 24.

Mary d. of Joseph Blyth & Hannah his Wife, late Hannah Howes
    spinster, born Aug 20 bap 24 (P.)

Maria d. of Sarah Bear, born Aug: 18 bap. 24.

P.51. Sarah d. of John Kiddle & Esther his Wife late Esther Barber
    spinster, born & bap Oct: 5.

Amelia d. of Alexander Robertson & Sarah his Wife late Sarah
    Gay spinster born Nov: 22. bap Dec: 7.

Eleanor d. of John Pentin & Eleanor his Wife, late Eleanor
    Nutt spinster, born Dec: 19. bap: 21.

Charles s. of Edward Watson & Margaret his Wife late Margaret
    Pentin spinster, born Nov: 18 bap 24 (P.)

Elizabeth d. of James Gladden & Elizab. his Wife, late Elizab.
    Peters spinster, born Dec: 23 bap 28.

1789. William s. of Wm Goodwin & Mary his Wife late Mary
    King spinster, born Jan: 2 bap. 5.

Thomas s. of John Watson & Hannah his Wife, late Hannah
    Heath spinster, born Jan 7. bap. 11. (P.)

P.52. Hannah d. of Matthew Jeckel & Phœbe his Wife late Phœbe
    Lubbock spinster, born Jan: 19 bap 25. (P.)

John s. of James Cook & Frances his Wife, late Frances Buddle
    spinster, born March 17. bap. 22 (P.)

Thomas s. of Thomas Greenwood & Ann his Wife, late Ann
    Rump spinster, born April 8 bap. 12. (P.)

Mary d. of John Stageman & Susannah his Wife, late Susanna
    Ulph spinster, born Apr. 26 bap. 27. (P.)

Philip s. of Diana Greenwood born May 20 bap: 24 (P)

Ama d. of Christopher Grix & Susannah his Wife, late Susannah
    Hammond[1] spinster born May 22 bap. 24[1]

P.53. Mary d of Thomas Smithson & Ama his Wife, late Ama Edwards
    spinster, born June 3. bap 14. (P.)

John s. of Wm Batchelor & Elizab: his wife, late Eliz: Skinner
    spinster, born June 12 bap. 14. (P.)

Laurina d. of Samuel Soame & Mary his Wife, late Mary Green-
    wood spinster, born Aug 2. bap 9.

---

[1] Torn off but restored from Transcript.

Elizabeth d. of Eliz[th] Greenwood born Aug 20 bap.[1] 23. (P.)

Ann d. of W[m] Hastings & Ann his Wife, late Ann Pye spinster, born Oct 29 bap Nov: 1.

John s. of John Lake & Susannah his Wife, late Susanna Lawes, spinster born Nov: 20 bap. 22. (P.)

Fra[-]ncis s. of John Watson & Judith his Wife, late Judith Sutton spinster born *Dec: 11*[2] bap Dec 13. (P.)

P.54. Elizabeth d. of John Gaze & Mary his Wife, late Mary Playford spinster born Dec : 19 bap. 20.

Joshua s. of Christin Jeckell, born Dec 18 bap 20. (P.)

1790. John s. of Caleb Blyth & Alice his Wife, late Alice Colman spinster, born Feb 19 bap. 21. (P.)

John s. of John Davey & Sarah his Wife, late Sarah Watson spinster, born Feb 25 bap March 1. (P.)

James s. of John Watson & Hannah his Wife, late Hannah Heath spinster, born Feb 28 bap March 1 (P.)

Sarah d. of James Crotch & Lucy his Wife, late Lucy Crow spinster, born March 25 bap 28.[1]

Sarah d. of Samuel Smyth & Martha his Wife, late Martha Rogers spinster born Apr. 15. bap. 18. (P.)

P.55. William s. of W[m] Palmer & Sarah his Wife, late Sarah Bear spinster, born April 23 bap. 25.

Peter s. of Rob[t] Rhodes & Susannah his Wife, late Susanna Everett spinster, born June 17 bap. 20. (P.)

Robert s. of Jonathan Ulph & Frances his Wife, late Frances Gold spinster, born June 10 bap 13. (P.)

Elizabeth d. of John & Mary Ann Sutton born June 28. bap. July 4.

Laurina d. of Samuel Soame & Mary his Wife, late Mary Greenwood spinster, born Aug : 6. bap. 8.

John-King, s. of W[m] Goodwin & Mary his Wife, late Mary King spinster, born Aug : 9 bap. 22.

Robert s. of Thomas Smithson & Ama his Wife, late Ama Edwards spinster, born Aug : 15 bap. 22.

Esther d. of Robert Edwards & Eliz[th] his Wife, late Eliz[th] Blythe, born Sep : 2 bap. 12. (P.)

---

[1] Delivered at the Generals.

[2] Torn off but restored from Transcript.

Flint, s. of Noah Stone & Ann his Wife, late Ann Durrant spinster born Sep: 4 bap 12. (P.)

P.56. John s. of John Watson & Ann his wife, late Ann Green spinster, born Sep: 11 bap 12. (P.)

John s. of Matthew Jeckel & Phœbe his Wife, late Phœbe Lubbock spinster, born Sep: 11 bap. 12 (P.)

James s. of James Gladden & Elizabeth his Wife, late Eliz: Peters spinster, born Oct: 4 bap. 11.

John s. of Henry Edridge & Ann his Wife, late Ann Smith spinster, born Oct: 14 bap 17.

Philip s. of John Panten & Elanor his Wife, late Elanor Notts spinster, born Nov. 4 bap 7. (P.)

Mary d. of John Kiddle & Esther his Wife, late Esther Barber spinster, born Nov: 14 bap 14.

1791. Isaac s. of Joseph Blythe & Hannah his Wife late Hannah Howes spinster, born Jan: 7 bap 9. (P.)

Ann d. of Wᵐ Payne & Elizabeth his Wife, late Eliz: Dix spinster, born Jan: 7 bap 9. (P.)

Thomas s. of Richard Bunn & Mary his Wife, late Mary Jeckel spinster born Jan 17 bap 23. (P.)

P.57. Francis s. of William Basey & Mary Ann his Wife, late Mary Ann Newman sp., born Feb 6 bap 6. (P.)

Frances, d. of Edward Watson & Margaret his Wife, late Margaret Pantin spinster, born Feb 25 bap Mar 6. (P.)

Elizabeth d. of John Bramsby & Mary his Wife, late Mary Plane spinster, born March 8. bap 27. (P.)

Sarah d. of John Gaze & Mary his Wife, late Mary Playford spinster, born & bap March 28.

Grace, d. of James Steerman & Abigail his Wife late Abigail Leake sp., born & bap Apr. 17.

Robert s. of Charlotte Marsham, born Apr. 9 bap. 17. (P.)

Martha d. of Lydia Crome born Apr. 9 bap 17.[1] (P.)

P.58. Caroline d. of Alexander Roberts & Sarah his Wife late Sarah Gay spinster, born May 3 bap 6.

Ann d. of John Amys & Phillis his Wife, late Phillis Jekyl spinster, born May 19. bap 20. (P.)

---

[1] Delivered at the Visitation.

Mary-Page, d. of John Finch & Eliz^th his Wife late Eliz^th Page
spinster, born Aug: 26 bap 28. (P.)

Thomas s. of Charles Whighton & Eliz^th his Wife, late Eliz^th
Stockings spinster, born Aug: 10 bap Sep: 4.

James s. of Sarah Palmer, born Aug 30 bap Sep: 4 (P.)

James s. of John Watson & Hannah his Wife, late Hannah
Heath spinster, born Sep 11. bap. 13. (P.)

Elizabeth d. of Thomas Grix & Martha his Wife, late Martha
Plumb spinster, born Sep: 16 bap 18. (P.)

Elizabeth d. of Mary Marsham, born Oct 13. bap 14. (P.)

P.59. Elizabeth d. of Thos Smithson & Ama his Wife late Ama
Edwards spinster, born Oct 15. bap. 16. (P.)

Hannah d. of John Watson & Judith his Wife, late Judith Sutton
spinster, born Oct: 20 bap 23. (P.)

Joseph s. of Wm Hastings & Ann his Wife, late Ann Pye spinster,
born Dec: 14 bap 15.

Mary d. of Elizabeth Barker born Dec: 5 bap 18. (P.)

1792.   Sarah d. of Wm Palmer & Sarah his Wife, late Sarah
Bear spinster born Dec: 21. 1791 bap Jan 1. 1792 (P.)

Christmas s. of Samuel & Martha Smith born Dec 25. 1791 bap
Jan: 1. (P.)

John s. of John Watker & Margaret his Wife, late Margaret
Crotch spinster, born Jan: 6 bap. 8. (P.)

Esther d. of John Kiddle & Esther his Wife, late Esther Barber
spinster, born & bap. Jan: 15.

P.60. Susannah d. of Lilly Whiley born Jan 8. bap 22 (P.)

Henry s. of Wm Goodwin & Mary his Wife, late Mary King
spinster, born March 7 bap. 11.

Christopher, s. of John Stageman & Susannah his Wife, late
Susannah Ulph sp., born Mar. 29 bap Apr. 1. (P.)

Margaret d. of John Panten & Eleanor his Wife, late Eleanor
Knot, born March 29 bap Apr. 1.[1] (P.)

Jacob s. of Robert Watson & Ann his Wife, late Ann Watson
spinster, born April 6 bap 8. (P.)

James s. of James Crotch & Lucy his Wife, late Lucy Crow
spinster, born April 6. bap 8. (P.)

---

[1] Delivered at the General.

Sarah d. of James Gladden & Eliz[th] his Wife, late Eliz[th] Peters spinster, born & bap. April 15.

Sarah d. of James Cook & Frances his Wife, late Frances Buddle spinster, born Apr: 20 bap 23 (P.)

Ann d. of Samuel Soame & Mary his Wife, late Mary Greenwood spinster, born April 20 bap 22.

P.61. Sarah d. of James Hastings & Eliz[th] his Wife, late Eliz[th] Sutton spinster, born Aug: 1 bap. 24. (P.)

William-Reynolds, s. of John Cutting & Ann his Wife, late Ann Baker spinster, born Nov: 8 bap 11.

Susannah d. of Thomas Smithson & Amy his Wife late Amy Edwards spinster, born Dec: 2 bap. 9. (P.)

Sarah d. of John Laws & Eliz[th] his Wife, late Eliz[th] Barker, Born Dec. 15 bap: 25 (P.)

Christmas s. of Richard Bunn & Mary his Wife, late Mary Jeckel, born & bap Dec: 25. (P.)

1793. Joseph s. of Joseph Blythe & Hannah his Wife, late Hannah Howes, born Feb 12 bap. 17. (P.)

Samuel s. of Eliz[th] Case born & bap. Feb 22. (P.)

Esther d. of Joseph Blythe & Eliz[th] his Wife, late Eliz[th] Green spinster, born Apr. 8 bap. 10 (P.)

P.62. Christopher s. of Christopher Grix & Susannah his Wife late Susanna Hammond, born March 10 bap.[1] 24 (P.)

Sarah d. of Henry Edridge & Anne his Wife, late Anne Smith, spinster, born April 16 bap 21.

Susannah d. of John Gaze & Mary his Wife, late Mary Playford spinster, born March 20. bap 29.

Charles s. of Charles Whighton & Eliz[th] his Wife, late Eliz[th] Stockings spinster, born May 2. bap. 5.

Charles s. of John Sutton & Mary his Wife, late Mary Riches spinster, born May 2. bap. 5.

Benjamin s. of Thomas Grix & Martha his Wife, late Martha Plumb spinster. born July 5. bap 16 (P)

Esther d. of John Bramsby & Mary his Wife, late Mary Plane spinster, born July 17 bap. 21. (P.)

---

[1] Delivered at the General,

P.63. Catherine d. of James Greenwood & Frances his Wife, late
Frances Penton spinster, born Aug: 24 bap. Sep: 1.

Henry-Edward, s. of Samuel Soame & Mary his Wife, late Mary
Greenwood, born Aug 30 bap. Sep: 1.

Edward s. of Edward Watson & Margaret his Wife, late Margaret
Penton born Sep: 16. bap 29. (P.)

Thomas s. of George Cook & Ann his Wife, late Ann Page, born
& bap Sep: 29. (P.)

Catharine d. of John Pantin & Eleanor his Wife, late Eleanor
Knot, born & bap Sep: 29. (P.)

James s. of James Gladden & Eliz: his wife, late Elizth Peters,
born Oct: 25. bap 27.

John s. of Wm Payne & Elizth his Wife, late Elizth Dix, born
Nov: 13. bap. 17. (P.)

P.64. Joseph, s. of Elizth Watson, born Nov: 20. bap 24. (P.)

Barbara-Carolina, d. of John Kiddle & Esther his Wife, late
Esther Barber, born Dec: 11. bap. 15.

Ann d. of John Laws & Elizth his Wife, late Elizth Barker, born
Dec: 22. bap. 29. (P.)

1794.   Mary, d. of Wm Hastings & Ann his Wife, late Ann Pye
spinster, born Jan: 16 bap. 19. (P.)

James s. of Timothy Blythe & Susannah his Wife, late Susannah
Roberts, born Jan: 14. bap. 19 (P.)

Phillis d. of John Amis & Phillis his Wife, late Phillis Jeckel,
spinster, born Jan: 25. bap. 26. (P.)

William s. of James Cook & Frances his Wife, late Frances
Buddle born Feb: 26. bap. 28.

P.65. John-Baker s. of James Moore & Elizth his Wife, late Elizth
Baker, born March 14. bap. 16.

Sophia d. of Wm Palmer & Sarah his Wife, late Sarah Bear, born
Feb 26 & bap 28. (P.)

William s. of Caleb Blythe & Alice his Wife, late Alice Colman
spinster, born March 8. bap. 9.[1] (P.)

James s. of Christopher Grix & Susannah his Wife, late Susannah
Hammond, born Apr. 11 bap. 13 (P.)

Henry s. of Judith Watson, born June 28 bap July 6. (P.)

---

[1] Delivered at the Visitation.

Margaret d. of John Watson & Ann his Wife, late Ann Green
spinster, born June 30. bap July 6. (P.)

Thomas s. of Thomas Smithson & Ama his Wife late Ama
Edwards, born Sep: 2. bap. 7. (P.)

P.66. Philip s. of Philip Garrard & Diana his Wife late Diana Greenwood spinster, born Oct: 1. bap 5. (P.)

Susannah d. of James Hendson & Eliz[th] his Wife late Eliz[th]
Fish spinster, born Nov: 15. bap. 23.

John s. of John Stageman & Susannah his Wife late Susannah
Ulph born Dec: 13. bap. 14 (P.)

Job s. of James Hastings & Eliz[th] his Wife, late Eliz[th] Sutton
spinster born Dec: 11. bap. 14.

Robert-Peters s. of James Gladden & Eliz[th] his Wife, late Eliz[th]
Peters, born Dec: 14 bap. 21.

1795.   John s. of John Cutting & Ann his Wife, late Ann Baker,
born Jan: 8. bap 11.

Charles s. of Eliz[th] Greenwood, born & bap. Jan 11.

Francis s. of W[m] Goodwin & Mary his Wife, late Mary King
spinster, born Jan: 26. bap. Feb: 1.

George s. of John Laws & Eliz[th] his Wife, late Eliz[th] Barker,
born Jan: 29 bap. Feb: 1.

P.67. Mary d. of Thomas Delph and Ann his Wife, late Ann Grand
spinster, born Feb: 5 bap. 13.

Harriet d. of Richard Bunn & Mary his Wife, late Mary Jeckel
spinster, born March 10. bap. 15.

Maria d. of Thomas Lake & Ann his Wife, late Ann Jeckel
spinster, born March 10. bap. 18.

Esther d. of Edward Delph & Esther his Wife, late Esther Grix
spinster, born & bap. April 5.[1]

Thomas s. of Henry Edridge & Ann his Wife, late Ann Smith
spinster, born May 22. bap. 25.

P.68. Sophia d. of James Crotch & Lucy his Wife, late Lucy Crow
spinster, born May 23. bap. 25.

Sophia d. of Charles Whighton & Eliz[th] his wife, late Eliz[th]
Stockings, born June 2. bap. 7.

Elizabeth d. of John Gaze & Mary his Wife, late Mary Playford
spinster, born & bap. 21 June.

[1] Delivered at the General.

William s. of Lilly Whiley, born June 21. bap. 28.

Robert s. of Elizth Rudd born June 26. bap 28.

William s. of Samuel Gladden & Mary his Wife, late Mary
Barnard spinster, born June 30 bap. July 5.

Mary d. of Edmund Jerry & Mary his Wife, late Mary Pain
spinster, born Aug: 15. bap. 16.

Mary d. of Thomas Grix & Martha his Wife, late Martha Plumb
spinster, born Aug: 21 bap: Sep: 6.

Isaac s. of Robert Watson & Ann his Wife, late Ann Watson
spinster, born Oct. 6. bap: 11.

P.69. Emmeline d. of John Kiddle & Esther his Wife, late Esther
Barber, born Dec: 9. bap. 10.

Elizabeth d. of James Cook & Frances his Wife, late Frances
Buddle, born Dec: 12. bap. 13.

1796. James s. of James Greenwood & Frances his wife, late
Frances Panton, born Jan: 8. bap 10.

Elizabeth d. of Christopher Grix & Susannah his wife, late
Susannah Hammond, born Feb 12. bap. 13.

David s. of Wm Hastings & Ann his wife, late Ann Pye spinster,
born March 1. bap. 6.

Caleb s. of Caleb Blythe & Alice his wife, late Alice Colman
spinster, born March 2. bap. 6.

Sophia d. of James Gladden & Elizth his wife, late Elizth Peters,
born March 5. bap. 9.

P.70. Mary d. of John Sutton & Mary his wife, late Mary Riches
spinster, born March 13. bap. 20.

William s. of James Smithson & Tabitha his Wife, late Tabitha
Shreeve spinster, born March 30 bap Apr. 3.

Stephen s. of William Smithson & Ann his Wife, late Ann
Bowles spinster, born April 21 bap 24.

William s. of John Edwards & Elizth his Wife, late Elizth Watson spinster, born April 25. bap. May 1.

Sarah d. of John Amys & Phillis his wife, late Phillis Jeckyl
spinster born June 20. bap. 26.

Luke s. of Robert Edwards & Mary his wife, late Mary Palmer
spinster, born July 6. bap 10.

William s. of James Moore & Elizth his Wife, late Elizth Bear,
born July 22. bap. 24.

P.71. Christopher s. of John Laws & Eliz[th] his wife, late Eliz[th] Barker,
born Aug : 1. bap. 2.

Mary d. of Thomas Delph & Ann his Wife, late Ann Grand
spinster, born Aug : 17 bap. 21.

Peter s. of Edward Watson & Margaret his wife, late Margaret
Penton spinster, born Oct : 17 bap. 23.

Matthew s. of John Penton & Allen his wife late Allen Knott
spinster, born Oct : 23. bap. 30.

Judith d. of Thomas Smithson & Ama his Wife, late Ama
Edwards spinster, born Nov : 8. bap. 13.

Benjamin s. of James Grix & Ann his Wife, late Ann Barnard
spinster, born Nov : 25. bap. 27.

David s. of W[m] Pain & Eliz[th] his Wife, late Eliz[th] Dix spinster
born Dec : 6. bap. 11.

P.72. Dinah d. of Eliz[th] Cawston, born Dec : 6. bap. 11.

Mary-Ann d. of W[m] Goodwin & Mary his Wife, late Mary King
spinster, born Dec : 7. bap. 11.

Sarah d. of Edward Delph & Esther his wife, late Esther Pye
widow, born Dec : 8. bap. 11.

1797.   Thomas s. of John Gaze & Mary his wife, late Mary
Playford spinster, born & bap Feb 1.

Edward s. of John Cutting & Ann his Wife, late Ann Baker
spinster, born Feb : 7. bap. 12.

James s. of James Greenwood & Frances_his wife, late Frances
Pantin, born Feb : 13. bap. 19.

Ann d. of Christopher Grix & Susannah his wife, late Susannah
Hammond born March 22. bap. 26.

Combe-Miller s. of William Race & Sarah his wife, late Sarah
Chapman spinster, born March 24. bap. 26.[1]

P.73. Rebecca d. of Tho[s] Hastings & Eliz[th] his Wife, late Eliz[th] Sutton spinster, born April 21. bap. 30.

Amelia d. of Ann Bear, born May 3. bap. 7.

John s. of Thomas Cooper & Mary his wife, late Soames, bap
May 16.

Mary d. of Richard Bunn & Mary his Wife, late Jekyll bap. May
28.

---

[1] Delivered.

George-Thompson s. of Edward Gallant & Mary his wife, late Mary Thompson spinster, born June 4. bap. 11.

Samuel Barnard s. of Samuel Gladden & Mary his wife, late Mary Barnard, born June 13. bap. 18.

William s. of Robt Haselup & Mary his Wife, late Mary Jeckel spinster, born Aug : 19. bap. 20.

Amelia d. of Henry Edridge & Ann his Wife, late Ann Smith spinster, born Oct : 6. bap. 8.

Timothy s. of Joseph Blyth & Hannah his wife, late Hannah Howes spinster, born Oct 13. bap. 15.

P.74. Elizabeth d. of John Stageman & Susannah his wife, late Susannah Ulph, born Oct : 26. bap 29.

Sarah d. of John Edwards & Elizth his wife, late Elizth Watson spinster, born Oct : 31 bap Nov : 5.

John s. of Edmund Jerry & Mary his wife, late Mary Pain spinster, born & bap. Nov : 26.

Sarah d. of Caleb Blythe & Alice his wife, late Alice Colman spinster, born Dec : 11. bap. 17.

1798.   Mary d. of John Watson & Hannah his Wife, late Heath spinster, born Jan : 14 bap. 21.

George s. of John Kiddle & Esther his wife, late Esther Barber, spinster, born Feb : 13. bap 18.

Thomas s. of Elizth Greenwood, born Feb : bap. 25.

John s. of John Grix & Elizth his Wife, late Elizth Bear, born March 4. bap same day.

P.75. Rose d. of Ann Wittington, born March 16. bap. 18.

Elizabeth d. of Henry Drory & Susannah his Wife late Susannah Ives born & bap March 25.[1]

Samuel s. of Samuel Jacobs & Sarah his Wife, late Sarah Moore, born April 8. bap. 9.

Arthur s. of Thos Lake & Ann his Wife, late Ann Jeckel, born June 17. bap. 21.

Horace s. of Wm Batchelor & Judith his Wife, late Judith Watson widow, born & bap. June 24.

Elizabeth d. of Wm Pain & Elizth his wife, late Elizth Dix, born June 17 bap. 24.

---

[1] Delivered.

James s. of James Smithson & Tabitha his wife, late Tabitha
  Shreeve, born July 1. bap. 4.

Edward s. of James Moor & Elizth his wife, late Elizth Baker,
  born & bap. July 5.

Jane d. of John Pantin & Allen his wife, late Allen Knott, born
  July 20. bap 22.

P.76. Robert s. of Robt Watson & Ann his Wife, late Ann Watson,
  born July 25. bap. 29.

William s. of Richard Bunn & Mary his Wife, late Mary Jeckell,
  born Aug : 9. bap. 12.

Isodora d. of Shadrach Ives & Phœbe his Wife, late Phœbe
  Matishall, born Aug : 28. bap. Sep. 2.

Robert s. of John Sutton & Mary his Wife, late Mary Riches,
  born Aug : 29. bap. Sep. 2.

Rebecca d. of James Hastings & Elizth his Wife, late Elizth
  Sutton, born Oct 12. bap. 14.

Elizabeth d. of Wm Goodwin & Mary his Wife, late Mary King
  born & bap. Dec : 2.

William s. of Thomas Delph & Ann his wife, late Ann Grand
  born & bap. Dec : 2.

Matthew s. of John Amis & Phillis his wife, late Phillis Jeckell,
  born Dec : 15. bap. 16.

1799.   Sarah-Thompson d. of Edward Gallant & Mary his wife,
  late Mary Thompson, born Jan : 9. bap. 14.

P.77. Mary-Ann d. of John Cutting & Ann his wife, late Ann Baker,
  born Feb : 16. bap. 17.

John s. of Wm Hastings & Mary his Wife, late Mary Breeze,
  born Feb : 21. bap. 28. [1]

Elizabeth d. of James Crotch & Lucy his Wife, late Lucy Crow
  spinster, born April 16. bap. 19.

Elizabeth d. of Robert Edwards & Mary his Wife, late Mary
  Palmer spinster, born April 22. bap. 28.

Martha d. of Samuel Soame & Mary his Wife, late Mary Greenwood spinster, born May 27, bap. June 2.

Mary-Ann, d. of Samuel Watson & Margaret his Wife, late
  Margaret Blackburn sp., born June 14 bap. 15.

Elizabeth d. of Lilly Whila, born June 28. bap. 30.

---

[1] Delivered.

P.78. William s. of Jeremiah Fish & Sarah his Wife, late Sarah Hayne spinster, born July 13. bap. 14.

Sarah d. of John Bransby & Sarah his Wife, late Sarah Grix spinster, born July 13. bap. 14.

Elizabeth d. of Edward Watson & Margaret his Wife, late Margaret Penton spinster, born July 13. bap. 14.

John s. of Wm Skinner & Eunice his Wife, late Eunice Edwards spinster, born Aug: 13. bap. 18.

Susannah d. of Christopher Grix & Susannah his Wife, late Susannah Hammond, born Aug: 15. bap. 18.

Jonathan s. of John Stageman & Susannah his wife, late Susannah Ulph, born Aug: 19. bap. 25.

Mary-Ann, d. of David Shreeve & Elizth his wife, late Elizth Bayfield spinster, born Sep: 7. bap. 8.

P.79. George s. of Peter Jonas & Elizabeth his wife, late Elizth Edwards widow, born Sep: 7. bap. 8.

Mary-Ann d. of Thos Barber & Hannah his wife, late Hannah Wittington spinster, born Sep: 27. bap 29.

Thomas s. of John Edwards & Elizth his wife, late Elizth Watson spinster, born Dec: 1. bap same day.

Mary-Ann, d. of James Moore & Elizth his Wife, late Elizth Baker spinster, born Dec: 10. bap. 15.

Luke s. of Richard Edwards & Ann his wife, late Ann Bear spinster born & bap. Dec: 15.

1800. William s. of Wm Race & Sarah his Wife, late Sarah Chapman spinster, born Jan: 27. bap. Feb: 2.

James s. of Amy Stageman born Jan: 26 bap. Feb: 2.

James s. of John Grix & Elizth his Wife, late Elizth Bear spinster born Jan: 28. bap. Feb: 2.

P.80. Mary d. of Henry Drory & Susannah his Wife, late Susannah Ives spinster, born Feb: 24 bap March 2.

Robert s. of Wm Hastings & Ann his Wife, late Ann Breeze spinster, born Feb: 24. bap. March 2.

Elizabeth d. of Edmund Jeary & Mary his Wife, late Mary Payne spinster born Feb: 26. bap. Mar. 2.[1]

John s. of Thomas Hunt & Elizth his Wife, late Elizth Nobbs spinster, born April 5. bap. 6.

---

[1] Delivered.

Mary d. of Thomas Cooper & Mary his Wife, late Mary Soame
  spinster, born May 2. bap. 4.

Elizabeth d. of Wm Goodwin & Mary his Wife, late Mary King
  spinster, born May 23. bap. 25.

Ann d. of Richard Bunn & Mary his Wife, late Mary Jeckel
  spinster, born May 28. bap June 1.

Harriot d. of John Kiddle & Esther his Wife late Esther Barber
  spinster, born June 19. bap. 22.

P.81. Herriot d. of Henry Edridge & Ann his Wife, late Ann Smith
  spinster, born July 4. bap. 6.

Diana d. of James Greenwood & Frances his Wife, late Frances
  Penton spinster, born Aug : 14. bap. 17.

Stephen s. of Stephen Smithson & Lucy Martha his wife, late
  L. M. Carter spinster, born Oct : 8. bap. 12.

Frances d. of John Cutting & Ann his Wife, late Ann Baker
  Spinster, born Oct : 12. bap. 19.

Edward s. of Samuel Gladden & Mary his Wife late Mary Barnard
  Spinster born Nov : 21 bap. 25.

1801. William s. of Tobias Pulley & Martha his Wife, late
  Martha Lavender, born Jan : 7. bap. 10.

Sarah d. of Charles Gibbs & Sarah his Wife, late Sarah Hastings
  spinster, born Jan : 20 bap. 25.

P.82. Edward s. of Edward Gallant & Mary his Wife late Mary
  Thompson spinster, born Jan : 20. bap 25.

James s. of John Watson & Hannah his Wife, late Hannah
  Heath, born Feb : 13 bap. 15.

Susannah d. of Thos Lake & Ann his Wife, late Ann Jeckell
  spinster, born Feb : 16. bap. 22.

Sarah d. of Jeremiah Fish & Sarah his Wife, late Sarah Hayne
  spinster, born March 9. bap. 15.[1]

Maria d. of James Moore & Elizth his Wife, late Elizth Baker
  spinster, born March 29. bap. Apr. 5.

William s. of Richard Jeckell & Martha his Wife late Martha
  Daines spinster, born Feb 17 & bap Feb : 22 * omitted
  by mistake till now.

Esther d. of Wm Kelligrew & Ann his Wife, late Ann Rudd
  spinster, born April 7. bap. 12.

---

[1] Delivered at the Visitation.

P.83. Samuel s. of Elizth Jeckell, born June 5. bap. 7.

Ann d. of John Sutton & Mary-Ann his Wife, late Mary-Ann Riches, born June 14 bap. 21.

Susannah d. of Amy Watson, born June 22. bap. 28.

William s. of Thos Hunt & Elizth his Wife, late Elizth Nobbs spinster, born Sep: 15. bap. 17.

John s. of Nathan Stuart & Sarah his Wife, late Sarah Thompson spinster born Nov: 6. bap. 8.

David s. of James Smithson & Tabathy his Wife, late Tabathy Shreeve spinster, born Nov: 9. bap. 15.

Henry s. of John King & Frances his Wife, late Frances Pratt spinster, born Nov: 24 & bap. 29.

1802.   James s. of David Shreeve & Elizth his Wife, late Elizth Bayfield spinster, born Feb: 11: bap. 21.

Luke s. of Robert Edwards & Mary his Wife, late Mary Palmer spinster, born Feb: 15 bap. 21.

P.84. Maria d. of Edmund Jeary & Mary his Wife, late Mary Payne, born Feb: 28. bap. March 7.

Elizabeth d. of John Cutting & Ann his Wife, late Ann Baker spinster. born March 12. bap. 14.

Thomas s. of John Edwards & Elizth his Wife, late Elizth Watson spinster, born March 20. bap. 28.[1]

Elizabeth d. of Samuel Grapes & Ann his wife, late Ann Blyth spinster, born April 3. bap. 4.

James s. Edwd Skinner & Ann his wife, late Ann King spinster, born May 5. bap. 9.

Martha d. of Richard Edwards & Ann his Wife, late Ann Bear, spinster, born & bap. June 23.

Joshua s. of Caleb Blyth & Alice his Wife, late Alice Collman spinster, born June 25. bap. 27.

Mary d. of Mary Sutton, born July 16. bap. 18.

Lydia d. of Henry Drory & Susannah his Wife, late Susannah Ives, born Aug: 7. bap. 8.

Isaac s. of Robert Fiddy & Susannah his Wife, late Susannah Willmot, born Aug: 9. bap. 12.

Thomas s. of Thos Hastings & Mary his Wife, late Mary Paine spinster, born Aug: 15. bap. 22.

---

[1] Delivered.

Samuel s. of Edward Watson & Margaret his Wife late Margaret Penton spinster, born Sep. 8. bap. 12.

P.85. William s. of John Grix & Eliz^th his Wife, late Eliz^th Bear spinster, born Sep : 12. bap. 19.

James s. of James Moore & Eliz^th his Wife, late Eliz : Baker, spinster, born Sep : 30 bap. Oct. 8.

Elizabeth d. of Wm Hastings & Mary his Wife, late Mary Breeze, born Oct : 30. bap. 31.

Matthew s. of Richard Jeckel & Martha his Wife, late Martha Dains spinster, born & bap. Nov : 21.

Thomas s. of Thos & Mary Roberts, late Pey, born Nov : 27 : bap. 30.

Ann d. of Jno King & Frances his Wife, late Pratt spinster, born Dec : 26. bap. 27.

John Bransby born Oct : 3. 1759. bap. Nov : 29. 1802.[1]

1803. Moses s. of Thos & Ann Delph, late Grand spinster, born Feb : 5 bap. 6.

Richard s. of Richard & Mary Bunn, late Jeckell spinster, born Feb : 9. bap. 20.

Mary, & Ann, dd. of Jeremy & Sarah Fish, late Hearn spinster, born Jan : 3. bap. 4.

P.86. Robert, s. of John & Esther Kiddle, late Barber, born Jan : 26. bap. 30.

Peter s. of James & Eliz^th Gladden, late Peters spinster, born Feb : 18. bap 20.

Britannia d. of James & Amy Spink, late Vertegans spinster, born March 2. bap. 6.

John s. of James & Mary Howard, late Lubbuck spinster, born March 25. bap. April 17.[2]

John s. of Isaac & Phebe Greenwood, late Gold spinster, born April 3. bap. 17.

Mary d. of Saml & Mary Gladden, late Barnard spinster, born & bap. April 24.

Eliza d. of Henry & Ann Edridge, late Smith spinster, born April 29. bap. May 1.

---

[1] This entry & the two next noted as out of order.
[2] Delivered.

Elizabeth, d. of Sam¹ & Mary Gipson, late Key spinster, born
    May 9. bap. 14.

Martha d. of Ja^s & Frances Greenwood, late Pentein spinster,
    born May 26. bap. 29.

John s. of W^m & Sarah Race, late Chapman spinster, born May
    30. bap. June 5.

Robert, s. of John & Susanna Stageman, late Ulph spinster, born
    June 13. bap. 20.

P.87. James s. of Susannah Jeckell, born Aug : 8. bap. 21.

Robert s. of W^m & Martha Jeckel, late Pulley Widow, born Sep :
    3. bap. 18.

James s. of W^m & Unice Skinner, late Edwards spinster, born
    Sep : 26. bap. Oct : 16.

Mary d. of Edward & Ann Skinner, late King spinster, born Oct :
    9. bap. 30.

Ann d. of James & Maria Pierce, late French spinster, born Dec :
    7. bap. 8.

Martha d. of John & Eliz^th Gareberith, late Dains, spinster, born
    Dec : 10. bap. 18.

1804.   John s. of Robt & Mary Roberts, late Pye spinster, born
    Nov : 28. 1803 bap. Jan : 1. 1804.

Robt. s. of John & Ann Cutting, late Baker, born Dec :—,[1] bap.
    Dec : 29. 1803.

Eldred s. of Jeremiah & Sarah Fish, late Hain spinster, born
    Jan : 26 bap. Jan : 29.

Matthew s. of Lydia Clark, born & bap. Jan : 31.

Thomas s. of Timothy & Susannah Blyth, late Roberts spinster,
    born Dec : 9. 1803 bap. Jan : 16. 1804.

Carolina d. of John & Mary Sutton, late Riches spinster, born
    March 15. bap 18.

Francis s. of John & Eliz^th Watts, late Reynolds spinster, born
    March 18. bap 20.[2]

P.88. Thomas s. of Thomas & Mary Cooper, late Soames spinster, born
    Apr. 14. bap. 18.

William s. of Edmund & Mary Jeary, late Pain, born April 16.
    bap. 22.

---

[1] Left blank.
[2] Delivered.

James s. of Joseph & Mary Grix, late Scarle, born April 30. bap
May 6.

Ann d. of George & Eliz^th Jonas, late Palmer, born July 26.
bap. 28.

Margaret-Leach d. of Joseph & Mary Leach belonging to the
parish of Walberton in the County of Devonshire, born
July 30. bap. July 30.

Sophia d. of John & Eliz^th Grix, late Bear, born Sep: 1. bap. 2.

John s. of James & Tabitha Smithson, late Shreeve, born Sep:
1. bap. 2.

Henry s. of W^m & Mary Hastings, late Breeze, born Oct: 6.
bap. 7.

Mary-Ann d. of Ann Greenwood born & bap. Oct. 6.

Robert s. of Robt & Mary Edwards, late Palmer, born Oct: 27.
bap. 28.

James s. of Thomas & Ann Lake, late Jeckell, born Nov: 1.
bap. 4.

P.89. John s. of John & Frances King, late Pratt, born Nov: 17. bap.
18.

1805.   John s. of John & Mary Penton, late Ash, born Dec: 25.
1804. bap. Jan: 6. 1805.

Mary d. of John & Rose Soame, late Fish, born Jan: 16.
bap. 20.

Elizabeth d. of Benjamin & Ann Smith, late Penton, born Jan:
23. bap. 27.

Thomas s. of Caleb & Alice Blyth, late Collman, born Jan: 30.
bap. Feb: 3.

Matilda d. of James & Elizabeth Gladden, late Peters, born
March 22. bap. 23. [1]

John s. of Henry & Susannah King, late Soame, born March 29.
bap. 31.

William s. of Benjamin & Elizabeth Skipp, late Blyth, born
April 22. bap. 28.

William s. of Thomas & Mary Hastings, late Paine, born April
28 bap. 28.

Thomas s. of Joseph & Mary Roberts, late Pye, born May 2.
bap. 11.

---

[1] Delivered.

Isaac s. of John & Mary Oliver, late Willett, born April 30 bap. May 13[1]

P.90. Henry s. of Samuel & Mary Gibson, late Key, born & bap. May 19.

Ann d. of Henry & Ann Edridge, late Smith, born May 14. bap. 21.

Elizabeth d. of Edmund & Susanna Fiddy, late Willimot, born May 23. bap. June 2.

Robert s. of Edwd & Margaret Watson, late Penton, born & bap. June 10.

John s. of Thos & Ann Delph, late Grand, born June 25. bap. 30.

Sophia d. of Thos & Lydia Williamson, late Greenwood, born July 4. bap. 7.

Lydia d. of Timothy & Susanna Blyth, late Roberts, born June 18. bap. July 12.

Frances d. of Maria Sutton, born June 16. bap. July 21.

Frances d. of Isaac & Phœbe Greenwood, late Gold, born Aug: 22. bap. Sep: 15.

Needham d. of John & Elizth Watts, late Reynolds, born Oct: 4 bap. 6. *This Registration should have been " Needham son of John Watts &c.," as certified by John Watts the father & Benjamin Smith godfather. N.B. the Certificate is lodged in ye Bishop's Office—Ja^s Bingle March 5. 1831.

Philip s. of Elizth Penton, born & bap. Oct: 13.

P.91. Sarah d. of Saml & Sarah Penton, late Ubbins, born Oct: 16. bap. Nov: 3.

Sophia d. of Saml & Ann Cook, late Roberts, born & bap. Dec: 5.

Henry s. of Saml & Ann Smith, late Watson, born Dec: 14 bap. 16.

1806. Edward s. of John & Esther Kiddle, late Barber, born Jan: 17. bap. 19.

Sarah d. of John & Ann Cutting, late Baker, born Jan: 27. bap. Feb: 2.

---

[1] Delivered.

Matthew s. of Thomas & Mary Cooper, late Soame, born March 16. bap. 21.

Sarah d. of Henry & Susanna Drorey, late Ives, born March 17. bap. 23.

Charlotte d. of James & Eliz^th Hall, late Cook, born May 3. bap. 4.

Zachariah s. of John Fisher Hunt & Charlotte his wife, late Pye, born May 23. bap. 25.

Sarah d. of John & Eliz^th Grix, late Bear, born May 31. bap. June 8.

Matilda d. of James & Eliz^th Gladden, late Peters, born June 10. bap. 12.

William s. of John & Frances King, late Pratt, born Aug: 31, bap. Oct: 12.

Sarah d. of Joseph & Mary Grix, late Scarls, born Oct: 1. bap. 19.

1807.   Robert s. of Robert & Patience Pottle, late Edridge, born Dec: 13. 1806 bap. Jan: 11. 1807.

P.92. Henry s. of Henry & Susanna King, late Soame, born Dec: 26. 1806 bap. Jan: 25. 1807.

John s. of Samuel & Mary Gibson, late Key spinster, born Jan: 26. bap. March 8.

Betsy d. of Samuel & Susanna Pye, late Speakman spinster, born Feb: 18. bap. March 15.[1]

Mary-Ann d. of W^m & Eunice Skinner, late Edwards spinster, born March 6. bap. May 3.

Mary-Ann d. of John & Susanna Newman, late Jeckel, born Apr. 24. bap. May 17.

John s. of Eliz^th Blyth, born May 22. bap. 31.

Samuel s. of Saml & Sarah Pentein, late Cook, born Apr. 10. bap. June 14.

Ann d. of Edmund & Mary Jerry, late Pain, born June 2. bap. 14.

John s. of Ja^s & Mary Spink, late Vertegans, born May 29. bap. June 28.

George s. of George & Eliz^th Jonas, late Palmer, born Dec. 8. 1806. bap. Aug: 9. 1807.

---

[1] Delivered.

Ann d. of Benjamin & Ann Smith, late Panton, born July 11. bap.
Aug: 9.

Lydia d. of Lydia Clark, born Aug: 14. bap. Oct: 4.

Mary d. of Benjⁿ & Elizth Skipp, late Blyth, born Sep: 3. bap.
Nov: 1.

Harriot d. of Ja^s & Lucy Crotch, late Crow, born July 23. bap.
Nov: 1.

Joshua s. of Thos & Ann Delph, late Grand, born Nov: 29. bap.
Dec: 13.

James s. of John & Elizth Watts, late Reynolds, born Nov: 13.
bap. Dec: 27.

1808.   Benjamin s. of John & Elizth Grix, late Bear, born Jan:
25 bap. Feb: 14.

P.93. Thomas s. of James & Tabitha Smithson, late Shreeve, born
Jan: 3. bap. March 6.

William s. of John & Frances King, late Pratt, born Apr: 12.
bap. 18.

Thomas s. of John & Ann Cutting, late Baker, born Apr. 3. bap
May 1.[1]

Susanna d. of Saml Smith & Ann his Wife, late Ann Watson,
born May 5. bap. 29.

Mary d. of Isaac Greenwood & Phœbe his Wife late Phœbe Gold,
born Nov: 29. 1807. bap June 12. 1808.

Sarah-Soame d. of Thos Cooper & Mary his Wife, late Mary
Soame, born Feb: 5. bap. June 12.

Mary d. of John Soame & Rose his Wife, late Rose Fish, born
Jan: 16. 1805 received July 3. 1808.

Samuel, s. of John Soame & Rose his Wife, born June 25. 1806
bap. July 3.

Sarah d. of John Soame & Rose his Wife, born March 11. 1808.
bap. July 10.

Thomas s. of Joseph Roberts & Mary his Wife, late Mary Pye,
born May 2. 1805 received July 10. 1808.

Margarett d. of Joseph Roberts & Mary his Wife, born June 7.
1808 bap. July 10.

John s. of Richd Bunn & Mary his Wife, late Mary Jeckell, born
Dec: 28. 1807. bap. Oct: 9. 1808.

---

[1] Delivered.

William s. of Thos Lake & Ann his Wife, late Ann Jeckell born
Sep: 20. bap. Oct: 9.

Francis s. of Edwd & Peggy Watson, late Pentein, born Oct: 22
bap. Nov: 13.

Peter s. of James Gladden & Eliz^th his Wife, late Eliz^th Peters
born Dec: 6. bap. 7. received 11.

1809. James s. of Henry Drory & Susanna his wife, late
Susanna Ives, born Jan: 19. bap. 29.

Mary-Ann d. of Wm Hastings & Mary his wife, late Mary Breeze,
born Feb: 7. bap. 12.

Elizabeth d. of Saml Neave & Hannah his wife, late Hannah
Amis, born Feb: 25. bap March 5.

Benjamin s. of Thos Hastings & Mary his Wife, late Mary Pain,
born March 14 bap. 19.

P.94. Robert s. of Edmund Jerry & Mary his Wife, late Mary Pain,
born Apr. 10. bap. 16.[1]

John s. of James & Maria Blackburn, late Maria Sutton, born
April 22. bap. May 21.

Harriot d. of Robert & Patience Pottle, late Patience Edridge,
born May 21. bap. 28.

William s. of Joseph & Mary Grix, late Mary Scarles, born May
6. bap. 28.

Elizabeth d. of W^m & Eunice Skinner, late Eunice Edwards,
born May 8. bap. June 25.

Isaac s. of Samuel & Sarah Penton, late Sarah Ubbins, born Feb:
19 bap. July 9.

Sarah d. of W^m & Sarah Wattson, late Sarah Drory, born July
14. bap. 23.

Thomas s. of James & Sarah Richardson, late Sarah Stone, born
Aug: 20 bap. Sep. 3.

Mary-Ann d. of Isaac & Phœbe Greenwood, late Phœbe Gold,
born July 29. bap. Oct: 1.

Esther d. of John & Susanna Newman, late Susanna Jeckell,
born Sep: 12. bap Oct: 1.

Elizabeth d. of James & Elizabeth Moore, late Eliz: Baker,
born June 5. bap. Oct. 15.

---

[1] Delivered at the General.

Mary d. of Mary Davey born Dec: 8. bap. 12.

John s. of George & Eliz^th Jonas, late Eliz^th Palmer, born Nov: 24 bap. Dec: 24.

1810.   Mary d. of John & Charlotte Hunt late Charlotte Pye, born Dec: 20. 1809. bap Jan: 23, 1810.

Elizabeth d. of Esther Panton born Jan: 10. bap. 23.

Elizabeth d. of John & Rose Soame, late Rose Fish, born Nov: 6. 1809. bap Feb: 4. 1810.

Charles s. of Benjamin & Eliz^th Skipp, late Eliz: Blyth, born Jan: 21 bap. Feb: 18.

Charles s. of Thomas & Ann Delph, late Ann Grand, born March 7 bap. 18.

Robert s. of James & Amy Spink, late Amy Vertegans, born Feb: 10 bap. April 1.

Edward s. of John & Frances King, late Frances Pratt, born Apr. 11. bap. 17. received May 13.[1]

P.95. Charles s. of John Cutting & Ann his wife, late Ann Baker, born May 4. bap. June 3.

James s. of Robert Edwards & Mary his wife, late Mary Palmer, spinster, born June 29 1807. bap June 10 1810.

John s. of Robert Edwards & Mary his wife, born March 6. 1810. bap. June 10.

James-Furnace s. of Margaret Greenwood born July 12. bap. 22.

Samuel s. of Saml Howard & Eliz^th his Wife, late Eliz^th Pain, born July 12. bap. Aug: 5.

John s. of James Hall & Eliz^th his wife, late Eliz: Cook, born July 8. bap. Aug: 18.

George s. of John Rice & Hannah his Wife, late Hannah Lake spinster, born July 11 bap. Aug: 19.

William s. of Joseph Roberts & Mary his wife, late Mary Pye, born June 10. bap. Aug: 23.

Benjamin s. of Benjamin Smith & Hannah his Wife, late Hannah Panton spinster born July 5. bap. Sep: 30.

Mary-Ann d. of Wm Cully & Sarah his wife, late Sarah Smithson spinster, born Sep: 15 bap. 30.

1811.   Mary d. of Eleanor Panton, born Sep 22. 1810 bap. Feb: 3. 1811.

---

[1] A Bill delivered.

Robert s. of James Smithson & Tabitha his wife, late Tabitha Shreeve, born Feb : 20. bap. Mar. 3.

Ann d. of Samuel Neave & Hannah his Wife, late Hannah Amis, born Apr. 13. bap. 28.

Samuel s. of Samuel & Ann Smith, late Ann Watson, born Apr. 18. bap May 12.[1]

William s. of John Watts & Eliz[th] his wife, late Eliz[th] Reynolds, born May 29. 1810 bap. June 23. 1811.

Mary-Ann d. of James Blackburn & Maria his Wife, late Maria Sutton, born May 28. bap June 23.

Jane d. of W[m] Jeckell & Martha his wife, late Martha Pnily, born Oct : 12. 1804 bap. Sep. 15. 1811.

Ann d. of Samuel Panton & Sarah his wife, late Sarah Ubbins, born June 30. bap. Sep : 15.

John s. of Thomas Hastings & Mary his Wife, late Mary Pain, born Aug : 25 bap. Sep : 15.

Robert s. of John Grix & Eliz[th] his Wife late Eliz[th] Bear, born June 24. bap. Sep : 15.[2]

P.96. Hannah Frostick d. of James Moore & Alice his Wife late Alice Barthram, born Aug : 24 bap. Sep. 22.

Mary d. of James Richardson & Sarah his Wife, late Sarah Stone, born Sep : 25. bap : Oct : 6.

Ann d. of Robert Pottle & Patience his Wife, late Patience Edridge, born Sep : 16 bap. Oct : 27.

John s. of Joseph Grix & Mary his wife, late Mary Scarles, born Sep : 15. bap. Oct : 29.

Mary d. of Richard Edwards & Ann his Wife, late Ann Bear, born Oct 27. 1809. bap. Nov : 3. 1811.

James s. of Isaac Greenwood & Phœbe his Wife, late Phœbe Gold, born Sep : 22. bap : Nov : 10.

1812. Sarah d. of John Newman & Susanna his Wife, late Susanna Jeckell. born Oct : 28. 1811. bap. Jan : 5. 1812.

William s. of Tho[s] Grix & Martha his Wife, late Martha Plumb, born Aug : 1. 1797. bap. Feb : 2. 1812.

John s. of Robert Mack & Mary his Wife, late Mary Amis, born Jan : 21 bap. Feb : 2.

---

[1] Delivered at the General.

[2] This page & the next signed James Bingle, Curate.

Harriot d. of Edmund Jerry & Mary his Wife, late Mary Pain,
    born Jan : 14 bap. Feb : 9.
Mary d. of Samuel Barrett & Eliz^th his Wife, late Eliz^th Oliver,
    born Jan : 14. bap. Feb : 9.
John s. of Wm Lake & Hannah his wife, late Hannah Blyth,
    born Mar. 29. bap. Apr. 11. rec^d May 3.
Charlotte d. of John & Frances King, late Pratt, born Mar. 29.
    bap. Apr. 11.
Leonard Drory s. of W^m & Sarah Watson, late Sarah Drory,
    born Apr. 26. bap. May 3.
John s. of Samuel Cook & Hannah his Wife late Hannah
    Roberts, born May 1 bap. 10.
Amelia d. of John Soame & Rose his Wife, late Rose Fish, born
    March 25 bap. May 31.
Thomas s. of Thomas Delph & Ann his Wife late Ann Grand,
    born May 19 bap May 31.[1]
Thomas s. of Lily Wiley, born May 4. 1808. bap June 28 1812.
William & Mary, Twins, s. & d. of Eliz^th Gabbareth, born Apr.
    27. bap June 28.
Margarett, d. of Willm Hastings & Mary his Wife, late Mary
    Breeze, born Aug : 20. bap. 30.
John s. of Willm Cully & Sarah his wife, late Sarah Smithson
    born sep. 19 bap. oct : 11.
Mary d. of Nelly Panton, born July 17. bap. oct : 4.
P.97. Mary d. of Joseph Grix & Mary his Wife, late Mary Scarles, born
    Oct : 26 bap. Nov : 22. 1812.[1]

P. 1. [2]   BURIALS 1738—1812.

1738.   Elisabeth Everard was buried April 5.
        James Sherwood was buried March 1.
        Edward Peartree was buried June 6.
        Mary Oats was buried June 11.
        Ann Watts was buried October 10.
        Mary Jeckel was buried November 11.

---

[1] Delivered at the Generals.
[2] The Burials follow the Baptisms but are paged independently.

Nath : Greenwood was buried November 21.

James Jeckel was buried March 10.

1739.   Elisabeth Jeckel was buried April 22.

Ursula Jeckel was buried June 2.

William Davy was buried June 3.

Francis Barns was buried July 23.

Lucy Oats was buried September 18.

Sarah Greenwood was buried September 24.

John Fox was buried October 2.

Thomas Barns was buried October 12.

1740.   Elizabeth Woods was buried April 8.

Elisabeth Harding was buried April 9.

William Farmer was buried May 20.

Samuel Lubbock was buried July 8.

Edmund Jeckel was buried July 20.

Richard Jeckel was buried December 26.

P. 2. 1742.   John Green an old man was buried Jan^{ry} 21.

Edward Green, s. of the said John was buried Feb^{ry} 14.

1743.   Isaac Ward buried April 29.

John Saunders October 16.

Elizabeth Thompson October 19.

1744.   John Pearson February 15.

1745.   Amy Green an old woman was buried May 9.

1747.   *Christiana Woods buried June 1.*[1]

John Watson buried June 3.[1]

Philippa Bly buried June 29.[1]

Ann Bly buried June 29.[1]

1747.   John Ward August 9.

John Oats August 10.

Jonathan Everet August 24.

Ann Everet August 24.

Lucy Oats August 27.

Robert Oates September 2.

Tryphena Everet September 3.

Sarah Barker September 24.

Ann Oliver October 25.

[1] Supplied from Transcript in Diocesan Registry.

P. 3.　　John Ward November 9.
John Delph November 10.
Rebekah Ward December 6.
Ann Bly December 23.
Ann Lubbock January 3.
1748.　Caleb Everet April 4.
Hannah Watson an Infant October 11.
Robert Peartree a man October 30.
William Brier a young man December 8.
James Daines an Infant February 8.

SAM^L DYBALL　　　　　　　　　NATH^{EL} PONDER
JOHN GREEN—CHURCHWARDENS.　　RECTOR.

1749.　Robert Harding a Man July 15.
Lydia Hartley a Woman[1] August 8.
Anne d. of Sarah Manning an Infant Sep: 21.
Mary, Wife of Samuel Wiley October 28.
Robert Tramplett a Man December 28.
Mary Scott an old Woman February 6.
Edward Stageman an Infant Feb^{ry} 11.
Martha Jeckel, widow February 20.
John s. of Luke & Sarah Thompson Feb^{ry} 27.
John Oates an old Man March 9.
[2]Robert *Olfe an infant March 20.*
P. 4. 1750.　Thomas Page an old man June 20.
Susanna Mitchell a woman May 13.
Mary Green an Infant September 8.
Anne Lubbock a young woman Sep: 29.
Elizabeth Hastings a woman October 2.
Ellen Doughty a Woman November 14.
Robert Mann an Infant December 6.
John Marsham an Infant December 18.
Rose Scotto an old woman Jan^{ry} 13.
Legget Legget a Lad January 31.

---

[1] *Widow* in Transcript.
[2] The rest of this entry has been cut off by the binder, but is supplied from the Transcript at Norwich.

Sarah Farmar an old Woman February 10.

SAM^L DYBALL CHURCHWARDENS.   NATH^L PONDER
JOHN GREEN   RECTOR.

1751   Anne Smithson an Infant March 28.
       Henry Harper a Man April 15.
       John Wattson a Man May 22.
       John Hunt a Man June 7.
       Robert Amplefer a Man June 11.
       Jacob Blyth a Man July 2.
       Anne West an Infant July 5.
       Anne Man a Woman September 11.
       Mary Bailey an Infant from Briston Sep : 15.
       Susanna Barnes a young Woman Novr 1.
       Matthias Stageman an Infant December 10.
       Isaac Blyth a man December 15.[1]
P. 5. [1740.[2]   Elisabeth Blyth was buried Jan : 4.
       Susanna Delf was buried March 1.
       John Hains was buried March 27.]
1751.   Frances Gedge an old Woman Decem : 25.
1752.   John Jeckel an old Man Jan : 28.[3]
       John Medler an old man March 6.
       Mary Jeckel, widow, an old Woman March 26.
       John Delph a Man April 9.
       Elizabeth Olfe an Infant April 9.
       Thomas Spantin an Infant May 12.
       Edward Peartree an Infant May 16.
       Sarah Everett an old woman July 1.
       Samuel Wily an Infant July 29.
       John Green a Man August 23.
       Samuel Dyball, gent, August 25.
       Abigal Thompson an Infant August 25.
       James Sturman an Infant Decr 5.
       William Sparin an Infant Decr 10.

---

[1] Cut by binder, but verified.
[2] These 3 entries in same hand & ink as rest of 1740.
[3] New style begins.

Robert Pert a man Decr 14.
Nicholas Mann a man Decr 31.

JOHN VERTEGANS CHURCHWARDEN.   NATH^{EL} PONDER
RECTOR.

P. 6. 1753.   John Jeckell an old man March 24.
Anne Pierson a young Woman March 28.
Jonathan Daines an Infant June 4.
Amy Bacon a young woman June 10.
Amy Green an Infant August 11.
Mary Jeckell, wife of Richd Jeckell Aug: 23.
Honour Greenwood an Infant Sep: 10.
Elizabeth Doughty an Infant October 9.
Thomas Davy an Infant October 12.
Sarah Wattson an Infant October 29.
Mary Hastings a young Woman Novr 4.
Matthew Penteny[1] an Infant Novr 5.
John Marsham a Lad Novr 12.
Andrew Gibson a Man Decem: 2.

JOHN VERTEGANS CH. WARDEN.   NATH^{EL} PONDER REC^{TR}

1754.   Mary Oates a young Woman January 19.
Samuel & Robert Wily, Infants & Twins Jan: 23.
Robert Wattson a Man February 9.
Joseph Barker an Infant February 14.
Elizabeth Hunt an Infant February 17.
James Bear a young Man February 22.[2]
Jemima Barker a Woman March 10.
Robert Bear an old man March 25.
Sarah Bear a young Woman March 28.
John Barney an old man April 12.[3]

P. 7.   James, illeg^{te} s. of Susanna Woods, an Infant Apr: 1.
Samuel Lubbock a Man April 2.
Mary Barker an Infant April 22.
Thomasin Oats a young woman April 27.

---

[1] *Spantin* in Register Bill.
[2] "Son of Robert & Tryphena, aged 28."—M.I.
[3] Cut by binder.

Robert Oats an Infant April 29.
Richard Oates a man May 3.
Richard Jeckell an Infant May 19.
Kezia Barker an Infant June 11.
Luke Tompson a man July 3.
Amy Stageman an Infant July 15.
Sarah Doughty an Infant August 5.
William Lubbock an Infant Sep : 16.
John Edwards an Infant Sep : 22.
Mary Scott an Infant from Blickling Sep : 22.
Mary Thornton a Woman Sep : 23.
Honour Lubbock an Infant Sep : 27.
Elizabeth Wiley a Woman October 1.
Elizabeth Shaftin an old woman October 11.
Martha Davidson an old woman October 18.
Anne Jeckell a' young woman October 21.
Sarah West a Girl November 7.
Frances Penteny an Infant November 16.
Elizabeth Blyth widow November 26.
Sarah Wattson a young woman November 27.
Francis Penteny an Infant November 28.
Sarah Betts an Infant December 22.
William Brier Bunn an Infant Decr 24.

P. 8. 1755.   Jacob Wiley an Infant Jan : 9.
Robert Olfe an Infant Feb^{ry} 7.
Alice Collman an old woman April 15.
Mary Gedge an old woman April 19.
William Wattson a young man April 30.
James Gaze an Infant May 8.
Mary, the wife of Thomas Scott May 10.
William Sparin an Infant May 11.
Sarah Fox an Infant May 13.
Mary Peartree an old woman May 18.
Barbara Ward an Infant June 8.
John Ward a Man from Dilham June 22.
Mary Marsham a young Woman July 18.
John Delph an Infant August 2.
Sarah Herring an Infant August 8.

Elizabeth Edwards an Infant August 19.
Thomas Burrage a young man Aug: 31.
Richard Edwards an Infant Sep: 2.
Michael Wilde an Infant Sep: 4.
Robert Wattson a Man Sep: 12.
Samuel Lubbock an old man & Parish Clark Sep: 14.
David Lubbock a young man Sep: 17.
Mary Jeckell an Infant October 23.
William Greenwood a young man Nov[r] 10.
Richard Berney a young man Nov[r] 12.
Henry Danna a man October 28.
John Davidson an old man Nov[r] 30.
James Jolly an old man December 9.

P. 9. 1756.   John Lubbock an Infant February 6.
Thomas Wattson an Infant March 16.
Mary Jeckell an old woman March 16. `
Mary Betts an Infant April 2.
William Marsham an old man April 3.[1]
Edward Stageman an Infant June 13.
John Thompson an Infant June 25.
Thomas Harding an old man July 9.
William Lubbock a Man and Parish Clark July 15.
Martha Morris a married woman Sep: 19.
An Infant of Will[m] Dunnett[2] Sep: 19.
Nathaniel Ponder Rector of this Parish Oct[r] 23.
Sarah Laxion Dec[r] 11.

1757.   Mary Oats Jan: 2.
Jemima Woods, Infant—Jan: 6.
Elizabeth Greene—Jan: 30.
Sarah Bear aged 85—March 23.
Ursula Tramplin aged 84—March 25.
Robert Wattson, Infant—April 14.[3]
Ann Pearson, Infant June 23.
Christopher Stageman Infant July 31.
Janet Gordon, Infant August 21.

---

[1] A Bill carried to the Generals May 7.
[2] *William Dunnett an Infant*, in Reg[r] Bill.
[3] A Bill carried to the Generals May 13.

Thomas Watson, Infant Sep : 4.
Robert Ward, Infant Sep : 8.
Samuel Everett Oct[r] 9.
William Betts Nov[r] 13.
Elizabeth Press Nov[r] 14.
P. 10. John Watson December 4.
George Alexander Dec[r] 6.
1758. William Laxton Jan : 3.
Sarah Alexander Jan : 27.
Esther Greenwood March 5.
James Greenwood April 20.
Bridget Pearson May 7.
Thomas Scott May 15.
William Watson, Infant, May 19.
Elizabeth Watson Sep : 3.
Mary Jeckel, Infant Oct[r] 9.
Thomas Pearson Nov[r] '8.
Hammond Smithson Nov[r] 28.
1759. Christian Fox Jan : 6.
Christian Neeve Feb : 14.
Richard Hannant March 8.
Robert Jeckil March 11.
John Hammond, Infant April 30.[1]
Samuel Greene, Infant May 13.
Susanna Lake May 14.
Ann Watson July 3.
Daniel Everet July 16.
Frances Gazeley July 26.
Elizabeth Boswell August 14.
Robert Bloy, Infant Aug : 16.
William Hammond Aug : 19.
Thomas Smith Sep : 3.
Sarah Ward Sep : 7.
P. 11. Susanna Jeckel Sep : 18.
Elizabeth Watson Sep : 21.
Elizabeth Bunn, Infant Oct : 10.

---

[1] A Bill carried to the Generals, May 11.

1760.   Elizabeth Spink April 30
       Stephen Davy May 12.
       Ann Port June 3.
       Mary Hastings June 14.
       Sarah Stageman July 16.[1]
       Sarah Watson Aug: 31.
       Elizabeth Watson, Infant, Sep: 16.
       Thomas Grix Sep: 14.
       Elizabeth Doughty Oct: 26.
       Phœbe Ward Oct: 28.
       Susanna Lake Nov: 10.
       Andrew Hastings Nov: 17.
       Elizabeth Whiley Nov: 21.
       Ann Harding Dec: 14.
1761.   Mary Hammond Jan: 7.
       Elizabeth Dains Feb: 26.
       Edward Peartree May 3.
       Elizabeth Barker June 22.
       Mary Saunders Aug: 3.
       Ann Lubbock Aug: 16.
       Margaret Barney Sep: 2.
       Margaret Jeckell Sep: 18.
       Richard Pain, Infant, Sep: 18.
       John Mack, Infant, Sep: 30.
       Sarah Betts Oct: 4.
       Mary Everet Oct: 16.
       James Crotch Dec: 2.
       Rebecca Crotch Dec: 18.
P.12. 1762.   John Sutton Jan: 10.
       John Collison April 4.
       John Ollfe April 13.
       John Wiley April 19.
       Mary Dey June 13.
       James Starling July 1.
       Mary Woods Aug: 19.
       Sarah Davy Aug: 29.

---

[1] A Bill carried to the Generals.

Thomasin Browne Sep: 19.
Isaac Harding Oct: 7.
John Blyth, Infant, Nov: 8.
Margaret Doughty Nov: 19.
Sarah Fox, Infant, Dec: 9.
Christian Earl Dec: 12.
Ann Earl Dec: 12.
Robert Oats Dec: 19.
1763.   Sarah Lubbock Jan: 9.
Susanna Lake Jan: 23.
James Ollifer Jan: 23.
Richard Delph Jan: 31.
Arthur Lake Feb: 1.
Jane Ollifer Feb: 1.
Sarah Ward Feb: 3.
Elizabeth Whiley Feb: 27.
Elizabeth Stageman March 20.
Timothy Blyth March 29.
Elizabeth Jeckell April 1.
James Dains May 1.
Phœbe Grand May 1.
Ursula Harding May 3.
John Betts May 8.[1]
P. 13.   Isaac Fox June 8.
Elizabeth Medler Aug: 3.
Caleb Blyth a married man Aug: 11.
Ann Wattson Sep: 26.
Mary Davy Oct: 8.
Thomas Fox Oct: 30.
Samuel Greene, Infant, Nov: 28.
Susanna Wild Dec: 9.
1764.   Elizabeth Pain, Infant, Jan: 26.
James Newman, Infant Feb: 2.
William Watson, Infant, March 11.
Samuel Root, Infant, March 28.
William Everet, Infant, April 15.

[1] A Bill carried to the Bp's Visitation.

Margaret Fox April 22.
Robert Peartree April 30.[1]
Sarah Edwards June 23.
? Aron Delph July 20.
John Watson July 30.
Ruben Peartree, Infant, Aug : 26.
Mary Lake, an infant, Sep : 17.
Arthur Lake, an infant, Octob : 10.
John Vertegans Dec : 20.
1765.   Joseph Grix Feb : 3.
Joseph Jeckell Feb : 5.
William Blyth Feb : 12.
Mary Ward March 24.
Rachel Amplefer April 3.
John s. of John & Mary Bloy May 10.[1]
P. 14.   Elizabeth Jeckell buried May 24.
Stephen Everett buried June 9.
John Moll buried June 12.
Ann Lake buried June 21.
Benjamin Jeckell, Infant, buried July 7.
Jonathan Ulph buried July 25.
Webster Everett buried Aug : 8.
James Riches buried Aug : 28.
Sarah Crome buried Oct : 13.
1766.   Robert Ivory, Infant, buried Feb : 2.
Robert Pain, Infant, buried Feb : 17.
Mary Marsham buried March 6.
Robert Tompson buried March 21.
John Fletcher buried May 7.[1]
Charles Watson buried May 20.
Sarah Hart buried May 26.
Phœbe Edwards buried June 8.
John Key buried July 7.
Benjamin Ulph buried Nov : 18.
Robert Thornton buried Dec : 12.
1767.   Amy Vertegans buried Jan : 13.

---

[1] A Bill carried to the Generals.

James Grix buried Feb: 24.
John Watson, Infant, buried March 1.
Mary Durrant buried April 6.
Rose Riches buried April 23.
Mary Boswell buried April 28.[1]
Mary Moll buried May 17.
William Jeckell buried May 24.
Grace Lubbock buried June 9.
P. 15.   John Lubbock buried June 14.
James Tompson buried June 14.
Jacob Wood buried June 14.
Rachel Greenwood buried June 14.
Rebecca Harding aged 87 buried June 17.
Rachael Jeckell buried June 28.
Benjamin Ulph buried July 5.
John Pain buried July 8.
Fanny Pain buried July 8.
Ann Scott buried Aug: 4.
Elizabeth Rud buried Aug: 9.
Elizabeth Davison buried Oct: 11.
Elizabeth Earle buried Nov: 19.
John Moll buried Nov: 29.
1768.   John Spink buried Jan: 13.
Thomas Mann buried Jan: 17.
Tryphena Bear buried Feb: 7.
Mary Hammond buried Feb: 1.
Judith Browne buried April 13.
Ann Earle buried April 27.[1]
Sarah Scott buried May 5.
Mary Wiley buried May 12.
Thomas Wattson buried May 20.
Thomas Wiley buried May 25.
Roger Hammond buried Sep: 11.
Moses Delph buried Sep: 18.
Robert Jeckell buried Oct: 20.
Judith Jeckell buried Nov: 25.
1769.   Mary Wattson buried March 26.

---

[1] A Bill carried to the Generals.

Francis Palmer buried April 14.
Aaron Key buried May 18.
James Rudd buried May 18.[1]
P. 16.   Mary Dyball buried May 26.
Ann Lubbock buried May 28.
Susan Weddlock buried June 25.
John Crow buried July 18.
Phœbe Everet buried Nov: 9.
John Vertegans buried Nov: 17.
1770.   John Mack buried Jan: 23.
Robert Tramplett buried Feb: 4.
Mary Newman buried March 4.
Mary Earle buried May 6.
Elizabeth Wattson buried May 22.
Hannah Lubbock buried June 15.[2]
Susan d. of Ann Fox buried Aug: 5.
Ann Smithson buried Oct: 14.
Robert Laxton buried Nov: 4.
John Miller Vertegans buried Nov: 4.
Ann Barnard buried Nov: 4.
Rachel Watson buried Nov: 14.
Thomas Watson buried Nov: 14.
Hannah Watson buried Dec: 2.
Sarah Grix buried Dec: 6.
Ann ? Rose buried Dec: 30.
1771.   Charles Fox buried Jan: 20.
Mary Daines buried March 10.
Charlotte Pye buried March 13.
Mary Harding buried March 27.
Elizabeth Harding buried April 14.
Elizabeth Grix buried May 5.
Ann Lubbock buried May 5.[1]
Peggy Lubbock buried July 7.
Elizabeth Clift buried July 24.
P. 17.   Elizabeth Spantin buried Sep: 8.

[1] A Bill carried to the Generals.
[2] A Bill carried to the Visitation.

William Wattson buried Sep : 15.
Ann Dewing buried Oct : 29.
Spicer Crow buried Nov : 10.
1772.   Bridget Greene buried Jan : 19.
Elizabeth Bloy buried Jan : 19.
Charles Southgate buried Feb : 18.
William Crow buried Feb : 23.
Paul Thurston buried Feb : 23.
William Jeckell buried March 22.
James Key buried April 5.[1]
Edmund Jeckell buried April 19.
Stephen Stone buried May 3.
Ann Fox buried May 26.
Samuel Wiley buried June 2.
John Everet buried June 2.
John Vertegans buried June 28.
Elizabeth Key buried Aug : 5.
Ann Watson buried Aug : 11.
Richard Jeckell buried Sep : 10.
John Jeckell buried Nov : 8.
Judith Smithson buried Dec : 10.
1773.   Robert Woods, Infant, buried Jan : 5.
Thomas Lake buried Feb : 7.
Ann Durrant buried Feb : 28.
Susanna Durrant, Infant, buried Feb : 28.
Stephen Jeckell buried April 7.
Richard Edwards buried May 11.
Robert Jeckell buried May 18.[1]
John Rose, Infant, buried June 13.
Jonathan Everett buried Oct : 6.
Elizabeth Blyth buried Nov. 15.
1774.   Nathaniel Key buried Jan : 16.
Francis Manning buried April 10.
P. 18.   Jane Jeckell buried May 1.[1]
William Pearson buried May 18.
Elizabeth Daines buried May 22.
William Colman aged 84 buried Aug : 5.

---

[1] A Bill delivered at the Generals.

Amy Vertegans buried Aug : 8.
John Crow buried Aug : 14.
Ann Laxton buried Sep : 1.
John Smith buried Sep : 8.
Denys Jeckell buried Sep : 25.
Judith Jeckell buried Oct 23.
Theophilus Pye buried Nov : 2.
Thomas Grix buried Nov : 29.
Mary Saunders buried Dec : 6.

1775.   William Bear buried Feb : 5.
William Parker buried March 19.
Sarah Key buried April 9.
Samuel Smith buried April 9.
Benjamin Jeckell buried April 24.[1]
Joshua Everett buried Aug : 20.
Phœbe Marsham 89 years old buried Oct : 2.
Joseph Pain buried Oct : 29.
Robert Spurrell buried Nov : 29.
William Dunnitt buried Dec : 17.
Richard Bunn buried Dec : 20.

1776.   Elizabeth Bullock buried Jan : 17.
Elizabeth Barker buried Jan : 31.
Sarah Oats buried March 10.
Robert Rudd buried March 26.[1]
Mary Vertegans buried May 28.
James Woods, Infant, buried June 29.
Elizabeth Everett buried July 12.
John Earle buried July 31.
Hannah Smith, Infant, buried Aug : 7.
Mary Laxton buried Aug : 13.

P. 19. 1777.   Samuel Smith Jan : 26.
John Aldridge buried Feb : 9.
Mary Dunnitt buried Feb : 9.
Phœbe Marsham buried March 16.
Esther Case buried March 16.
James Ward buried March 19.
William Jeckell buried May 12.

---

[1] A Bill delivered at the Generals.

Phœbe Grand buried May 15.
Ann Stageman buried May 18.
William Grand, Infant, buried May 25.[1]
John Woods, an Infant, buried July 2.
John Jeckell buried July 27.
Samuel Ward buried Aug: 22.
Elizabeth Sterman buried Sep: 24.
Sarah King, Infant, buried Sep: 24.
Sarah Sterman buried Oct: 5.
Edward Denny buried Nov: 4.
Richard Jeckell buried Dec: 18.
1778.   Samuel Watson buried March 1.
Richard Delph buried March 8.
Mary Killigrew buried March 11.[2]
Thomas Gazely buried May 29.
Thomas Sterman, Infant, buried Aug: 20.[2]
1779.   Ann Harding buried June 13.
John Burrell buried July 18.
William Thompson buried Nov: 7.
Elizabeth Gazley buried Nov: 12.
Susanna Durrant buried Dec: 5.
1780.   John Pyle buried Feb: 25.
John Lubbock buried March 1.
Sarah Delph buried March 21.[2]

P. 20.   Sarah. illeg[te] d. of Mary Greenwood buried July 18.
Phœbe Pearson buried July 25.
Sarah Harris buried Aug. 15.
William Thain buried Sep: 11.
Elizabeth Hunt buried Sep: 17.
Isabella Killigrew buried Oct: 1.
Martha Smith buried Oct: 20.
Susanna Pain buried Nov: 5.
Ann Watson buried Dec: 24.
1781.   Sarah Newman buried Jan: 21.
Ann Rhodes buried March 4.
Robert Rudd buried March 25.[2]

---

[1] A Bill delivered at the Visitation.
[2] A Bill delivered at the Generals.

Sarah Pye buried July 15.
Mary Coman buried Sep : 9.
Sarah Gibson buried Oct : 22.
Samuel Lubbock buried Nov : 11.
Shadrach Ives buried Dec : 4.
Mary Lubbock buried Dec : 11.
William Edwards buried Dec : 25.
1782.   Rebecca Seaman buried Feb : 3.
Ann Sutton buried March 3.
Richard Deeker buried March 17.[1]
William Barnard buried April 18.
John Barthram buried April 24.
Mary Ann Smithson buried June 2.
Elizabeth Beaver buried June 23.
John Smith buried July 14.
John Bloy buried Aug : 6.
Elizabeth Pentein buried Aug : 22.
George Jonas buried Sep : 1.
Mary Barker buried Sep : 13.
Ann Jonas buried Sep : 17.
Elizabeth Bunn buried Sep : 22.
P. 21.   Richard Killigrew buried Sep : 29.
Samuel Smith buried Oct : 2.
Deborah Killigrew buried Oct : 8.
John Barker buried Oct : 13.
Elizabeth Everett buried Oct : 15.
Ann Fletcher buried Oct : 27.
Mary Edwards buried Oct : 29.
Isaac Blyth buried Nov : 8.
Frances Palmer buried Nov : 13.
Philemon Palmer buried Dec : 3.
Sarah Daines buried Dec : 13.
Melinda Killigrew buried Dec : 13.
William Jeckel buried Dec : 14.
Pettis Delph buried Dec : 19.
Edmund Jeckell buried Dec : 23.
1783.   Rose Davy buried Jan : 13.

---

[1] A Bill delivered at the Generals.

Elizabeth Jeckell buried Jan : 15.
Elizabeth Lubbock buried Feb : 20.
Thomas Doughty buried Feb : 26.
Paul Deeker buried Feb : 27.
Rebecca Sursham buried March 8.
Joshua Ward buried March 9.
Robert Watson buried March 14.[1]
Margaret Key buried May 11.
Ann Thompson buried May 23.
John Daines buried June 1.
Elizabeth Pentein buried June 25.
Amy Pentein buried July 20.
Frances Ann Page buried Aug : 3.
Susanna Jeckell buried Aug : 17.
Mary Saunders buried Sep : 6.
William Middleton buried Sep : 21.
Michael Whiley (Collectioner, no Tax) buried Dec : 1.
William Collison buried Dec : 3.
Sarah Minns buried Dec : 7.
John Davy buried Dec : 19.
Hester Davy buried Dec : 19.
William Smith buried Dec : 21.

P.22. 1784.   Sarah Batchelor buried Jan : 22.
Elizabeth Grand, Collectioner, buried Feb : 3.
Isaac Blyth buried March 4.
Sarah Narbroo, Collectioner, buried March 9.
Joseph Blyth buried March 12.
John Hunt buried March 27.[2]
James Woods buried June 2.
Samuel Jeckell buried June 21.
Mary Smith buried Sep : 26.
Michael Davy, buried Sep : 30.
Hannah Blyth, Collectioner, buried Oct : 3.

[Rec[d] 3 shillings for the Duty on Burialls from Oct 1. 1783 to Oct 1.
1784—Robert Francis for John Gay Jun[r] Collector.]

---

[1] A Bill delivered at the Generals.
[2] A Bill delivered at the Visitation.

Joseph Lubbock, Collectioner, buried Dec : 22.

1785.   John Greene, Collectioner, buried Jan : 14.

John Green buried Jan : 14.

Isaac Vertegans, Collectioner, buried Jan : 20.

Mary Jeckell buried Feb : 9.

Jane Cawston, Collectioner, buried Feb : 22.

Sarah Delph buried March 14.

Grace Sterman buried March 27.

Judith Jeckell, Collectioner, buried March 27.[2]

Mary Peartree was buried May 8.

Margaret Watson, Collectioner, buried June 26.

Thomas Morrill, Infant, buried July 21.

William Pain buried Aug : 5.

William Marsham buried Sep : 7.

John Crow buried Sep : 8.

Mary Rhodes buried Sep : 18.[1]

Henry Sterman buried Oct : 9.

William Bear buried Oct : 17.

Jane Meads buried Oct : 23.

John Dains, Collectioner, buried Nov : 20.

William Peartree buried Nov : 21.

1786.   Martha Gaze buried Jan : 24.

Robert Durrant, Collectioner, buried March 31.[2]

Jane Daines, Collectioner, buried June 11.

P. 23.   Robert Thompson, Collectioner, buried June 28.

Susanna Barker, Collectioner, buried July 16.

Richard Sterman buried Aug : 24.

Robert Thompson, Collectioner, buried Sep : 3.

Mary Woods buried Sep : 3.

Elizabeth Morrill buried Sep : 8.

Elizabeth Barnard, Collectioner, buried Oct : 1[3]

Sarah Hunt buried Oct : 15.

Robert Smith buried Nov : 26.

1787.   Mary Sutton buried Jan : 29.

Maria Middleton buried Feb : 15.

---

[1] Duty P^d to 1 Oct. 1785.
[2] A Bill delivered at the Generals.
[3] Duty P^d to 1 Oct 1786.

Elizabeth Dunnett buried Feb: 21.

James Key buried Feb: 25.

Sarah Bear buried March 6.

Ann Pain buried March 11.

Esther Blyth, Collectioner, buried March 16.

William Jeckell buried April 1.[1]

Elizabeth Lubbock, pauper, buried April 24.

Davy Shreeve buried April 28.

John Jonas buried May 29.

Mary Fletcher buried May 29.

Samuel Tungate aged 48 years buried Aug: 1.[2]

Elizabeth wife of James Hastings, late Eliz[th] Comau spinster, aged 46 years, buried Nov: 5.

John Dains aged 48 years buried Dec: 25 P.[3]

Susannah wife of John Dains buried Dec: 28. P.

1788. Thomas Gazely aged 36 years buried Jan: 26. P.

Sarah d. of Rob[t] Smithson & Sarah his Wife buried April 6.[4]

W^M JEWELL, CURATE.[5]

Elizabeth Dunnett, wife of John Dunnett, late Eliz: Grix spinster buried May 11. aged 29. P.

Thomas s. of John & Sarah Davy, late Sarah Watson, buried June 17 aged 6 years. P.

Rose Medler, wife of W[m] Medler of Hevingham, aged 68 years buried July 4.

John s. of Samuel & Martha Smith, late Martha Rogers, an Infant, buried July 27. P.

Christopher Stageman aged 67, buried Aug 20. P.[6]

Sarah, wife of John Lawes, late Sarah Davidson, aged 39, buried Oct: 31.

Ann d. of W[m] & Ann Hastings, late Ann Pye, an infant, buried Dec: 14.

---

[1] Delivered at the Generals.

[2] Duty P[d] to 1 Oct. 1787.

[3] P.—pauper.

[4] Delivered.

[5] This page & the following 10 so signed.

[6] Duty Pd. to October 1. 1788.

Mary Thompson, widow, aged 35, buried Dec: 21.

1789.   Thomas s. of Isaac & Hannah Watson, late Hannah Heath, buried Jan: 25. *P.*

P. 25.   Elizabeth, wife of John Pantin aged 60, bur. Mar. 10.

Hannah d. of Matthew Jeckle & Phœbe his Wife, late Phœbe Lubbock, an infant, buried Mar. 15. *P.*

Diana d. of Samuel & Mary Soame, late Mary Greenwood, an infant, buried Mar. 29.

Ann Moppitt, aged 71, buried April 8.

Hannah Gazely, widow, buried April 27.

Lorina d. of Samuel & Mary Soame, late Mary Greenwood, an infant, buried Sep: 8

Thomas Mack buried Sep: 28.[1]

1790.   Elizabeth d. of John & Mary Gaze, late Mary Playford, buried Jan: 25 an Infant.

P. 26.   Philip s of Philip Garrett & Dinah his wife late Dinah Greenwood, an infant, bur. Feb: 7. *P.*

William Jeckell aged 49, buried Feb: 11. *P.*

Sarah, wife of John Davey, aged 36, bur. March 1.[1]

Rachel d. of James Greenwood & Hannah his wife, an infant, buried April 25. *P.*[1]

Ann d. of Abraham & Mary Blyth, late Mary Lubbock, aged 6 years, buried July 6. *P.*

Sarah d. of Samuel & Sarah Smith, an infant, buried 20 July. *P.*

Sarah wife of John Blythe, late Sarah Rudd, buried Sep: 28 aged 33 years. *P.*

1791.   Henry s. of James Cook & Frances his wife late Frances Buddle, aged 10 years, bur. Jan: 17.

P. 27.   Phillis Colman wife of John, aged 60, bur. Feb: 20.

John s. of Matthew & Phœbe Jeckel, late Phœbe Lubbock, an infant, buried March 20.

John s. of John & Sarah Blythe, late Sarah Rudd, aged 2 years, buried March 28. *P.*

John Daines, aged 20 years, buried March 30. *P.*

James s. of James & Eliz[th] Gladden, infant, bur. May 1.

---

[1] **Delivered at the General.**

William Boswell, aged 59, bur. May 17. *P.*[1]

George Drory, aged 51, bur. Oct 7. *P.*

Laurina d. of Sam[l] & Mary Soame, infant, Nov: 20.

P. 29. Robert, s. of Rob[t] Edwards & Eliz[th] his wife, late Eliz:
Blythe, bur. Nov: 23, aged 46.

William Riches, aged 58, bur. Dec: 15.

1792. Ann Fletcher, aged 84, bur. March 11.[2]

Elizabeth Ward, aged 75, bur. July 3. *P.*

Frances Crotch, aged 93, bur. Oct. 14. *P.*

George s. of John & Mary Bransby, infant, bur. Oct: 15.

Elizabeth wife of Edward Delph, late Eliz: Rice, buried
Nov: 2, aged 49. *P.*

1793. Sarah Palmer, widow, aged 69, bur. Feb: 19. *P.*

Samuel s. of Eliz[th] Case, infant. bur. Feb: 24. *P.*

Hannah widow of Rob[t] Durrant bur Mar: 12. *P.*[2]

P. 29. Stephen Davy, of Aylesham, aged 70, bur. Apr. 19.

Mary d. of W[m] & Eliz[th] Marsham, aged 22, bur. Apr: 19.

David s. of W[m] & Eliz[th] Paine, late Eliz: Crotch, aged 14
years, buried May 30. *P.*

Robert Edwards, aged 79, bur. Sep: 3. *P.*

James s. of Joseph & Ann Newman, late Ann Barnes, bur.
Oct: 22, aged 28 years.

Ann, widow of Christopher Stageman, aged 82, buried Oct:
23. *P.*

1794. Noah Laxon, aged 50, bur. Jan: 21. *P.*

Ann d. of John & Eliz[th] Laws, late Eliz: Barker, infant,
bur. Feb: 5. *P.*[3]

P. 30. Thomas s. of Tho[s] & Ann Smithson, late Ann Edwards, an
infant, bur. Sep. 25. *P.*[2]

1795. Mary d. of John & Mary Bramsby, late Mary Plane, bur.
May 3. aged 40 years.

Phillis d. of Abraham & Mary Blythe, late Mary Lubbock,
bur. May 18 aged 14 years.

Mary d. of Tho[s] & Ann Delph, late Ann Grand, bur. June 7,
an infant.

---

[1] Delivered at the Visitation 1791.
[2] Delivered at the General.
[3] Delivered at the Visitation.

Joseph Hastings, aged 70, bur. August 5.

Richard s. of John & Susanna Lake, bur. Dec: 6 aged 18
years. [1]

1796.   Ruth Ash aged 97 bur. May 2.

Caleb s. of Caleb & Alice Blythe, infant, bur. May 2.

P. 31.   Mary, wife of Robt Smithson, late Mary Smith spinster,
buried May 8, aged 61 years.

Mary Crome, aged 67, buried May 10.

Isaac s. of Robt & Susanna Watson, late Susanna Watson
spinster, aged 21, buried Aug: 3.

Christopher s. of John & Elizth Laws, infant bur. Aug: 3.

Elizabeth, wife of John Laws, aged 43, bur. Aug: 23.

Stephen Ward, aged 86, buried Oct: 8.

John s. of W^m & Mary Goodwin, late Mary King, buried
Oct: 21, aged 6 years.

Henry s. of W^m & Mary Goodwin, bur. Nov. 21, aged 5 yrs.

P.32. 1797.   Charles Davison, aged 78, bur. Jan: 22.

Thomas s. of John & Mary Gaze, infant, bur. Feb: 5. [2]

Mary Dyball d. of Samuel & Mary Dyball aged 58, buried
April 15.

Davy s. of Wm Payne & Elizth his wife, late Elizth Dix, an
infant, bur. April 17.

William Cory, aged upwards 60 years, bur. Apr. 19.

Mary Lubbock, aged 64 years, bur. Aug: 3.

Ann, wife of John King, late Ann Vertegans, bur. Aug: 7.,
aged 63 years.

Rebecca d. of James & Elizth Hastings, bur Aug: 11, an
infant.

Sarah Steward, aged (?) 38, bur. Sep: 3.

William s. of Robt Hasslelup & Mary his wife, buried Sep:
10, an infant.

P.33. 1798.   Isaac s. of Isaac & Ann Blythe, bur. Jan: 31. aged 14.

Isaac Blythe, aged 48, bur. Feb: 18.

Thomas Hunt, aged 56, bur. March 1.

John s. of Sarah Grix, aged 9, bur March 11. [3]

---

[1] Delivered at the General.

[2] Delivered.

[3] Delivered at the Generals.

Sarah Palmer, aged 30, bur. April 3.

Susanna Whiley, aged 22, bur April 5.

Richard Jeckel, aged 78, bur. April 12.

Ann Fox, aged 64, bur April 22.

Mary Bridgeman, wife of—[1] Bridgeman aged 29, bur. April 22.

Mary, Wife of Stephen Jeckel bur May 10 aged 64 years.

Lydia, d. of George & Ann Drory, bur May 21, aged 14.

P. 34.   Esther d. of John & Mary Bransby, late Mary Plane, bur. June 17, aged 3 years.

Sarah wife of Robt Jeckle, late Sarah Gibson, bur. July 4, aged 59 years.

James s. of James & Frances Greenwood, bur. August 28, aged 3 years.

Luke, s. of Robt & Mary Edwards, buried Sept 11, aged 4 years.

Timothy s. of Joseph & Hannah Blyth bur. Oct: 31., aged 3 years.

Thomas Dains bur. Dec: 15, aged 50 years.

Stephen s. of Christopher & Susannah Grix bur. Dec: 17, aged 6 years.

1799.   Stephen Jeckell bur. Jan: 1, aged 60.

Ann Smithson bur. Jan: 7, aged 30.

Mary Blyth bur Jan: 9, aged 70.

Elizabeth Watson bur. Feb: 7, aged 83.

Joshua Blyth bur. Feb: 28, aged 44.[2]

Mary Hunt bur. Apr. 21. aged 84.

Judith d. of Thos & Amy Smithson, late Amy Edwards, bur. April 29, aged 2 years.

Elizabeth, d. of Abraham & Mary Blyth, late Mary Lubbock, bur. May 2, aged 22 years.

Elizabeth d. of W^m & Mary Goodwin, late Mary King, bur. May 17, an infant.

Elizabeth, wife of James Rudd, bur. June 12, aged 60.

William s. of Robert & Mary Smithson late Mary Smith, bur. June 19, aged 26.

Elizabeth, wife of James Hastings, bur June 20 aged 39.

----

[1] Left blank in Register.
[2] Delivered.

Ann, wife of John Woods, late Ann Bear, bur. Sep : 22, aged 49.

Sarah Jeckell bur. Oct : 30, aged 29 years.

Mary, Widow of Richard Delph late many years Clerk of this Parish, bur. Dec : 8, aged 84.

P.36. 1800.　Ann d. of John & Judith Watson bur. March 12, aged 15 years. [1]

Ann d. of Mary Watson bur. May 4, Infant.

John King bur. May 30, aged 65.

Elizabeth d. of W^m & Mary Goodwin bur. Aug : 7. Inf^t.

Jane, wife of Charles Dugdale bur. Aug : 17, aged 24.

Elizabeth, wife of Henry Stirman bur. Aug : 31, aged 64.

Joseph Watson bur. Nov : 27, aged 69.

Ruth Dugdale bur. Nov : 29, aged 23.

1801.　Mary, wife of Wm Goodwin, late Mary King, bur. Jan : 12, aged about 31 years.

Thomas Cawston bur. Feb : 22, aged 70.

James Key bur Feb : 26, aged 82.

William s. of Richd Jeckell & Martha his wife bur. March 17. an infant. [2]

P. 37.　John Sutton bur. June 7, aged 74.

Martha d. Saml & Mary Soame bur. June 8, aged 2 years.

Robert Smithson, bur. Sep : 27, aged 71.

Amy Lubbock bur. Oct : 16, aged 69.

Noah Stone bur. Dec : 15, aged 78.

John Penton bur. Dec : 20 aged 79.

Mary Greenwood bur. Dec : 20, aged 72.

Susannah Watson bur. Dec : 28, aged 70.

1802.　Robert Bear bur. Feb : 9. aged 73.

Samuel s. of Ann Jeckel bur. Feb : 28, Infant. [1]

Ann, Wife of Joseph Newman bur Apr. 20 aged 60.

Elizabeth, Wife of John Vertegans, bur. May 5, aged 36.

Ann, Wife of Edwd Reynolds bur. July 4, aged 40.

Elizabeth, Wife of Joseph Grix bur. July 30, aged 23.

Mary d. of Ann Greenwood bur. Oct : 5. Infant.

---

[1] Delivered.
[2] Delivered at the Visitation.

1803. Nathan s. of Nathan Steward & Eliz[th] his Wife bur.
March 1 aged 16 years.
Sarah Jones d. of Rob[t] Bowles bur. March 13 aged 40.
Ann, d. of Jeremy & Sarah Fish bur. Mar 14 Infant [1]
Robert Jeckell bur. April 2, aged 22.
John Smith bur. April 27, aged 70.
Mary Crotch bur. May 7, aged 67.
John Coleman bur. May 25, aged 79. [2]
P. 38. Stephen Cawston bur. July 1, aged 6½ years.
Ann Wattson bur. Aug : 20, aged 74.
Frances Ulph bur. Nov : 16, aged 50.

1804. Thomas Roberts bur. Feb : 5, aged 1 year.
Joseph Newman bur. Mar : 21, aged 67.
John Lubbock bur. March : 25, aged 79. [1]
John Murrell bur. April 19, aged 11 years.
Martha Jeckell bur. Aug : 14, aged 28.
Thomas Dugdale bur. Sep : 28, aged 63.
Matthew Dugdale bur. Oct : 2, aged 34.
William Fish bur. Nov : 29 aged 67.

1805. Mary Vincent bur. Jan : 22, aged 61.
Matilda Gladden bur. March 25, Infant.
Mary Barnard, bur May 17, aged 66. [1]
Elizabeth Hastings bur. June 9, aged 76.
Esther Pile bur. June 12, aged 76. [1]
Joshua Blyth bur. July 28, aged 19 years.
Sophia Williams bur. July 28, Infant.
Peter Gladden, bur. Nov. 13, aged 2 yrs.

1806. Amy Watson bur. Jan : 10, aged 30.
William Nichols bur. Jan : 31, aged 46.
Henry Goaty bur March 2 aged 2 yrs.
Christian Hodge, bur. May 23, aged 77.
Matthew Jeckel, s. of Richard & Martha, late Martha Daines,
bur. Nov : 13, aged 4 yrs.
Ann, Wife of James Grix, late Ann Sutton. bur. Nov : 16,
aged 73.

---

[1] Delivered.
[2] This page and 4 following signed, JAMES BINGLE CURATE.

John Cook, Bachelor, s. of Bel & Sarah, late Sarah Roofe, bur. Nov: 22 aged 57.

P. 39.   John Watson, married man, s. of Tho⁸ & Ann late Ann Case, bur. Nov: 28, aged 70.

William Goodwin, widower, s. of Wᵐ & Mary, bur. Dec: 4 aged 36.

1807.   Deborah d. of Wᵐ & Deborah Bitten bur Jan : 29. aged 76.

Mary Cook spinster, d. of Bell & Sarah, late Sarah Roofe bur, Feb : 16 aged 41.[1]

John Hodge widower bur. Apr : 9 aged 74.

Samuel Gibson, married man, s. of Samˡ & Ann, bur. May 24, aged 47.

Margaret wife of Henry Key, late Margaret Green bur. June 2. aged 53.

Lydia Dugdale, widow of Matthew, late Lydia Barnard spinster, bur. July 17 aged 32.

Matthew Jeckel married man s. of Richᵈ & Judith late Judith Smithson, bur. July 17, aged 60.

Samuel s. of Edwᵈ & Peggy Watson, late Peggy Pentein, bur. Aug: 9 aged 5 years.

William s. of John & Frances King, Inft, bur. Sep: 6.

Ann Crow, widow, bur Oct 11, aged 67.

1808.   Elizabeth Pain, widow, bur Feb: 14, aged 73.[1]

Ann, wife of Jno Everitt, late Ann Jerry, bur. June 3, aged 60.

James Hastings, widower, s. of Joseph & Elizᵗʰ late Elizᵗʰ Wood, bur. June 13, aged 56.

P. 40.   Mary d. of Isaac & Phœbe Greenwood bur. July 7. Infᵗ

Barbara Press bur. Nov: 20 aged 66.

1809.   John Ebbs bur. Feb: 17 aged 75.

Mary, widow of Wᵐ Jeckel, bur. Mar. 4, aged 72.

Elizabeth, widow of John Lubbock bur May 3, aged 72.

Abraham Bligh, married man, s. of Isaac & Eliz : bur. May 5, aged 62[1]

John Burrows, married man, s. of Wᵐ & Mary late Mary Crisp, bur. June 29, aged 46.

Thomas s. of Tho⁸ & Jane Morrill, late Jane Thornton, bur. Nov: 1, aged 15 years.

Ann, wife of Noah Stone, late Ann Durrant, bur. Nov : 16 aged 44.

Thomas Grix, widower, bur. Dec : 13, aged 74.

James Rudd, married man bur. Dec : 14, aged 72.

James Greenwood, married man, s. of James & Mary, late Mary Lake, bur. Dec : 24, aged 51.

Hannah Doughty, widow, bur. Dec : 28, aged 68.[1]

1810. William Jeckel married man, s. of W^m & Jane, bur. June 12, aged 60.

William s. of Thomas & Jane Morrill bur. July 6, aged 9 years.

Phœbe Jeckel, widow of Matthew, late Phœbe Lubbock, bur. July 8, aged 58.

Mary-Ann, d. of Thos & Jane Morrill, bur, Aug 15. aged 7.

William s. of Joseph & Mary Roberts bur. Nov : 1. Inft.

1811. John Daines bur. Feb : 22. aged 64.

P. 41. Elizabeth, wife of Solomon Shreeve, late Eliz : Tompson, bur. March 15, aged 71.

Mary d. of Robert & Sarah Fuller, late Sarah Cook spinster, bur. April 10, aged 55.[1]

Susan d. of Christopher & Susan Grix, late Susan Hammond, bur. July 1, aged 11 years.

Mary d. of Eleanor Pentein, Infant, bur. July 1.

Henry s. of Henry Coldham & Elizth his Wife, late Elizabeth Anth bur. July 7, aged 2 years.

James Crotch bur. Sep. 4, aged 76.

Sarah Stone bur. Oct. 9 aged 84.

John s. of Joseph & Mary Grix, late Mary Scarles, bur. Nov : 3. Infant.

Ann d. of George & Elizth Jonas bur. Nov : 28 aged 7.

Mary, Wife of Edmund Witterton bur. Dec : 3, aged 65.

1812. John Smithson, married man, s. of Robert & Mary, bur. Jan : 27, aged 52.

Susan, widow of John Smith bur. Mar. 12, aged 82.

Eliz^{th,} wife of Wm Edwards, bur. Mar. 26, aged 44.[1]

James Sturman married man, s. of Rich^d & Grace late Grace Page, bur June 8, aged 57.

---

[1] Delivered at the General.

Richard Pain, Bachelor, s. of W^m & Eliz^th late Eliz : Dix,
  bur. Aug 9, aged 28.
John Edridge, Batchelor, s. of Henry & Ann late Ann
  Smith, bur. Aug : 14 aged 21.
Sarah, widow of James Rudd, bur. Aug 21 aged 71.
Frances, widow of James Greenwood bur. Sep : 17 aged 55.
Ann d. of Robt & Patience Pottle bur. Nov. 19 aged 1 yr.
Edward Killegrew, a married man, bur Dec : 23, aged 71.[1]

[Book 5.]

Marriages 1754—1812.[2]

No. 1. Roger Bammond of Little Barningham, singleman and
  Mary Green, of Marsham, widow, March 25 1754.[3]

No. 2. Richard Jeckell, widower, and Elizabeth Wattson singlewoman, both of Marsham, August 23. 1754.

No. 3. Robert Thompson, singleman, and Anne Key, singlewoman, both of Marsham, October 20 1754.

No. 4. William Payne, singleman, and Elizabeth Crotch,
  singlewoman, both of Marsham, January 8. 1755.

No. 5. Theophilus Pye singleman, and Sarah Tompson, widow,
  both of Marsham, February 10. 1755.

No. 6. Charles Blyth, singleman, and Margaret Green, singlewoman, both of Marsham, February 24. 1755.

No. 7. John Reeve, widower, of St Laurence, Norwich, and
  Sarah Manning, widow, of Marsham, Jan^ry 11. 1756.

No. 8. Robert Dix, singleman, and Anne Lake singlewoman,
  both of Marsham, April 6. 1756.

No. 9. Joseph Leak, singleman, of Brampton, and Susanna
  Leak, singlewoman, of Marsham, Aug : 23. 1756.

No. 10. John Barker, widower, and Susanna Woods, singlewoman, both of Marsham, April 8. 1757.[4]

---

[1] Delivered at the General.

[2] This book is in the form prescribed by Act of Parliament, and the names
and Dates only are extracted.

[3] N°s 1 to 9. solemnised by Nath. Ponder. Rector.

[4] N°s 10—42 solemnised by William Gordon, Curate.

No. 11.   Francis Rochester, widower, of St George's, Norwich, and Sarah Nichols of Marsham, singlewoman, October 2. 1757.

No. 12.   Thomas Hunt, singleman, of St Faiths, and Elizabeth Spink, singlewoman, of Marsham, October 9. 1758.

No. 13.   James Grix, singleman, and Ann Sutton, single woman, both of Marsham, November 2 1758.

No. 14.   William Parker, Bachelor, and Elizabeth Gravener, spinster, both of Marsham, Oct : 11. 1759.

No. 15.   William Jeckell, singleman, and Mary Braddock, both of Marsham, November 4. 1759.

No. 16.   Andrew Harris, widower, of Oxned, and Sarah Watson, widow, of Marsham, November 19. 1759.

No. 17.   Isaac Jeckell, singleman, and Sarah Hix, single woman, both of Marsham, February 4. 1760.

No. 18.   Thomas Balls, singleman, of Aylsham, and Ann Symonds, singlewoman, of Marsham, April 1. 1760.

No. 19.   John Lake, singleman, and Ann Crow, singlewoman, of Marsham, October 13. 1760.

No. 20.   Noah Stone, singleman, and Sarah Davy, singlewoman, both of Marsham, October 27, 1760.

No. 21.   James Crotch, singleman, and Rebekah Boswell, singlewoman, both of Marsham, Nov : 18. 1760.

No. 22.   John Everett, singleman, and Elizabeth Pearson, singlewoman, both of Marsham, November 20. 1760.

No. 23.   John Moll, singleman, and Mary Harding, singlewoman, both of Marsham, January 5. 1761.

No. 24.   James Rudd, singleman, of Horsted, and Elizabeth Watson, singlewoman, of Marsham, July 12. 1761.

No. 25.   Samuel Wild, widower, and Elizabeth Lubbock, widow, both of Marsham, July 19. 1761.

No. 26.   John Daines, widower, and Mary Smith, widow, both of Marsham, October 5. 1761.

No. 27.   William Peartree, singleman, and Mary Hartley, singlewoman, both of Marsham, Nov: 7. 1761.

No. 28.   William Grand, singleman, and Phœbe Ward single woman, both of Marsham, November 15. 1761.

No. 29.   Isaac Fox, widower, and Ann Peartree, single woman, both of Marsham, February 22. 1762.

No. 30. William Bear, singleman, and Sarah Hartley, single
        woman, both of Marsham, August 18. 1762.
No. 31. Webster Everett, singleman, and Elizabeth Sutton
        singlewoman, both of Marsham, October 18. 1762.
No. 32. William Riches, singleman, and Lydia Lake, single-
        woman, both of Marsham, March 8, 1763.
No. 33. Thomas Doughty, widower, and Hannah Pain, single-
        woman, both of Marsham, April 5. 1763.
No. 34. Joseph Watts, singleman, of Hevingham, and Lydia
        Needham, single woman, of Marsham May 5. 1763.
No. 35. Thomas Caston, singleman, and Jane Bloom single-
        woman, both of Marsham, July 24, 1763.
No. 40.[1] Luke Edwards, single man, and Sarah Burridge,
        singlewoman, both of Marsham April 16. 1764.
No. 41. William Jeckell, singleman, and Mary Dunn single
        woman, both of Marsham, May 28. 1764.
No. 42. Tobias Field, singleman, of Blickling, and Elizabeth
        Gazeley, singlewoman, of Marsham, May 29. 1764.
No. 43. Edward Delph, singleman, and Elisabeth Rice, spinster,
        both of Marsham, November 7. 1764.[2]
No. 44. Elisha Aldridge, singleman, and Martha Carr single
        woman, both of this Parish, Nov : 20. 1764.
No. 45.[3] Robert Rose, singleman, and Elizabeth Peartree,
        widow, both of Marsham, May 6. 1765.
No. 46. John Crome, widower, and Elizabeth Porter, widow,
        both of Marsham, May 26. 1765.
No. 47. Stephen Westney, singleman, of Lamas, and Mary
        Sterling, singlewoman, of Marsham, June 17. 1765.
No. 48. John Davy, widower, and Esther Blyth, widow, both
        of Marsham, August 4. 1765.
No. 49. John Bartram, singleman, and Elizabeth Ulph single-
        woman, both of Marsham, October 21. 1765.
No. 50. Richard Jeckell, widower, and Mary Gedge, single-
        woman, both of Marsham, December 5. 1765.

----

[1] There is no Gap, but the Nos. of the Marriages and the Banns are now
made to correspond for a few entries.
[2] This No. and the next solemnised by W. L. Bennett,
[3] No[s] 45—137 by William Gordon, curate, except where noted otherwise.

No. 51.   Richard Sendall, singleman, and Abigall Lake, single-woman, both of Marsham, July 21. 1766.

No. 52.   Edward Benett, singleman, and Mary Everett single woman, both of Marsham, October 11. 1766.

No. 53.   Thomas Colls, widower, of Hanworth, and Elizabeth Fox, widow, of Marsham, November 11, 1766.

No. 54.   John Lake, widower, and Susanna Laws, single woman, both of Marsham, November 17. 1766.

No. 55.   John Daines, singleman, and Susanna Clarke, single woman, both of Marsham, November 25. 1766.

No. 56.   Samuel Lubbock, single man, and Elizabeth Spantin, single woman, both of Marsham, May 10. 1767.

No. 57.   Roger Hill, bachelor, of Itteringham, and Mary Fletcher, spinster, of Marsham, Sep: 29. 1767.

No. 58.   James Vertegans, Bachelor, and Frances Gladden, spinster, both of Marsham, October 16. 1767.

No. 59.   Edmund Palmer, single man, of St Stephens, Norwich, and Frances Greenwood, single woman of Marsham, April 8. 1768.

No. 60.   Luke Edwards, widower, & Elizabeth Everett, widow, both of Marsham, October 24. 1768.

No. 61.   William Medler, widower, of Hevingham, and Rose Collison, widow, of Marsham, November 15. 1768.

No. 62.   Thomas Soame, singleman, of Aylsham, and Mary Gladden, single woman, of Marsham, Nov: 30. 1768.

No. 63.   William Collison, single man, and Mary Thompson, single woman, both of Marsham, February 13. 1769.

No. 64.   Abraham Blyth, single man, and Mary Lubbock, single woman, both of Marsham, May 29. 1769.

No. 65.   Joshua Everett, singleman, and Mary Moll, widow, both of Marsham, July 24. 1769.

No. 66.   Christopher Southgate, single man, of St Michael at Thorn Norwich, and Rebecca Ward, single woman, of Marsham, Aug: 21. 1769.

No. 67.   John Shreeve, singleman, of Horsham St Faith, and Lucy Denford, singlewoman of Marsham, October 8. 1769.

No. 68.   William Jeckell, singleman, and Susanna Adams, singlewoman, both of Marsham, October 11, 1769.

No. 69. William Boswell, single man, and Sarah Watson, single woman, both of Marsham, November 28. 1769.

No. 70. Thomas Daines, singleman, and Sarah Thirtle, single woman, both of Marsham, June 10. 1771.

No. 71. Robert Jeckell, single man, and Sarah Gibson, single-woman, both of Marsham, October 17. 1771.

No. 72. Henry Mann, single man, and Susanna Waller, both of Marsham January 15. 1772.[1]

No. 73. Richard Jeckell, single man, and Mary Everet single woman, both of Marsham, March 24. 1772.

No. 74. Matthew Jeckell, singleman, and Phœbe Lubbock single woman, both of Marsham, April 27. 1772.

No. 75. James Greenwood, single man, and Anne Watson single woman, both of Marsham, June 8. 1772.

No. 76. John Woods, single man, of Scottow, and Anne Bear, a minor, & single, of Marsham, June 14. 1772.

No. 77.[2] John Arterton, single man, and Margaret Hastings, spinster, both of Marsham, October 12. 1772.

No. 78. Isaac Blyth, single man, and Ann Jeckell, single woman, both of Marsham, November 2. 1772.

No. 79. Thomas Abbs single man, and Susanna Greenwood single woman, both of Marsham, November 2. 1772.

No. 80.[2] Charles Saunders, single man, and Mary Gilbert single woman, both of Marsham, January 15. 1773.

No. 81. John Barker single man and Susanna Barber single woman, both of Marsham, April 7. 1773.

No. 82. Robert Durrant widower, and Hannah Watson single woman, both of Marsham, May 3. 1773.

No. 83. Edmund Jeckell single man, and Elizabeth Bennet, single woman, both of Marsham, October 18. 1773.

No. 84. John Wattson, single man, and Judith Sutton single woman, both of Marsham, October 25. 1773.

No. 85. Stephen Jeckell single man, and Mary Narborow single woman, both of Marsham, November 1. 1773.

No. 86. Robert Rodes, singleman, and Susanna Everit single woman, both of Marsham, November 15. 1774.

---

[1] This one solemnised by "Robt. Parr, a Minister."
[2] Nos 77 and 80 by Robert Parr, Minister.

No. 87. Joseph Blyth single man, and Elizabeth Greene single woman, both of Marsham, January 17. 1775.

No. 88. William Hastings single man, and Ann Pye single woman, both of Marsham, April 17. 1775.

No. 89. James Dunnett single man, and Mary Ward single woman, both of Marsham, July 4. 1775.

No. 90. John Pentein widower, and Elizabeth Jeckell widow, both of Marsham, October 2. 1775.

No. 91. William Barker single man, and Mary Palmer single woman, both of Marsham, November 21. 1775.

No. 92.[1] Noah Webster, single man, and Elizabeth Pye single-woman both of Marsham, December 25. 1775.

No. 93. John Mack single man, and Elizabeth Greene single woman, both of Marsham, January 31. 1776.

No. 94. John Dains widower, and Elizabeth Parker widow both of Marsham, May 6. 1776.

No. 95. John Pentein single man, of Aylsham, and Ellen Knott single woman, of Marsham, May 13. 1776.

No. 96. Joshua Ward single man, and Thomasin Ward single woman, both of Marsham, August 4. 1776.

No. 97. John Sterman bachelor, and Mary Jeckell widow, both of Marsham, September 15. 1776.

No. 98.[1] Edward Watson single man, and Ann Dunnett single woman, both of Marsham, June 9. 1777.

No. 99.[1] John Grout single man, and Elizabeth Marsham single woman, both of Marsham, September 15. 1777.

No. 100. Christopher Hardingham, single man, of Runton, and Mary Wiley single woman, of Marsham, Nov: 3. 1777.

No. 101. Richard Bulwer single man, and Barbara Gazely single woman, both of Marsham, May 4. 1778.

No. 102. John Amys single man, and Phyllis Jeckell single woman, both of Marsham, October 12. 1778.

No. 103. Samuel Soame singleman, and Mary Greenwood single woman, both of Marsham, October 14. 1778.

No. 104.[1] Christopher Gricks singleman, and Susanna Hammond single woman, both of Marsham, October 19. 1778.

---

[1] These four by William Jewell.

No. 105.   Edward Killigrew widower, and Deborah Palmer single woman, both of Marsham, Nov: 30. 1778.

No. 106.   Henry Key single man, and Margaret Greene single woman, both of Marsham, December 26. 1778.

No. 107.   Joseph Blyth single man, and Hannah Howes, single woman, both of Marsham, January 4. 1779.

No. 108.   James Greenwood single man, and Frances Penten single woman, both of Marsham, January 4. 1779.

No. 109.   John Laws single man, and Sarah Davidson single woman, both of Marsham, February 22. 1779.

No. 110.   John Minns single man of Hackford, and Sarah Longe single woman, of Marsham, May 11. 1779.

No. 111.   Theophilus Pye single man, and Esther Grix single woman, both of Marsham, May 31. 1779.

No. 112.   Joseph Hastings single man, and Ann Ward single woman, both of Marsham, July 12. 1779.

No. 113.   James Silence widower, of Aylsham, and Mary Johnson, singlewoman, of Marsham Nov: 1. 1779.

No. 114.   John Childes single man, and Susanna Bird single woman, both of Marsham, November 4. 1779.

No. 115.   John Meek singleman, and Rose Chamberlaine single woman, both of Marsham, Nov: 9. 1780.

No. 116.   John Davy, singleman, and Sarah Wattson single woman, both of Marsham, December 3. 1780.

No. 117.   John Smithson singleman, and Susanna Jonas single woman, both of Marsham, March 14, 1782.

No. 118.   Charles Dack single man, of Hevingham, and Elizabeth Palmer single woman, of Marsham, April 10. 1782.

No. 119.   John Hunt widower, of Hainford, and Mary Bunn single woman, of Marsham, Sept: 17, 1783.

No. 120.   Henry Edridge single man, and Ann Smith single woman, both of Marsham, December 8. 1783.

No. 121.   John Cooper widower, of Knapton, and Hannah Fletcher spinster, of Marsham, January 26, 1784.

No. 122.   Thomas Youngman single man of Barney, and Lydia Smith single woman, of Marsham, April 19. 1784.

No. 123.   John Dunnett single man, and Elizabeth Grix single woman, both of Marsham, April 23. 1784.

No. 124. Edward Wattson widower, and Margaret Pentein single woman, both of Marsham, June 1. 1784.

No. 125. John Everett widower, and Ann Jary single woman, both of Marsham, December 2. 1784.

No. 126. John Appleton single man, and Leah Greenwood, both of Marsham. April 4. 1785.

No. 127. John Ownes, *alias* Warnes, single man, of Aylsham, and Judith Greene single woman, of Marsham, April 4. 1785.

No. 128. Samuel Tongett single man, and Hannah Orstick single woman, both of Marsham, August 2. 1785.

No. 129. Jonathan Ulph widower, and Frances Gould single woman both of Marsham, August 2. 1785.

No. 130. Henry Sterman widower, and Elizabeth Daius widow, both of Marsham, August 2. 1785.

No. 131. John Kiddle single man, and Esther Barber single woman, both of Marsham, August 3. 1786.

No. 132. John Bligh single man, of Hunworth, and Sarah Rudd single woman, of Marsham, August 19, 1786.

No. 133.[1] Charles Saunders widower, and Honour Wattson single woman, both of Marsham, October 14. 1786.

No. 134. William Wegg, widower, of Hevingham, and Sarah Sexton widow, of Marsham, November 6. 1786.

No. 135. William Jeckell single man, of Alborough, and Sarah Bayfield single woman, of Marsham, December 4. 1786.

No. 136. Richard Bunn single man, and Mary Jeckell single woman, both of Marsham, December 8. 1786.

No. 137. Thomas Mann single man, of Aylsham, and Mary Hammond single woman, of Marsham Feb. 20. 1787.

No. 138.[2] Caleb Blyth single man, and Alice Colman single woman, both of Marsham, April 18. 1787.

No. 139.[3] Robert Buck single man, and Elizabeth Sutton single woman, both of Marsham, May 21 1787.

No. 140. John Watson single man, and Hannah Heath single woman, both of Marsham, July 9. 1787.

---

[1] By Wm Jewell, Clerk.

[2] This one by C. L. Bennett, R. of Hevingham.

[3] Nos. 139 to 209 by William Jewell, Curate, except where noted otherwise.

No. 141.   John Sutton widower, and Hannah Tungate widow,
both of Marsham, October 11. 1787.

No. 142.   John Sutton single man, and Mary Ann Riches, single
woman, both of Marsham, February 18. 1788.

No. 143.   William Goodwin singleman, and Mary King single
woman, both of Marsham, April 14. 1788.

No. 144.   Thomas Smithson single man, and Amy Edwards
singlewoman, both of Marsham, January 5. 1789.

No. 145.   William Palmer single man, and Sarah Bear single
woman, both of Marsham, January 6. 1789.

No. 146.   James Crotch single man, and Lucy Crow single
woman, both of Marsham, March 9. 1789.

No. 147.   Philip Garrod single man, and Diana Greenwood
single woman, both of Marsham, July 13. 1789.

No. 148.   Robert Smith single man, and Elizabeth Watts spinster,
both of Marsham, October 19. 1789.

No. 149.   Robert Edwards single man, and Elizabeth Blyth,
spinster, both of Marsham, October 19. 1789.

No. 150.   Joshua Blyth singleman, and Christian Jekyll single
woman, both of Marsham, December 9. 1789.

No. 151.   Henry Coxton single man, and Mary Palmer single
woman, both of Marsham, April 20. 1790.

No. 152.   Noah Stone single man, and Anne Durrant single
woman, both of Marsham, May 18. 1790.

No. 153.   Robert Skinner single man, and Mary Peartree single
woman, both of Marsham, May 7. 1790.

No. 154.   Augustine Dewing widower, of Cawston, and Elizabeth
Pye single woman, of Marsham Nov: 18. 1790.

No. 155.   William Basey single man, of Hevingham, and
Marianne Newman single woman, of Marsham, Dec: 21.
1790.

No. 156.   Robert Jekyl singleman, and Charlotte Marsham
singlewoman, both of Marsham, May 24. 1791.

No. 157.   William Watker single man, of Hevingham, and
Margaret Crotch single woman, of Marsham, July 25.
1791.

No. 158.   Thomas Delph single man, and Ann Grand single
woman, both of Marsham, August 14. 1791.

No. 159. James Hastings widower, and Elizabeth Sutton single
woman, both of Marsham, November 4. 1791.

No. 160. Thomas Betts single man, of Ingworth, and Sarah
Crotch, single woman, of Marsham, November 7. 1791.

No. 161. Robert Wattson single man, and Ann Watson single
woman, both of Marsham, November 25. 1791.

No. 162. John Laws widower, and Elizabeth Barker, single
woman, both of Marsham, September 24. 1792.

No. 163.[1] Henry Drory single man, of Marsham, and Susanna
Ives, single woman, of Brampton Nov : 5. 1792.

No. 164.[1] Thomas Lake single man, and Ann Jeckell single
woman, both of Marsham, December 24. 1792.

No. 165. Timothy Blyth single man, and Susannah Roberts
single woman, both of Marsham, September 24. 1793.

No. 166. James Grix singleman, and Ann Barnard single
woman, both of Marsham, January 5. 1794.

No. 167. Edward Delph widower, and Esther Pyé, widow, both
of Marsham, January 20. 1795.

No. 168.[1] Edmund Jerry of Oxned, and Ann Pain of Marsham
both single, June 29 1795.

No. 169. Robert Edwards single man, and Mary Palmer single
woman, both of Marsham, August 17. 1795.

No. 170. Theophilus Hastings[2] single man, of Letheringsett,
and Jemima Barker single woman, of Marsham, Oct : 1.
1795.

No. 171. John Edwards single man, and Elizabeth Watson
single woman, both of Marsham October 6. 1795.

No. 172. John Jacob single man, and Mary Smith single
woman, both of Marsham, October 11. 1795.

No. 173. William Smithson single man, and Anne Bowls single
womam, both of Marsham, November 16. 1795.

No. 174. James Smithson single man, and Tabitha Shreeve
single woman, both of Marsham, November 16. 1795.

No. 175. Thomas Cooper single man, and Mary Soame single
woman, both of Marsham, November 26. 1796.

No. 176. Edward Killigrew widower, and Elizabeth Cawston
single woman, both of Marsham, January 4. 1797.

---

[1] These three by Wm Taswell, Minister.
[2] He signs Theophilus Pye Hastings.

T

No. 177.   James Dains single man, and Hannah Marsham single woman, both of Marsham, January 9. 1797.

No. 178.   William Batchelor widower, and Judith Watson widow, both of Marsham, February 7 1797.

No. 179.   John Grix single man and Elizabeth Bear, single woman, both of Marsham, May 8. 1797.

No. 180.[1]   Edward Gallant singleman of Oulton, and Mary Thompson single woman, of Marsham, May 15. 1797.

No. 181.   John Bransby widower, and Sarah Grix single woman, both of Marsham, May 16. 1797.

No. 182.   Samuel Jacob of Aylsham, and Sarah Moor single woman, of Marsham, June 5. 1797.

No. 183.   Peter Jonas single man, and Elizabeth Edwards widow, both of Marsham, July 13. 1797.

No. 184.   Robert Hasslclup single man, and Mary Jeckell single woman, both of Marsham, July 17. 1797.

No. 185.   Matthew Dugdale single man, of Hevingham, and Lydia Barnard single woman, of Marsham, Oct: 10. 1797.

No. 186.   Nathan Steward widower, and Sarah Thompson single woman, both of Marsham, Nov: 13. 1797.

No. 187.   Thomas Story single man, of Aylesham, and Elizabeth Thompson single woman of Marsham, January 2. 1798.

No. 188.   Benjamin Grix single man, and Mary Blyth single woman, both of Marsham, March 23. 1798.

No. 189.   John King widower, and Ann Reynolds widow, both of Marsham, May 15. 1798.

No. 190.   Benjamin Newman widower of Cawston, and Mary Edwards single woman, of Marsham, June 28. 1798.

No. 191.   John Laws widower, and Sarah Pratt widow, both of Marsham, July 3. 1798.

No. 192.   John Vertegans single man, of Hevingham, and Elizabeth Rudd single woman, of Marsham, Oct: 15. 1798.

No. 193.   Charles Dugdale singleman, and Jane Jeckel single woman, both of Marsham, October 30. 1798.

---

[1] This one by C. L. Bennett.

No. 194.   David Shreeve single man, and Elizabeth Bayfield single woman, both of Marsham, December 3. 1798.

No. 195.[1]   Daniel Briggs single man, and Frances Cook single woman, both of Marsham, December 17. 1798.

No. 196.   Joseph Grix single man, and Elizabeth Key single woman, both of Marsham, December 24. 1798.

No. 197.   Richard Edwards single man, and Ann Bear single woman, both of Marsham. November 2. 1799.

No. 198.   Jonathan Pain single man, and Sarah Burrell single woman, both of Marsham, November 10 1799.

No. 199.[2]   Samuel Cook single man, and Hannah Roberts single woman, both of Marsham, December 17. 1799.

No. 200.   Richard Jeckell single man, of Marsham, and Martha Daines single woman of Felmingham, Feb 25. 1800.

No. 201.   James Rudd widower, and Sarah Dains widow, both of Marsham, October 6. 1800.

No. 202.   John Hunt single man, and Charlotte Pye, single woman, both of Marsham, November 4. 1800.

No. 203.   Charles Gibbs single man, and Sarah Hastings single woman, both of Marsham, December 24. 1800.

No. 204.   William Killigrew single man of Great Bircham, and Ann Rudd single woman, of Marsham, Dec : 30. 1800.

No. 205.[3]   Minns Stagg widower of Corpusty & Ann King widow of Marsham June 29, 1801.

No. 206.   Henry Stirman widower & Lydia Riches widow both of Marsham September 13 1801.

No. 207.   Edward Skinner single man and Ann King single-woman both of Marsham, October 15, 1801.

No. 208.   Thomas Hastings single man and Mary Pain single woman both of Marsham Nov : 2. 1801.

No, 209.   Samuel Grapes single man and Ann Blythe single woman both of Marsham March 2. 1802.

No. 210.[4]   James Howard single man and Mary Lubbock single woman both of Marsham June 7 1802.

---

[1] This one by Joseph Alderson, minister.
[2] This one by Wm Taswell, minister.
[3] This one by John Dashwood, minister.
[4] This one by Francis Ed. Arden.

No. 211.[1]   John Vertegans widower and Mary Grix single woman, both of Marsham Nov : 1. 1802.

No. 212.   Joseph Grix widower and Mary Scarles single woman both of Marsham July 4 1803.

No. 213.   John Willimott of Hevingham single man and Mary Watts of Marsham single woman July 8 1803.

No. 214.   Henry King single man and Susanna Soame single woman both of Marsham July 19 1803.

No. 215.   William Jeckell widower and Martha Pulley widow both of Marsham August 14 1803.

No. 216.   Francis Watts single man and Sophia Hook single woman both of Marsham October 27 1803.

No. 217.   Benjamin Skip single man and Elizabeth Blyth single woman both of Marsham Nov : 7. 1803.

No. 218.   George Jonas single man and Elizabeth Palmer single woman both of Marsham Nov : 10 1803.

No. 219.   John Watts singleman and Elizabeth Reynolds single woman both of Marsham Dec : 1803.

No. 220.   Benjamin Smith single man and Ann Pentene single woman both of Marsham April 9. 1804.

No. 221.   Henry Suffolk of Lamas single man and Ann Colman of Marsham single woman June 12. 1804.

No. 222.   Samuel Smith of Cawston single man and Ann Watson single woman of Marsham Oct : 18. 1804.

No. 223.   Isaac Ward of Colchester, Essex, single man and Lydia Edridge of Marsham single woman Dec : 23. 1804.

No. 224.   Samuel Pentein single man and Sarah Hobbaus widow both of Marsham Jan : 17. 1805.

No. 225.   Thomas Williamson of Scottow single man and Lydia Greenwood of Marsham spinster May 18. 1805.

No. 226.   John Newman single man and Susanna Jeckell single-woman both of Marsham Oct : 14. 1806.

No. 227.   Samuel Pye single man and Susanna Speakman single woman both of Marsham Oct : 18. 1806.

No. 228.   Thomas Greenacre of Aylsham widower and Mary Shreeve of Marsham single woman Nov : 23. 1807.

---

[1] This & following, to 239 by James Bingle, Curate.

No. 229. James Blackburn single man and Maria Sutton single-woman both of Marsham August 8. 1808.

No. 230. Joseph Bowman of Stratton Strawless widower and Christiana Seaman widow of Marsham Aug : 30. 1808.

No. 231. Joseph Cook widower and Mary Maris widow both of Marsham Dec : 6. 1808.

No. 232. William Wattson single man and Sarah Drory single woman both of Marsham Jan ; 22. 1809.

No. 233. William Culley single man and Sarah Smithson single woman both of Marsham Dec : 17. 1809.

No. 234. William Mann single man and Grace Sturman single woman both of Marsham April 23. 1810.

No. 235. John Dunham of Costessey singleman and Mary Smithson of Marsham single woman Apr : 24. 1810.

No. 236. Joseph March of Aylsham widower and Ann Medler of Marsham widow Dec : 9. 1811.

No. 237. William Lake single man and Hannah Blythe single woman both of Marsham Jan : 18. 1812.

No. 238. James Blyth single man and Mary Gibson widow both of Marsham May 30. 1812.

No. 239. James Tortice of Aylsham singleman and Ann Parmer single woman of Marsham Nov : 20. 1812.

[Book 6.]

MARRIAGES 1813 TO 1832.

No. 1. Stephen Woodcock of Hainford and Honour Watson of Marsham, 11 October 1813.[1]

No. 2. John Greenwood and Elizabeth Neal both of Marsham 19 November 1813.

No. 3. Joseph Edwards *alias* Watson and Katherine Panton both of Marsham, 11 April 1814.

No. 4. Philip Panton and Sarah Grix both of Marsham 2 May 1814.

---

[1] Nos. 1 to 79 by James Bingle, Curate.

No. 5.   Charles Sutton and Mary Ann Piggott both of Marsham, 28 November 1814.

No. 6.   Daniel Drory and Sarah Bransby both of Marsham, 1 February 1815.

No. 7.   Thomas Dodman of Aylsham and Sarah Grix of Marsham, 6 February 1815.

No. 8.   William Elden of Tuttington and Elizabeth Wighton of Marsham 15 May 1815.

No. 9.   James Abbs of Buxton and Ellen Panton of Marsham, 29 May 1815.

No. 10.   Thomas Marsham and Frances Watson both of Marsham 23 October 1815.

No. 11.   Joseph Grix and Sarah Watson both of Marsham 4 May 1816.

No. 12.   Jacob Watson and Lydia Marsham both of Marsham 3 June 1816.

No. 13.   George Drory and Mary Foster both of Marsham 24 September 1816.

No. 14.   John Cooke and Elizabeth Jarvis both of Marsham 11 October 1816.

No. 15.   Matthew Jeckel and Lydia Clark both of Marsham 26 November 1816.

No. 16.   Peter Spink and Elizabeth Blyth both of Marsham 30 June 1817.

No. 17.   William Elvin of Marsham and Hannah Masterson Boult of Great Yarmouth 9 August 1817.

No. 18.   Benjamin Culley and Elizabeth Cook both of Marsham 6 January 1818.

No. 19.   Benjamin Grix and Mary Pulley both of Marsham 21 January 1818.

No. 20.   Francis Goodwin and Elizabeth Reynolds both of Marsham 26 May 1818.

No. 21.   Christmas Smith and Mary Ann Goodwin both of Marsham 12 November 1818.

No. 22.   Arthur Lake and Parnell Steward both of Marsham 26 December 1818.

No. 23.   George Ives and Mary Greenwood both of Marsham 14 January 1819.

No. 24. William Blyth and Mary Delph both of Marsham 8 February 1819.

No. 25.[1] John Dunnett single man of Tuttington and Elizabeth Grix single woman of Marsham 6 March 1820.

No. 26. Edmund Abbott single man and Maria Coleman single woman, both of Marsham 21 Aug : 1820.

No. 27. Thomas Wighton single man and Mary Ann Moore single woman both of Marsham 13 November 1820.

No. 28. Thomas Shreeve single man of S[t] Peter Mancroft in Norwich and Sarah Delph single woman of Marsham 4 Dec : 1820.

No. 29. Lovett Amos single man and Esther Blyth single woman both of Marsham 1 February 1821.

No. 30. Samuel Gladden single man and Mary Boult single woman both of Marsham 13 February 1821.

No. 31. George Jonas single man and Mary Ann Walter single woman both of Marsham 24 May 1821.

No. 32. William Bunn single man and Sarah Souther single woman both of Marsham 11 June 1821.

No. 33. Thomas Cook single man and Mary Tompson single woman both of Marsham 27 July 1821.

No. 34. Henry Nickels single man of Suffield and Sarah Blake single woman of Marsham 21 July 1821.

No. 35. Thomas Sturman single man and Amelia Edwards single woman both of Marsham 27 November 1821.

No. 36. Edward Moore single man and Elizabeth Walter single woman both of Marsham 25 December 1821.

No. 37. John Grix single man and Mary Blake single woman both of Marsham 14 February 1822.

No. 38. Edward Gladden single man and Maria Walter single woman both of Marsham 19 March 1822.

No. 39. William Spink single man and Ann Sutton single woman both of Marsham 27 May 1822.

No. 40. William Forrow single man and Mary Wattson single woman both of Marsham 14 Oct : 1822.

No. 41. William Frankland widower of N. Walsham and Elizabeth Edridge single woman of Marsham 12 May 1823.

[1] This one by W[m] Jewell Off[g] Min[r.]

No. 42. David Smithson single man and Jane Panton single woman both of Marsham 20 May 1823.

No. 43. Robert Sutton single man and Susanna Lake single woman both of Marsham 23 September 1823.

No. 44. Anthony Woodhouse Ireland single man of Wood Dalling and Sarah Howlett of Marsham single woman 21 October 1823.

No. 45. James Watson single man and Elizabeth Coman single woman both of Marsham 1 Dec : 1823.

No. 46. William Wiley single man and Sarah Edwards single woman both of Marsham 22 Dec : 1823.

No. 47. John Smithson single man and Ann Grix spinster both of Marsham 24 January 1824.

No. 48. Thomas Lake single man and Elizabeth Cutting spinster both of Marsham 9 June 1824.

No. 49. Henry Pike single man of Aylsham and Emma Howlett spinster of Marsham 4 Aug : 1824.

No. 50. William Shreeve single man and Lydia Blyth spinster both of Marsham 22 October 1824.

No. 51. William Thompson Storey of Holt batchelor and Ann Watts of Marsham spinster 17 March 1825.

No. 52. Thomas Reynolds single man and Sarah Drory spinster both of Marsham 21 November 1825.

No. 53. Charles Sutton widower and Ann King spinster both of Marsham 24 November 1825.

No. 54. John Pooley of N. Walsham widower and Harriet Bunn of Marsham spinster, 5 Dec : 1825.

No. 55. Christopher Stageman single man and Mary Dring spinster both of Marsham 13 Dec : 1825.

No. 56. Charles Neale single man and Sophia Cooke spinster both of Marsham 8 May 1826.

No. 57. John Peel of Letheringsett single man and Mary Wickham of Marsham spinster 16 Oct : 1826.

No. 58. John Steward single man and Elizabeth Edwards spinster both of Marsham 27 Nov : 1826.

No. 59. William Randall of Aylsham bachelor and Elizabeth Moore of Marsham spinster 16 Jan : 1827.

No. 60. John Culley of Aylsham single man and Dinah Killegrew of Marsham spinster 25 Oct : 1827.

No. 61. Isaac Blyth of Horstead widower and Susanna Wiley of Marsham spinster 29 October 1827.

No. 62. James Grix single man and Caroline Sutton spinster both of Marsham 25 December 1827.

No. 63. Moses Delph single man and Mary Sutton single woman both of Marsham 20 Sept: 1828. [1]

No. 64. Zachariah Hunt single man and Mary Drory spinster both of Marsham 10 November 1828.

No. 65. John Moore of Burrough single man and Mary Ann Newman of Marsham spinster 28 Nov: 1828.

No. 66. Thomas Blyth single man and Charlotte Applegate spinster both of Marsham 12 December 1828.

No. 67. John Jones single man and Phœbe Neale single woman both of Marsham 17 Feb. 1829. [2]

No. 68. Henry Gibson singleman and Martha Matthewson spinster both of Marsham 30 March 1829 [2]

No. 69. Joshua Blyth single man and Maria Chaplin single-woman both of Marsham 29 May 1829. [1]

No. 70. Thomas Wiley of Buxton single man and Elizabeth Soame spinster of Marsham 19 Jan 1830.

No. 71. Robert Stageman single man and Mary Skipper spinster both of Marsham 21 April 1830. [1]

No. 72. James Moore bachelor and Sophia Gittoes widow both of Marsham 14 July 1830.

No. 73. Charles Skipper single man and Jane Jex spinster both of Marsham 11 November 1830.

No. 74. William Skipper widower and Mary Jex spinster both of Marsham 23 May 1831.

No. 75. Henry Fox single man and Mary Ann Culley spinster both of Marsham 24 August 1831.

No. 76. Charles Delph single man and Anne Randall single woman both of Marshan 7 November 1831. [3]

No. 77. Robert Spink single man and Sarah Grix both of Marsham 8 December 1831.

No. 78. Robert Grix single man and Harriet Steward single woman both of Marsham 26 December 1831.

---

[1] These three by George Jarvis Off[s] Min[r].
[2] These two by F. C. Fowler Off[s] Min[r].
[3] This one by Edward Holley, Off[s] Min[r].

No. 79.   James Edwards single man and Mary Ann Blackburn single woman both of Marsham 26 Dec : 1831.

No. 80.   Thomas Catton widower and Margaret Garrad widow both of Marsham 20 Feb : 1832.[1]

No. 81.   James Drory singleman and Ann Smith spinster both of Marsham 6 March 1832.

No. 82.   Edward King singleman and Rose Wittleton spinster both of Marsham 25 June 1832.

No. 83.   Isaac Penton singleman and Sophia Grix spinster both of Marsham 30 July 1832.

No. 84.   Edmund Gall singleman and Sophia Oliver spinster both of Marsham 16 October 1832.

No. 85.   George Neale singleman and Susan Blogg spinster both of Marsham 21 November 1832.

[Book 7.]

No. 1.   John William Ladell Spaul a Minor and Anne Edridge spinster both of Marsham 18 July 1833.[2]

No. 2.   George Willimott singleman and Eliza Steward spinster both of Marsham 9 October 1833.[3]

No. 3. Robert Smithson singleman and Ann Hastings spinster both of Marsham 26 Feb. 1834.

No. 4.   Thomas Wighton widower of Marsham, and Maria Smith spinster of Buxton 21 April 1834.

No. 5.   John Delph singleman of Marsham and Mary Sall spinster of Aylsham 22 Sept : 1834.

No. 6.   Thomas Greenwood singleman and Elizabeth Nobbs singlewoman both of Marsham 5 Nov : 1834.

No. 7.   Stephen Mack singleman and Harriet Crotch spinster both of Marsham 17 Nov : 1834.

No. 8.   Henry Thos Soame singleman and Hannah Moore spinster both of Marsham 25 Dec : 1834.

No. 9.   Robert Taylor singleman of N Walsham a private in the 3rd Light Dragoons and Sarah Ann Pottle singlewoman of Marsham 10 March 1835.

---

[1] This and No. 81 to 85 by Henry Evans, Curate.

[2] Nos. 1 to 11 by H. Evans except where otherwise noted.

[3] This one by Jacob Snelgar clk Hevingham.

No. 10.   Hercules Bradfield singleman and Mary Sexton spinster both of Marsham 13 Oct 1835.

No. 11.   John Cook singleman and Sophia Nobbs spinster both of Marsham 3 Nov: 1835.

No. 12.   James Spink of Burgh next Aylsham singleman and Harriet Mack of Marsham singlewoman 9 Nov 1835.[1]

No. 13.   Samuel Smith singleman and Tabitha Middleton singlewoman both of Marsham 14 Feb 1837.[2]

No. 14.   Robert Blake singleman and Charlotte Lake singlewoman both of Marsham 26 December 1837.[2]

---

[1] This one by James Carver, R. of Hevingham.

[2] These two, by William Atthill, curate, are printed because they conclude the book.

Book 8

Baptisms[1] 1813.

Feb 28 Ann d. of George and Elizabeth (Palmer)[2] Jonas.[3]
Feb 28 Sarah d. of John & Charlotte (Pye) Hunt.[4]
Feb 28 Rebekah d. of Henry & Mary Ann (Newman) Atthowe.[5]
March 28 Deborah d. of James & Elizth (Cook) Hall.[6]
April 4 Mary d. of Ann Garrad spinster.
May 16 Elizabeth d. of John & Elizth (Reynolds) Watts.[7]
June 6 Mary Ann d. of Edmund & Mary (Leegood) Davy.[8]
June 13 James s. of Edward & Margaret (Pentein) Watson.[9]
July 11 Maria d. of Samuel & Sarah (Hobbing) Penton.[9]
Sept. 19 Ann d. of Henry & Hannah (Smith) Roberts.[10]
Sept. 19 James s. of James & Mary (Gibson) Blyth.[9]
Sept 26 Sarah d. of Samuel & Hannah (Amis) Neave.[7]
Oct. 24 Robert s. of Wm & Mary Ann (Basey) Laskey.[11]
Nov. 14 Robert s. of Mary Blake spinster.
Dec. 5 James s. of James & Sarah (Webster) Gooch.[7]
Dec. 5. Charles s. of James & Maria (Sutton) Blackburn.[9]
Dec 19 Robert s. of Nathan & Sarah (Tompson) Steward.[9]
Dec. 25. Samuel s. of Saml & Elizth (Oliver) Barrit.[9]
1814 Feb 27. Elizabeth d. of John & Susanna (Jeckell) Newman.[4]
April 10 Mary Ann d. of Samuel & Ann (Watson) Smith.[9]
April 10 Maria d. of James & Sarah (Stone) Richardson.[9]
April 10 Stephen s. of Robert & Mary (Amis) Mack.[5]
May 1. Mary d. of John & Frances (Pratt) King.[7]
May 1 John s. of Joseph & Harriot (Head) Blyth.[9]
May 22 Elizabeth d. of Thomas & Mary (Pain) Hastings.[5]
May 22 Maria d. of Richard & Ann (Bear) Edwards.[4]
June 12 John s. of John & Elizabeth (Neal) Greenwood.[9]
June 19 Ann d. of Wm & Hannah (Blyth) Lake.[9]

---

[1] Performed by J. Bingle, Curate, to 1832; then by H. Evans, Curate, except where otherwise noted.
[2] The maiden names of the wives are printed in brackets.
[3] Pensioner. [4] Weaver. [5] Carpenter. [6] Laborer.
[7] Farmer. [8] Stock-jobber. [9] Husbandman. [10] Tailor.
[11] Toll-Gatherer.

July 10 Joseph W^m s. of Isaac & Mary (Watson) Panton.[1]
Oct. 2 Thomas s. of Isaac & Phœbe (Gold) Greenwood.[2]
Oct. 2. Anne d. of W^m & Sarah (Smithson) Culley.[2]
Nov 28 Susanna d. of Thomas & Mary (Soame) Cooper.[3]
Dec. 18 Mary Ann d. of Thomas & Ann (Jeckell) Lake.[2]
1815. Feb 12. John s. of Benjamin & Hannah (Panton) Smith.[4]
Feb. 26. Ann d. of W^m & Sarah (Drory) Watson.[2]
March 19. John s. of Elizabeth Cook spinster
March 19 John s. of John & Charlotte (Pye) Hunt.[5]
April 23. John s. of Philip & Sarah (Grix) Panton.[6]
May 14. Louisa d. of Charles & Mary Ann (Piggott) Sutton.[2]
June 11. Thomas s. of Joseph & Mary (Scarls) Grix.[2]
June 18. John s. of Henry & Elizabeth (Auth) Coldham.[2]
June 20. Lydia d. of John & Elizabeth Watts.[7]
July 9. Maria d. of Peter & Sarah (Soame) Soame.[7]
Aug: 13. James s. of Thomas & Sarah (Grix) Dodman.[8]
Aug: 27. Thomas s. of Edmund & Mary (Pain) Jeary.[2]
Sept: 3 Mary Ann d. of James & Tabitha (Shreeve) Smithson.[2]
Oct 1. Mary Ann d. of James & Mary (Gibson. widow) Blyth.[2]
Oct 15. John & Thomas twins ss. of W^m & Mary (Larn) Oliver.[2]
Nov 5. Sophia & Ann twins dd. of Edwd & Sarah (Ives) Proudfoot.[8]
Nov 19. Hannah d. of James & Elizabeth Hall.[2]
Dec 17. John s. of Daniel & Sarah (Bransby) Drory.[2]
1816. Jan. 28. Robert s. of W^m & Phœbe (Marsham) Spink.[2]
Feb. 11. Joseph s. of John & Susanna Newman.[5]
March 10. Susanna d. of W^m & Hannah Lake.[2]
March 24 Frances d. of Daniel & Frances (Skery) Frostick.[2]
April 7. William s. of Sarah Edwards spinster.
May 5. Lœtitia d. of W^m & Sarah (Fowler) Warner.[9]
June 2. William s. of James & Maria Blackburn[2]
June 9 John s. of Samuel & Hannah Neave.[7]
July 14 Robert s. of Samuel & Sarah Penton.[2]
July 28 Harriet d. of Joseph & Sarah (Watson) Grix.[2]

---

[1] Corporal 1st Reg^t of Foot.   [2] Husbandman.   [3] Tailor.
[4] Thatcher.   [5] Weaver.   [6] Private 1st Reg^t of Foot.
[7] Farmer   [8] Carpenter.   [9] Mason.

Sept 22. George s. of W^m & Sarah Cully. [1]
Oct 6. Harriet d. of Robert & Mary Mack. [2]
Oct. 6 James s. of George & Elizabeth Jonas. [3]
Oct. 20 Ann d. of Thomas & Mary Hastings. [2]
Oct 20. William s. of Isaac & Phœbe Greenwood. [1]
Nov. 3 Mary Ann d. of Edward & Mary (Drory) Stone. [1]
Dec. 1. Elizabeth d. of John & Elizabeth Greenwood. [1]
Dec 15 John Foster s. of George & Mary (Foster) Drory. [1]
1817.   Feb 23. Harriet d. of Thomas & Sarah Gooch. [4]
March 2. Edward s. of James & Sarah Richardson. [1]
March 9 Harriet d. of Samuel & Ann Smith. [1]
May 25 Phillis d. of John & Elizabeth Watts. [4]
June 1. Mary Ann d. of John & Eliz^th (Jarvis) Cook. [1]
June 15 Samuel s. of W^m & Sarah (Caston) Ducker. [1]
Aug 10. Ann d. of W^m & Eleanor (Shreeve) Smithson. [1]
Aug: 24 Ann d. of Daniel & Sarah Drory. [1]
Sept. 21. Peter s. of Henry & Elizabeth Coldham. [1]
Sept 21. Joseph & Ann twins s. & d. of John & Susanna
          Newman. [5]
Oct 19. Edmund s. of Edward & Sarah Proudfoot. [2]
1818.   Feb. 17 Ann d. of Isaac & Dinah (Sparks) Watson. [1]
Feb 22. Katharine d. of Philip & Sarah (Grix) Penton. [1]
March 8 William s. of James & Mary Blyth. [1]
April 19 John s. of Charles & Mary Ann Sutton. [1]
June 28. Peter s. of Peter & Elizabeth (Blyth) Spink. [1]
July 5. Theophilus s. of John & Charlotte Hunt. [5]
July 12 William s. of W^m & Hannah Lake. [1]
July 26. Benjamin s. of John & Frances King. [4]
Aug: 23. Emma Gladden d. of Elizabeth Walter.
Sept. 6. Robert Hannant s. of Mary Blake.
Sept 27. Charlotte d. of Richard & Mary (Laws) Watson. [1]
Nov. 29. Eliza d. of William & Phœbe Spink. [1]
Nov. 29. John s. of Thos & Julia (Johnson) Edridge. [2]
Dec. 13. Anne Sophia d. of Thos & Eliz^th (Watson) Spink. [1]
Dec 27 John s. of Benjamin & Mary (Pulley) Grix. [2]

---

[1] Husbandman.   [2] Carpenter.   [3] Pensioner.
[4] Farmer.   [5] Weaver.

1819.   Jan. 24. Edward s. of Robert & Mary Mack.[1]

Jan. 24. Mary d. of John & Eliz[th] Greenwood.[2]

Feb 17. Joshua s. of James & Maria Blackburn.[2]

March 7. Elizabeth d. of Joseph & Sarah Grix.[2]

March 21 Rachel d. of Samuel & Hannah Neave.[3]

May 2. Harriet d. of Benjamin & Elizabeth (Cook) Cully.[1]

May 16. Uriah s. of Isaac & Mary Penton.[2]

May 16. William s. of W[m] & Mary (Delph) Blythe.[4]

June 6 George s. of Isaac & Phœbe Greenwood.[2]

June 20 William Frederick s. of Amelia Edridge.

July 25. Martha Sophia d. of Peter & Sarah Soame.[3]

Aug: 22. Mary Ann d. of William & Sarah Ducker.[2]

Aug: 29. Elizabeth d. of Thomas & Mary Hastings.[1]

Sept: 19. Maria d. of Kezia Grix.

Oct: 3. Elizabeth Ann d. of W[m] & Frances Amelia (Wighton)
        Larne.[5]

Nov: 20 Henry Johnson s. of Thomas & Julia Edridge.[1]

Dec: 12 Honour d. of Isaac & Dinah Watson.[2]

Dec: 12. John s. of John & Elizabeth (Jarvis) Cook.[4]

1820.   Jan: 16. Henry Coleman s. of William & Mary Ann
        (Coleman) Sparks.[1]

Jan: 30 Sophia Hindry d. of John & Eliz[th] (Hindry)
        Grix.[2]

March 26 Ann Goodwin d. of Christmas & Mary Ann (Goodwin)
        Smith[4]

April 2. Robert s. of Benjamin & Eliz[th] (Blyth) Skipp.[7]

April 2. George s. of Richard & Mary Watson.[2]

April 2. James s. of Philip & Sarah Penton[2]

May 14. Sarah d. of Thomas & Eliz[th] Spink.[2]

May 19. John s. of Joseph & Sarah Grix.[2]

May 21. William s. of Susanna Steward.

May 21. John s. of Samuel & Ann Smith.[2]

May 21. Charlotte d. of Arthur & Parnell (Steward) Lake.[7]

June 25. George s. of Benjamin & Mary Grix.[1]

June 25. William s. of John & Susanna Newman.[7]

---

[1] Carpenter.   [2] Husbandman.   [3] Farmer.   [4] Bricklayer.
     [5] Cordwainer.   [6] Weaver.   [7] Shepherd.

July 9 James s. of William & Hannah Lake.[1]
July 26 Henry s. of George & Mary Drory.[2]
Aug : 27 Henry s. of W[m] & Susanna (Watson) Grix.[1]
Nov : 26 Joseph s. of Peter & Eliz[th] Spink.[2]
Dec : 10. Sophia d. of Tho[s] & Mary Ann (Moore) Wighton.[5]
Dec : 24. Eliza Ann d. of Charles & Mary Ann (Shreeve) Green-
        wood.[2]
1821.   Feb : 18. George s. of Robert & Mary Mack.[4]
March 4 John s. of Margaret Watson.
March 7. Henry s. of Henry & Elizabeth Coldham.[1]
June 10. Joseph s. of Daniel & Sarah Drory.[1]
June 19. Thomas s. of Tho[s] & Julia Edridge.[4]
July 22. Caroline d. of James & Maria Blackburn.[1]
Sep : 2. Hannah d. of William & Sarah Ducker.[1]
Sept : 2. John s. of George & Mary Ann (Walter) Jonas.[5]
Oct : 14. William s. of Ann Garrod.
Nov : 11 Charles s. of Thomas & Mary Ann Wighton.[3]
Nov : 11 Edward s. of Thomas & Sarah (Delph) Shreeve.[2]
Nov : 11 Matilda d. of Samuel & Mary (Bolt) Gladden.[1]
Nov : 11 Joshua s. of William & Mary Blyth.[6]
Dec : 2. Jacob s. of Isaac & Dinah Watson.[2]
Dec : 30 Henry s. of Sam[l] & Mary Ann (Temple) Chubbock.[7]
1822.   Jan : 8 Charles s. of Charles & Mary (Roberts) Lake.[2]
Jan 20. Sarah d. of Richard & Mary Watson.[2]
Feb : 7 William s. of Francis & Eliz[th] (Reynolds) Goodwin.[1]
Feb : 24. James s. of Charles & Mary Ann Greenwood.[2]
[9]March 3. Mary d. of Samuel & Hannah Neave.[8]
[9]March 3. Charlotte d. of W[m] & Mary Ann Sparks.[4]
[9]March 3 John s. of Thomas & Elizabeth Spink.[1]
March 19. Henry s. of Ann Drory.
April 21. Robert s. of Benjamin & Eliz[th] Skip.[2]
May 3. Ursula Bowman d. of W[m] & Eleanor Smithson.[1]
May 10. Sarah d. of John & Mary (Crotch) Gardner.[10]
May 12. Martha d. of Christmas & Mary Ann Smith.[11]
May 12. Thomas s. of Ann King.

<table>
<tr><td>[1] Husbandman.</td><td>[2] Weaver.</td><td>[3] Publican.</td><td>[4] Carpenter.</td></tr>
<tr><td>[5] Cordwainer.</td><td>[6] Bricklayer.</td><td>[7] Shepherd.</td><td>[8] Farmer.</td></tr>
<tr><td>[9] These 3 by Robert Jay.</td><td>[10] Waiter.</td><td>[11] Thatcher.</td><td></td></tr>
</table>

May 19. Elizabeth Ann d. of George & Lucy (Fish) Drory.[1]
May 19 Susanna d. of Sarah Edwards.
May 26. Mary d. of W[m] & Hannah Lake.[2]
June 19. John s. of Amelia Edridge.
June 30 Lydia d. of Christmas & Sarah (Baker) Bunn.[1]
July 7. Peter s. of Peter & Elizabeth Spink.[1]
July 14. David s. of Will[m] & Hannah Masterson (Boult) Elvin.[3]
July 28. Martha d. of Samuel & Sarah Penton.[2]
July 31. William s. of Mary Grix.
Aug: 18 William s. of William & Ann (Sutton) Spink.[1]
Aug: 25 Henry s. of Isaac & Phœbe Greenwood[2] (born 28 Feb:
    1821).
Sept. 1. Edward Thomas s. of Edw[d] & Eliz[th] (Walter) Moore.[4]
Sept. 15. George s. of William & Susanna Grix.[2]
Sept. 22. Mary Ann d. of W[m] & Sarah (Souther) Bunn.[2]
Nov: 10. Samuel s. of Edward & Maria (Walter) Gladden.[2]
Dec: 22. Maria d. of Arthur & Parnell Lake.[1]
1823.   Jan: 5. Elizabeth d. of John & Elizabeth Cook.[5]
Jan: 5. James s. of Thomas & Amelia (Edwards) Sturman.[1]
Jan: 26. Frances d. of Daniel & Sarah Drory.[2]
Feb: 2 Elizabeth Amy d. of John & Eliz[th] Grix.[2]
Feb: 2. Benjamin s. of John & Eliz[th] (Mack) Lake.[2]
March 12. Susannah d. of Tho[s] & Sarah (Reynolds) Claxton.[6]
April 20. Eliza d. of George & Martha (Edwards) Jopson.[1]
April 27. Mary Ann d. of Tho[s] & Mary Ann Wighton.[7]
April 27. Mary Amelia d. of George & Mary (Gladden) Rayson.[8]
May 11. Francis s. of Susanna Lake.
May 18. Ryson & George twin ss. of Henry & Eliz[th] Coldham.[2]
May 25. Mary Ann d. of Sam[l] & Mary Ann (Vincent) Chubbock.[9]
June 1. Benjamin s. of Lydia Drory.
June 1. Elizabeth d. of James & Maria Blackburn.[1]
June 8. Sarah d. of Isaac & Phœbe Greenwood.[2]
June 22. Maria d. of Isaac & Dinah Watson.[1]
June 29. Matilda d. of Charles & Mary Ann Greenwood.[1]
Aug: 3. James s. of Samuel & Mary Gladden.[2]

---

[1] Weaver.	[2] Husbandman.	[3] Miller.
[4] Butcher.	[5] Brickmaker.	[6] Tailor.
[7] Inn-keeper.	[8] Carpenter.	[9] Shepherd.

Aug : 31. Robert d. of Robert & Mary (Amis) Mack.[1]
Sep : 7. Robert s. of Thomas & Eliz[th] Spink.[2]
Nov : 23. George s. of George & Mary Ann Jonas.[3]
Nov : 23. Louisa d. of David & Jane (Panton) Smithson.[4]
Nov : 23 Henry s. of William & Sarah Bunn.[4]
Nov : 30. Ann d. of William & Ann (Garrad) Skinner.[4]
Dec. 14 David Elvin s. of John & Martha (Crane) Colman.[5]
Dec : 21. James s. of Christmas & Sarah Bunn.[6]
Dec : 26 William Pike s. of Amelia Edridge aged 3½ yrs.
1824.   Jan : 18 Isaiah s. of Edward & Eliz[th] Moore.[7]
Feb : 1. Susanna Russell s. of Francis & Eliz[th] Goodwin.[8]
Feb 1. Hannah d. of Joseph & Sarah Grix.[4]
Feb 8. Mary Ann d. of Philip & Sarah Panton.[4]
Feb : 29. Robert s. of Rob[t] & Mary (Brown) Watson.[6]
April 11. John s. of William & Ann Spink.[6]
April 16. James s. of Samuel & Hannah Neave.[8]
May 23. Edmund s. of William & Sarah Ducker.[4]
May 30. Eliza d. of William & Hannah Lake.[4]
June 6. Thomas s. of John & Mary (Cooper) Coman.[9]
June 6. Frances d. of William & Mary Blyth.[10]
June 9. Amelia d. of Mary Ann Spink.
July 3. Lydia d. of Arthur & Parnell Lake.[6]
Aug : 22. Mary Ann d. of James & Eliz[th] (Larwood) Shreeve.[6]
Aug : 30. Elizabeth Ann d. of Tho[s] & Hannah (Postle) Jarred.[11]
Sept. 5. Caroline d. of John & Eliz[th] (Mack) Lake.[4]
Sept : 20. William Boult s. of Samuel & Mary Gladden,[4]
Oct : 10. Eliza d. of George & Martha Jopson.[6]
Nov : 7. Mary Ann d. of Elizabeth Edwards.
Nov : 21. Elizabeth d. of Christmas & Mary Ann Smith.[12]
1825.   Jan : 23. Elizabeth d. of Tho[s] & Mary Ann Wighton.[13]
Feb : 23. Charles s. of Isaac & Dinah Watson.[6]
Feb : 27. Judith Smithson d. of W[m] & Sarah (Smithson) Culley.[4]
Feb 27. W[m] Bolt s. of W[m] & Hannah (Bolt) Elvin.[5]
March 13. Harriet d. of John & Elizabeth Cook.[10]
March 13. Mary Ann d. of W[m] & Susanna Grix.[4]

---

[1] Carpenter.   [2] Servant.   [3] Cordwainer.   [4] Husbandman.   [5] Miller.
[6] Weaver.   [7] Butcher.   [8] Farmer.   [9] Blacksmith.
[10] Bricklayer.   [11] Dyer.   [12] Inn-keeper.   [13] Thatcher.

March 15. William Medler s. of Mary Wickham.

March 27. Elizabeth d. of Isaac & Mary Panton.[1]

March 27. Ann d. of William & Ann Spink.[2]

April 3. James s. of Frances Blackburn.

April 3. Ann d. of George & Mary (Greenwood) Ives.[2]

[3]April 24. Harriet d. of Tho[s] & Julia Edridge.[4]

May 12 James s. of Benj. & Mary Grix[4] (born 22 June 1823).

May 12. Alfred s. of Benj: & Mary Grix.[4]

June 19. Samuel s. of Sam[l] & Mary Ann Chubbock.[5]

July 10. John s. of David & Jane (Panton) Smithson.[2]

July 17 Joseph s. of Joseph & Catherine (Panton) Edwards.[1]

July 27. Mary Ann d. of James & Eliz[th] (Comer) Watson.[2]

July 28. Mary Ann d. of Joseph & Mary Ann (Nichols) Blyth.[7]

[6]July 31. Samuel s. of Daniel & Sarah Drory.[8]

[6]Aug: 7. Caroline d. of John & Eliz[th] Lake.[1]

Sept: 25.   Alice d. of Henry & Elizabeth Coldham.[1]

Oct: 11. John s. of Christmas & Sarah Bunn.[2]

Oct: 16 Alfred s. of Maria Walter (born 26 Feb 1818).

Oct: 16. Mary Ann d. of Edward & Maria Gladden.[9]

Oct: 23. James s. of James & Eliz[th] (Cutting) Lake.[2]

Oct: 23. William John s. of W[m] & Eliz[th] (Raymes) Soame.[2]

Oct: 30. John Reynolds s. of Francis & Eliz[th] (Reynolds) Goodwin.[10]

Oct: 30. Arthur s. of Arthur & Parnell Lake.[2]

Oct: 30. Sarah Ann d. of Harriet Steward.

Nov: 6. Francis s. of Rob[t] & Susanna (Lake) Sutton.[2]

Nov: 20. Mary d. of John & Eliz[th] Grix.[1]

Dec: 18. Deborah d. of Edward & Elizabeth Moore.[11]

Dec: 18. Robert s. of Tho[s] & Sarah (Melton) Appleton.[1]

1826.   Jan: 17. Thomas s. of Sarah Edwards.

Jan: 17. Elizabeth d. of W[m] & Sarah (Edwards) Wiley.[1]

Feb: 19. Charles s. of Benj. & Lydia (Drory) Grix.[1]

Feb: 26 Mary Ann d. of Daniel & Margaret (Basey) Hannant.[1]

March 5. Tho[s] Wiley Rounce s. of Benj. & Ann (Newstead) Rounce.[10]

---

[1] Husbandman.   [2] Weaver.   [3] This 1 by George Jarvis.   [4] Carpenter.
[5] Shepherd.   [6] These by J. D. Parmeter.   [7] Bricklayer.   [8] Broom Maker.
[9] Miller.   [10] Farmer.   [11] Butcher.

March 12 Mary Ann d. of Caroline Sutton.

March 26. Martha d. of Robert & Mary Mack. [1]

March 26 William s. of Tho[s] & Mary Ann Wighton. [2]

April 9 Henry s. of Ann King.

April 9. Sarah d. of James & Maria Blackburn. [3]

April 23. Frances d. of Robert & Mary Watson. [4]

May 7 Mary Ann d. of James & Eliz[th] Shreeve. [4]

May 7. Francis s. of Philip & Sarah Panton. [3]

May 21. Henry s. of Thomas & Julia Edridge. [1]

June 4 John s. of John & Mary Coman. [5]

June 4. Esther d. of George & Mary Ann Jonas. [6]

Oct: 22. Martha d. of Joseph & Sarah Grix. [3]

Dec: 3 Samuel s. of Samuel & Mary Gladden. [3]

1827.   Feb: 11 Robert s. of Francis & Christiana (Forrow) Watts. [4]

March 25 Philip Garrard s. of W[m] & Ann (Garrard) Skinner. [3]

Apr. 8 Eliz[th] d. of Geo. & Charlotte (Cobb) Gooch, [3] born 21 Ap.
        1826.

May 13 Sarah d. of Joseph & Ann (Elmer) Pottle, [3] born in 1813.

May 13 Herriott d. of Joseph & Ann Pottle, [3] born in 1819.

May 20 Henry s. of Edward & Maria Gladden. [3]

May 20 Martha d. of Mary Ann Newman.

May 27. George s. of Richard & Mary Watson. [3]

June 10 Sophia d. of Maria Bishop.

June 10 Susanna d. of Samuel & Hannah Neave. [7]

June 17 Robert s. of W[m] & Susan (Watson) Grix. [3]

Sept: 2. Thomas s. of Arthur & Parnell Lake. [4]

Sept: 9. John s. of William & Ann Spink. [4]

Sept: 9. Hannent Thomas s. of Charles & Mary Lake. [4]

Sept: 30. Joseph s. of W[m] & Hannah (Blyth) Lake. [3]

Oct: 7. Henry s. of Thomas & Julia Edridge. [1]

Oct: 21 Thomas s. of William & Mary Blyth. [8]

Nov: 4 Richard s. of George & Charlottte Gooch. [3]

Nov: 11. Mary d. of Francis & Eliz[th] Goodwin. [9]

Dec: 2. Sarah Ann d. of James & Eliz[th] Lake. [4]

Dec: 16 Mary d. of John & Phillis (Gotterson) Raymes. [10]

1828.   Jan: 6. Louisa d. of John & Eliz[th] Grix. [3]

---

[1] Carpenter.   [2] Innkeeper.   [3] Husbandman.   [4] Weaver.   [5] Blacksmith.
[6] Cordwainer.   [7] Cooper.   [8] Bricklayer.   [9] Farmer.   [10] Servant.

Jan : 6. James s. of Mary Randal.
Jan : 20 James s. of John & Maria (Moore) Bartram. [1]
Jan : 27 Hannah d. of Francis & Christiana Watts. [2]
Jan : 27 Mary Ann d. of John & Ann (Cadderma) Oliver. [2]
Feb : 24 Mary Ann d. of Christmas & Mary Ann Smith. [3]
Feb : 24. James s. of John & Ann (Grix) Smithson. [2]
March 9. Robert s. of Robert & Mary Mack. [4]
March 11 Elizabeth d. of Elizabeth Soame.
April 6 Theodorick s. of Theodorick & Frances (Starling) Terry. [5]
April 20 Charles s. of James & Elizabeth Shreeve. [2]
May 25 Charles s. of Francis & Eliz[th] (Grix) Bullock. [2]
May 25 Elizabeth d. of W[m] & Sarah Ducker. [2]
May 26 William s. of Christmas & Sarah Bunn. [6]
[7]June 22. Robert s. of Charles & Ann (King) Sutton. [6]
June 29. John s. of Daniel & Margaret (Basey) Hannant. [2]
June 29 Mary d. of William & Sarah (Edwards) Wiley. [2]
July 20 Henry s. of Benj[n] & Sarah Grix. [6]
July 27. Elizabeth d. of James & Caroline (Sutton) Grix. [6]
July 27. Elizabeth d. of Joseph & Mary Blyth. [8]
Aug : 24. Mary d. of Samuel & Mary Gladden. [2]
Sept : 7. Elizabeth Ann d. of Robert & Mary Watson. [6]
Sept. 21. Mary Ann d. of George & Mary Ann Jonas. [9]
Oct : 5. Edward s. of Edw[d] & Eliz[th] Moore, [10] born 20 Jan 1826.
Oct 5. Elizabeth d. of Edw[d] & Eliz[th] Moore.
Oct. 19. Elijah s. of Benj[n] & Mary (Pully) Grix. [4]
1829.   Feb : 8 James s. of John & Dinah (Killegrew) Culley. [9]
Feb : 22. Elizabeth d. of John & Mary Ann (Newman) Moore. [4]
March 8. William s. of George & Charlotte Gooch. [6]
March 15. Ann Charlotte d. of Benjamin & Ann Rounce. [11]
March 22. Caroline d. of Christmas & Mary Ann Smith. [3]
May 10. John s. of Sam[l] & Mary (Davidson) Poll. [12]
May 17. Mary d. of Joshua & Maria (Chaplin) Blyth. [6]
June 7. Letitia d. of Arthur & Parnell Lake. [6]
June 7. Josiah s. of Henry & Sarah (Blake) Nichols, [9] born 4
        Nov : 1821.

---

[1] Miller.   [2] Husbandman.   [3] Thatcher.   [4] Carpenter.   [5] Steward.
[6] Weaver.   [7] This one by Hammond Roberson off[g] Min[r].   [8] Bricklayer.
[9] Cordwainer.   [10] Butcher.   [11] Farmer.   [12] Laborer.

June 7. Eliz[th] Blake d. of Henry & Sarah Nichols born 15 Dec
  1826.
June 7. Mary Ann d. of Henry & Sarah Nichols.
1829.   Jan : 15. Ann d. of W[m] & Susanna Grix.[1]
Sept 21 Lydia d. of Thomas & Charlotte (Applegate) Blyth.[2]
Oct 18 John s. of William & Sarah Wiley.[1]
Nov : 22 George s. of Sarah Grix.
Dec : 13 Margaret s. of Philip & Sarah Panton.[1]
1830.   Jan : 31. James s. of Henry & Martha (Mathewson)
  Gibson.[2]
Feb : 7. Robert s. of Benjamin & Mary Grix.[3]
Feb : 21. Maria d. of Joseph & Sarah Grix.[1]
Feb : 21 Mary Ann d. of Francis & Christiana Watts.[1]
March 7. Emma Maria d. of William & Ann Spink.[2]
March 7. Robert s. of William & Ann Skinner.[1]
March 21. John s. of Elizabeth Drory.
March 21. Rose d. of John & Phillis Raymes.[4]
April 4. Vallatta d. of Samuel & Mary Gladden.[1]
April 4 Mary Ann d. of Christmas & Sarah Bunn.[2]
April 18 Moses s. of Moses & Mary (Sutton) Delph.[1]
April 18. John s. of William & Mary Blyth.[4]
June 13 Eliza d. of W[m] & Mary (Bulman[5]) Skipp *alias*
  Skipper.[6]
Aug : 8. Harriet d. of Joseph & Mary Blyth.[4]
Aug : 22. Charlotte d. of Robert & Mary Mack.[3]
Aug : 22. Robert s. of Thomas & Julia Edridge.[3]
Sept : 19 Charlotte d. of John & Eliz[th] (Mack) Lake.[1]
Oct : 3. Martha d. of W[m] & Sarah Ducker.[1]
Oct : 31. William s. of Joseph & Katherine (Panton) Edwards.[1]
Nov : 28 John s. of John & Dinah Culley.[6]
Dec : 19 Mary Ann d. of Rob[t] & Maria (Bishop) Edwards.[1]
1831.   Jan : 9. Harriet d. of George & Charlotte Gooch.[2]
Jan : 16. Robert s. of James & Caroline Grix.[2]
Jan : 16 Nathaniel s. of Nathan[l] & Sarah Stewart.[2]
Jan : 16 Thomas s. of Nathan[l] & Sarah Stewart.[2]
Jan : 16. David s. of James & Sarah Shreeve.[2]
Jan : 23. Sarah Ann d. of John & Ann (Grix) Smithson.[1]

---

[1]. Husbandman.   [2] Weaver.   [3] Carpenter.
[4] Bricklayer.   [5] Widow.   [6] Cordwainer.

Feb 20 Robert s. of Charles & Mary Ann (Spink) Sutton.[1]

March 27 Isaac s. of Thos & Katharine (Twea) Greenwood.[2]

May 2. Stephen s. of Wm & Sarah (Smithson) Culley.[2]

June 5. John s. of Zechariah & Mary (Drory) Hunt.[1]

July 31. John s. of Benjn & Frances (Dike) Smith.[3]

July 31 Mary d. of Christmas & Mary Ann Smith.[3]

Aug: 7 Eliza d. of Jennis & Eliza (Jex) Jex.[2]

Oct: 2 Elizabeth Rogers d. of Wm & Hannah Elvin.[4]

Oct: 2. Robert s. of Robt & Ann (Mouney) Thompson.[2]

Oct: 2. Henry d. of Thos & Elizth (Soame) Wiley.[2]

[5]Nov: 27 Sarah Ann d. of Joseph & Catherine Edwards.[1]

[6]Dec: 8. James s. of Robt & Mary (Skipper) Stageman.[2]

[6]Dec: 18 John s. of James & Mary (Mount) Thompson.[7]

[8]1832.   Jan: 8. Jonathan s. of John & Mary Grix.[1]

[8]Jan: 8 Sophia d. of John & Mary Grix, born 30 July 1825.

[8]Jan: 8 Isaiah s. of John & Mary Grix.

[8]Jan: 8. Hannah d. of Moses & Mary Delph.[7]

Jan: 15. Marianne d. of Frances Sutton, born 25 Dec 1831.

Feb: 19 Maria d. of James & Caroline Grix,[1] born Jan: 19.

Feb: 19. Amy d. of Wm & Susan Grix,[2] born 31 Dec 1831.

Feb: 26 Sarah Ann d. of Zephaniah & Sarah Smithson,[10] born
 Feb: 13.

March 11. William s. of Thos & Elizth Wiley,[2] born Feb: 26.

March 18. Robert s. of George & Mary Anne Jones,[11] born 15
 Nov 1830.

March 18. Francis s. of Saml & Hannah Neave,[12] born 13 Oct 1831.

Apr. 8. Ann d. of Charles & Ann Delph,[2] born Apr. 5.

Apr. 16 Britannia d. of Charles & Mary Anne Sutton,[2] born Feb 13.

April 29. Lydia Ann d. of Philip & Sarah Panton,[2] born Ap. 16.

April 29. Susanna d. of Henry & Mary Fox,[13] born Ap. 19.

May 20. Benjamin s. of Wm & Mary Skipper,[11] born Ap. 28.

June 10. Mary Anne d. of Wm & Mary Blyth,[14] born 5 Dec 1831.

June 10. Sarah d. of Thos & Sarah Shreeve,[2] born 23 Nov 1823.

June 10. George s. of Thos & Sarah Shreeve,[2] born 17 June 1826.

June 10 Ann d. of Thos & Sarah Shreeve,[2] born 16 May 1828.

---

[1] Weaver.   [2] Husbandman.   [3] Thatcher.   [4] Miller.   [5] This one by J. Perowne Offg Minr.   [6] These 2 by Edwd Holley Offg Minr.   [7] Labourer.   [8] These 4 by Saml Fisher Offg Minr.   [10] Barber.   [11] Shoemaker.   [12] Farmer.   [13] Baker.   [14] Bricklayer.

June 10. William s. of Tho⁸ & Sarah Shreeve,[1] born 26 Oct 1830.
June 17 Thomas s. of Rob[t] & Maria Edwards,[2] born 9 June.
June 17 Sarah Amelia d. of Benj[n] & Emily Grix,[2] born 17 June 1831.
Aug : 5. Samuel s. of Isaac & Sophia Panton,[2] born 3 Aug :
Aug : 5. William s. of Rob[t] & Sarah Spink,[2] born 11 July.
Aug : 26 Elizabeth d. of James & Ann Drory,[3] born 11 Aug :
Sep : 2. Mary Ann d. of Tho⁸ & Deborah Brown,[4] born 12 Aug :
Sept : 9. Robert s. of James & Maria Blackburne,[1] born 13 Aug.
Sept : 16 Eliza d. of Samuel & Mary Gladden,[1] born 13 Aug.
Sept : 25 Eliza d. of Charles & Jane Skipper,[2] born 18 Sept.
Oct : 14 Harriet d. of Christmas & Sarah Bunn,[2] born 6 Oct :
Oct 14, Maria d. of Robert & Mary Mack,[5] born 29 Sept :
Dec : 23 Dinah d. of Tho⁸ & Catharine Greenwood,[1] born 25 Nov.

[Bk. 8.]

1833.   Jan 5. Robert s. of Nathaniel & Sarah Steward,[1] born 28
Oct 1832.
Feb : 17. Harriet d. of Francis & Christian Watts,[1] born 16 Jan :
Feb : 17 James s. of W[m] & Ann Spink,[2] born 15th Feb :
Feb : 24. Harriet d. of James & Eliz[th] Shreeve,[6] born 25 Dec 1832.
March 17. Elijah s. of Tho⁸ & Emily (Edwards) Stearman,[2] born
12 Feb.
April 14 Hannah d. of Moses & Mary Delph,[1] born 1 April.
April 14 Zephaniah s. of Benj[n] & Emily (Soame) Grix,[1] born 6 April.
April 14 Mary d. of W[m] & Sarah Wiley,[1] born 27 Nov : 1832.
April 14 Matthew s. of Rob[t] & Sophia (Oliver) Jeckel,[1] born 11th.
April 21. Edward s. of Tho⁸ & Eliz[th] (Soame) Wiley,[1] born 25 Feb.
April 28. Eliz[th] Ann d. of Benj[n] & Frances Smith,[7] born 28 Mar.
May 12. James s. of W[m] & Sarah Ducker,[1] born 16 May 1832.
May 12 Thomas s. of Joseph & Sarah Grix,[1] born 25 Feb :
May 26 Isaiah s. of John & Mary (Blake) Grix,[1] born 28 Apr.
May 26. Henry s. of George & Mary Ann Jones,[8] born 28 Feb.
June 2. Matilda d. of Sam[l] & Eliz[th] (Berney) Wells,[9] born 4 May.
June 2. Henry s. of Henry & Martha Gibson,[2] born 27 May.
June 2. William s. of James & Eleanor (Penton) Abbs,[2] born 2 March
June 9. Sarah Ann d. of W[m] & Ann Skinner,[6] born 3 July 1832.
June 30. Joseph s. of Ann Penton, born 10 May.
July 7. Thomas s. of Tho⁸ & Sarah Shreeve,[1] born 12 June.

July 14 Henry s. of Rob[t] & Mary Stageman,[1] born 15 June.

July 21. Mary Ann d. of Tho[s] & Charlotte Blyth,[1] born 4 Feb:

Aug: 4. Robert s. of Ja[s] & Mary (Blackburn) Edwards,[1] born 3 July.

Aug: 4 Stephen s. of Charles & Mary Sutton,[2] born 30 June.

Sept: 1. Mary Ann d. of Robert & Susan Sutton,[2] born 16 Ap.

Sept: 8. Charles s. of Charles & Ann (Randall) Delph,[2] born 5[th.]

Sept: 22 Edward s. of Edw[d] & Maria Gladden,[2] born 15 Aug:

Sept: 22. Susan Eliz[th] d. of James & Sarah (Rivett) Drory[3] born 2nd.

Oct: 13. John s. of Zephaniah & Sarah (Watson) Smithson[4] born 20 Sept:

Nov: 3 Henry s. of Zechariah & Mary Hunt,[1] born 4 Oct:

Nov: 10. Joseph s. of Joseph & Mary Blyth,[5] born 8 Oct:

Nov: 10. James s. of Edmund & Sophia (Oliver) Gall,[2] born 14 Oct:

Nov: 24. Eliz[th] Smith d. of Ja[s] & Anne (Smith) Drory,[6] born 4 Oct:

Nov: 24. Anne Maria d. of Tho[s] & Deborah Brown,[7] born 21 Nov 1830.

Dec: 25. Mary d. of John & Ann (Grix) Smithson,[2] born 23 Nov.

1834.   Jan 19. Rebecca d. of W[m] & Mary Skipper,[3] born 19 Dec 1833.

Jan: 26. Eliza Ann d. of Ja[s] & Mary Ann Thompson,[2] born 6 Jan:

Feb: 9 Henry s. of George & Charlotte Gooch,[1] born 24 Jan:

Feb: 16. William s. of Henry & Sarah Nichols,[3] born 10[th.]

March 2. Charles s. of Geo. & Eliza (Steward) Willimott[8] b. 8 Feb.

April 27. Esther d. of Francis & Christian Watts,[2] born 31 Mar.

May 18 Emma Harriet d. of John & Harriet Howlett,[9] b. 17[th.]

May 18 Samuel Mack s. of Sam[l] & Mary Gladden,[2] born 24 Ap.

June 29. Matilda d. of W[m] & Sarah Wiley,[2] born 5 May.

July 20. William s. of Christmas & Mary Smith,[10] born 25 June.

Aug: 19. Matilda d. of Rob[t] & Sarah Spink,[1] born 8[th.]

Sept: 14 Margaret d. of Christmas & Sarah Bunn,[1] born 3[rd.]

Sept: 21. Thomas s. of Elizabeth Willimott, born 4 July.

Sept: 28 Thomas s. of W[m] & Mary Blyth,[5] born 27 July.

---

[1] Weaver.   [2] Husbandman.   [3] Shoemaker.   [4] Barber.   [5] Bricklayer.
[6] Fuller.   [7] Baker.   [8] Blacksmith.   [9] Farmer. [10] Thatcher.

Oct: 12. Comely d. of W^m & Susan Grix,[1] born 5 Feb:

Oct: 12. Eleanor d. of Thomas & Maria Wighton,[2] born 1st.

Oct: 19. Ann Jane d. of Charles & Mary Lake,[3] born 24 May.

Oct: 19 Robert s. of James & Caroline Grix,[4] born 23 Aug:

Nov: 16. Benjamin s. of Benjn & Mary Grix,[5] born 26 Oct 1833.

Nov: 16. Eliza d. of Robert & Mary Mack,[5] born 10 Oct:

Nov: 20 Charlotte d. of W^m & Maria (Nobbs) Morter,[1] born 20 Oct:

1835.   Jan: 4. William s. of Robt & Mary Stageman,[4] born 27 Dec 1834.

Jan: 11. William s. of Isaac & Sophia Penton,[4] born 11 Dec 1834.

Jan: 11 Edmund s. of Ja^s & Mary Ann (Bell) Watson,[1] b. 17 Dec 1834.

Feb 8. Joseph s. of Nathaniel & Sarah Steward,[1] born 14 Jan:

March 8. Thomas s. of Jacob & Mary (Smith) Bowman,[1] b. 19 Feb.

March 8. Eliza d. of Thos & Eliza (Nobbs) Greenwood,[1] b. 8 Feb.

March 8. Mary Ann d. of Henry & Martha Gibson,[1] born 22 Feb.

March 10. Elizabeth d. of Charles & Jane Skipper,[4] born 24 Feb.

March 15. Eleanor Alice d. of Henry Thomas & Hannah (Moore) Soame,[6] born 15 Feb.

March 15. James s. of Martha Soame, born 7th.

May 2 Charlotte d. of George & Susan (Blogg) Neale[1] born 30 April.

May 13. Ellen twin d. of John & Harriet Howlett,[3] born 11th.

May 13 Anna, twin d. of John & Harriet Howlett, born 11th.

May 17. John s. of Ann Penton, born 14th.

May 21. Barnard s. of Philip & Sarah Penton[1] born 21st.

May 24 Edmund s. of Edmund & Sophia Gall,[1] born 1st.

June 7. William s. of W^m & Sarah Ducker,[1] born 30 Dec. 1834.

June 14 Caroline d. of W^m & Amy (Sutton) Spink,[4] born 21 May.

June 23. Susan d. of Thos & Eliz^th Wiley,[1] born 22nd.

June 28. Ellena d. of Thos & Esther (Bullen) Smithson[1] born 19th.

June 28 Sarah Ann d. of Benjn & Emily Grix,[1] born 6 March.

July 5. Henry s. of George & Charlotte Gooch,[4] born 21 June.

July 19 Matilda d. of James & Eliz^th Shreeve,[3] born 6th.

Aug: 16. Elizabeth d. of Robt & Susan Sutton,[4] born 3rd.

---

[1] Husbandman.	[2] Innkeeper.	[3] Farmer.
[4] Weaver.	[5] Carpenter.	[6] Cabinet Maker.

Sept : 6. Frederick s. of Maria Edwards, born 22 Aug :

Sep : 6. William s. of Saml & Eliz^th Wells,[1] born 30 Aug :

Sept : 27. Isaac s. of Thos & Catherine (Twee) Greenwood,[2] b. 27 Aug :

Oct : 11. Maria d. of Rebekah Naylor, born 22 Sept.

Oct : 11 Eliza Mary Anne d. of Geo. & Eliza Willimott,[1] b. 2nd.

Oct : 11 Harriet d. of Charles & Ann Delph,[2] born 6th.

Oct : 18 Susan d. of John & Mary (Sall) Delph,[2] born 5th.

Nov : 22 Henry s. of Edwd & Maria Gladden,[2] born 26 Oct.

Dec : 6. Sarah Elizabeth d. of John & Mary (Soame) Spaul[2] born 4 Nov :

Dec : 6. James s. of Benjn & Frances (Dyke) Smith,[3] b. 22 Oct :

Dec : 25 Elizabeth d. of Henry & Mary (Forrow) Middleton,[2] born 20th.

1836. Jan 3. Jacob Edridge s. of Elizabeth Bowman, b. 3 Dec 1835.

Jan : 10 Jane d. of Benjn & Mary Grix,[4] born 5 Dec 1835.

Feb : 7. William s. of Hercules & Mary (Sexton) Bradfield,[5] born 2nd.

Feb : 7. Henry s. of Maria Spaul, born 22 Feb 1835.

Feb : 14 Elizabeth d. of Ja^s & Mary Anne Thompson,[2] b. 10 Jan :

March 27. Mary Ann d. of Ja^s & Ann (Savage) Blyth,[2] b. 23rd.

March 27. Mary Ann d. of George & Mary Ann Jones,[6] b. 2 Feb.

April 10. James s. of W^m & Sarah Wiley,[2] born 23 Feb :

April 24. Rachel d. of Thos & Sarah (Delph) Shreeve,[7] born 20 Feb.

June 7. Caroline d. of Ja^s & Mary Ann (Blackburn) Edwards[8] born 3rd.

June 12 William s. of Robert & Sophia (Oliver) Jeckell,[2] b. 25 May.

June 26 Harriet d. of Charles & Mary Ann Greenwood,[9] b. 13 May.

July 3 John s. of Philip & Sarah Penton,[2] born 11 June.

July 3. Philip s. of Catherine Penton, born 25 Nov 1835.

July 10. John Hammond s. of John & Harriet Howlett,[9] born 7th.

July 17. Henry s. of Robert & Sarah Spink,[8] born 24 June.

July 24 Isaac s. of John Wright & Eliz^th (Skipper) Jex[2] born 16th.

---

[1] Blacksmith.	[2] Husbandman.	[3] Thatcher.
[4] Carpenter.	[5] Servant.	[6] Shoemaker.
[7] Gardener.	[8] Weaver.	[9] Farmer.

July 31. Matilda d. of Robt & Mary Mack,[1] born 11$^{th.}$

Aug : 14 Elizabeth Mary d. of Francis & Elizth Goodwin,[2] b. 18 March.

Aug : 21 Harriet d. of Edmund & Sophia Gall,[3] born 18$^{th.}$

Sept : 4. Sarah d. of Robt & Maria Edwards,[3] born 30 Aug :

Sept 11. Mary Ann d. of Francis & Christian Watts,[3] born 17 Aug :

Nov : 27 Mary Anne d. of John & Lydia Mack.[4]

[Book 9.]

BURIALS 1813 TO 1832.[5]

1813.   Jan 8 John Gibson aged 77.

Feb 14 William Grand of Mattishall aged 78.

May 17 Elizabeth Jerry aged 13.

Aug : 6. Lydia Grix aged 2.

Nov : 9 Robert Jeckell, Buxton Ho. of Industry, aged 80.

Dec : 8 Sarah Buck, of St Mich : Thorn, Norwich, infant.

1814.   Jan : 27. John Lake, aged 75.

Feb : 17 Francis Watson aged 22.

March 7. Mary Hunt aged 65.

May 29 Grace Mann aged 23.

Nov : 30. Elizabeth Edwards, Buxton Ho. of Ind^y, aged 80.

Dec : 21 Robert Blake, infant.

Dec : 25 James Crotch aged 48.

1815.   Jan : 6 Robert Floyd aged 70.

Feb 14. John Everett, Buxton Ho. of Industry, aged 80.

March 21. Susanna Dains aged 53.

March 24 James Greenwood aged 88.

April 11 Samuel Ward aged 40.

Aug : 8 William Shreeve of Blickland,[6] aged 83.

Aug : 14 Susanna Thompson aged 71.

Aug. 18 Wm Henry Elvin aged 3.

Aug : 31. Philip Panton aged 9.

Sept : 27 Mary Jeary aged 42.

---

[1] Carpenter.   [2] Farmer.   [3] Husbandman.   [4] Weaver.
[5] The first 218 entries by J. BINGLE, Curate.   [6] Blickling.

Nov: 9 Thomas Jeary infant.

1816.   Feb : 1 Robert Steward aged 2.

March 27 James Gladden aged 52.

April 12 Thomas Grix aged 1.

May 26 Ann Watson aged 1.

June 2 Sarah Bransby aged 56.

Dec : 1 Joseph Newman infant.

1817.   Feb 26. Elizabeth Fish, of Hevingham, aged 72.

March 19 Elizabeth Watts aged 42.

March 27 Flint Stone aged 26.

April 13. Sophia Proudfoot aged 1.

June 1 Elizabeth Edwards aged 56.

June 17 Sarah Watson aged 84.

July 13 Elizabeth Pain aged 19.

July 29 Thomasin Ward aged 66.

Aug : 4. Edward Watson aged 64.

Aug : 30 Phillis Watts infant.

Sept. 14. Solomon Shreeve, of North Walsham, aged 78.

Dec : 4 Mary Lubbock aged 69.

1818.   Jan : 11. Isaac Coman, Buxton Ho. of Industry, aged 70.

Feb : 25 Mary Sutton aged 21.

April 14 Mary Oats, Buxton Ho. of Industry, aged 70.

April 9 Edward Stone aged 25.

Sept 12 Elizabeth Hastings aged 4.

Sept 24 Anna Sophia Pike aged 39.

Oct : 4. Elizabeth Buck, of Norwich, infant.

Dec : 10 John Sutton aged 55.

Dec : 17 Ann Greenwood aged 68.

1819.   Jan 31.   William Matthews Goodwin, of Buxton, Inf[t.]

March 12 Elizabeth Grix, infant.

May 13 Elizabeth Crotch aged 20.

May 24 *Uriah Penton,*[1] infant.

Aug : 16 William Frederick Edridge,[1] infant.

Oct : 13. Harriet Edridge, of Hingham, aged 19.

Dec : 30 Robert Lubbock aged 45.

1820.   Jan : 20 Mary Jeckel, aged 95.

March 10. Stephen Grix, of Norwich, aged 53.

[1] Torn out, but supplied from Transcript.

March 10 Edmund Witterton aged 78.
April 2. Bridget King aged 45.
April 26 Joseph Blyth —— —[1]
—— —[1] Jane Amis —— —[1]
May 19 Amy Grix aged 32.
June 16 Robert Skipp infant.
June 25. Henry Key, Buxton Ho. of Industry, aged 70.
July 31. Henry Drory infant.
Sept 3. Eunice Skinner aged 45.
Oct: 9. Mary Ann Willimot aged 15.
Oct: 20 William Blyth infant.
Nov: 5. Maria Edwardes, of Tuttington, infant.
Nov 27 George Watson infant.
Dec: 16 Mary Ann Blyth aged 5.
Dec: 26. Peter Spink aged 2.
1821.   Jan: 5. Charles Saunders aged 72.
Jan: 15 Christopher Grix aged 64.
March 5. Samuel Bunn aged 32.
July 1. Benjamin Lake aged 38.
July 15 Robert Edwards aged 52.
July 20 David Stone, of Hevingham, aged 25.
Nov: 1. Ann Edridge aged 59.
1822.   Jan: 14 Susanna Lake aged 76.
March 13 James Greenwood infant.
March 19 Luke Edwards, Buxton Ho. of Indy. aged 78.
April 20. Sarah Drory aged 79.
April 20. Mary Grix aged 28.
April 25 John Laws aged 84.
June 19. Sarah Gardner infant.
July 8. Peter Spink infant.
July 8. Lydia Watts aged 83.
July 12 Phillis Amys aged 66.
Aug: 9. William Grix infant.
Sept: 3. Henry Johnson Edridge aged 2.
Sept: 16. Edward Thomas Moore infant.
Nov: 16 Sarah Kiddle aged 24.
Nov: 25 John Edridge infant.

---

[1] Torn out.

Dec : 25 John Panton aged 18.

1823.   Jan : 9. Meliza Edwards, of Norwich, aged 2.

Jan : 19. Mary Neave aged 1.

Jan : 22. Mary Shreeve aged 61.

Jan 29 Mary Ann Sutton aged 35.

Feb : 11 Thomas Witterton aged 51.

May 25 Ryson Coldham infant.

May 25 John Dory aged 6.

May 31. Eliza Jopson aged 1.

June 21. Maria Houghton, of Lakenham, aged 35.

June 26. Elizabeth Walsingham aged 78.

July 19 Mary Ann Meeds aged 72.

Nov : 9 Samuel Panton aged 16.

Dec : 1 Sarah Laws, Buxton Ho. of Industry, aged 72.

1824.   Feb : 2. Ann Lake aged 54.

April 29. John Spink infant.

May 2. William Gamaliel Skidmore aged 25.

May 16. Robert Hastings aged 24.

June 15. Sarah Greenwood aged 1.

June 15 Thomas Blyth aged 19.

June 27. Frances Marsham aged 38.

July 6. Lydia Lake infant.

July 13. Esther Delph aged 70.

July 19. Aaron Delph aged 43.

July 20. Sarah Boswell aged 80.

July 29. Mary Lubbock aged 59.

July 30. Richard Edwards aged 52.

Aug : 5. Edward Delph aged 81.

Aug : 21. Mary Blyth aged 10.

Sept : 5 Sarah Carr, of Norwich, aged 69.

Sept : 22. Caroline Lake infant.

Oct : 3 Mary Ann Stone aged 8.

Oct 19 Martha Grix aged 64.

Nov : 1. Francis Lake infant.

Nov : 8. William Amis aged 63.

Nov : 11 Sarah Panton aged 48.

Nov : 29. Maria Panton aged 11.

Dec : 12. Mary Ann Edwards infant.

Dec : 14. Hannah Blyth aged 70.

Dec : 25. Robert Panton aged 8.

Dec : 28. John Amis aged 75.

Dec : 29. Isaac Greenwood aged 48.

1825.   Jan 2 Ann Blyth aged 74.

Feb : 2. John Howlett aged 73.

March 22. William Medler Wickham infant.

May 10 John Hunt aged 84.

June 21. Samuel Chubbock infant.

July 20 Jonathan Ulph aged 75.

Aug : 1. John Stageman aged 76.

Aug : 2. Samuel Drory infant.

Aug : 14. Mary Ann Shreeve aged 1.

Oct : 11. Henry Sturman aged 87.

Nov : 2. Elizabeth Cory aged 87.

1826.   Jan : 15. Lucy Shreeve aged 86.

April 23. Alice Coldham infant.

May 19. Judith Carr of Hevingham aged 74.

June 18. Henry Edridge infant.

June 27 Deborah Moore infant.

July 13 Mary Ann Gladden infant.

July 31. Robert Jeary of Oughton[1] aged 18.

Aug : 29 William Wighton infant.

Oct : 28. Matilda Gladden, of Reepham, aged 21.

Nov : 12. Sarah Soame aged 46.

Dec : 23 Sarah Neave aged 92.

1827.   Jan 20 Elizabeth Drory, of Hevingham, infant.

March 5. John Newman aged 65.

March 29 Mary Ann Wighton aged 27.

April 5. Edward Smith, Buxton Ho. of Industry, aged 70

Aug : 23 Mary Greenwood aged 18.

Sept : 21 Mary Blyth, of Aylsham, aged 83.

Nov : 5. Joseph Roberts, of Cawston, aged 51.

Nov : 27.   John Bransby, of Hevingham, aged 70.

Dec : 16 Elizabeth Pain aged 71.

1828.   Feb : 25. Mary Soame, of Aylsham, aged 70.

March 11. Mary Ann Smith infant.

Perhaps **Houghton, or Oulton.**

March 15. Samuel Gladden aged 1.

March 17 Peters Gladden, of Wangford Suff[k] aged 19.

May 20 Ann Neave aged 17.

May 24. Charles Wighton aged 68.

May 26 Sarah Ann Lake infant.

July 8 Robert Sutton infant.

Aug : 14 Elizabeth Lake aged 26.

Aug : 31 Ann Sutton aged 25.

Oct : 7. Elizabeth Ash, Buxton Ho. of Industry, aged 84.

Oct : 17. David Shreeve aged 52.

Nov : 1. William Gittoes aged 82.

Nov : 21. Robert Jackson infant.

Dec : 30. Mary Ann Goodwin aged 1.

1829.   April 7. Mary Whiley aged 1.

June 30. William Skipp infant.

June 30. Elizabeth Grix infant.

July 31. Sarah Ann Skinner aged 1.

Dec : 17. Peter Grix infant.

Dec : 22. Maria Grix infant.

1830.   Jan : 4. Susan Stageman aged 74.

Jan : 23 William Fiddy, of Catton, aged 2.

Feb : 24 John Wright aged 77.

April 18. Mary Skidmore aged 55.

June 16 John Lake aged 18 ([1]or 78.)

June 17. John Drory infant.

June 17. Abigail Sturman, Buxton Ho. of Ind[y,] aged 77.

June 19. Samuel Smith aged 87.

June 23. Mary Skipp *alias* Skipper aged 30.

July 20. Mary Gabbarent *alias* Gabbareth of Hainford, aged 18.

Aug : 1. William Bunn aged 2.

Sept : 10. Eliza Skipp *alias* Skipper infant.

Oct : 11. Joseph Edwards aged 4.

Oct : 20 William Hastings aged 25.

Oct : 29. Ann Bowles aged 93.

Oct : 29. Amy Smithson aged 68.

Nov : 30. Elizabeth Blyth aged 82.

---

[1] Figures obscure.

1831.   Jan : 22. Robert Edridge infant.
        Jan : 22. Robert Grix infant.
        Feb : 4 Julia Edridge aged 36.
        Feb : 4. Thomas Blyth aged 3.
        Feb : 12. Lydia Sturman aged 90.
        April 21. Benjamin Grix aged 60.
        June 3. William Edwards aged 2.
        Sept : 25 William Pain aged 74.
        Oct : 2. Ann Hastings aged 76.
        Oct : 23. James Moore aged 29.
        Nov : 17 Samuel Lubbock aged 89.[1]
        Nov : 17 Philip Garrad aged 37.[1]
        Nov : 19. Elizabeth Gladden, of Reepham, aged 66.[1]
        Nov : 25 William Shreeve aged 63 years.[1]
        Nov : 27 James Dunnet aged 81 yrs.[2]
        Dec : 31 Sarah Elvin aged 81 yrs.
1832.   Jan : 8 Susan Smithson aged 72.[3]
        March 21 Hannah Delph aged 15 weeks.[4]
        April 1 Caroline Blackburn aged 10 yrs.
        April 1. William Wiley aged 1 month.
        May 3 Isaiah Grix aged 47 weeks.
        June 10 Sarah Abbs aged 15 yrs.

[Book 10.]

1833.   Jan^{ry} 7 Joseph Edwards aged 39 years.
        Jan^{ry} 13. Thomas Edwards aged 6 months.
        Jan^{ry} 22 Mary Bunn aged 61 years.
        Jan^{ry} 23 Susan Barker aged 95 years.
        Feb^{ry} 17 John Shreeve aged 87 years.
        March 7 James Cook aged 80 years.
        May 17 Sarah Watson aged 53 years.
        June 4 Mary Abbs aged 20 years.

---

[1] These 4 by W. J. Blake Off^g Min^r.
[2] This 1 by J. Perowne Clk.
[3] This 1 by Saml Fisher Off^g Min^r.
[4] The rest of this book by H. Evans, curate.

June 13 Christian Bowman aged 90 years.

June 30 Sarah Grix aged 9 weeks.

July 18 William Abbs aged 4 months.

July 25 Israel Neale aged 20 years

September 1. Hannah Watts aged 5 years.

Septʳ 22 Eleanor Penton aged 80 years.

October 6. Benjamin Skipper aged 21 years.

December 8. Mary Hastings aged 49 years.

December 25 John Watson aged 84 years.

1834. April 15 John Watson aged 43 years.

May 25 John King aged 64 years.

July 3 Anne Watson aged 81 years.

July 21 Edmund Jeary, of Oulton, aged 60 years.

October 5. James Gibson aged 5 years.

October 5 Mary Ann Gibson aged 3 years.

October 12 Mary Ann Jones aged 6 years.

October 12 Susan Neave aged 7 years.

October 15 Mary Ann Watts aged 4 years.

October 30 Matthew Moore aged 89 years.

October 30 Frederick Stone aged 2 years.

November 9 Matilda Spink aged 3 months.

November 16. Henry Gooch aged 9 months.

November 20 Charles Willimott aged 9 months.

November 20 Benjamin Grix aged 1 year.

November 25 Henry Gladden aged 7 years.

December 2 Mary Grix aged 41 years.

December 4 Robert Skinner aged 4 years.

December 4 Samuel Neale aged 4 years.

1835. Jan : 2. John Edwards, Buxton Ho. of Industry, aged 63 years.

Feb : 5. Elice Blyth aged 72 years.

March 5. William Hastings aged 84 years.

April 12 Martha Jeckell aged 75 years.

May 3 Joseph Blyth aged 86 years.

May 18 Ellen Howlett aged 4 days.

May 18 Anna Howlett aged 4 days.

May 21 Sarah Ann Edwards aged 3 years.

June 8 Mary Hunt aged 35 years.

June 9 Mary Ann Sutton aged 9 months.

June 23 Sarah Coman, Buxton Ho. of Industry, aged 80 yrs.

July 5 Susan Wiley aged 12 days.

July 14 Mary Miller, wife of Wm Miller, of Hellesdon aged
20 years.

July 15 John Jary, of Aylsham aged 37 years.

July 19 Barnard Penton aged 2 months.

August 14 Thomas Greenwood, Buxton Ho. of Industry,
aged 85 years.

August 16 Honour Saunders aged 77 years.

October 2 William Wyley aged 64 years.

October 11 Martha Smith aged 87 years.

October 25 Eliza Willimott aged 2 weeks.

November 13 Mary Ann Blyth aged 2 years.

November 25 Mary Ann Blyth aged 35 years.

1836.　　February 14 James Smith aged 2 months.

February 21 Elizabeth Thompson aged 13 months.

March 6 Caleb Blyth, of Belaugh aged 75 years.

March 8 Harriet Mack aged 28 years.

March 20 Benjamin Smith aged 63 years.

April 24 Robert Stageman, Buxton. H. I., aged 33 years.

May 15 Mary Ann Bunn aged 6 years.

June 21 Elizabeth Killigrew aged 67 years.

July 16 James Grix aged 71 years.

Sept 22 Harriet Gall aged 5 weeks.

Nov : 13 Lydia Shreeve aged 31 years.

Dec : 4 Henry Spinks aged 6 months.

Dec : 18 Anne Wittleton aged 65 years.

Dec : 19 Joseph Blythe aged 82 years.

APPENDIX.

Note 1. The Bells.

The following Note in the handwriting of the Rev. Samuel Otes is found in the First Register Book, (page 21).

> A note what the olde three bells weighed before they were shott w^h was in the year 1621.

A note what the olde three bells weighed before they were shott w^h was in the year 1621.

The weight of the litle bell was seaven hundred & half a iust, & no more.

The weight of the second bell was nine hundred fifty four poundes and a half.

The weight of the grett bell was thirteene hundred & a half & one and twenty poundes.

The old Brasses weighed fourtie five poundes.

The weight in all cam to thirtye hundred & a half & nineteene pounde.

A note what the 4 newe bells weighed after they wer newe shott att ye same time, and also of ye newe Brasses.

The Treble weighed when it was newe shott foure hundred and a half and half a pounde.

The second bell weighed six hundred iust.

The third bell weighed eaight hundred wantinge twenty three pounds.

The grett Bell weighed Ten hundred wantinge three pound, w^h cam to in all eaight and twenty hundred & thirtie pound.

The newe brasses weighed thirty seaven pound.

The rest of the mettle remaines still in the Bell founders hands towarde the charge of the shootinge.

per me Samuelem Otes parson here an eye witnesse to all this.

These four bells remained in use until 1824, when the old No. 3 became the Tenor, having been pared down and set in B.   Nos. 1, 2, and the "grett Bell," were cast by Dobson, of Downham, into Nos. 2, 3, 4, and 5 of a peal of six; the treble being supplied by the "Charles Newman" bell in the list given below.   This bell is said to have been sold by the people of Blickling, when the tower of their church became dangerous in the middle of the last century, but it was probably acquired by Marsham through Dobson in 1824. The present peal of eight was made up in 1842 by the addition of two bells purchased by subscription. The inscriptions on the eight bells now in the tower are as follows :—

1. and 2. THOMAS. MEARS. FOUNDER. LONDON. 1842.

3. CHARLES. NEWMAN. MADE. MEE. 1703.

4. and 5.   1824.

6. WILL^M. DOBSON. FOUNDER. DOWNHAM. NORFOLK. 1824.

7. W^M. GOODALL. RECTOR. JOHN. HOWLETT. THO^S. RAYSON. CHURCHW^DNS. 1824.

8. 𝕬𝖓𝖓𝖔. 𝕯𝖔𝖒𝖎𝖓𝖎. 1621. Arms of Brasyer, Norwich City, and Monogram of William and Alice Brend.

The weights are given by L'Estrange as : —

	cwt.	qr.	lb.		cwt.	qr.	lb.
1.	3.	1.	24.	5.	4.	1.	17.
2.	3.	0.	17.	6.	5.	0.	9.
3.	3.	2.	0.	7.	5.	3.	1.
4.	4.	0.	0.	8.	7.	2.	0.

But he has transposed the descriptions of Nos. 3 and 4, the "Newman" bell being in reality No. 3.

Note 2. A Right of Way.

The following memorandum is written on the spare pages at the end of the First Book. The Way now remains as a Footpath only.

" In perpetuam Rei Memoriam."

Know all men by these presents that we whose names are here underwritten, being ancient Inhabitants of Marsham, the first of which did at the Court in the former yeare 1698 give in his evidence and testimony to the Steward Colonell Justice John Ayd Esquire openly in the presence of all the Tenants and Inhabitants, and the rest of us which were ready to give in our evidence and testimony at the last Court October the 18th 1699 but prevented by the open acknowledgments of the proprietors of the lands through which the aforesaid way lieth, & which we are ready to depose most solemnly upon oath whenever we shall be required, before any Judge or Magistrate or Master of Chancery, that we have known this drift way to & from the old Parsonage as before mentioned for above fiftie years and never knew or heard anything to the contrary, but that it hath been time out of mind successively from age to age & from generation to generation : witnesse our hands this 27th day of December 1699.

ROGER MARTIN now foure score & five yeers old & came into this town at 34 yeares of age.

JOHN MEDCALFE (*his + marke*) being now threescore & twelve yeares of age borne in this towne & brought up in it & never out of it but one yeare, & M^ter Otes his Cart brought theire firing from the old Parsonage through that way.

CLEMENT JECKELL (his + marke) senior now threescore & eleven yeares of age borne & that alwayes lived in this Towne.

JAMES GEDGE (his + marke) being threescore & four or five yeares of age, borne in Hevingham, & came riding from the western part of Hevingham when a child of about ten yeares of age, & so forwards for severall yeares till at man's estate, that way through the whites to Balwick water mill, & particularly once or oftener with his sister, and all the neighbours of that part of Hevingham, and old Philip Watker continually the father of the present John Watker who declares that his father did it. As James Gedge now living & that hath lived about thirty yeares in Marsham & severall of the neighbours did, & know that he did *nemine contradicente* through Hevingham lane from Hevingham field, and crossing Marsham lane into a short lane of about threescore paces long that leades into Charles Bustinge's Pightle & so through the Whites.

MATTHEW GOSSE (his + marke) being now threescore & ten yeares old & came with his father John Gosse into Marsham at ten yeares of age & have lived threescore yeares in Marsham, & hath known it always so to be even whilest his father aforesaid was tenant to the Whites for 4 or 5 yeares & that he hath seen 20 times or more M^ter Otes then Rector his Cart come through the same in the time aforesaid with broome from the old Parsonage.

ALICE ALLEN (her + marke) being now threescore & one years of age borne at Balwick M^ill her father Oliver Smith, miller & wheelwright there, to which mill the inhabitants of the western part of Hevingham came for the time aforesaid § continually, out of Hevingham lane into the short leading lane into Parker's now Charles Bustinge's Pightle & so into & through the Whites and so into the camping land, in which † where (*sic*) she lived till she was 22 yeares old, & passing frequently that way hath seen passengers going & coming on horseback with theire corne & meale to & from her fathers mill that once was, & hath frequently seen M^ter Otes his Cart carrying when they had occasion to carry & bringing theire firing fuell, as wood, broome, furse, brakes, through that way.

§ Viz: from the feast of All Saints to the Feast of the Purification of the Blessed Virgin Mary.

† She lived with her mother in her first husband Dowsinge's house where Rich: Otes now liveth

ANNE ALLEN (her + marke) the mother of Richard Allen the present though absent husband of Alice Allen afores^d being four-score & 2 yeares old come midsummer next, borne in this house where she now liveth with her sonne Isaack Blyth & her daughter Anne his wife (now M^ter Adams') & hath always lived here saith the same, & further that it was layd open at shack‡ & never stopt up till Candlemas, & that M^ter Otes came through with his wood, broome, & furse, brakes from thence, & then besides innumerable times seeing it she frequently in morning heard their collar of bells with which their horses usually went: that her husband Charles Allen, & Philip Watker of Hevingham have both usually & frequently come with their carts out of Hevingham with broome & furse through the Whites to Marsham Towne & all strangers from that part of Hevingham come through that way all that time of the yeare, & that when Thomas Harwin M^ter Lyng's Tenant to the Whites desired his landlord's leave to ditch it in he refused saying that without the towns consent it would not be, for it was an old custome of shack & passage, & it could not be put by, said M^ter John Lyng the owner and a Counseller at Law, his Tenant Thomas Harwin afores^d living then where Edward Peartree the present Tenant of the same to M^ter Lancaster Topcliffe now liveth, onely the Smith's shop was not there then.

ISAAC BLYTH sonne in law of Anne Allen widdow afores^d that lived with M^ter Day Rector of Marsham that yeare in which he died which was anno Domini 1678 his hired servant carried with his Cart Ash-muck to the little pightle at the water ponds mouth at the further side of the Parsonage ground, & did sow it with white wheat that yeare, & brought with his Cart broome that way through the Whites *Nemine Contradicente.*

Note 3.　The Register-Bills.

As very sweeping assertions have been made as to the state of the Transcripts of Parish Registers, called in the Diocese of

‡ A local name for acorn harvest.

Norwich, Register Bills, it may be interesting to note the number which have survived in the case of this Parish. There are extant in the Registry of the Archdeacon of Norwich the following Marsham Register Bills, among a mass of others :—

1600, 1601, 1602, delivered by Sam. Otes, curate, Robert Pearce & John Withe, churchwardens.

1603. by Sam. Otes : John Wake, Tho⁸ Moses.

1606. by Sam. Otes : Tho⁸ Moses, Christopher Cotes.

1610. by Sam. Otes : Andrewe Dix, John Exham.

1623. by Sam. Otes : Tho⁸ Moses, Robert Vowte.

1629 (imperfect) by Sam. Otes : Richard Bell, James Horne.

1630 by Sam. Otes : Adam Chambers, John Green.

1633 by Sam. Otes : James Horne, Willᵐ Barnes.

1665, 1666, 1668, 1670, 1675, 1677. 1678 as printed above.

1684 by John Deyns, Rector. Edm. Hunt, Ja⁸ Gedge. Chʷ·

1686 by Matthew Bateman, John Jeckell, Ch. Wⁿˢ·

1688 by Daniel Wiseman, Rector.

1689, by Daniel Wiseman, Rʳ· ; Edwᵈ Jecks, Richᵈ Tills.

1692, by D. Wiseman : James Gedge, John Jeckill.

1694, by D. Wiseman : James Gedge, James Deeker.

1696, by D. Wiseman : Willy Jeckall, Charles Busting.

1700, by D. Wiseman : John Grand, Edw. Paretree.

1703, by D. Wiseman : Charles Die, Edward Jecks.

1704, by D. Wiseman : Edw. Jecks, John Bare.

1710, 1711, by Robert Dymes, Clerk.

1713, by Thomas Fuller, curate.

1717, by James Norris, Clerk. 1718 by James Norris : Isaac Vertegans. 1720, by James Norris.

1726, 1727, by James Norris : James Grix.

1730, 1731, 1732, 1733, 1737, 1742, as printed above.

1743, 1744, 1745, 1747, by G. Ray, curate.

1748. 1749, 1750, 1751, by Nathaniel Ponder : Samˡ Dyball. John Green. 1753, 1754, by N. Ponder.

1756, 1757, 1758, by W. Gordon.

1763, 1764, 1765, 1766, 1767, 1768, 1777, 1778, 1781, by Wᵐ Gordon.

1789, by Wᵐ Jewell. 1791 by Wᵐ Jewell curate : John Kiddle, Wᵐ Reynolds.

In all 61 Bills between 1600 and 1800, the whole of which have been carefully compared with the contents of the Registers, a work made comparatively easy by the admirable order in which the Bills have been arranged under Mr. Overbury's care.

In the Diocesan Registry are contained the Bills delivered in the years of the Bishops' Visitations, and we observed that Incumbents occasionally delivered the Bills of preceding years, probably because they had been prevented from attending the " General " to deliver them at the proper time. Among the Visitation years appear to have been, 1691, 1709, 1716,* 1723, 1728, 1735, 1740, 1747, 1763, 1770, 1777, 1784, 1791, 1794, 1801, 1806, &c. The packet of 1716 has been searched in vain. In that of 1735, we found the Bill of 1734—5 printed above. We also found in the packet of 1740, the Bills, 1 April 1738 to 1 April 1739, and 1 April 1739 to Visitation, both signed, Wm Harvey, Rector ; and in that of 1747, the Bill Easter 1746 to Easter 1747, signed G. Ray, curate. It may be safely assumed that a considerable proportion of Bills are preserved among the other packets, but the Registers being perfect, search was unnecessary. Since 1815 all Transcripts have been sent to the Diocesan Registry, and the blame for any missing years must be laid upon the Parishes and not upon the Registry, the methodical arrangement of which rendered easy the restoration of two torn entries of 1819.

INDEX.

291, 292 (bis), 294 ; William-Frederick, 287, 301 ; William-Pike, 290.

Edwards, (Edwarde,) Ama, Amy, 148, 196, 213, 214, 216, 217, 219, 221, 250, 272 ; Amelia, 279, 289 ; Ann, 224, 226, 235, 257, 284 ; Caroline, 299 ; Catherine, 291, 294, 295 ; Edward, 193 ; Elizabeth, 186, 192, 194, 200 (bis), 202 (bis), 203, 205, 214, 220, 222, 223, 224 (bis). 226, 242, 257, 263, 274, 280, 290, 300, 301 ; Emily, 296 ; Esther, 214 ; Eunice, 224, 228, 231, 233 ; Frederick, 299 ; James, 234, 281, 297, 299 ; John, 147, 148, 155, 170, 179, 188, 192 (bis), 196, 202, 220, 222, 224, 226, 234, 241, 273, 307 ; Joseph, 277, 291 (bis), 294, 295, 305, 306 ; Luke, 185, 200 (bis), 202 (bis), 203, 206, 220, 224, 226, 259, 266, 267, 302 ; Maria, 284, 294, 296, 299, 300, 302 ; Martha, 226, 289 ; Mary, 148, 185 (bis), 186, 187 (bis), 188, 190, 192, 193, 194, 196, 197, 198, 200, 220, 223, 226, 229, 234 (bis), 235, 259, 274, 297 ; Mary-Ann, 290, 294, 299, 303 ; Meliza, 303 ; Phœbe, 194, 246 ; Richard, 193, 202, 203, 224, 226, 235, 242, 249, 275, 284, 303 ; Robert, 115 (ter), 186, 187, 188, 190, 192, 193, 194, 197, 198, 200, 214, 220, 223, 226, 229 (bis), 234 (bis), 257 (ter), 259, 272, 273, 294, 296, 297, 300, 302 ; Sarah, 222, 246, 280, 285, 289, 291 (bis), 293, 300 ; Sarah-Ann, 295, 307 ; Susan, 24, 155 ; Susanna, 197, 289 ; Thomas, 224, 226, 291, 296, 306 ; William, 198, 206, 220, 263, 285, 294, 306.

Elden, Barbara, 177 ; William, 278.

Elmer, Ann, 292.

Elmore, Frauncis, 19 ; Marie, 19.

Elsing, Alice, 134 ; Gurtrude, 104.

Elson, —, 44.

Elvin, (Elvyn,) David, 289 ; Elizabeth-Rogers, 295 ; Hannah-Masterson, 289, 290, 295 ; Henrye, 3 ; John, 3, 11 ; Katherine, 66 ; Sarah, 306 ; William, 62, 278, 289, 290, 295 ; William-Bolt, 290.

Elwarde, Anne, 21 ; Edmonde, 21.

Elwin, (Elwings, Elwyn,) Adam, 13 ; Fraunces, 10 ; John, 7, 12 ; Margaret, 11 ; Marie, 9 ; Robert, 12 ; Thomas, 9 ; William, 29 ; wife of Wm., 29.

Emerson, Alyce, 24.

Emmes, Thomas, wife of, 57.

Engledow, Henry, 175.

Estwick, Cicelie, 25.

Eswick, Christopher, 112.

Everett, (Everard, Evererd, &c.,) Agnes, 212 ; Ann, 146, 212, 237, 262 ; Caleb, 186, 238 ; Daniel, 146, 151, 178, 243 ; Dorothy, 203 ; Elisabeth, 180, 183, 186, 195, 197 (bis), 198, 200, 236, 250, 252, 267 ; George, 123, 126, 141, 151, 167 ; Henry, 147 ; Isaac, 175 ; John, 200, 212, 249, 262, 265, 271, 300 ; Jonathan, 202, 237, 249 ; Joshua, 202, 203, 250, 267 ; Mary, 126, 163, 178, 183 (bis), 184, 186, 187 (bis), 198, 202, 203, 212 (bis), 244, 267, 268 ; Phœbe, 200, 248 ; Peter, 126 ; Robert, 85, 136 ; Samuel, 137, 178, 183, 186, 195, 243 ; Sarah, 133 (bis), 136, 137, 140, 144, 146, 239 ; Stephen, 197, 246 ; Susanna, 186, 214, 268 ; Thomas, 79, 131, 133, 136, 137, 140, 144, 146, 180 (bis) ; Tryphena, 184, 237 ; Webster, 183, 197, 246, 266 ; William, 197, 245.

Ewinch, Johann, 7.

Exham, Agnes, 35, 36 ; Alice, 69 ; Amie, 72 ; Andrewe, 54, 84 ; Anne, 35, 41 (bis), 45, 58, 59, 63, 69 (bis), 77, 88, 91 ; Bennet, 85 ; Brigett, 72 ; Christopher, 60 ; Edmoud, 105 ; Elizabeth, 54, 58, 79 (bis), 83 ; Faithe, 47, 76, 91 ; Frances, 105 ; John, 31, 33, 35, 36, 40, 41 (bis), 42, 44, 45 (bis), 47, 49 (bis), 51, 54, 58, 61, 63, 72, 75, 76, 77, 79 (bis), 82, 84, 86, 89, 98, 119 ; Judeth, 58, 79 ; Katherine, 81, 85, 86 ; Margaret, 31, 49 (bis), 54, 56, 61, 72, 82, 86, 88, 145 ; Margery, 37, 86 ; Mary, 105 ; Nicholas, 36, 42, 54, 56, 58, 60, 69, 77, 79, 88 ; Oliver, 44, 76, 83 (bis), 84, 86, 91 ; Peter, 76 ; Robert, 33, 51, 59, 63, 72, 78, 84, 85, 88, 89, 91, 94, 103 ; Samuell, 61, 72 ; Wife of Oliver, 83 (bis) ; William, 36, 37.

Farclay, Robert, 10.

Farmar, (Farmer,) Sarah, 239 ; William, 180, 237.

Farror, (Farrar, Farrow, &c., see also Ferror,) Adam, 4 ; Avis, 15, 16 ; Clement, 6 ; Clemes, 6 ; Edmunde, 4, 6, 8, 17 ; Helene, 6, 8 ; Johann, 11 ; Margaret, 4, 8, 9, 10 ; Margerie, 8 ; Martha, 201 ; Mary, 201 ; Thomas, 11, 15, 16, 17 ; William, 201.

Feak, Whitehead, 177.

Fen, (Fenne,) Amie, 90 ; Robert, 25, 67 ; "widow," 63, 89.

Ferror, (see also Farror, &c.,) Alyce, 12 ; Edmunde, 12.

Caroline, 293, 294, 295, 298; Charles, 291; Christopher, 207, 208, 210 (bis), 213, 217 (bis), 218, 220, 221, 224, 259, 263, 269, 302; Comely, 298; Elijah, 293; Elizabeth, 183, 184 (bis), 194, 209, 216, 220, 222, 224, 227, 229, 231, 232, 235, 248, 255, 260, 270, 279, 287 (bis), 289, 291, 292, 293 (bis), 301, 305; Elizabeth-Amy, 289; Emily, 296 (bis), 298; Esther, 210, 219, 270; George, 287, 289, 294; Hannah, 290; Harriet, 285; Henry, 288, 293; Isaiah, 295, 296, 306; James, 172 (bis), 179, 180 (bis), 192, 193, 194, 195, 196, 198 (bis), 200 202, 206, 218, 221, 224, 229, 247, 261, 265, 273, 281, 291, 293, 294, 295, 298, 308; Jane, 299; John, 200, 208, 212 (bis), 222 (bis), 224, 227, 229, 231, 232, 235 (bis), 258, 263, 274, 279, 286, 287 (bis), 289, 291, 292, 295 (ter), 296; Jonathan, 295; Joseph, 184, 206, 211, 229, 231, 235, 236, 246, 260, 263, 275, 276, 278, 285 (bis), 287 (bis), 290, 292, 294, 296; Kezia, 287; Louisa, 292; Lydia, 291, 300; Maria, 287, 294, 295, 305; Martha, 211, 212, 216, 217, 220, 235, 292, 303; Mary, 181, 207, 220, 229, 231, 233, 235, 236 (bis), 263, 276, 285, 286, 287, 289, 291 (ter), 293, 294, 295 (ter), 296 (bis), 298, 299, 302, 307; Mary-Ann, 290; Peter, 305; Robert, 235, 281, 292, 294 (bis), 298, 306; Sarah, 172, 180, 184, 195, 209, 212, 224, 231 (bis), 248, 258, 274, 277, 278, 281, 285 (ter), 286, 287 (bis), 290, 292, 293, 294 (bis), 307; Sarah-Amelia, 296; Sarah-Ann, 298; Sophia, 229, 282, 295; Stephen, 259, 301; Sophia-Hindry, 287; Susanna, 207, 208, 210 (bis), 213, 217, 218, 220, 221, 224 (bis), 259, 263 (bis), 288, 289, 290, 292, 294, 295, 298; Thomas, 151, 160, 183 (bis), 184 (bis), 193, 196, 211, 212, 216, 217, 220, 235, 244, 250, 263, 285, 296, 301; William, 210, 227, 233, 235, 288, 289 (bis), 290, 292, 294, 295, 298, 302; Zephaniah, 296.

Gronie, (Grony, Grunny, &c., see also Gurny,) Amie, 52 (bis); Anne, 30; Barbarie, 77; James, 22, 29; Johan, 27; John, 21, 22, 23, 27, 29 (ter), 30; Margaret, 29; William, 23, 29.

Groome, Elizabeth, 149.

Grout, John, 269.

Gruuye, see Gronie.

Gryme, (Grym, Grime, &c.,) Anne, 51, 96, 131; Dorothy, 136; Henry, 86; Mary, 131, 136, 139; Robert, 83, 86; Thomas, 83, 96, 131, 136, 139 (bis); Ursula, 132.

Guggle, Mary, 121.

Gurny, (see Gronie, &c.,) Thomas; William, 67.

Gymby, Thomas, 114.

Haber, Thomas, 9, (see also Haver).

Hackett, William, 5.

Hagon, John, 117.

Hall, Alice, 101; Charlotte, 231; Deborah, 284; Elizabeth, 231, 234, 284, 285; Grace, 101; Hannah, 285; James, 231, 234, 284, 285; John, 90, 234; Mary, 134; Robert, 86, 88; Samuell, 82, 83 (bis); Stephen, 77; Thomas, 80 (bis), 81, 82, 83, 86, 88 (bis), 90, 101 (bis); William, 88.

Hallifax, Anne, 43, 65; Erasmus, 58, 59 (bis), 62, 65, 73, 79, 81, 82; John, 59, (bis); Laurence, 73, 79; Mary, 51, 62, 73, 81; Thomas, 59.

Halott, Elizabeth, 12.

Hambleton, Anne; Martin; 44.

Hammond, Ann, 194, 195; John, 194, 243; Mary, 191, 193 (bis), 194 (bis), 195, 197, 199 (bis), 244, 217, 271; Robert, 197; Roger, 191 (bis), 193 (bis), 194 (bis), 195, 197, 199, 247; Susan, 156, 193, 213, 217, 218, 220, 221, 224, 269; William, 193, 243.

Hanes, (Hayne, Haynes,) Amy, 104, 107; Anne, 76, 164, 165, 167, 168; Brigett, 20; Elizabeth, 80, 104, 107, 110, 118, 120, 132 (bis), 154, 158 (bis), 159, 160, 162, 164, 165; Faithe, 86, 99; Frances, 149, 168; John, 104, 107, 110 (bis), 118, 120, 132, 150, 153, 154 (bis), 158, 160, 165, 239; Mary, 88, 118, 157, 161, 177; Robert, 40; Sarah, 149, 153, 224, 225, 228; Thomas, 89; William, 76 (bis), 80, 83, 86, 89, 99 (bis), 100, 153.

Hannant, Daniel, 291, 293; John, 293; Margaret, 291, 293; Mary-Ann, 291; Richard, 243.

Harding, (Hardinge,) Anne, 38, 50, 85, 134, 165, 194 (bis), 200, 244, 251; Bridget, 31 (bis); Cicely, 82; Dorathie, 35, 45, 66; Edmund, 41, 83; Elizabeth, 50, 53, 55, 78 (bis), 82, 87, 89, 90, 97, 129, 134, 165, 166, 172, 174, 178, 182, 184, 186, 200, 237, 248; Isaack, 93, 105, 108, 114, 115, 119, 124, 127 (bis), 162, 163, 165, 182, 245; James, 186; John, 28, 32, 65, 72, 74 (ter), 82, 85, 87, 88, 89; Margaret, 29, 86; Mary, 64, 69 (bis), 73, 91, 93, 105, 114, 134, 151, 193,

Johnson, Julia, 296; Mary, 270.

Jolly, (Jollie, &c.,) Anne, 153; Edmund, 74, 75, 77, 78, 81, 86, 99; James, 100, 242; John, 76, 77, 78; Mary, 117; Nicholas, 81, 100, 166; Rachell, 74; Thomas, 86.

Jonas, (Jones,) Ann, 196, 199, 200 (bis), 202, 220, 252, 263, 284; Elizabeth, 224, 229, 231, 234, 263, 284, 286; Esther, 292; George, 196, 199, 200, 202 (bis), 224, 229, 231 (bis), 231, 252, 263, 276, 279, 284, 286, 288, 290 (bis), 292, 293, 296, 299; Henry, 296; James, 286; John, 234, 255, 286, 288; Mary-Ann, 288, 290, 292, 293 (bis), 295, 296, 299 (bis), 307; Peter, 196, 224, 274; Robert, 295; Stephen, 199; Susanna, 270.

Joonys, William, 15 (bis).

Jopson, Eliza, 289, 290, 303; George, 289, 290; Martha, 289, 290.

Jordan, Marrian, 44.

Keed, (Keede,) Dorathie, 69, 77; Elizabeth, 36, 65, 71; Frauncis, 73; Johan, 22; Mary, 62, 77; Philip, 36; Thomasine, 69; William, 68, 69, 73, 77.

Kemp, (Kempe,) Agnes, 37; Ann, 170; Stephen, 37 (bis), 39 (bis); William, 39 (bis).

Kent, Edmond, 134; Elizabeth, 130; Judith, 145.

Key, Aaron, 201, 248; Anne, 264; Elizabeth, 171 (bis), 206, 249, 275; Ezra, 191; Henry, 187, 206, 207, 209, 210, 211, 262, 270, 302; James, 171 (bis), 187, 189, 191, 193, 211, 249, 255, 260; John, 168, 171, 189, 197, 246; Margaret, 187, 189, 191, 193, 206, 207, 209 (bis), 210, 211, 253, 262; Mary, 207, 228, 230, 231; Nathaniel, 202, 249; Richard, 167, 197, 199 (bis), 201, 202; Samuel, 193, 210; Sarah, 168, 171, 197, 199, 201, 202, 250.

Kiddle, Barbara-Carolina, 218; Edward, 230; Elizabeth, 211; Emmeline, 220; Esther, 211 (bis), 213, 215, 216 (bis), 218, 220, 222, 225, 227, 230; George, 222; Herriot, 225; John, 211 (bis), 213, 215, 216, 218, 220, 222, 225, 227, 230, 271; Mary, 215; Robert, 227; Sarah, 213, 302.

Killegrew, (Kelligrew, Killigrew,) Ann, 225; Deborah, 206, 207, 209, 252; Dinah, 280, 293; Edward, 204 (bis), 205, 206, 207, 209, 263, 270, 273; Elizabeth, 308; Esther, 225; Frances, 207; Isabella, 205, 251; Mary, 204, 205, 251; Melinda, 209, 252; Richard, 252; William, 206, 225, 275.

Kinge, (King,) Agnes, 18; Alyce, 15; Ann, 211, 226, 227, 228, 258, 275 (bis), 280, 288, 292, 293; Benjamin, 287; Bridget, 302; Charlotte, 236; Ciselie, 2 (bis), 25; Edward, 234, 282; Frances, 226, 227, 229, 231, 232, 234, 236, 262, 284, 287; Frauncis, 19; Henry, 36, 226, 229, 231 (bis), 276, 292; John, 226, 227, 229 (ter), 231, 232, 234, 236, 258, 260, 262, 274, 284, 287, 307; Joseph, 211; Margaret, 15 (bis); Mary, 51, 213, 214, 216, 219, 221, 222, 225, 259, 260, 272, 284; "Moother," 25; Peter, 7; Richard, 25, 43; Sarah, 251; Susan, 18, 37, 229, 231; Thomas, 2, 5 (bis), 289; William, 51, 231, 232, 262.

Knapp, Elizabeth, 160.

Knott, (see also Nott,) Allen,* 221, 223; Eleanor,* 216, 218; Ellen,* 269; Helen,* 211.

Kotes (see also Cotes, &c.,) Margaret, 23.

Lacey, Thomas, 176.

Lake, (Leake, Lecke,) Abigail, 120, 162, 164, 168, 182, 192, 211, 215, 267; Anne, 195, 197, 201, 219, 222, 225, 229, 233, 264, 284, 285, 303; Anne-Jane, 298; Arthur, 118, 121, 140, 178, 180, 182, 185 (bis), 188, 197, 203, 222, 245, 246, 278, 287, 289, 290, 291 (bis), 292, 293; Benjamin, 210, 289, 302; Caroline, 290, 291, 303; Charles, 288 (bis), 292, 298; Charlotte, 283, 287, 294; David, 163, 165; Edward, 157, 160, 162, 164; Eliza, 290; Elizabeth, 185 (bis), 289, 290, 291 (bis), 292, 294, 305; Francis, 289, 303; Hannah, 234, 236, 284, 285, 286, 288, 289, 290, 292; Hannaut-Thomas, 199; James, 116, 207, 211, 229, 288, 291 (bis), 292; John, 106 (bis), 113, 115 (bis), 116, 118, 120, 121, 127, 131, 132, 137, 140, 145, 160 (bis), 161, 163, 182, 194, 195, 197, 199 (bis), 200, 201, 203, 205, 207, 208, 210, 211, 214 (bis), 236, 258, 265, 267, 289, 290, 291, 294, 300, 305; Joseph, 192, 194, 264, 292; Letitia, 293; Lydia, 131, 133, 154, 166, 266, 290, 303; Maria, 219, 289; Mary, 106, 113, 115, 116, 118, 120, 121, 127, 131, 133, 137, 140, 158, 159, 167, 173, 195, 246, 263, 288, 289, 292, 298; Mary-Ann, 285; Parnell, 287, 289, 290,

Needham, Lydia, 266.

Newman, Ann, 195, 197, 199, 200, 201, 203, 257, 260, 286; Benjamin, 274; Elizabeth, 284; Esther, 233; James, 197, 245, 257; John, 195, 231, 233, 235, 276, 284, 285, 286, 287, 304; Joseph, 195, 197, 199 (bis), 200, 201, 203, 257, 260, 261, 285, 286, 301; Martha, 292; Mary, 200, 248; Mary-Ann, 201, 215, 231, 272, 281, 284, 292, 293; Sarah, 203, 235, 251; Susanna, 231, 233, 235, 284, 285, 286, 287; William, 287.

Newstead, Ann, 291.

Newton, Michael, 142.

Nichols, (Nickels, Nicolls, &c.,) Agnes, 5, 9; Anna, 7; Anne, 176; Avis, 17; Elizabeth-Blake, 294; Henry, 279, 293, 294 (bis), 297; Jane, 17; Josiah, 293; Mary-Ann, 292, 294; Sarah, 265, 293, 294 (bis), 297; William, 261, 297.

Nickerson, Edward, 56, 57; Mary, 57.

Nobbs, Eliza, 298; Elizabeth, 224, 226, 282; Maria, 298; Sophia, 283.

Norris, Ann, 162, 163, 164, 165, 166 (bis), 167; James, 162, 163, 164, 165, 166 (bis), 167, 170; John, 162, 163, 165; Judith, 168; Thomas, 164, 166; William, 166.

North, Elizabeth, 67.

Notts, (see also Knott,) Eleanor, 215.

Nun, Augustine, 47.

Nurse, Margaret, 169.

Nutt, (see also Knott), Eleanor, 213.

Oakes, Mary, 94; Richard, 48; William, 48, 49 (bis), 121.

Oates, (Oats, Otes,) Anne, 40, 41, 45, 48 (bis), 51, 55, 61, 86, 95, 111 (bis), 114, 119; Dionis, 79; Dorathie, 90; Elizabeth, 32, 33 (bis), 71, 84, 88, 97, 100, 101, 138; John, 39, 45, 68, 71, 74, 77, 78 (bis), 79 (ter), 80 (ter), 83, 84, 86, 88, 90 (bis), 97, 105, 145, 146 (bis), 149, 152, 179, 186, 237, 238, 244; Katherine, 35, 38 (bis), 46, 74, 77; Lucy, 237 (bis); Margrett, 51, 150; Martha, 38; Mary, 98, 105, 107, 109, 114, 120, 131, 146, 149, 152 (bis), 180, 181, 184 (bis), 236, 240, 242, 301; Matthewe, 71; Reuben, 187; Richard, 55, 87 (bis), 89, 98, 100, 101, 103 (bis), 104, 105, 107, 109, 111, 114, 119, 120, 131 (bis), 139 (bis), 167, 184, 241; Robert, 21, 61, 149, 181 (bis), 183 (bis), 185, 187, 190 (bis), 237, 241, 245;

Samuel, 39, 40 (ter), 41 (bis), 45, 48, 51, 55, 61, 80, 86, 89, 90, 119; Sarah, 142, 183, 186, 187, 190, 250; Simont, 83, 95, 97, 138, 162; Thomasin, 240; Timothy, 19, 36; Titus, 19, 107, 109; Ursula, 120; William, 33 (bis), 71, 84, 88, 97, 100, 101, 138.

Ogden, Diana; John; 179.

Olfe, (see also Ulph,) Anne, 186, 187, 189, 190 (bis), 191, 193; Benjamin, 173, 187, 188, 189, 190, 193, 194, 196; Elizabeth, 189, 194, 239; James, 190; John, 188, 193; Jonathan, 189, 196; Joseph, 187; Robert, 186 (bis), 187, 189, 190, 191 (bis), 193, 238, 241; Sarah, 187; Susanna, 187, 188, 189, 190, 193 (bis), 194, 196.

Oliver, (Olifer,) Abigail, 171, 178; Anne, 47, 185, 237, 293; Elizabeth, 18, 236, 284; Isaac, 230; James, 130, 168 (bis), 171 (bis), 179, 187, 245; Jane, 245; John, 129, 130, 133, 170, 185, 187, 230, 293; Margaret, 185, 187; Martha, 130; Mary, 167, 230, 285; Mary-Ann, 293; Sophia, 282, 296, 297, 299; Thomas, 47.

Orstick, (? Frostick,) Hannah, 271.

Osborne, Anne, 41, 47; Joane, 36; Margerie, 33; Mary, 39; Rebecca, 43; Richard, 43; Robert, 33 (4), 35 (4), 36, 37 (bis), 39; William, 38, 39 (bis), 40, 43, 52.

Ownes, *alias* Warnes, John, 271.

Owsin, Susanna, 173.

Page, Ann, 209, 218; Elizabeth, 216; Frances-Ann, 209, 253; Grace, 263; Joseph, 209; Thomas, 238.

Pain, (Payne,) Ann, 211, 215, 253, 273; David, 206, 221, 257, 258; Elizabeth, 192, 193, 194, 195 (ter), 196, 197, 198, 199, 200, 201, 202, 204, 206, 207, 208, 209, 211, 212, 215, 218, 221, 222 (bis), 234, 245, 257, 258, 264 (bis), 306; Fanny, 194, 247; Hannah, 266; James, 193; John, 199, 200, 218, 247; Jonathan, 202, 275; Joseph, 250; Mary, 204, 208, 220, 222, 224, 226 (bis), 228, 229, 231, 233 (bis), 235, 236, 275, 284, 285; Richard, 195, 196, 209, 244, 264; Robert, 197, 201, 246; Susanna, 207, 251; Thomas, 192, 212; William, 192, 193, 194 (bis), 195 (bis), 196, 197, 198, 199, 200, 201, 202, 204, 206, 207, 208, 209, 211, 212, 215, 218, 221, 222, 254, 257, 258, 264 (bis), 306.

Southgate, Charles, 195, 249; Christopher, 267; John, 194, 195; Susanna, 194, 195; Townshend, 194.

Soway, Edmund; Thomas; 6.

Sower, Margerie, 15; Robert, 44; Thomas, 15; 'widow,' 29.

Sowthes, (Sowthies, see also Sothis,) Bennet, 24; Doritie, 19; Elizabeth, 20; Martha, 22; Thomas, 25; William, 25.

Spantin, (Spanton, see also Pautin, Peuton,) Amy, 195; Anne, 70, 82; Clement, 62, 70, 75, 82, 85; Elizabeth, 189, 190, 193, 195, 197, 248, 267; Francis, 190, 193; John, 189, 190, 193, 195, 197; Margrett, 75; Mary, 70; Peggy, 97; Thomas, 189, 239.

Sparin, (Spearing.) Anne, 189; Elizabeth, 187, 189, 191, 192; John, 192; William, 187 (bis), 189, 191 (bis), 192, 239, 241.

Spark, (Sparke, Sparks,) Charlotte, 288; Dinah, 286; Edmund, 97, 158; Elizabeth, 162; Henry-Coleman, 287; Mary-Ann, 287, 288; William, 287, 288.

Spaul, Henry, 299; John, 299; John-William-Ladell, 282; Maria; Mary; Sarah-Elizabeth, 299.

Speakman, Susanna, 231, 276.

Spearing, see Sparin.

Spencer, Elizabeth, 104, 105; John, 104, 105; Thomas, 105.

Spicer, Alice, 19; Barbarie, 20; John, 25; 'widow,' 39.

Spink, (Spinke,) Amelia, 290; Amy, 227, 234, 298; Ann, 289, 290, 291 (bis), 292, 294, 296; Ann-Sophia, 286; Britannia, 227; Caroline, 298; Edmunde, 27; Eliza, 286; Elizabeth, 241, 265, 286 (bis), 287, 288 (bis), 289, 290; Emma-Maria, 294; Henry, 308; James, 227, 231, 234, 283, 296; John, 231, 247, 288, 290, 292, 303; Mary, 152 (bis), 181, 231; Mary-Ann, 290, 295; Matilda, 297, 307; Peter, 278, 286 (bis), 288, 289 (bis), 302 (bis); Phœbe, 285, 286; Robert, 234, 281, 285, 290, 296, 297, 299; Sarah, 287, 296, 297, 299; Thomas, 286, 287, 288, 290; William, 27, 152, 279, 285, 286, 289 (bis), 290, 291, 292, 294, 296 (bis).

Spooner, Thomas, 142.

Springall, Anne, 57, 62, 175; Nicholas, 53, 57; Thomas, 57, 58.

Spurrell, Elizabeth, 185; John, 185; Margaret, 175; Robert, 185 (bis), 250; Susan, 185 (bis).

Stageman, Amy, 181, 190, 208, 224, 241; Ann, 187, 188, 190, 191, 192, 194, 196, 198, 209, 251, 257; Christopher, 160, 187, 188, 190, 191, 192 (bis), 194, 196, 198, 217, 242, 255, 257, 280; Edward, 187, 191, 238, 242; Elizabeth, 196, 222, 245; Henry, 297; James, 198, 207, 224, 295; John, 160, 163, 164 (bis), 207, 208, 209, 211, 213, 217, 219 (bis), 222, 224, 228, 304; Jonathan, 224; Mary, 213, 295, 298; Matthias, 188, 239; Robert, 228, 281, 295, 297, 298, 308; Sarah, 160, 164, 169, 194, 211, 244, 297; Susanna, 207, 208, 209, 211, 213, 216, 219, 222, 224, 228, 305; William, 298.

Stagg, Minns, 275.

Stains, (Staines, Staynes,) Alice, 72, 119; John, 72, 76, 81, 84 (bis); Margrett, 76, 94; Mary, 81, 95; Thomas, 72.

Stamp, William, 132.

Stangroome, Christopher, 111.

Starling, (Sterling,) Ann, 104, 107, 137, 139; Elizabeth, 102, 139; Frances, 293; James, 102, 104, 107, 115, 116 (bis), 125, 137, 139 (ter), 167, 244; John, 95, 98, 99; Mary, 115, 116, 125 (bis), 137, 139 (bis), 155, 266; Robert, 95, 97, 115; Thomasin, 95; 'widow,' 98; William, 107.

Starly, Elijah, 157; Thomas, 96 (bis).

Stearman, (Sterman, Stirman, Sturman,) Abigall, 210, 215, 305; Amelia, 291; Ann, 183 (bis); Elijah, 296; Elizabeth, 251, 260; Emily, 296; Grace, 187, 188, 191, 251, 254, 263, 277; Henry, 210, 254, 260, 271, 275, 304; James, 188, 210, 215, 259, 263, 289; John, 191, 205, 207 (bis), 269; Lydia, 304; Mary, 205, 207; Philip, 101; Richard, 187 (bis), 188, 191, 254, 263; Sarah, 251; Susanne, 101; Thomas, 100 (bis), 183, 251, 279, 289, 296.

Sterling, see Starling.

Sterman, see Stearman.

Steward, (Stewart, Stuart,) Eliza, 282, 297; Elizabeth, 185, 261; Harriet, 281, 291; John, 226, 289; Joseph, 298; Mary, 185; Nathan, 226, 261 (bis), 284, 294 (ter), 296, 298; Parnell, 278, 287; Robert, 284, 296, 304; Sarah, 226, 258, 274, 284, 294 (bis); Sarah-Ann, 291; Susanna,

INDEX CHIEFLY TO CLERGY, CHURCHWARDENS, AND PARISHES.

[*No. of Copy   .*]